ASSASSINS OF RIAZ

By

Michael Drakich

Amazon Edition

Copyright © Michael Drakich
ISBN-13: 9781775166535

First Edition Traanu Enterprises, October, 2018

Editor: Kate Richards
Cover: Ted Kruzsely

CAST OF CHARACTERS

LYMOS, CAPITAL CITY OF RIAZ

Assassin Lord – Mysterious powerful warlock leader of the assassin guild
Kero – 15 yr. old ward of the Assassin Lord
Maresh – Cook at Rock House, inn owned by the Assassin Lord
Derak – 14 yr. old friend of Kero
Bashar – Accountant employer of Kero
Lazaan – Powerful warlock member of the assassin guild
Stod – Member of the assassin guild
Petrius - Member of the assassin guild
Bokko - Member of the assassin guild
Quinto Hamak – Patriarch of the Hamak family and leader of the merchant guild
Alban Hamak – Oldest son of Quinto Hamak
Janina – Daughter of a Lymos fisherman
Lasha – Friend of Janina
Orvest – Merchant of Lymos

MORENCE, CAPITAL CITY OF MORICA

King Jessop – Ruler of Morica
Prince Brumaine – 19 yr. old fourth son of the king
Prince Doren – Oldest son of the king
Prince Cassan – Second oldest son of the king
Lieutenant Varamanthu – Appointed guardian/mentor to Prince Brumaine
Commander Oberus – Top commander of all military forces in Morica

VISK, NORTHERN CITY OF SECHLAND

King Devron – Ruler of Sechland
Darlee – 15 yr. old powerful witch
Captain Brusk – Commander of the military in Visk and foster
father to Darlee
Silk – Demoness bride to Captain Brusk and foster mother to
Darlee
Daphora – Witch and tutor to Darlee

LIA, CAPITAL CITY OF PIAXIA

Queen Tessia – Ruler of Piaxia
Regent Tarlok – Warlock husband to the queen
Commander Savan – Commander of the military in Piaxia and
older brother to Tarlok
Frollence – Head of the Piaxian merchant guild and father to
Queen Tessia
Prattrow – Master warlock of Lia
Gar – Powerful warlock and brother to Darlee

CHAPTER 1

Kero slipped quietly from behind one stack of wooden crates to another, keeping an eye on the men on the pier to ensure none spotted him.

They were too busy moving cargo halfway down the dock toward a ship he knew to be flying the colors of Morica. At such a late time, at least five or six hands after sundown, they toiled in near darkness as the moon already had made its pass for the night and no torches lighted their work. Smugglers. He was sure of it. What contraband lay in those crates was definitely something the men didn't want the harbormaster to see.

Where was the night patrol, and why were all the lanterns out? He scanned the dock, a wooden structure fifteen paces across stretching over one hundred paces out into the bay, parallel to the shore on his left. He spotted the two constables in Riaz colors of gold and silver standing somewhat away from the others. Their constant furtive glances told him all he needed to know. They were paid off. Boats were not allowed to tie up to the pier at night. No loading was permitted after dark. An alarm should have been raised.

The tip he'd learned that afternoon proved true. Ordered to investigate, he'd hidden amongst the crates of Riaz red wine awaiting shipment. Careful not to jostle the wine, it had taken all his willpower to stay awake.

The telltale sparks of flint and the sudden glow of an oil lamp illuminated the captain of the ship. He halted the men at the base of the gangplank leading aboard his vessel. "Let's see the stuff. I'll not sail with it first and discover later I've been misled."

There were four cases in all, each four hands by eight, and eight again long. The men carrying them pried open the lids for the captain to see in. At the first, he reached in and pulled out a stick the length of Kero's forearm. Short roots extended from the base and its overall configuration looked somewhat warped and twisted. From each of the other containers he withdrew more of the same.

For Kero, it was easy to recognize the stuff. Grape vines. More than likely, the four varieties exclusive to the island state of Riaz. Serious contraband, indeed. His master was not going to be pleased.

He knew what he was supposed to do should he find such a serious violation. Making sure of a clear line of sight to the top of the hill behind him, he waved his arm in a planned pattern. Some thirty or forty paces up there in the darkness, his master waited. At such a distance in the dark, there was no way Kero could see his master, but there remained no doubt his signal had been seen. Now, it was only a matter of time.

No matter how many occasions he witnessed the arrival of his master's creations, they still gave him chills. From the hill and down the lane they came. Dark huge manlike things, half again as tall as a man, comprised of mud, sticks, and rocks. Golems—six in total.

They moved silently, occasionally leaving small parts of themselves in their wake—a twig here, a pebble there, a small clump of clay staining the cobblestones. During the day, whenever villagers found such tailings, much muttering amongst the people would occur for they knew his lord had once again been working his dark magic.

By their reaction, the first to see the golems were the two guards. Rather than warn the others, they took off running in the opposite direction and dove into the bay, making a swim for the shore. There was little other choice. No other way from the docks existed than the road the golems walked.

The consecutive splashes were enough noise to make the smugglers and the ship captain look around. Like the two sentries, the four smugglers dropped their parcels and made for the end of the dock and the waters beyond. Kero didn't know for sure, but a rumor existed the golems could not survive in water. More than likely, the men would rather chance drowning in the bay than being caught by his master's minions.

As they ran, the ship captain held his ground and called for them to come back. When such a return became unlikely, he called up to his ship for his crew to come help load the containers. Men holding lamps crowded at the rail, but none ventured down the ramp.

The captain drew his sword and pointed it at the nearest four men. "Get down here and pick up these crates, or I'll have you keelhauled on the way home."

The four moved, albeit slowly. Kero glanced to his left and the passing golems then back at the sailors. *They'd better hurry or they're going to get caught.*

He was right. The sailors had barely hoisted the cases when the first of the golems set upon them. The creatures carried no weapons but relied on their hands to do damage. In place of fingertips, they sported stones sharp enough to cut the flesh from any man. Despite the stabbing thrusts of the captain into the midst of the things, they lacerated one man badly while the others dropped everything and dashed back up the gangplank. The foolish captain was wasting his time. The creatures had no internal organs. His efforts were useless.

The fool was obviously determined not to go home empty-handed and dragged one of the crates toward the plank while trying to fend off the golems with his sword. When one of them managed to rake the captain's face, he howled in pain and dropped his load to scramble up and join his shipmates.

The golems ascended the plank. The sailors tried in vain to dislodge the board, but the weight of the creatures must have been too much for them to move it. From the far side of the ship, Kero could hear splashes as the crew must be abandoning ship.

In a swirl of black cloak and robes, his master entered the dock area. In the language reserved for his creations, something filled with a lot of hisses and growls, he called out to the golems who stopped their climb and returned the way they'd come.

It took a while for the docks to be cleared of the creatures, but, eventually, only his master remained near the four discarded cases and the dropped oil lamp. Seizing the thing, he poured its contents over the four cases then touched the lit wick to them. Flames erupted, consuming the crates and what they contained. His master passed his hand over the blaze, and the intensity of the fire multiplied tenfold. In a matter of moments, everything was reduced to ash.

His master looked up toward the ship and the retreating gangplank. "Begone from this port before I decide to sink your vessel. I have no qualms of treating thieves like you without mercy."

As if on cue, the boat, untied from the dock, drifted away. The captain, holding a cloth to his ravaged face, stood at the rail. "We're going. Spare us your wrath."

Only when the boat was beyond arrow shot did Kero venture forth and study his master. "You let them go."

His master turned on a heel and walked away. "Politics. The merchant's guild has asked for a measure of tranquility in the days to come. They have something big in the works. As much as I wanted to, the destruction of that ship would have soured their event considerably. I've been asked not to disrupt things. For this time, I relented."

Before attempting to catch up, Kero glanced at the fallen man on the dock. Sprinting, he caught a handful of his master's cloak and gave a gentle tug. "Master…the sailor."

His liege stopped and looked back. "What of him?"

Moments like this always caused Kero some trepidation. Should he ask? What if it made his lord angry? It wouldn't be the first time, and memory of the cuff he'd once received gave him pause. "Should you leave him to die?"

His lord sighed. "Do not test me, Kero. The man wrought his own demise. I have no pity for fools."

He let go of the cloak, clasped his hands before him, and bowed his head in an attempt to look submissive. "Then…with your permission…may I try?"

"You are still young—barely fifteen. Your mana has yet to fully blossom. I do not believe you would be successful."

He'd expected such a retort. Although his master had begun training him early when traditionally such schooling did not occur until after a youth reached sixteen, the age of ascension, he knew his skills were still limited as, like puberty, his mana growth was yet incomplete. "Perhaps, but it would be good practice. You can evaluate my progress." It was his hope wording the request the way he did would grant him some leniency.

His master gripped his shoulders then, as he stood several hands taller than the average man, crouched to level the black eyes in his gray, rocky face with Kero's own. "There is much you need to understand of the ways of men. Pity and mercy will lead only to trouble. Such is their darkness where they would abuse those things. Do not fall prey to their wiles. Leave him be."

Mercy was not a quality his liege tolerated. His master straightened and continued his exodus from the area.

Kero turned once more to look back at the fallen man. Too dark to see much at that distance, he conjured a small ball of light and directed it to float over the wounded sailor. The unconscious man's breath, visible in the cool night air, was shallow and short, with each perceptibly slower than the previous. It didn't take much longer. The cessation of white mists from the sailor's mouth informed Kero what he knew to be true. The man had died. *I might have saved him.*

From the direction of the top of the hill, his master's voice carried to him. "Come Kero. We must dally here no longer. There is nothing left to be done. Do not try my patience."

He released his hold on the light orb, and it winked out of existence. Turning, he hastened to catch up with his lord. He knew better than to anger the leader of the guild of assassins.

CHAPTER 2

Advanced accounting. How Kero hated the class. Why his master insisted on Kero's extracurricular education was beyond him. His sixteenth birthday was coming soon. It would entitle him to choose his own path, and accounting wasn't the one he'd seek.

Every afternoon, he attended the home of Bashar, senior accountant for the Hamak family, to continue his studies. Supposedly, it was to learn the intricacies of trade financing in a country where the merchant's' guild ruled and the island served as a trade hub for countries on either side of the Great Sea.

Instead, Bashar had him toiling away, entering countless transactions into huge ledgers. It was *really* boring. That day was no different. As he neared completion of one stack, his tutor entered to drop a fresh one on the desk beside him.

"More documents to be recorded, Kero. Let's not dawdle. A good accountant does not let his work pile up."

With the time it would take to transcribe everything, he would be lucky to finish before dusk. Perhaps he could sway his tutor to let him leave early. "Sir, today my master expects me to return to him no later than the tenth hand of light. I would not want to disappoint him."

Bashar blinked a few times. "No, er, no, I wouldn't want to do that." He lifted away half of the stack. "You can do these tomorrow. Please inform your master that your training is coming along well."

If it was, Kero didn't see it. "Is it really? It seems all I do is post entries."

"You think that's all?" Bashar grabbed one of the ledgers and flipped to the last page of posts then stabbed a finger at the second last thing recorded. "Here you spotted the double entry of a planting transfer from one farm to another. It was well concealed in numerous documents, but find it you did. Where the goods have disappeared to is another matter, one taken up with the farm manager to the tune of fifteen lashes. In my opinion, the penalty was lenient. The Hamak family will normally not tolerate theft. Alban's decision to forgo having him killed probably did not sit well with his father, Quinto. It's lucky for him they did not employ the services of your master to deal with the issue."

If anything, the merchants were diligent in their recordkeeping. Everyone must sign for and submit notes daily describing any goods or money exchanges. The manager in question attempted to detail transferring the stuff to another farm, but that manager never provided a receipt record. The system worked well. "Yes, I understand that. I was just wondering if there was something more. Something…exciting."

"Oho! So it's excitement you're after!" He slapped Kero across the back. "You must live vicariously through the actions that result from your work. I found the success of your find, along with the accolade given by my superiors when I reported it this morning, most exhilarating."

He had never really met any of the Hamaks. Alban Hamak, the oldest son of the household, often came to visit Bashar, but never spoke with Kero. His visitations were always held behind a closed door. Sure, Kero had seen the rest in the market square and, of course, at the summer solstice celebrations where everybody turned out. This year, he would have the opportunity to submit his application to the Assassins Guild. Then he wouldn't just be a servant, but an actual assassin. The idea exhilarated him, not the boring life of an accountant. "I suppose so."

Bashar smiled and rested a hand on Kero's shoulder. "I see you do not share my passion. You are young. Perhaps in time, you will come to appreciate what I do." He lifted the rest of the stack away. "Go. I'll do the postings today. Enjoy the afternoon sun. 'There'll still be plenty to do tomorrow."

He jumped up from his seat and bowed. "Thank you, sir. I will, and tomorrow I'll redouble my efforts in an attempt to find the joy in the work."

Bashar laughed and gave Kero a kick in his behind as he headed for the door.

"Do not attempt to win my approval through glib

commendations. I am immune to such praise."

"Yes, Sir." Rubbing his sore backside, he scooted out the door and out into the courtyard. He nodded toward the guard at the gate and moved out onto the street.

Bashar lived in the wealthy district of town. Everyone here had security. Kero made his way across town to the neighborhood he called his own. Not exactly slums, as everyone in Lymos worked if they wanted to. Most jobs didn't pay all that well, but they paid fairly. No employer took unjustified deductions for fear of reprisal from the Merchants Guild. The system in place ensured they stayed in power. No public strikes or underground revolts brewed in Riaz. Everyone accepted the status quo.

Then there were the assassins. In the employ of the merchants, their mere existence kept many wary. One of the great skills a warlock possessed was the ability to read the surface thoughts of those nearby. Fear of being found in opposition to the will of those in power kept the malcontents in line.

Most warlocks were members of the Assassins Guild. A handful of others took up practice as local doctors using their skill in healing to meet the need. An honorable trade, but, outside of the top merchant families, the real power lay with the assassins. That's the life Kero wanted. Ever since he was old enough to understand why he had no real parents, he craved the ability to wield magic. Lucky for him, his mana was sufficient to do so. The chance that led to his being in the care of the most powerful warlock in all the land, who trained him, made such a goal attainable.

As he neared Rock House, the inn he called home, he noted Lazaan, a member of the Assassins, with his back toward him, leaning idly against the doorframe, chatting with Stod, another of the guild. The assassins frequented Rock House because it was considered sanctuary for them. He stopped to ponder whether to brush past the two men or wait until they moved. Lazaan *always* gave him a hard time.

"What do you think of this new edict he wishes to impose on us? This is unacceptable. It's our trade."

Stod made eye contact with Kero then returned his attention to

Lazaan. "We must heed this one, Lazaan. It's not just *our* guild master who wants this. It's the Merchants Guild as well."

He liked Stod, a unique rarity among the guild. Without a lick of magic, the fellow relied on his skills with the bow, sword, and knife. Unlike Lazaan, a weasel of a person smaller than Kero, Stod was a big man whose muscles bulged and flowed when he moved.

In a fight, despite his size, Stod would probably lose, as it was generally accepted that, next to the master, Lazaan was the most powerful assassin in the guild. Too bad. He would have liked to see Stod pummel the smaller man into the ground.

Lazaan poked a finger into Stod's chest. "That's the trouble…letting others think for you. I may be a member, but I cut my own path as well. I'm no one's pawn. Mark my words. One of these days there'll be a new leader of the guild. Decisions like this will sooner or later be our current one's downfall."

Stod laughed. "And who would replace him…hmm? You? You wouldn't stand a chance against his magic."

"I wouldn't be so hasty to judge. Fortunately, our guild laws prevent putting such a thing to the test."

Stod waved a hand in dismissal. "You know that's not what they say. The rules only apply to family members. They are off limits. If one assassin is contracted to kill another, there's nothing preventing them. It's a code the guild boss demands. We're supposed to protect each other. It makes sense. If we start killing one another, we'll be down to one left in no time. We only avoid such contracts for our own self-preservation. You're just too afraid to try."

"There's a difference between fear and cunning."

Kero knew it was time to go by them. Despite what jibes Lazaan may give when he passed, his presence would remind the two that the master had eyes and ears everywhere and such talk would not be countenanced. He stepped between the two men as he made for the door. "Good day."

Both took a half step back as he crossed between them, but before he could enter the tavern, Lazaan grabbed him by the collar.

"And just where does the royal pet think he's going?"

He brushed off Lazaan's grip. "Inside. Where else?"

"I think not. You are not of age."

A sudden seizure of his muscles temporarily stopped Kero where he stood. He recognized the spell and concentrated to break it. It disappointed him that, without concentrating, his magical defenses weren't strong enough to resist the spell in the first place. His master told him how, in time, his defensive skills would automatically block such attacks. "Stop it, Lazaan. You know I live here. I have duties to attend to, and you wouldn't want the master discovering you interrupted them."

The pull of the spell disappeared, and Lazaan sneered. "Always the pampered whelp. When you do become a man and are no longer under the guard of the guild master, I'll teach you some respect."

Stod gave Kero a gentle shove toward the door. "Leave him be, Lazaan. Don't you already have enough things to worry about without the guild master breathing down your neck?"

"Perhaps. Come, until the meeting later, let's slake our thirst down the street at the Fisherman's Well instead of here. I'm afraid the mead might be somewhat tainted."

The two headed off toward the low end of town near the wharf. Kero was glad to see them go. It interested him to know there was a meeting later. His master never informed him when they would occur.

He headed into the smoky haze generated from the firepit of the main room. Built on an outcrop of granite, with rough-hewn stone walls, the place was appropriately named as the back corner featured a large natural stone ledge where his master and a few of the senior guild members often sat. At the moment, his master sat alone.

The room had its usual assortment of regulars, but all in all was fairly empty as would be wont so early before dusk. He made his way over to the ledge. His tutor, who was leaning back in his seat, had his eyelids shut, his breathing shallow. As always in public, his master was covered from head to toe, with gauze to see through. Had Kero not known better, he would have thought the outfit stifling. Rather than wake him, he decided to head for the kitchen and see if there was something he could get to eat. He didn't manage two steps before he heard a rustle behind him.

"You're home early today. Have you disappointed Bashar that he would send you away?"

He turned to face the accusation squarely. "No. In fact, he was most pleased about my discovery yesterday of the mislaid plantings. As a reward, he gave me the rest of the day off."

"Then you should go outside and enjoy the day." He reached into his pocket, withdrew a copper coin, and flipped it toward Kero. "Buy yourself a sweet. Like Bashar, I should reward you. You and your friends are my eyes and ears in this town."

Kero deftly caught the coin. His master referred to the other street youths he associated with who prowled the town market and the city's back alleys day and night. "If it's all right with you, I'd rather stay indoors. I smell some good cooking from the kitchen and would rather have a proper meal first."

"Stay, if you wish, but know this, there is a meeting within the hand of the guild and you cannot be present, as you are not a member."

He knew, but he had every intention of listening in. As much as he would have enjoyed meeting up with some friends in the town square, it was why he was staying. "I shall retire to my room upstairs before the meeting starts."

"See that you do...and Kero...draw the shade on your window. The light from it seeps through the small hole you have bored in the floor to eavesdrop."

With his cheeks aflame, Kero made for the kitchen. Once there, he snuck up on the old lady who cooked for Rock House. He waited until he was right behind her shoulder in hopes of startling her. Laid out on the counter were a large number of meat pies, still steaming and with light brown gravy oozing out from under their tops. Their aroma was intoxicating. She was busy trying to ladle the spillage back into the open cuts in the crusts. "What's cooking, Maresh?"

He didn't move fast enough, and the wooden spoon in her

hand caught him across the ear.

"You're a brat, young Kero. What the master sees in you I'll never understand."

He rubbed at the side of his head. Not only did his ear throb some, but his hair was sticky from a splash of gravy. "He has a penchant for taking in stray boys and old ladies alike."

She crossed her arms and sighed. "Aye, that he does. Rock House has been home to me for nigh on twenty-seven years now. If he hadn't taken me in, I'd be long dead in a gutter somewhere, more than likely the one he found ya in when you was just a three-year-old whelp. Ta think I've had ta spend the last twelve years helping raise such a one as you does my heart no good."

The ache abating, he grabbed a kitchen cloth and wiped at the wet spot on his head. "I think you've done a fair job keeping me in line."

She waggled the spoon at him. "Not enough, in my mind. He lets you get away with far too much. Now I suppose ya be wanting to get some dinner?"

Finished with the cleaning, he placed the cloth back on the table. "If you wouldn't mind. Master has said I have to eat in my room as there's a meeting tonight."

"*I* know that." She waved at the food. "What do ya think I've been doing all day? That's what these pork pies are for. I'm just letting them cool a little so the gravy don't leak all over. Come back when I'm done serving, and I'll get you a plate."

The smell of the food was too good for him to wait. "Aw, Maresh, you know you always prepare enough to feed half the town. Surely you can cut me a slice now."

She studied the pies. "Aye, I suppose so." With a hitch in her step she claimed came from a bad hip, she made her way to one end of the counter and the pie farthest away. "This one's been cooling the longest. I suspect it might to safe to cut into it."

One thing for sure. Maresh knew her cooking. She'd been a cook in the Piaxian royal castle back in Lia prior to the warlock rebellion. Stowing aboard a boat bound for Riaz, she'd escaped the purge where many in the castle were put to death, but being a foreigner here, she'd had little luck finding employment until the master took her in. As she sliced into the pie, making sure he got a hefty piece, she loaded the rest of his board with rye bread and goat's cheese.

Using the back stairs, he made his way up to his room. There, he dived into his meal with gusto and listened to the goings on in the common room below him.

As he completed his repast, the sounds picked up. The members of the guild were showing up. This was going to be a special meeting because, for the first time, every member was in town. Normally, at least half a dozen or more were overseas fulfilling contracts. People came from far and wide to hire the assassins as they didn't want the hiring to be traceable in their homeland.

Of late, Lazaan had been pushing for a restructuring of guild operations. His master never agreed. That usually resulted in an argument, making the small man combative. Even through the floor, Kero could hear the boisterous voice of Lazaan complaining about the slow service. It wouldn't be long until the meeting started.

Remembering his master's words of warning, he pulled the shade across his window, blocking the last rays of light coming in, and settled down in the near darkness next to the chest in which he kept his meager belongings. Pushing on it, he uncovered the spy hole and stretched out on the floor to optimize his ability to hear the voices filtering up.

As he pressed his eye to the hole, he could make out most of the room. Many of the twenty members were already seated. It looked like the pork pie was a big hit as boards were empty and Maresh was gathering them up with many a compliment coming her way. He must remember to thank her as well. It was something he always forgot.

Once Maresh left the room, his master rapped his fist on the table, getting everyone's attention.

"We are here today to discuss the latest request from the Merchant's Guild."

Lazaan, seated at the end of the same table, stood up. "You mean you're going to dictate to us the latest request. These meetings are a sham. There's never anything but you telling us what we can and cannot do."

His master continued to stare out at the crowd. "They have requested there be no killings, *of any kind whatsoever*, until after the trade meeting they have scheduled a fortnight from now. As I understand it, there are already agents from many of the invited countries here now working to ready accommodations for their people. From what I am told, there are many delicate issues to be resolved in these negotiations, and the merchants do not want anything to taint them."

Lazaan also glared out at the crowd. "And I take it you have already given the merchants your assurances we will comply."

Kero watched his master finally acknowledge Lazaan with a glance. "In fact, I have. It is a contract I have taken on behalf of all. What would *you* have me do?"

Here it comes. The same old argument. When would Lazaan learn? A people's right to choose had never been successful anywhere. Might always ruled, and no one was mightier than his master.

"A vote. Let the members decide."

His master rose from his seat to his full height, towering over the much smaller man. "So be it. All of those who support Lazaan, *and* are against me as leader of this guild, raise your hand."

No one moved. Not a single hand was raised. No, wait, there was one. Stod. Lazaan's face went beet red. He plopped down in his seat and crossed his arms over his chest.

His master turned toward the lone dissenter. "Stod, you stand against me as well?"

Stod looked around then stood. "No, I do not. The question was worded in such a way that it left me in a quandary. I want to support my friend but not to oppose you. As my vote mattered not in the final tally, I decided on the former so he would not stand alone. Surely you can see my reasoning."

His master nodded. "I can. Friendship is precious. It is a gift in which I am lacking. If I were you, I would counsel my *friend* not to take any more foolhardy steps lest he encourage my darker side." He sat down, and for a moment, glared at Lazaan.

"I shall take your suggestion under advisement." Stod also sat and exchanged nods with Lazaan.

His master grabbed hold of a sheaf of papers and passed them to his left. "Back to business. Here are the rules for this period. All that remains to discuss is how to enforce them."

The man who received the papers handed them, minus one, to the next man, and the stack circled the room until all were dispersed. Once everyone had a chance to peruse them, the members were allotted sectors of the city in which they were to keep watch. None would dare engage in their trade, contracts were sacrosanct, never to be breached upon penalty of death, but it would be necessary to ensure normal citizens likewise were kept in check.

The meeting ended, and most of the men departed. Kero noted that more than Stod exchanged quiet words with Lazaan as he exited the building.

CHAPTER 3

Darlee hoisted her skirt to allow her bare bottom to be in contact with the hard rock on which she sat. The magic worked better that way.

For the past month, since the snow melted, she'd made the trek every five days to this rocky outcrop near her hometown of Visk in Sechland. She checked the sky. The time looked right. Holding her hand at arm's length to measure the sun, it was about one hand past the zenith. It was time to try and contact her brother Gar.

Concentrating, she reached out through the rock toward the distant city of Lia, capital of the country of Piaxia to the north. It took a few moments, but eventually, she felt the connection she sought. Now came the tricky part—getting it to manifest as an image before her.

At first like looking into a snowstorm, the white flecks eventually cleared away and coalesced into a vision of her brother. "Gar! It's great to see you."

Her brother smiled. "Hey, Darlee. Your magic is getting stronger every day, and you still only fifteen. I wouldn't be surprised you catch up to me."

Her brother was the most powerful warlock in Piaxia, even if he wasn't free to use his skills. Since the war with the other kingdoms in the seven realms, he was held prisoner there. "Catch you? I intend to pass you."

"Ha! I sincerely doubt it. Where you have only one teacher, I've half a dozen. In fact, I've trained with another student—a lad with Warlock Lord level mana like us. He's the first one born in the kingdom in forty-three years. Well, not born...let's see, he's sixteen so that makes it...hmm...seventeen?"

Her brother never was the brightest. It was why he got into so much trouble before. That whole thing with the demon stones was nothing but a nightmare. So much was lost—their parents, grandfather Pap, the farm, Gar's freedom.

She touched the patch over her left eye. Another thing lost in it all. For a moment, the memories of all that was forever gone soured her. No, she needed to keep up appearances for her brother. If he felt she was in need of help, he might do something stupid again like try and escape to come to her. She forced a smile. "No, Gar. Twenty-seven. I *did* pass you in school, don't forget that."

Gar's expression changed to a pensive one. "How is Captain Brusk treating you?"

Always the same question. Her foster parents were never anything but gold to her, doting constantly. "Nothing's changed since you asked that last time, or the time before that, or the time—"

"Okay, okay, I get the message. You know I constantly worry about you, don't you?"

If there was anything she was sure of, it was how much he loved her. "Yes, Gar. I'm fine. In fact, he's told me he has a surprise for me. Only the gods know what it could be because they've already bought me everything I could ever want."

"Whatever it is, you deserve it. He's a good man. I know it. I should have listened to him more when I had the chance."

She didn't want to dredge up old memories, and the drain on her to maintain the conversation was becoming palpable. "I need to go now, Gar. My mana's just about used up. I can feel it. I'll talk to you tomorrow."

"Bye, Darlee. Give my regards to the captain and Silk."

"Will do." She severed the link. The taxing of her magical skills ceased, and she could already feel the natural regeneration occurring within her.

She got up and made for home. Her foster mother, Silk, always chided her for coming home so late when school ended at the sun's zenith. Her usual excuse was meeting with friends in the town square, but that ruse had been exposed already, so she needed a different one. Her new favorite was to state she visited the old farmstead. In truth, she had not returned to the place since last year. There were too many painful memories. She must go soon and plant flowers at the graves of her parents and Pap. They deserved her respect.

As she neared the gatehouse on the way back into town, she spotted her friend Jango on duty. During the day, the gates were open and the citizens came and went as they pleased. The guards usually just watched unless they saw a stranger or suspected something. She needed to decide now whether to hurry past or stop and say hi.

Jango was in love with her. That much she was certain of. She didn't feel the same. Although she was only fifteen and he couldn't ask her to wed, as the age of ascension was required, nevertheless, it didn't stop him from trying to court her. She sighed. He needed to give it up. It was putting a strain on their friendship. She decided to be polite and visit, but only for a moment.

She stopped at the booth. "Hello, Jango. Catch any criminals today?"

"The only thing I'm looking to catch is you, Darlee."

Here we go. "I'm too young. You know that. Surely there must be some other girl who catches your eye."

"None so fair."

The temptation to laugh was there, but she didn't want to insult him. With scars on her arms and legs and missing an eye from her torture, skinny and small, she was no prize. Not that Jango was, either. He, too, lacked any size or girth, but that was beside the point. She needed to move on. "You'll find one. You just aren't looking hard enough."

The other guard, snarling, gave Jango a tug. "Stay away from that witch. She's nothing but trouble."

Although King Devron had removed the statutes outlawing magic, people were still uncomfortable with the concept. As a result, she trained in private at her home. Darlee knew of no one in town aware of her skills, but she was guilty by association. Her foster mother was a demon. Because her foster father was in command of the troops in Visk, none dared challenge his choice of mate. It simply led to a fair amount of muttering whenever she encountered anyone who felt contrary to the situation.

After a quick, hard glance at the other guard, she waved bye to

Jango. "Listen, I've got to go. *Captain* Brusk is waiting for me." She glanced at the guard again to see if her veiled threat showed any effect. The man frowned, released his hold on Jango, and turned away. Her ploy had worked.

Before her friend could respond, she dashed toward home. Not palatial by any means, but a good-sized residence in a nice neighborhood. She found her foster mother tending the garden in the small courtyard fronting the house.

Silk may be a demoness, but another reason many resented her relationship with the captain was due to her being simply the most stunning woman in the city. As tall as any man in town, possessed of an amazing figure, especially heavy on the top and, despite her slate-gray skin and lack of hair, a face as beauteous as could be. Whenever they attended a social function in town, Darlee could tell by the expressions of those who believed the captain and Silk weren't watching how every man lusted after her and every woman jealous.

She examined her own meager assets. If only her magic could give *her* such a figure, then more than Jango would be interested. "Hello, Silk. Is Brusk around?"

Silk pointed into the house. "He's in his study."

"Thanks." She dashed in the door and headed straight to where her foster father would be. Exactly as Silk described, she found him at his desk, poring over some documents. When she entered, he looked up and smiled.

"Darlee girl, I've got something to talk to ye about."

A quick glance at the room showed nothing out of the ordinary. If there was a gift involved, it wasn't in there. "What is it?"

He motioned to a nearby chair. "Have a sit."

Following instructions, she pulled the chair a little closer to him and plunked down with her hands clasped on her knees. "Okay, I'm sitting. What's up?"

He handed her a document. She unfurled it from its post and scanned it. It was a missive from the king. Brusk had been named emissary to Riaz in the upcoming trade talks. Besides, instructions to work out details regarding the routes trade would take were also concerns regarding the protection of such routes. It looked like an important job. This meant he would be gone for quite some time.

Daphora, her tutor in the magical arts, had left for the capital city, Sechwisk, days ago. If he left as well, she would be alone. Obviously, he was planning some kind of boarding situation for her while he was gone. *So much for a gift.* "How long will you be gone?"

"A few fortnights, to be sure, maybe four. It's a mighty responsibility the king has entrusted me with."

She handed back the document. "As well he should. You taught him all he knows. There's no one in all of Sechland he should trust more."

Brusk chuckled. "Not all. I daresay that lass Daphora has taught him a thing or two, not to mention what else has been forced on him since his decision to take the throne. In my day, he was just a lieutenant under my command."

Her foster father was modest, as always. "A crown that might not have been there had you not held the city."

"Let's not forget the part your brother and those demons played, but enough chitchat. I'm going away, and there's the matter of what to do with you."

He had already left her behind once when he attended the winter solstice meeting in Lia. "I know. I have to stay at your cousin's' place once more. They treat me like a child. Can't I stay home alone? I'll take care of the place. I promise, *Father*, I will."

Brusk reached out and patted her on the knee. "You only call me that when you want something." He chuckled. "I don't think so. Now, what do you think Silk will do if you start doing her chores. You know how territorial she is about that stuff."

She glanced to her left as a moment of confusion set upon her then focused once more on her patron. "Silk? Isn't she going with you?"

"We've had a talk on this and decided it best if she not go. She, being what she is, is sure to upset a few folk there from some of the other countries. No, she's staying home. In fact, she's the one who's suggested it might be right for ye to see a bit of the world and for me to take you with me. I decided to agree with her that it might be a good idea."

Darlee's foster mother's laughter from behind her surprised her, for she had not heard her enter. Silk's laughter had the most interesting and distinctive tinkling sound to it. It always put Darlee at ease. She suspected there might just be a bit of magic there. Silk's power was, after all, the ability to draw, or feed willpower to anyone.

"It took me half the night to get that agreement. You know how stubborn Brusk can be."

She jumped up in joy at the prospect of traveling overseas to Riaz. She'd never been on a boat, or for that matter even seen the ocean. She glanced back and forth between Silk and Brusk, trying to decide which one to hug first. As Silk was standing, and the fact it was her idea, she started there. "Thank you, oh, thank you. I'm going to ride on a sailing ship. How exciting!"

Silk returned the hug, smothering her in her ample bosom. "You're growing up fast. You need to see the world before your life becomes too complicated."

Extricating from Silk's embrace, she skipped over to Brusk to give him one as well. "And thank you! A foreign country, and you an important emissary. This is going to be amazing. Will I get to see royalty? Go to a fancy ball? I can hardly wait."

Brusk rose, turned her toward the door and gave her a gentle pat on her rear. "You won't have to wait long. Start packing. We leave at first light tomorrow."

She giggled and did as asked, dashing to her room and sorting through her clothes. Most everything she owned was fairly new. The homespun clothes of her youth had been lost in the fire that consumed her family home. Brusk and Silk had taken her shopping more than once, and Daphora had as well. When it came to shopping, her tutor was the best. The woman had exquisite taste. She would pack everything Daphora picked out.

As she folded the last few items into her travel bag, she studied her room to try and think if there was anything she was missing, then it hit her. Gar. She wouldn't be able to let him know she was gone. Only Daphora knew about the secret chats, and, unlike Darlee, she didn't have the necessary mana to do them herself. Perhaps she might get lucky on the road and find some bare bedrock to send a message, but the chances were slim to be able to do so at the appointed time.

She had to hope her brother would wait out her absence.

CHAPTER 4

Ankle deep in the sand of the middle of the practice ring, Brumaine feinted to his left, dropped his right knee down then thrust his sword toward the right thigh of his opponent in hope of scoring some kind of mark. The ruse didn't work as his tutor, Varamanthu, special second lieutenant to the throne, easily deflected his blade and left his own hovering perilously close to Brumaine's right ear.

Varamanthu stepped back, sheathed his weapon then extended a hand to help Brumaine rise. "A sloppy move, young sire. Though, from here, I could not strike a killing blow, the damage would have more than incapacitated you. What did you hope to gain with such a maneuver? The point of your blade into my thigh would only be, in the heat of battle, the slightest of flesh wounds. Any man engorged by bloodlust would, despite such a wound, strike you across the skull."

Brumaine bent to dust off his knee and then sheathed his sword. "It's not fair, Var. I sought to prove to myself that I could, at the very least, draw some measure of blood, no matter how tiny, from an officer of the elite guard. My skills are no match for one such as you. I failed."

"Firstly, sire, you are royalty. It is my job to ensure that *I* am at my best in order to protect you. Second, do not be so quick to discount your own skills. Of good height, fit, trained, you should be more than adequate in a fair fight. I daresay there are men in my own cadre who would fail in a contest with you."

He doubted what his instructor said to be true. In the previous year, during the war against Sechland, his father forbade him from serving in the army stating he'd received word Brumaine's skills weren't up to surviving a pitched battle.

Tired of training, he measured the sky. "In a couple of hands, it will be dark. Let's resume this at our usual time tomorrow. For now, I'd like to slake my thirst and perhaps get a bite to eat."

"Not that tavern again. You know the king is not fond of you frequenting such establishments. You're eighteen now. You should know better. Mixing with the commonry is below your station...and then there is the matter of your safety."

His father, King Jessop of Morica, was always making new rules that interfered with his fun. "What does he care? It's not as if anyone at court wants to associate with me. I'm the fourth son. My oldest brother already has two sons of his own. I'm so far down the hierarchy, no one thinks I'm worth a damn. The only place I get any respect is among the people."

Var placed a hand on Brumaine's shoulder. "That's where you're wrong. It's *because* he cares about you that he imposes such rules. Come with me back to the castle."

He smiled. If there was anyone who truly cared about him, it was his tutor. "I know you mean well. Send someone to accompany me if you must. Hub will do."

His mentor laughed. "Not Hub. The last time he went with you, he got so drunk the city guard discovered him the next morning passed out in an alley, and you were nowhere to be found, although there was some mention of a certain tavern wench who lived somewhere nearby. The only question is whether it was him or you who spent the night with her. You must take care, sire. A child would be the death of your mother."

It had been him, but he was careful. He knew better than to get some serving girl pregnant. "Then let it be you, if you are so worried."

Before Var could answer, a soldier arrived and saluted. "Lieutenant, your presence is required by the king."

His tutor nodded. "I will be there shortly."

As the soldier turned to leave, Var grabbed the man by the elbow. "Hold a moment."

His instructor returned his attention to him. "I would, if not needed in the throne room tonight. Besides, you know I do not drink. Alcohol weakens the spirit and the reflexes."

Var pulled the soldier near. "Attend the prince this evening, wherever he goes. Make sure he does not get into any trouble."

The soldier saluted once more. "Yes, sir."

His trainer smiled. "There. That matter has been settled. I will see you in the morning."

Var headed off toward the castle. Brumaine turned to face his new shadow. "What's your name, soldier?"

"Zubrius, Sire, though my friends call me Zub."

The comedy of the closeness of name was not lost on him. He chuckled and draped an arm over the man's shoulders. "Come, Zub. The nightlife is calling us."

***

Well into his fourth mug of Riaz red wine, Brumaine considered the possible shapeliness of the tavern girl on his knee. Her homespun clothes lacked the necessary refinements to properly display her figure, but between the cinching of a leather belt at her waist and the tight fit at the girl's hips, there was more than enough revealment to tell him the night should be pleasurable.

Zub, on the other hand, was less enjoyable as a drinking partner. The man was taking the job too seriously. Still nursing his first mug of mead, the constant scowl on the man's face told Brumaine all he needed to know about what the soldier thought of his actions. He nudged the fellow. "Cheer up. This has got to be the easiest job you've ever been assigned."

Zub carefully placed his drink on the table. "No, sire. This is not. I have half a mind to—"

His chaperone jumped up and stared in the direction of the door. Brumaine turned to follow the man's line of sight. Striding toward them was Var. *Great. There goes my night.*

Zub saluted. "Lieutenant. I have been keeping careful watch on Sire Brumaine here. In fact, I was just about to take away his wine."

Var waved him off. "Don't worry, soldier. The fact the prince is still here tells me you have done a more than adequate job. Normally, by this time in the evening, he's slipped off into the clutches of one female or another who is hoping to become a consort to royalty. You are dismissed."

Zub saluted again, nodded, then made for the door.

Obviously sensing she wasn't welcome anymore, the girl on Brumaine's knee rose just enough to slink away toward the far end of the tavern.

With the loss of a night of pleasure, he wasn't in the mood to be jovial with the lieutenant. Hopefully, he could quickly deal with whatever it was his mentor wanted then go in search of the girl once more. "What is it, Var? What's so important you need to chase me down in here?"

From a nearby table, Var snatched a jug of water then grabbed Brumaine by his upper arm and pulled him to a standing position. "Come, sire. You are wanted in the throne room."

The throne room? His father hadn't summoned Brumaine there since his sixteenth birthday to announce to the ladies and gentlemen of the court that his fourth son was now a man and entitled to the respect and civilities due a prince of the realm. There had been much celebration and congratulations, but that had been midday. This was night, and the type of business conducted at this hour often involved secret issues of state. "What does he want?"

Var stayed silent until they were out the door then handed him the water pitcher. "Here. Drink as much as you can. It will sober you some. You'll need your wits about you for what's to come."

He did not feel drunk, but obeyed the instruction and drank deeply. Finishing, he wiped the water that had sloshed his face with the back of his hand then tossed the empty ewer aside. In the time it took to drink the water he came to the conclusion Var knew more than just the mere summons. "What's this all about? Am I in some kind of trouble?"

Var waved for him to proceed. "I'm not at liberty to say anything. The only thing I can tell you is, it's important."

He sighed then turned and trudged toward the castle some eight blocks away. With the cloudless sky, the moon and the stars illuminated the towers enough for Brumaine to make out the building's silhouette. Rising several stories above the surrounding homes and occupying several city blocks, the lit windows and terraces helped to highlight the structure. The throne room was on the fourth level. As they walked in silence he studied the windows and determined which one was it. *There—the one with the wide, lit balustrade. I can even see people on it. I wonder who is with my father?*

As he entered the castle, he acknowledged the perfunctory salutes with his usual simple nod, a routine practice he normally performed almost absentmindedly, but tonight he carefully observed each guard they passed for any kind of inkling as to what awaited him. Did they show any anxiety? Any nervous motion?

Nothing was out of the ordinary. Whatever awaited, these simple soldiers had no idea. Nevertheless, a certain amount of uneasiness settled into his stomach as he worked his way through the halls and up the stairs.

By the time he reached the large double doors leading in, between the wine and the water, combined with the trepidation he felt, he needed to resist the urge to find a chamber pot room and relieve his bladder. Because the page at the doors ran in to announce him, there was no time to make the side trip. He would have to hold it.

The page returned to escort him in. His father stood near one of the map tables showing all of the seven realms and Piaxia to the north. Near him were his military commander, Oberus, his pompous oldest brother, Doren, a few other officers, a scribe in one corner, and a trio of men he had not met before. The three were expensively dressed, and Brumaine drew the first assumption that they were wealthy merchants.

His father looked over to Var. "Ah, Lieutenant, you've found him. Good. Now we can begin in earnest."

He approached the table and, after a quick glance into the faces of those gathered, bowed, clasped his hands behind his back, and did his best to stand regally. Despite the king being his father, he needed to show subservience. "What is it you need of me, Your Highness?"

"A mission of importance. Your brother, Doren here, is to lead as emissary to the trade negotiations in Riaz. I want you to accompany him to learn the art of diplomacy and to provide whatever input you can to the process."

Diplomacy? Until now, no one, including my father, cared one bit about my opinion. His father's focus was intent on him, obviously waiting for some kind of acknowledgment. On Doren's face, did he detect a flicker of a sneer? Why had Cassan not been picked? He was the second oldest. Until he figured out what was going on he knew he must accept the duty. There was always the possibility he was finally going to be given his due. "I am honored at the chance to prove my worth. Will I have any specific duties assigned solely to me?"

"Yes, we've given a number of them to you." His father glanced at the scribe. "Note keeper—provide the prince with his list."

The servant rose from a desk covered in various documents and handed Brumaine a scroll. He unfurled it and scanned through. Without too much detail, it appeared the majority of his duties involved the management of supplies and goods necessary for the journey. Not exactly the kind of responsibility he was hoping for. Still, it was something. He rolled up the scroll and stuffed it inside his doublet. "I look forward to commencing these duties. When is this trade meeting to take place?"

"The conference takes place in Riaz twelve days from now. You, your brother, and these gentlemen here representing the Merchant's League, along with a proper contingent of the commander's men will depart from the port town of Pero five days from now. It's expected the sea voyage will take anywhere from four to six days depending upon prevailing winds. That should place you in their capital, Lymos City, anywhere from one to three days early."

With Pero a four-day journey, it only left him a single day to make ready. "So soon? Did we not have further advance notice of this conference than that?"

His father came to stand beside him and placed a hand on Brumaine's shoulder. He pointed down at the map. "Look carefully. To both the north and the west, Piaxia and Sechland, we have enemies. To the south is Fermia whose neutral status leave us surrounded, without a friend. Know that all of these countries will also have representatives at this meeting. Not counting those realms farther south, our last strong trading partner to whom we have friendly lanes of trade is Riaz. No doubt there are forces at work looking to choke off that last line of support. It is imperative these meetings result in protecting what is needed. It is why you are entrusted with what may at first seem trivial duties. Much of our future rides on this mission."

There was something in what his father said. The idea of efforts made to slow such notification did not seem so far-fetched. A scribe paid to be tardy in his delivery to a messenger who, in turn, might be handsomely rewarded to delay his own delivery, and a week's notice could suddenly be reduced to days. He could understand the urgency in ensuring such an undertaking proceed without difficulty.

A pang in his side reminded him of another urgency demanding his attention. Forced to wince and react with a hand to the affected area, he drew his father's attention.

"What is it, Brumaine? Are you ill? Is this going to prevent you from going on this trip?"

He gave a weak smile. "No, merely the requirement of a natural bodily function to be performed is demanded of me."

A number of others nearby, his brother and the commander amongst them chuckled. His father gave him a gentle slap on the shoulder. "Go, then. We shall finish up without you. Report to the commissary in the morning and show your orders."

Bowing once more, he made for the door with Var close behind. Knowing the castle by heart, he headed directly for the chamber pot room. The relief he felt as he voided his bladder made him weak in the knees. As he did, he could hear Var pacing behind him.

"There is danger in this mission."

Startled at the statement, he missed his aim and he sprinkled one foot. *Damn!* He finished and buttoned up his pants then faced his mentor. "Why do you say that? No one would act with malice at such a conference. It would be foolhardy."

"Perhaps, but prudence is still required. You must take all precautions. I will not be with you."

Var had been assigned to Brumaine since he was five years old. In the thirteen years since, he had trained him, educated him, and schooled him in the duties expected of a prince. He was also his personal guardian. Sure, he gave Brumaine the space he needed to go on his own when he wanted to, but deep down the idea that Var would be there when necessary had, until now, seemed unshakeable. "Why?"

"I've been assigned to protect the merchants on this mission. They will be sailing in the comforts of their own vessel, whereas you will be on a navy one. We will meet up in Lymos, but much can happen in the intervening time."

He extended his hand, and Var did the same, taking his forearm in a soldier's clasp. "You have watched over me since I was a child and taught me what you could. I'll survive until then. Besides, that time will be spent either on Morica soil or one of her warships. What could go wrong?"

Var gave one last squeeze then released the grip. "Perhaps, but it is my nature to consider all possibilities. Just be careful."

He studied the intensity in Var's eyes. There was great seriousness there. "I will."

"Good. Let's get you to your rooms."

He followed the second lieutenant out of the door and through the castle toward his private suite. *Var's just being overly cautious. There's nothing to worry about.*

CHAPTER 5

The weekend always energized Kero. No school and no advanced accounting classes. It was a time to socialize with his friends and wander the city market. He still carried the copper his master had given him a few days before and was scouting various sweet sellers to see if something caught his eye. True, he carried a small purse filled with other coppers and a couple of silvers besides the coin in his pocket, but those were his master's and meant for different things.

Rambling alongside was his friend Derak. Though a year younger and a hand shorter, his pal's endless energy, matching the acuity of red in his shock of hair, was more than enough to compensate whenever they decided to do anything. Today, instead of looking to buy a fancy treat with his copper, he scouted for ones that were two for the price. If his master knew of his intention to give the second away, he would get another scolding. Small rebellions like this gave Kero cause to smile. Despite his master's teachings, he liked to have friends and to treat them well.

After picking out two pastries and handing one to Derak, a swirl of black cape seen from the corner of his eye startled him. Was that the master? Had his act of kindness been seen? Impossible. The master never came to the city market.

Still, the idea he had been found out made turning to look difficult. His breath caught in his throat as he searched for the cape. Only after he espied the wearer did he finally exhale. Like his master, the man was dressed all in black with the exception of purple piping on his sleeves and trousers and the same purple as an edging band around his cape.

Not an outfit he had seen before, especially in warm weather such as the day bore. Obviously, the man was not a resident of the city. Older, and with a graying beard, the stranger was scanning the crowd. For the briefest of moments, their eyes met, and Kero thought he detected the slightest of nods.

Why? He did not know the man. It bothered him he had been

identified.

A nudge in his ribs broke his concentration.

"Whatcha looking at?"

Derak smiled at him, chewing away at the treat, a ring of powdered sugar round his mouth. He pointed out the man in black. "That man. See how he's dressed? I first thought it was the master, but you can see it isn't. Who do you think he is? Where is he from?"

Finished eating, Derak wiped his mouth with his sleeve. "Don't know, but maybe merchant Orvest does. See? The man is standing between Orvest and another older man. They're together."

Derak was right. Kero's focus on the man in black had been so intense, he'd failed to notice the proximity of the other two. Orvest was fairly new to Lymos. Arriving only a couple of years before, the trader had quickly established a thriving business in town. Kero suspected his success was not endearing him to the five main families running the Merchant's Guild.

Trading in things Kero never bought, he had no reason to ever visit the man's stall, but that never stopped him and his friends from wandering through, just being nosy. Unlike other merchants, rather than shoo them out in a derogatory way, Orvest always treated them politely. As a result, none of Kero's cohorts ever pocketed anything during their brief sorties in his shop.

One of the tasks assigned to Kero was to garner as much information as he could and report back. His master would probably like to know why someone would dress the same, even if there was some purple trim. Like his other friends, Derak knew Kero wanted to know things, and if the information was good there would be a copper in it for them. "I think we need to find out who they are and why they're here."

"I'm on it." Derak took off at a run straight for Orvest's stall.

Kero sauntered after his friend, giving Derak the time to cause whatever ruckus he intended to do. So as to appear nonchalant, he gazed into the various stalls as he passed them. Simple wooden structures, stacked side by side, some three or four paces across and six or seven deep, with walls only enclosing the back half leaving the front open to all passersby. The merchants would have many goods prominently displayed on tables easily accessible from the main open area where hundreds of market goers wandered.

Kero paid little attention to the various stocks of foods, clothing, trinkets, jewelry, and such while keeping Derak within his peripheral vision. His friend reached Orvest's stall without difficulty and dashed in. With the distance, he could not hear what was being said, but Orvest's reaction was not one of his usual calm demeanor. Derak's intrusion was not welcome, that was certain.

Picking up his pace, Kero still did not make it to the stall prior to his friend being apprehended by the man in black. Maybe it was his friend's plan to ascertain who the stranger was, but he doubted that. From steps away, he heard his friend's protestation at being held.

The man in black shook Derak. "Why do you need to know who I am?"

Kero stepped into the stall. "Hey Derak, what's all the fuss?"

"Kero, tell this man to unhand me. I was just looking at the stuff here."

The man released his friend and closed the gap between them. "So you're Kero. I read in your friend's mind that it is you who seeks the information. Your guard is up, young warlock. I cannot read you. Tell me, before I resort to more drastic measures, why must you know who I am?"

Orvest placed a hand on the man's arm. "Let him be, Warlock Prattrow. This one is a favorite of the Assassin Guild leader."

A warlock. That only made sense. More than likely, the man identified Kero's own mana level as comparable, hence the nod. Another skill he had yet to learn. He wondered when Orvest had become aware of his affiliation with the master. With many guild members knowing, it was a logical deduction word would get out. There was no sense in hiding the facts. "My master likes to know the comings and goings of strangers in our city."

Prattrow spat to his left. "Assassins. They have no honor. I will not satisfy his curiosity with an answer."

The third man stepped between the warlock and Kero. "This

one does. He cannot be bought. Many years ago I tried—only because I feared for my own life from those in the guild employed by my competitors. I wanted assurances none would strike against me if I made certain promises. He told me bluntly to go and negotiate with the five, something we merchants are good at. Making deals."

Kero eyed the man. Nondescript in physique, attire, or his clean-shaven facial features, yet with an appearance of smooth confidence, as if nothing rattled him and no challenge was too great. Older, yes, but still fit and youthful looking. "And you are…?"

The fellow chuckled. "Still at it, are we? No matter. Tell your master merchant Frollence is in town for a visit. A mere dalliance, I can assure him. My friend and I"—he nodded at Warlock Prattro—"are here to garner accommodations for the Piaxian delegation. I figured while I was here I would pay a visit to Orvest, a former employee of mine. It heartens me to see him doing well. It's been a long time since my last visit, but I expect I will still be well received at a house or two of the five. Over the decades, we've done a lot of business."

What was implied in the history lesson? Was this man at odds with the master? If so, why was he still alive? The master never let anyone who crossed him survive. Perhaps the man escaped across the sea before such penance had been exacted. More information was needed. "If your life is forfeit to him and you are hoping the master will not collect, you are sadly mistaken. He never forgets, or forgives."

"Twenty years more gone, and he still hasn't mellowed, has he? How long has he ruled the assassin guild with an iron fist? It seems like forever. When I plied my trade in this city all those years ago, he was ancient. Such an incredibly long life is not normal. Until a year ago, I would have thought that impossible, but seeing a real live demon for myself, I now know time has no meaning to them."

Kero wondered what the man was talking about? Demons? With the exception of Maresh, no other had ever laid eyes on so much as a finger of the master. As to demons, he had no idea what they looked like so perhaps there might be some truth to it. Nevertheless, he could not let such a slight go. "Demons are things of myth. Your aspersion is unwarranted and unwelcome."

Frollence bowed. "My apologies. No slight was intended. I only think of the smooth-skinned, slate-gray, hairless creatures, with pointed ears and teeth, incarcerated in Lia, and the lore that surrounds them—invincible to weapons and magic, un-aging, and never sleeping. It was an improper supposition. I stand corrected."

Hearing the description provided, Kero knew the man to be mistaken. "I can assure you no such description is even remotely accurate."

Frollence bowed again. "Then, with your leave, I must go, as there are still many matters to attend to and the days only so long." He pulled a silver coin from a belt pouch and tossed it in the direction of Derak who, a gleam in his eye, caught it with both hands. "Take your worthy friend and enjoy the day. Young ones such as you should not worry over such mundane matters as food and lodging for foreigners."

With a "harrumph" from Prattrow, the men turned away and continued a discussion with Orvest over the exact things Frollence had just mentioned. Derak grabbed Kero's arm and yanked him from the stall.

"A whole silver! Can you believe it? Come on. Let's go shopping."

He followed his friend for a couple of steps, but stopped when he noted Lazaan a few stalls down. How long had the man been watching? He reached out to halt his friend's headlong charge. "Come. Let's go the other way."

Derak did a double take to follow Kero's line of sight. "Oh. I see. Okay, let's do that."

Kero led the way in the opposite direction for several stalls, glancing back occasionally to see whether Lazaan followed. On the third glance behind him, he ran into someone.

"Oof! Watch where you're going, Kero."

Stod blocked his way. "Sorry, Stod. I should have been paying more attention to where I was going."

Stod put a hand on each shoulder of Kero and gazed into his face. "Are you okay? Something troubling you?"

He glanced back once more. Lazaan was no longer visible. "No. My friend and I are out shopping is all."

"As am I." Stod lifted a satchel strapped across his shoulders. "Have you seen any good deals? Some of these merchants would take my last coin if given the chance. I gather there was nothing in merchant Orvest's as you have come out empty handed."

So Stod saw him there as well. Was every assassin in Lymos following his movements? "No. Nothing that caught my eye."

"Good to know. I would hate to have to do my shopping there, him being a foreigner and all."

He vacillated between Stod and the three men in Orvest's stall. What was Stod on about? Orvest had always been polite, except maybe today. "What's wrong with foreigners?"

"They wish to strip Riaz of its wealth. Where do you think Orvest's profits go? His home, compared to other merchants of his prowess, is modest. Yet, every fortnight a ship from Piaxia laden with nothing more than leathers, animals, and dairies arrives, but when that ship departs, oh ho, only the finest of goods that pass through this port are on board."

As he stared once more in Orvest's direction, he wondered whether such a claim was true. Though Stod was a friend, his master had always taught him to never take anything as entirely correct without verifying the details—a detail further entrenched by accountant Bashar.

His reverie was broken by Derak, who slapped him on the arm.

"Told you I'd find out who those guys were."

"Plbbt! All you did was get caught by that warlock, and *he* told me who he was, not you."

"No, not him, the other guy."

Frollence? The man was polite and generous, but not the subject of his query. Warlock Prattrow was most concerning his attention. "What about him?"

"As I ran in, I heard Orvest ask how fared his daughter, the queen. The guy's royalty, or at least the father of a royal, and a queen no less. I bet he has power." Derak went into one of his short celebrations where he skipped left and right with a finger in the air. "Woohoo, I'm good."

Stod grabbed hold of Derak, stopping the prancing. "The father of Queen Tessia, ruler of Piaxia, is it?" He looked at Kero. "High company Orvest keeps, wouldn't you say?"

Kero gave one last look at the three men. High company, indeed.

CHAPTER 6

There were many more foreign delegates in Lymos, and Kero made it his business to learn about all of them and where they were staying. A number of the coins in his master's purse were spent on the information to Derak and the other friends he relied on to scout out such details.

There was a side benefit to his accounting classes. He had learned to keep proper, copious notes. Creating his own special ledger on the subject, he charted where each delegation would be housed. Those from Piaxia were staying at the home of Orvest the merchant.

At Bashar's home, he learned the Moricans would be housed by the Hamak family in their palatial estate high up in the town's wealthy quarter. Alban had stated as much when chatting with Bashar in the hall before ensconcing into Bashar's private office once more.

Those from Storburg, Fermia, Gatway, Queensland, and Braxborough were staying at various inns located throughout the city, and the delegates from Sechland were to stay right at his own location, Rock House.

Already, one of their people had taken up residence in the room next to his. A portly fellow, it was Kero's opinion the only reason the Sechlander selected Rock House was for Maresh's cooking. Over the past few days he had noted the man constantly in the common room eating something or other.

With his list complete, Kero attended to his master in the private quarters the guild leader kept in a small room on the main floor. Through the wall from the common room, the granite ledge extended into this chamber, and seated on it his master reposed, stripped of his outer garments save a short set of leather breeches.

Compared to his own fair skin and dark hair, his master was the antithesis of normal. Against the facade behind him, the master almost blended in. His skin, if Kero could call it that, resembled ever so much the stones making up the wall. In those rare moments when he touched his master, that skin felt like the rocks he skipped into the bay—smooth, but hard. How it flowed like a man's when the master moved was beyond his understanding. He recalled those early days as a young boy snuggled in those arms. They weren't strange then, only comforting when he needed it.

After hearing of the existence of demons from the man Frollence, he wondered whether his master was of that kind. Although his hide displayed various shades of gray, the skin was mottled with black lines, and both his ears and teeth were blunted. Similarities—yes, but enough differences to wonder.

He presented the compiled list to his liege, including the accounting for the number of coins he'd needed to disburse to accumulate the data, and the master grunted acceptance then tossed over a small bag of coins, more than enough to replenish what he'd dispensed to his crew.

He remained standing there while his lord settled in to read the report. He continued to study his master until, finally, his continued presence was noticed.

"Why do you tarry, Kero? Is there something else?"

His intention had been to draw such a question, but his reply caught in his throat, and he gaped like a fish thrown on the pier.

"Out with it, boy, lest you try my patience."

Until then, the will to ask had eluded him, but now he felt spurred by the angry tone. "Are you a demon?"

The assassin lord sat quietly and studied Kero for a moment. He put the papers in his lap and placed his hands on his knees. "What makes you ask such a question?"

Though he mistrusted what Frollence had originally implied, the seed of doubt in him needed to be dealt with. "I spoke with a man from Piaxia a few days ago. Frollence. You'll find his name in the report. Apparently, he is father to the queen of their land. If such a position is true, then the man would have no need to lie to embellish his standing. He told me of demons in his homeland. He described them as, let me recite exactly, 'smooth-skinned, slate-gray, hairless creatures, with pointed ears and teeth.' He also stated they lived incredibly long lives. Though not exact, you bear some resemblance, and it is said you have been here for a very long time…longer than anyone can remember."

His liege picked up the papers once more and looked through them. "Frollence, you say? I think I remember such a man from long ago. He was a merchant in this city for a number of years. Tried to bribe me. Me! The audacity. Now that he is back in town, I think I should pay him a visit."

Kero waited patiently as his master continued to scour through the sheets. When what must have been the right page and the searching ended, he decided the time was right to ask. "Master…"

A simple grunt of acknowledgment answered him.

Kero was not to be put off. "Master…"

His liege looked up and blinked. "What *is* it, Kero?"

He inhaled a healthy breath, and then exhaled loudly to highlight his exasperation. "You have not answered my question."

This time, his lord put the papers aside, stood then paced. "Except perhaps Maresh, no one is more deserving of an answer than you. I keep myself covered from others to prevent the very hypothesis that others would apply toward me. I know my appearance would have many jump to such a conclusion. Understand, although I am ensconced on this island, word has reached me of the recent war amongst the seven kingdoms and Piaxia. News of the release of demons throughout their lands and as a cause for the war has also crossed the waters to me. I found it most disquieting."

His master paused to point a finger at Kero. "Understand this. I know of these demons. I know them well. I remember when they were freed on the land some one hundred years ago. Although I am not one of them, I consider them…kin. To hear of their imprisonment once more is disturbing. The fact that almost their entire lives have been one form of imprisonment or another is reasonable cause for some level of leniency that they are not afforded."

Once more, the pacing resumed. "If it lay within my power to free these creatures and bring them to Riaz to live freely without persecution, I would do so. Sadly, such a reality is only a dream.

First of all, those who hold the demons in captivity would resist such a release, then, even if I was successful in such a task, I would find it highly unlikely their presence would be tolerated here. No, the status quo is all I can expect—all the future holds for them...*and* for myself."

Sitting down, his liege once again perused the list provided. Kero recognized the silent dismissal and exited the room. The honest diatribe was more than he expected. It was probably best he left when he did.

An interesting detail learned was that his master existed way back then. One hundred years. How much older than that was his liege? He supposed it a question for another day.

The existence of demons and of wars fought across the sea so recently gave him a different perspective on the approaching summit. Surely, there were going to be parties attending who did not see eye to eye. Perhaps a closer tab on the delegates when they arrived would be necessary.

He discovered Maresh cleaning tables in the main room and at her behest assisted in the task. As he did so, the concept of his lord as something other than human roiled over and over in his mind. Ever since he was a child, he'd known his liege was different from others, but he never equated it to how. He had always been just...different. He'd never considered the concept of demon, monster, birth defect, curse, or any other of a number of plausible explanations as a possibility. Master was master. Now, with the new knowledge and a somewhat admission on his liege's part as to that difference, the reality of that variation sank home.

He glanced over at Maresh, who was scrubbing away. Grey, wrinkled, an old woman who had trouble walking, but with an endless loyalty that translated into immeasurable respect. Over the years she had also provided a certain amount of childrearing in Kero's life. Always though, her efforts were more like babysitting than parenting. Never one to get too close, her emotional aspect had always been missing.

His thoughts wandered to his own parents. Many a year had passed since he last wondered about them. In fact, he could no longer recall what they looked like. The reason they'd abandoned him was no longer a concern. His heart had hardened against such reasoning. A parent's job was to love and care for a child, no matter the circumstances.

He paused in his work to turn and face the door to his master's room. Behind it was a creature that was an enigma, not just to him, but the entire world—mysterious, unique, powerful, and dangerous. Such was Kero's lot in life to be flung in with such a pair. He had come to accept it a very long time ago.

As to what lay behind that door, all the other descriptions and aspersions from others were secondary to the one Kero applied. Father.

CHAPTER 7

From Brumaine's vantage point on the hill, Morica's seaport town of Halistor lay gleaming below him. Though not as large as Morence, the city was still a vibrant metropolis of some ten thousand or so citizens. Despite the surrounding defensive wall, from atop his mount, he could still make out the various sectors of the town. The residential neighborhoods, rich, common then poor, flowed down the slope toward the water's edge where the commercial area merged with the wharves and shipyards.

The ride of several days had been without incident, despite the concerns of Var. That night he would sleep in a proper bed with departure for Riaz planned the following morning.

The desire to increase his mount's speed to a trot was superseded by the duty of his assignment—to ensure the safe arrival of the supplies to the ships. Several wagons loaded with foodstuffs, pigeons, and more were marshaled behind him. That, and an order of priority on who should lead the way. Directly in front of him were his brother and Oberus, chatting about the upcoming voyage. Riding ahead would be a mild insult to his sibling.

In front of the wagons the three merchants traveled in a measure of luxury in a padded carriage. Throughout the trip, they'd requested several delays where they might stretch their legs and engage in midday meals and teas. As a result, the caravan had lost a whole day's travel. The idea of spending an afternoon in one of the local inns and imbibing to his pleasure would have to wait. It would take until dark to get the ships loaded.

His brother spurred his mount forward, and those in the column followed suit, taking the meandering road leading to the main gate. To his left, a gentle stream picked up speed as it flowed downhill toward its final destination, the sea. Once inside the walls, such waters would be siphoned off to various cisterns and aquifers to serve the homes below. For now, he breathed in the fresh smell the river infused in the air around him. What waters made it to the end would be spoiled with refuse and excrement, making proximity to it nauseating.

The clack of horse hooves on the cobblestones drowned out the voices of those chatting nearby. It allowed him the opportunity to concentrate on his own thoughts, not the mindless banter of others. Since leaving Morence, one item continued to nag at him. Why was he going to this conference at all? The argument of his learning diplomacy was without merit as there were still two brothers besides Doren who were older than he. Why weren't they sent?

The constant contemplation on this issue and how the whole trip interrupted the lifestyle he had become accustomed to, fueled his anger at having been selected.

So lost in thought, it came as a surprise when a shadow passed over him. Glancing up, he noted the archway over the open entry into the city through the outer wall. The portico must be at least seven, maybe eight paces from front to back. Deep enough to trap a wagon and its team of horses between the front solid wooden gate and the rear iron-bar one. A number of open slots above allowed a measure of sunlight to stream into this dark corridor, though he knew their intent was more for the allowance of arrows to be fired through rather than their current use.

As he cleared the iron gate, the town before him suddenly looked very crowded compared to the view from up on the hill. An open courtyard greeted him, but beyond lay stacked buildings of various sorts with narrow lanes running between. Glancing down them, the tight grouping of housing structures continued as far as the vista allowed until the streets turned enough to prevent any further examination.

His brother led the caravan down the road straight ahead versus the ones heading either left or right. It only stood to reason such a lane would lead directly to the marina and the ships awaiting their passage.

Var pulled Brumaine aside. "We're here, my lord. In the confines of the city, I no longer fear the perils of the open road. I think it safe to say my anxieties were without warrant. There should be no troubles in town before our ships hit the open water tomorrow. As you will be on the warship while I on the merchant, the likelihood of anyone at risk is greater with me than you."

Having experienced firsthand the largess with which the merchants suffered travel, he wished the positions could be swapped. "I suspect the only danger aboard the merchant ship would be getting too drunk and falling overboard, but I know your abstinence will prevent that. More than likely, there won't be a drop of drink available on the warship, and I only hope I do not wither and die before the voyage is over."

Var laughed. "Then we both shall arrive in Lymos sober and thirsty, you for drink, me for action, as the talk by the merchants will surely bore me stiff."

Brumaine joined his mentor in the mirth. "I suspect what you say is true. I had the misfortune of sitting with them for one meal. With the exception of constant praise for Doren for leading this mission, the conversation focused on the prices of silks and the various levels of quality and thread count. I could not finish eating fast enough so I could be excused."

"Then you know of the fate that awaits me. Combined with the queasiness I get when sailing, my stomach will suffer more than I can fathom."

Only having enjoyed pleasure crafts on the Lorne River close to home near Morence, he had never ventured on the large ships that plied the Great Sea. He had heard stories of seasickness so virulent causing men to be in a constant state of vomiting. Time would tell if his fortitude could stand up to the task ahead. Being so sick as to be unable to hold down a single morsel of food was not something he looked forward to. "I suppose it be best to get a good meal in us tonight before setting sail in the morning. Have you been in this town enough to know where it is best to dine?"

Var calmed, his smile disappearing. "Will you not sup with your brother and the others in the citadel?"

He shook his head. "No. I will have to be cloistered with them for the seven days of the journey aboard ship. I would prefer a night on my own before having to endure my brother's arrogance and Commander Oberus' haughtiness for such an extended period."

Var stared ahead, silent. He took several breaths before returning his attention. "So be it. I know of just the place. It is quite close to the marina. Once the boats are loaded, we will make our way there."

The laneway opened up before him, the wharf dead ahead. Beyond that, two ships sat moored. It was easy for him to identify which would be his mode of transportation. The merchant ship lay low, fat, and gaudily painted while the warship stood taller, sleeker, with two banks of oars, and fitted with a ram at the prow. On deck, he could identify ballistae set both fore and aft, whereas the merchant ship sported cabins, obviously for the comfort of the passengers.

The merchant ship boasted two sets of sails, so, in good weather, might travel well enough, but was subject to the winds. The handful of oars would be of little help except for steering. In short, the merchant vessel would take longer to navigate the gap from Halistor to Lymos but could definitely carry a much larger load of cargo. Undoubtedly, the warship, if necessary, could provide protection the entire way. As piracy on the Great Sea was often confined to small craft near shorelines, such defenses were unlikely to be needed. Var and a contingent of soldiers could more than defend an attack by any small craft on the huge merchant vessel.

Beyond, a large number of ships lay anchored in the bay. He was surprised to see so many ships. The bulk of the entire Morican fleet must be in the harbor. Perhaps this was the home port for the navy. If only he had been allowed to regularly attend his father's court, such details would be known to him.

The caravan pulled onto the wharf, and longshoremen joined with the drivers of the wagons to load the goods aboard both vessels. Brumaine needed to keep a sharp eye to ensure those goods destined for the warship did not get mixed with those headed for the merchant. Only when he was satisfied there were no errors did he take a moment to rest on a pier stanchion. A glance at the fading sun in the process of dropping below the horizon gave him satisfaction with the job done before dark.

His brother and many of the others had already headed for the citadel. Brumaine gave an excuse of doing a final inventory check for not accompanying them. The fact they showed no concern for his attendance made his decision not to show up all the easier. As long as a warm bed waited for him when his evening ended, that was all that mattered.

True to his word, Var steered him toward a neighborhood tavern filled with many common folk who lived and worked near the docks. Unlike in Morence, the knowledge he was royalty did not exist and, despite Var's uniform, they were able to mingle at ease with the people.

After an enjoyable repast of beef stew and rye bread, Var rose from his seat and gave Brumaine a nudge. "Come. Let us get some shut-eye. Morning will come all too soon. I would not want a delay in our voyage caused by your sleeping in."

He waved off his mentor. "If it's all right with you, I'm going to stay for a bit longer. I don't want to end what modest fun I'm going to get for the next little while."

Var glanced around the room. "Okay, just don't be too late. I don't see any young vixens around about to lead you astray, so I think it's safe to leave you be. You know the way to the citadel?"

He nodded. "Yes, I could see it from the docks. I'll find it."

"Right, then. I'm off. Good night."

Once Var was gone, he moved to sit with a few of the locals who, once he bought a round, accepted him into their group. As he sat there chatting, he was mildly amused by what constituted friendly banter in a port town. Most at the table were fishermen who spoke of little more than their trade. What waters were yielding the greatest catches, how much certain rarities were fetching at the market, the outrageous price for new nets and techniques to mending the old ones.

When they asked him what he was doing in town, he sloughed off their inquiries by stating he was just passing through and would be taking voyage in the morning to Riaz. This led to another whole round of complaining about Riaz fishermen infringing on their waters and the lengthy story from one about how he rammed a poacher and sent him to the bottom of the sea. His mates chastised him by stating the story was a fish tale to the extreme as his little craft couldn't sink a fish line float.

By the time he tired of hearing the stories and begged their excuse so that he may leave, upon standing he realized he might have had one or two libations too many. Thinking the night air might do him good, he staggered out the door into the street. *Now where is that darn castle?*

The buildings seemed to be crowded too close to him. He couldn't see over to try and espy his destination. Craning his neck to see, a moment of dizziness passed. He shook his head to clear it and breathed in deeply. That wasn't going to work. Deciding the best course of action was to return to the wharf and reacquire his bearings toward a waiting bed, he lurched down the road.

When he reached the docks, he took in the two boats still moored there. Dark out, there wasn't much to see, but not only were there two guards on patrol on the wharf, he could also make out at least one lit lantern on the warship. Somebody was on guard there as well.

The two guards, walking side by side, were passing the open gangplank to the merchant ship. When they were some ten paces past, Brumaine could swear he saw something scamper up it. Another dizzy spell had him blinking hard. Maybe he was seeing things. No, it was real. He did his best to run and made for the ramp. As he began to ascend, his steps must have alerted the guards as they turned and were calling for him to halt.

There was no time to explain. Ahead of him, he could just make out movement amongst the crates and cargo. Someone, or something, as what he saw could not have been more than a small child, but with extra-long arms and legs. Some kind of animal maybe? Not a dog, and too large for a cat, he could recollect no such creature that fit this description.

Making the deck, he stopped again to look and listen for his quarry. Whatever it was, it was now hiding. He would need to go slow and search carefully.

No sooner did he take two steps when rough hands grabbed him from behind.

"Hold there! You're under arrest for trespassing."

He tried to struggle free from the grasp of the guards, the taller one grabbing him at the shoulder whilst the shorter at his wrists. "Help me. There's some kind of animal loose on board."

The taller one converted his grasp to a bear hug. "The only thing we see is you trying to board this vessel."

This wasn't right. He was royalty. "Unhand me. I am Prince Brumaine. I command you to release me."

The shorter one, attempting to tie Brumaine's hands together, snorted. "Right...and I'm the king. Now hold still."

He twisted hard and broke free from their grip. "Such insolence will not be tolerated. I shall have you whipped. Now you will—"

The blow from the pommel of the tall one's sword as the man cracked him on the head forced Brumaine to his knees. As he tried to gather his wits, he was vaguely aware of his hands being tied together. While still dazed, he sensed he was moving then realized he was being pulled by the arms down the ramp and onto the wharf.

The soldiers dragged him into the guardhouse and deposited him in the gaol, locking its iron door. He could hear them talking as they walked away.

His head cleared some, and he made note of his surroundings with the little moonlight entering through the window bars. The cell was too small by several hands in either direction to accommodate his length. Against one wall lay a thin pile of straw. The men were gone, back to their rounds. There was no one to hear his plea. With no choice but to make the best of it, he decided to get some rest. His hands still tied behind his back, he struggled to lie down in the hay.

So much for getting a good night's sleep in a soft bed.

***

The door creaked open, letting in more light than Brumaine was ready for. Squinting against the brightness, he struggled into a sitting position. Maybe now, he could get this matter cleared up. Someone must recognize him. If not, the royal signet he carried on the chain round his neck would suffice. He should have thought of it the night before, but between the drink and the clubbing to his head, his mind was too addled.

"There you are."

Var. At least the comedy of his situation would end, though he bore no doubt about the ribbing he would receive. "Get me out of here. Those idiots on guard last night assaulted me. Me, a member of the royal family. I demand to speak to their superior officer."

His tutor drew a dagger from a sheath strapped to his thigh and cut the bonds holding Brumaine's wrists. "There's no time for retribution. We should have sailed two hands ago with the morning tide. It's only because of the guard change that we discovered you at all. There are more than a few persons upset our departure has been delayed."

As he rubbed his wrists to restore the lost circulation, the image of his brother sneering and ordering he be left behind was the first thing to pop into Brumaine's head. "Doren can bloody well wait. We'll depart only after I've had those two fools whipped."

Var pulled Brumaine to his feet. "Fortunately, your brother did not order a departure without you. In fact, it was he who was most adamant you be found. I know there is some bad blood between you two, but remember this, it is still the blood that binds a family. I cannot believe he would wish that much ill for you."

Stepping out onto the wharf, he made note of the six soldiers waiting just outside the guard house. Many a glance was exchanged. Brumaine suspected there would be much discussion of his incarceration—some with concern for their brethren, some with humor. It was the expected insults to his station that most perturbed him. The idea his arrest would be a point of ridicule amongst the men was something he would have to live with for a while. "Fine. Just get me aboard and let's be off then. I can deal with this matter when I return."

He followed Var toward the ramp leading to the warship, the soldiers falling in behind. Outside of a few gazes, most people on the wharf were ignoring them. Normal dock traffic was in play as two other ships were now in port with the off and onloading of cargo taking precedence.

Once he reached the ramp, the whole reason why he'd tried to board the merchant came back to him. He stopped to face Var. "Last night I saw an animal of some sort board your vessel. It's what I was after. A strange looking thing—small, like a child, but all arms and legs. It scampered up the ramp in the dark when the guards weren't looking. You need to find it."

Var nodded. "I shall conduct a thorough search. Have no fear. If it's aboard, I shall find it."

He knew Var's word to be trustworthy. "Good. When we dock in Lymos, you can tell me all about it. I am most curious to know."

Var left for the merchant ship and, as Brumaine climbed the ramp, he looked up to see his brother watching from the deck. Their eyes met then Doren turned away and began conversing with Oberus. The cold shoulder was more than acceptable to him. The last thing he needed was to be chided by his sibling. It was best he went aft and retired to the bunk assigned him in the officer's quarters. His sleep had been fitful. A change of clothes and a hearty meal followed by a nap beckoned him.

The quartermaster showed him around, got him a fresh uniform, and led him to the galley where the cook provided a warm stew. As he sat to eat, through his feet he could feel the sway of the boat moving. They were on their way.

CHAPTER 8

Brusk helped her down from the wagon. The whirlwind trip north from Sechland to Zon in Piaxia and across the country to the port city of Dun, though originally memorable, especially the many oddly ruddy-faced people near the dock, was now already forgotten as Darlee marveled at the merchant ship awaiting her boarding. It was about to come true, the voyage across the Great Sea to Riaz.

She tugged on her foster father's arm and pointed. "Up there. I see a lookout post at the top of the mast. Can I go up? I want to see everything from there."

Brusk turned his head, following the aim of her finger. "Up there? It looks awful tiny. I'd be afraid of you falling. Besides, it would be up to the captain to decide who goes up there, not me."

From where she stood, the platform looked to be about twenty hands square with the mast sticking through the middle. In her mind, there was plenty of space. There were advantages to being small. "Aw, please? I can fit on that easy. It would be so wonderful to do it. Won't you please ask? You're in charge of this mission. They'll let me if you say so."

Brusk sighed. "Let me make sure everything and everyone is aboard first. After that, I'll ask. I figure it'll take at least a hand before we're ready to go." He reached into a pocket on his belt and retrieved his coin purse, taking from it a small handful of coppers. "Here. I can see the town market square a block away up the hill. Go and buy yourself something sweet to eat to kill the time. Make sure you get extra to bring on board. The gods know what you'll get to eat on the voyage. I shudder at the thought of having fish every day until we get there."

"On second thought..." He pulled out a silver and handed it to her. "See if you can find a cured ham for me. No sense me taking any chances and getting sick on the way."

She pocketed the coins in her own purse and headed up to the market square. Unlike her hometown, Visk, where the street sellers gathered near the front gate to hawk their wares, here in Dun the market was close to the wharf. She could only guess the traffic from the docks outweighed the goods coming overland.

As expected, those merchant stalls closest to the wharf were selling exactly what her foster father had an aversion to. Fish. She'd seen him eat the stuff before, but he always did complain of being nauseous after. One time, when they ate some shellfish, he had been violently sick for a day. That was the day Daphora showed her how to heal someone. Together, they cured him of what her teacher said was akin to food poisoning. She explained that some people had food allergies and her foster father's must be certain types of seafood. Darlee had eaten more of the stuff than Brusk yet she never got sick. Obviously, such allergies did not apply to her. She loved fish.

Despite how good some of the catches looked, she knew better than to tarry at any of the displays but proceeded to that part of the market where the butchers were.

Once her purchases were complete, she worked her way through the busy throng of shoppers and was jostled by one young man who bumped into her hard, causing her to drop all. "Hey! Watch where you're going!"

Instead of apologizing, the fellow continued on his way into the crowd, ignoring her complaint. Irritated at the rudeness, she turned to continue her mission when she realized something didn't feel right.

Looking down, it didn't take long to spot that her pocket belt had been ravaged by a knife and her purse gone. Robbed in broad daylight! She spun quickly to try and spot the pickpocket.

With the man no longer in view, she remembered the direction he took and dashed that way in hopes of spotting him. There, some fifteen paces ahead, the individual she sought was walking briskly toward the far end of the market and a narrow lane between houses. If she lost him in the streets of an unfamiliar town, she didn't know if she would ever find him. "Stop, thief!"

He glanced back and then broke into a run. At the rate he was moving, there was no way she would catch up. She needed to slow him down and decided a decent tap on the shoulder with a weak lightning bolt ought to do the trick. Summoning the magic within her, she threw out a hand in the man's direction and let the bolt fly.

The nice thing about magical bolts, they never missed. Once hit, the robber cartwheeled through the air and landed with a thud on the ground. She made it to his side and retrieved her stolen purse from his weak grasp while he groaned in obvious pain. "That will teach you to steal from me."

A small crowd gathered, and she pointed down at the fallen thief. "This man tried to steal my purse." She pulled the slashed belt into better view. "See? He cut my belt and made off with my coins."

Two men, dressed in black with sea-green stripping, stepped through the gathered onlookers and approached her. The closest of the two, an older man with a beard, grabbed her arm. "Hold there! You're under arrest."

From previous encounters, both in Visk and Zon, she identified the men for what they were—warlocks. In Piaxia, they were the law. The incredulity of what was happening momentarily froze her in place. "Arrested? Me? Whatever for?" She nudged the fallen man with her foot. "This is the criminal. He attempted to rob me."

The second warlock heaved the groggy man from the ground, a firm grip on the thief's upper arm. "That he is, but it is illegal for women to practice magic. He might lose a hand. Your life is forfeit."

The horrifying time when she'd been held prisoner, tortured, burned, cut, beaten, with the final loss of one eye, rebounded in her mind. She would not let that happen again. "No!" Summoning magical fire, she created an aura of flame around her, singeing the man's hand clutching her wrist. He yanked it back with a howl.

The second warlock dropped the robber to the ground once more and unleashed a lightning bolt directly at her chest. It crackled and fizzled against her magical shield. Though it was of no effect, she identified the power of the blast to be lethal.

The crowd edged back quickly. More than likely, none wanted

to get caught in the crossfire of a magical duel. She studied the two warlocks as they separated in an obvious attempt to flank her. In her magical sight, both men glowed, perhaps focusing on their own defensive auras. She could summon enough magic to blast through the defense of either, but it would seriously weaken her and also result in the death of the warlock she targeted. She did not want to kill them, only incapacitate them.

She needed a boost. Glancing around, she spotted a location where bare rock protruded from the cobbled ground. She edged her way there, while the two warlocks moved to attain polar positions.

She stepped on the rock and felt it. The Key. It surged through her. The older warlock on her right's eyes went wide as he stopped moving.

"By the gods."

She allowed a tight smile to cross her face. "You will stand down. I do not wish to harm you. I am not of this country. I am from Sechland, and there it is legal for a woman to wield magic. I am here merely seeking passage from your port to Riaz. Allow me to retrieve the packages I have dropped, and I will be on my way."

The warlock squinted for a moment. "Do I have your word you will be gone from this city?"

The younger warlock, now to her far left, paused as well. "Craxius, what are you saying? We cannot let her go."

Craxius glared at his comrade. "Shama, open your eyes, you fool. Look at her aura. She's at Lord level. She has the Key. Standing on bedrock like that, she can kill you, me, and everyone in this square without breaking a sweat."

"That cannot be. She's only a child, only a…a female."

Now she was insulted. She gestured an open hand toward Shama then closed her fist while summoning her magic. The man's magical defensive aura shattered, and he crumpled to the ground. She seized control of his muscles. Shama could not move. "Proof enough?"

Craxius held his hands up in surrender. "Yes. Please…free him. He is new to the brotherhood and without knowledge or experience of one such as you. I give you my word you may go safely. Just don't hurt anybody."

Darlee released her hold on the man, and he scrambled to his feet then moved to stand beside Craxius. Her goods still lay where they fell. She pointed at them. "My packages?"

Craxius nudged his partner. "Go. Retrieve the lady her goods. The sooner we get her aboard her vessel, the better."

Shama scowled, but did as he was told. By the time he returned, a contingent of soldiers had arrived, weapons at the ready. The lieutenant of the troop joined up with Craxius while Shama once more picked up the thief from where he lay. "What goes here? I received an urgent summons that things were gone amok in the market and all I find is you faced off with this young lass. Should I be taking her into custody?"

"No. If you wish, you may accompany us to the docks. The lady is leaving for Riaz. She has the magic of a warlock Lord but claims she is a Sechlander, not Piaxian. She has promised no harm to anyone. I've given my word she may go peaceably. It would be best a clear path be provided so that no other incidents can occur."

The lieutenant snapped his fingers and pointed at her. His troop of ten men lined up five a side around her. "We shall assist you, but I will expect verification of her tale when we get to the docks."

Taking the lead in front of her, the lieutenant led his men down toward the wharf, clearing a path for her to walk. She gave a nod to Craxius, lifted her chin, and marched between the soldiers. To either side, the townsfolk whispered to each other, and she heard the word *witch* spoken now and then. Her only concern was what would Captain Brusk think when she arrived at the ship with such a retinue?

As they neared the vessel, the lieutenant signaled a halt to his men who closed ranks around her. While the troop commander engaged in a discussion with the ship's captain, she glanced up at the deck and spotted her foster father at the rail.

"Darlee girl, what's all this about?"

He dashed down the gangplank and would have charged into her had the lieutenant not intercepted him. "Hold there. Are you

Captain Brusk, the one accountable for those from Sechland seeking passage from here to Riaz?"

Brusk produced a document from inside his jacket and handed it to the lieutenant. "Aye, that I am. Why have you arrested my stepdaughter?"

Without answering, the lieutenant scanned the parchment. When he finished, he handed it back to Brusk. "All seems to be in order here. I am going to release this young woman back to you. Some advice, though. Witchcraft is illegal in Piaxia. You would be wise to respect our laws before bringing one such as her within our borders. As Master Craxius has promised her safe passage, I cannot hold her, but next time I might not be so lenient."

The lieutenant swirled a finger in the air at his men and led them away from the dock. Her foster father placed an arm round her shoulders and guided her up the gangplank. At the top, she paused to look back. Still standing at the base of the ramp was Craxius. He waved.

Surprised at this, she made a small wave back. She even smiled a little. Perhaps the warlock was not so bad, merely surprised. The same could not be said for his cohort who'd tried to kill her.

The ship's captain called out to make sail, and a number of sailors nudged her out of the way as they pulled the gangplank aboard.

She moved to the center of the deck with Brusk. He placed his hands on her shoulders. "Now, what's all this business about?"

It took time to explain everything that happened—from the thief robbing her to her zapping him and the ensuing magic battle with the warlocks until her final escort by the troops. She finished and awaited her punishment.

Her foster father sighed. "Well, outside of a cut belt, there's no damage done. We'll be leaving any moment and while you were away, I spoke with the captain, so up ya go."

She glanced at the main mast and the platform at its top then gave her foster father a hug. "Thank you. I was frightened they would imprison me. I couldn't bear that again."

He stroked her hair. "I know. It was terrible what happened to you before. No one will be taking you while I'm around. Go on up there and enjoy the view as we leave port."

He hoisted her to the ropes, and she clambered up toward the crow's nest. There was no rail. Instead, ropes ran through holes near the edge and were tied to the mast near its top. They gave her plenty to hold onto, and she could also wedge her feet to prevent them from shifting.

The boat moved away from the wharf and headed for the cove exit. Glancing back at the docks once more, she could still see the older warlock watching her leave. She wondered what he was thinking about. Perhaps her display of magic might have changed his opinion on whether women should be allowed to do so. She hoped so.

A fresh breeze caught the sail below her, and the ship quickened in its speed. As they cleared the breakwall, only open sea lay before her. Her hair billowed round her head. The taste of salt was in the air. She was going to enjoy this trip. Nothing would stop that now.

CHAPTER 9

The week passed with the excitement of new boats and dignitaries arriving every day. Kero, his friend Derak in tow, spent long afternoons wandering the pier listening to whatever snippets of information he could hear. Whenever something caught his attention, he would focus on the conversation and use his skill to read the surface thoughts of those talking.

Most times, there was nothing else of value to learn, but the odd extra detail would emerge. For example, the wariness of those from Storburg regarding what might be the real intentions of the summit. Without access to the sea except for the Lorne River, they feared the military aspect of the meeting would outweigh the trade portion and they would get shut out.

Those from Braxborough and Queensland were united in demanding a fair share of trade. Being as far south as they were and the trade route to them longer, they needed assurances their share would be protected.

The Gatway delegation seemed satisfied with the status quo and didn't want any changes at all.

Derak nudged him and pointed to the open waters beyond the harbor. "Hey, Kero, can you make out who that is?"

A trireme neared. From atop the mast, he could make out the purple and gold flag. "It's Piaxian. My guess it's strictly military. It looks like the deck is loaded with weapons, not cargo."

They waited for it to reach the pier and dock. As it tied up at the far end, they couldn't get close as guards cordoned off the area. They were relegated to stand amongst the fishermen as they brought in their catches for the day. Staring down the pier, Kero made out both Frollence and the warlock Prattrow waiting for those on board the Piaxian ship to disembark. From his previous encounter, he knew better than to get too close to them. The warlock would detect him.

The first to come ashore was a tall young man dressed all in black with purple piping, not like Prattrow as the youth wore no cloak, but similar enough to make Kero wonder whether he also was a warlock. This concept was further entrenched in his mind when he noted Prattrow nod in deference to the new arrival.

Behind him came another young man, dressed in full military uniform. From his facial features, Kero guessed him to be the older brother of the one in black. Both had dark hair, strong chin, and high cheekbones. Kero guessed the fellow was of some real high rank, perhaps commander. This was not surprising as both Storburg and Queensland had also sent their military leaders. What was surprising was the size of the man. Though the first was tall, this one was perhaps two hands above everyone. He had never seen anyone so big. Though not as heavily muscled as Stod, not shabby either. Combined with his height, the man was more than a match for anyone, perhaps even Stod.

Derak whistled. "Wow. They must feed them well in Piaxia. Look at the size of that guy. What do you say I see whether I can run circles round him?"

He put a staying grip on Derak's shoulder. "Not now. I don't want to get kicked off the dock."

Derak held out his hand toward the sun. "There's less than a hand before dusk. They're going to kick us off soon anyway."

Derak was right. Already, the last of the fishermen were packing up and heading into town. Soon their end of the dock would be empty and they would stand out as a couple of interlopers. Wanting to wait until the Piaxian delegation passed, he tugged Derak to follow him and hide amongst the fishing crates.

His friend held up and pointed out to sea. "Look. Two more boats coming in."

This was interesting. It would be lucky if the boats made it to the pier before the sunlight gave out. The rules in Lymos were simple. No boats docked on the sea side after sundown. The shore side was reserved for the local fishermen's boats, now all tied up for the night. What would the port authority do?

From the small house near the entrance to the pier, the dock masters came out and gestured toward the oncoming vessels. Five in total, one from each of the major merchants, they tallied all inventories that entered or left the docks. Kero crept closer so he might overhear the discussion.

Despite accidentally jostling some fishing crates, his approach appeared unnoticed as none looked his way, such was the heat of the argument. Three of the men wanted to call it a day and go home, but one was steadfast in allowing the docking while the fifth attempted to play peacekeeper. It didn't take Kero long to discern the holdout was from the Hamak family. He had seen the man a few times in the home of Bashar.

In the fading sun, he could not make out what colors flew on the two ships. As far as he knew, the only countries whose emissaries were yet to arrive were Sechland and Morica. Obviously, these were one of the two and, as he had already determined the house of Hamak would host the Moricans, it only made sense the two ships inbound bore those same people.

Finally, an agreement was made to solve the impasse. The ships could dock, but no goods, only people could come ashore. Once the emissaries were ashore, the boats were to anchor in the bay with the others. The peacekeeper agreed to ensure such occurred while the Hamak man strode onto the pier to greet the arrival and the three others headed up the hill toward their respective homes.

He made his way back to Derak's side and looked down the pier once more. "Anything happen?"

"Yeah, well, sort of. No real cargo, only people. Just a couple of small crates some of the Piaxian sailors are carrying. They've already untied but haven't moved. Everyone's pointing and looking at the two ships coming in. I guess they're waiting for them to dock."

Two more large ships. They should make for a tight fit. That would be interesting. With darkness descending, it should be difficult to maneuver without bumping the Piaxian ship. Would there be a flare-up? Having only learned of the recent war between Morica and Piaxia, something as innocent as an errant jostle may be all that was needed.

The dock lanterns were lit so the incoming boats should be

able to see the pier without problem. The far side of the Piaxian ship might be another matter. The young man in black raised his hands and sent a light orb up and over his ship. Question answered. A warlock indeed.

The Morican vessels were now visible. Oars out, they were rowing in, sails down. Over the water, he could hear the captains yelling orders to guide their boats. One ship was a merchant, the other a warship. The merchant pulled closest to shore, leaving a spot between it and the Piaxian vessel for the other. It was turning in to be nose to nose with the Piaxian. Both boats featured heavy rams out front.

He could see it now. Unless the Morican ship backwatered immediately, there would be no stopping a minor collision. The order came, but a moment too late. The ram of the Morican craft caught the Piaxian's, sending a shudder through the boat and causing it to bump hard against the pier.

The Morican ship settled into its berth, and the ramp was lowered. Kero noted Alban Hamak, along with a couple of men, probably employees of his, waited on the pier where the ramp landed.

The Piaxians moved to wait nearby while a host of people disembarked, the one in front dressed most regally. His garb told Kero this was a person of royalty. Most of the others were dressed in uniform with exception of one black-haired man also dressed well, but not quite so. Glancing back and forth, Kero came to the realization the two were brothers, the first one older. Their likeness was too close to bear any other interpretation. Interesting. Both countries had sent brothers to the talks, only their order reversed on who was in charge.

Alban greeted the royal. "Welcome, Prince Doren. I am pleased to meet you personally. I have brought with me two men to help you with your belongings. A wagon awaits to bring us to the estate."

"It is most gracious of you, Alban Hamak. We will be but a moment to unload and accept your hospitality. I have been told the house Hamak sets a most wondrous table."

The younger Piaxian brother, obviously leader of his delegation, moved toward the Morican prince. "Before you leave this dock, there is the unfriendly manner in which you have jostled our ship. I believe an apology is due."

Alban stepped between the men. "Do not exacerbate the situation, young Piaxian. I am sure no foul was meant."

Doren reached out and guided Alban out of the way. "Indeed, my sincerest apologies. It seems my ship's captain erred in his approach to the pier." He glanced at the Piaxian ship. "It appears there is no damage to your vessel. As a result, nothing more than a friendly bump."

Color came to the cheeks of the Piaxian. "Blind as well as dumb. I had shed enough light for him to see our vessel from the mouth of the harbor."

"Tsk, tsk, young man. You must not let such a triviality upset you so." He extended a hand. "Prince Doren of Morica. To whom do I have the pleasure of addressing?"

The man in black ignored the proffered hand. "Regent Tarlok of Piaxia. It seems we are to be combatants at the negotiations."

Tarlok's brother stepped quickly between the regent and the prince. "Here now, fighting is my forte." He spun to face his brother and in the act bumped Prince Doren hard to the ground. Turning, he proffered a hand to the fallen Morican. "Oh, my sincerest apologies. It seems I erred when turning." With little obvious effort, he hoisted the prince to his feet and dusted him off. "It appears you are unhurt. As a result, nothing more than a friendly bump. Commander Savan at your service."

A couple of the Moricans, with hands on the hilts of their swords, neared Savan, but Prince Doren, though red in the face, waved the men back. "Forsooth, a couple of friendly bumps in the night. To avoid any further instances, it be best we all resign ourselves from this pier. There will be daylight enough to see properly when the negotiations begin the day after tomorrow."

Regent Tarlok waved toward the city. "Come Savan. Let us quit first as is our right having docked first. The Moricans can wait until after we have left."

Alban moved to block Tarlok's path. "I would think as we are closer, such honor should be to the Moricans who are my guests."

"We are *all* your guests, or have you forgotten, Alban of the Hamak family? It is at your father's invitation we are here. Do not try to elevate one country over another."

Once more, Prince Doren pulled Alban aside. He motioned to the crates still being unloaded, including one filled with pigeons, their obvious distress at being moved while caged causing them to flutter and cry extensively. "It is of no consequence. We are not ready anyway. Let them pass."

The Piaxians marched up to Kero's location then stopped at Prattrow's urging. "There's someone behind the crates."

Derak winked. "It's me that guy senses. See you on the morrow."

His friend dashed out and danced in and around the Piaxians "It's me. I spent that silver and thought maybe I'd find you guys to see if any of you needed my help. Generosity such as yours is something I shouldn't forget."

He dashed in and out, tagging the men and pleading for a coin. When he got to Savan, the big fellow nabbed him. "Hold, little one. I'll engage your services. A nice silver to tell me all you know while leading me to the best tavern in Lymos."

Derak had struggled until Savan finished talking then looked up at the big man and smiled. "Sure thing, Sir. Rock House. No better place to wet one's throat. And Maresh, the cook there, is the best in all of Riaz, let alone Lymos. Follow me, and I'll lead the way."

Savan gripped wrists with his brother and then the group moved off and Kero returned his focus to the Moricans. They were now proceeding his way as well, all except the younger brother. The man was engaged in a spirited conversation with the peacekeeper member of the port authority. Despite all his requests, the man would not allow him to bring any goods ashore. The two were standing in front of the warship farther down the pier when movement to Kero's right caught his attention.

Just visible, clambering down the mooring rope from the

merchant ship was a gangly little creature. Small, and all arms and legs, it moved with alacrity, clinging to the rope with both hands and feet. He recalled the description Frollence gave of a demon. This looked like one.

Once on the pier, the thing bounded straight for him. Surely, his position hidden behind the crates was not visible to it? Despite his own self-assurances, the little beast climbed the crates and leaped for his head.

"Mana food. Hiss must eat!"

"Get off of me!" Kero grabbed at the demon and pulled to dislodge it from the grip it had on his head, but to no avail. With each limb he managed to pry free, the creature would move to once more secure his hold with the other three.

Something was happening. A weakness was overtaking him. He felt lightheaded. No longer able to pull at the creature, he dropped to his knees in surrender. Would his demise be at the hands of this vile demon imp?

CHAPTER 10

A flicker of movement down the pier toward the city had drawn Brumaine's attention away from the argument with the port authority officer.

What had just dashed from the merchant ship? The creature? Var had promised to search for it. Obviously, the thing had eluded even his tutor's thoroughness.

Leaving, in mid-sentence, the lecture he was receiving, he dashed down the pier toward some crates the thing had disappeared behind. He could hear shouting. While running, he pulled his sword. The animal might be dangerous.

As he rounded the crates, he came upon the thing crouched over the head of a young man lying prone. The little beast had hands placed on the lad's forehead. Hands! This was no odd dog. Upon close examination, he knew it to be one of the demons he had heard about. The thing had a soft blue glow.

There was no time to think, only act. Word of their immunity to weapons changed his assault from striking with his sword to kicking the thing as hard as he could. It grunted as the force of his kick sent it some three or four paces down the pier. For a moment it glanced back then scurried away off toward the city.

There was no point in chasing it. The demon moved way too fast for Brumaine to win a footrace. Instead, he knelt to check on the lad. The young man appeared drowsy, but unharmed save for a few scratches. "Are you all right?"

It took a moment for a dazed look to leave the youth's face. "Yes. I think so. I'm feeling a little weak. What happened?"

He chuckled and helped the lad to his feet. "I booted the thing off you. Right now I suspect it's off somewhere nursing some sore ribs, maybe even cracked ones. Why did the demon attack you? What did it want?"

The youth looked at his fingers then met Brumaine's gaze.

"So it *was* a demon. I thought so. My mana. Somehow it drained me of it all. It was saying something about eating mana.

Called itself Hiss. I became as weak as a newborn babe. Who should I thank for my rescue?"

"My name is Brumaine." Just to be sure, he checked the lad over once more, patting him down with his hands. "Well, you seem fit enough. When I get a chance, I'll inform the authorities to look for this Hiss creature. In the meantime, let's get you home. What's your name? Where do you live?"

"Kero. I live at Rock House. It's an inn a few blocks from here."

After glancing back to see whether the port authority official was looking for him, and seeing he wasn't, he gave Kero a light shove in the back. "Lead the way then. I'll turn you over to your parents there. I'm quite sure they would like to know you've been hanging around the docks after dark."

Kero started walking. "Okay. I'm going, but just so you know, I have no parents. I live with my guardian, and he *knows* what I'm up to. He sent me here. When we get there, it would be best you not try and speak with him. He is not the most easy-going of people. Let me do the talking. If I err in my story, then you can correct me."

He considered the young man walking before him. *A smart one, this one. He has me in a predicament before I've had a chance to assess the situation. I mustn't let him have the upper hand so easily.* "I'll be the judge of that. If what you say is true, it will be most evident to me when I get there."

The lad led him a few blocks to a three-story stone building set prominently on a corner. The wooden structures crowded against it were commercial shops, the second floors obvious abodes for the merchants. The sounds coming from the open door were those he was accustomed to in the taverns he frequented. He grabbed Kero by the shoulder. "Hold. This is your home? It's a drinking hole. As it is, I wonder whether you have reached the age of ascension yet to frequent such places, I find it unlikely you have told me the truth but intend to lose me within the crowd inside."

Kero shrugged away Brumaine's grip but stayed where he was. "The rooms to let occupy the top two floors. Mine is on the second. The main room serves as both restaurant and tavern for the customers as well as many of the locals including those in the guild. Follow me in, and you will see the truth."

He looked around. The shops were dark and shut against the night. Facing west across the street were simply more of the same, and farther on lay the marina he had just quit. He could see no other option than to go inside. "Very well. Introduce me to your guardian."

Kero stepped in the door and, as Brumaine followed, he scanned the room quickly to get a lay of the place. He guessed it to be about half of the main floor with only a handful of doors exiting from it. The floor was, in all actuality, two steps down, and comprised of a mosaic of stones arranged in something of a grid pattern with larger ones near the exterior walls and underneath the pillars supporting the upper floors. The balance, a smaller variety, tightly fit to give the impression of no gaps whatsoever but a tight, solid surface. None looked chiseled to fit but instead of exact size. The chance of such a collection being properly arrayed seemed most unlikely. An enigma for sure.

All throughout the room were tables of various sizes, occupied by mostly men, though he did note a few women in the crowd, even some to his liking. All were engaged in various conversations while either drinking or supping. At the back wall, a large granite bench, as if cut from the side of the hill, ran the width of the room, and seated at one end of the long table that fronted it was the large fellow from Piaxia, the one who'd knocked his brother down. Memory of the event made him smile. His brother deserved that.

An old woman emerged from one of the doors carrying two boards of food. She glanced at him and then at the lad.

"Kero. Where have you been? There's tables to be cleared. Get to work."

Brumaine needed no more proof as to the youth's attestations, but he still wished to see through his promise. He nudged Kero. "Is she also your guardian?"

"No. She is the cook." Kero waved to the woman. "Is the master here? This man would speak with him."

The woman shook her head. "He has gone to a meeting with the merchant's guild. I expect him back soon enough. You can talk to him then. Now, quit dawdling."

Before the question could be asked, Brumaine acknowledged the situation in his mind. He nodded toward the lad. "Go, attend to your duties. I will sit for a while until your guardian returns. When he does, we can talk. For now, something smells good. I think I'll dine here while I wait."

Kero nodded and set to work. Glancing around, Brumaine noted there were no empty tables. No matter, he would join one occupied by the locals. A round of drinks would make his acceptance an easy one.

It took another moment for him to realize even that plan wouldn't work. The place was so crowded there wasn't an empty chair to be seen. As it was, several people were already standing. *Popular place, the food must be real good.*

The only open space was at the back of the room. He would have to share a table with the Piaxian.

The idea was not one that appealed to him. Though he appreciated how the big fellow had taught his brother a lesson, fraternizing with him would be another thing altogether. After all, their respective countries fought a war last year. It would not sit well should his possible appearance of sharing a table with the enemy been seen by other Moricans.

Then again, the likelihood of that happening was small. They had all set off for the halls of the Hamak family. No doubt, by now, they were already fed and enjoying a bountiful amount of Riaz wine. Their hosts would likewise provide for him should he go. The only question was whether he wanted to. The company of his brother and Commander Oberus would spoil the meal.

A growl from his stomach decided for him. He made his way to the far end of the stone bench, near a door, farthest from the Piaxian, and sat down. The big man glanced his way then returned his attention to his own meal.

The old woman stopped in front of him. "Food or drink?"

"Both, if you don't mind. I'll have a plate of whatever is the fare tonight and a bottle of Riaz red."

"No bottles, only flagons. The master doesn't want any broken glass in the place. We're serving braised mutton stew. I'll send the lad with the wine and bring your meal when I can."

Meat. After a week of fish, nothing sounded so delicious. "That will do fine."

While waiting for the wine and the food, he decided to better observe the big man to his left. The Piaxian, now finished with his own meal, was chatting with a couple of lasses standing nearby. It was easy to see the young women were enamored by the fellow's station. Similar to the uniform worn by Oberus, the position of commander was prevalent in the insignia present. He recalled the name—Savan. One thing for sure, even seated, the man was big, probably another factor attracting the girls.

His wine arriving, Brumaine poured from the clay ewer into the same-made mug and watched Savan continue to woo the women. It became an eyebrow-raising moment when the big fellow suddenly pointed his way.

"Perhaps my ugly friend might be able to even the odds should the two of you wish to join our table."

Ugly? If anything, he knew his looks to be better than most, and certainly no worse than Savan's. Although a quick glance at the women showed both to be reasonably comely, and his libido aroused, the idea of the Piaxian procuring a date for him was more than he could accept. "I'm afraid I'll have to decline. I'm only here for the meal."

A tough-looking fellow, clean-shaved face and head, dressed in leathers, with a fair number of knives strapped to his ribs and thighs, suddenly pulled on the arm of one of the girls, yanking her away from the table. "It is not acceptable for the likes of you two foreigners to solicit our women."

As a couple more rough-looking men sidled in behind the one in leathers, the girl who was pulled back freed her arm. "Stod, leave me be. I'll talk to who I want."

The old woman arrived and placed the steaming food before Brumaine. He glanced down then at the three men across from him. "Whatever your argument, leave me out of it." He waved a thumb in Savan's direction. "I'm not with him."

Stod shoved the other girl out of the way. "It certainly looks like it to me. You're seated together, and I distinctly overheard the two of you planning on sharing our women."

This was getting ridiculous. He needed to get removed from this discussion. Shaking his head, he grabbed his spoon to begin working on the stew before him. Much to his chagrin, Savan reached over and clapped him on the shoulder, jostling the loaded spoon in his hand and causing the contents to spill onto his lap.

"Sure you are." The Piaxian squared toward Stod. "We're here together as guests of this fair land. You must be the welcoming committee. Are you asking us to dance?"

The scowl on Stod's face disappeared. "Dance?"

"Sure, let me lead." Savan grabbed the table and heaved it at the trio of men, sending Stod to the floor.

My supper!

There was no time to rue the loss of his meal as one of the men jumped at him, fist raised. He ducked below the blow and delivered a punch to the man's stomach. As the fellow collapsed, to the floor he stood to be able to better defend against any other attack as more people were joining the fray. Glancing Savan's way, he noted the big man sending a crushing blow to the jaw of the other man.

The Piaxian moved tight to him, fists at the ready. "Well, Morican, welcome to Riaz. Are we having fun yet?"

The statement made him glare at Savan, resulting in his inability to properly avoid the next punch from another who had joined the fray. As he whirled to recover, he noted two more jump at Savan, landing blows to his body. This was getting out of hand. He wondered if they would have to fight every able-bodied man in the place.

None of this would have happened if the Piaxian had kept a civil tongue and minded his own affairs. The once kind attitude he'd fostered for the man disappeared in his rage. The idea of leaving Rock House as a broken and beaten man blossomed in his thoughts. Or worse. He could end up leaving as a corpse.

A large shadow emerged from the door to his right. Busy wrestling with a fourth attacker he had no time to clearly see what this new threat was. He needed to be free of the hold his current combatant had on him. Using a move learned from Var, he slipped the grip by dropping a knee, then, free, reared back to throw a punch.

Then he froze where he was.

His muscles would not obey his will. He could get neither his arms nor legs to unlock from the awkward posture he held. Nothing made sense except for one possibility—magic.

A moment's panic set in. Would this dark work stop his heart as well? His lungs? No. He could still breathe. Though he could not move his head, the ability to roll his eyes left or right told him the affliction affected more than just him. Not only was Savan frozen, but almost every other male in the room.

"Who has broken my rule of sanctuary at Rock House?"

Straining to look, Brumaine could just see the stretched-out, black-clad arm and hand of whoever just spoke. The shadow was a man, bigger even than the Piaxian. Despite the clothing and the glove, the thickness of the wrist and sizes of the fingers were almost gargantuan. Such a human must be an abomination.

A small mid-aged man, unaffected by whatever spell held almost everyone, moved to stand before the caster. He pointed at both Savan and Brumaine. "The foreigners are the ones. They started the ruckus."

The female Stod forced aside also moved closer. "That's not true, Lazaan. They were goaded into action. What would you expect them to do when threatened by assassins?"

Assassins? Surely, Stod, the one with all the knives, looked the part, but the others were nothing more than local ruffians, the kind he had seen in more than one tavern over the years. Then again, there was always the aspect of cursed magic. More than just Lazaan were free of the freeze spell. He could only surmise such men possessed the necessary powers to resist.

The hand beside him dropped, and he stumbled free from his

frozen position, regaining his balance quickly then turning toward the monster man covered head to toe in black raiment. "I object to such treatment. I am a dignitary from Morica here on a peaceful agenda of negotiating a new trade deal with Riaz and others. I should be treated with respect. It is only because of the lad Kero that I am here in this place."

"What has Kero to do with this?"

The youth arrived to stand nearby. He placed a hand on Kero's shoulder. "It is a confidential matter between me and his guardian."

"Then you will tell me in private, for I am that guardian." The man extended an open hand toward the door he had emerged from.

Recognizing the invitation to enter, Brumaine stepped into the room. A small chamber, it featured an extension through the wall of the stone bench on which he had sat, a small table, a brazier glowing with coals, and another door. He suspected such a door exited into the alley behind Rock House, which would account for how the man entered without coming through the common room.

As Kero entered, the giant of a man paused to look back into the hall. "I will broach no more trouble in Rock House. You have all been warned." He closed the door and, fist on hips, faced Brumaine. "Now then, you will tell me what I need to know, all you know, without relent lest I pull it from you forcibly."

A small skittering sound from under the table urged him to bend and look. There, clinging to one of the back legs, was the demon imp Hiss.

CHAPTER 11

Following Brumaine's example, Kero bent to look below the table. The creature. It was here. He moved to put his lord between him and the vile little thing. "Master. There is a demon in the room."

"I know. I have brought him here. He was in need of my assistance." He also bent to look. "Come out, little one. No one will hurt you here."

The thing came out from under the table and moved to cling to the master's leg. "Hiss here, Gragnishozar."

No one had ever called his liege that. Was it his name? "Gragnishozar?"

It had been a long time since his guardian had last struck him, so when the blow came, he wasn't prepared. It sent him to the floor with alacrity, a pain in his left cheek.

"You will not speak that name." His master reached down and grabbed Hiss, shaking him hard. "Nor you. I will not have my name known."

"But who you are! What me to call you?"

His lord tossed the imp to the stone bench. "You will call me Master, as deserved." He then bent and helped Kero to his feet, a hand to his cheek. "My apologies, Kero. It was a spontaneous action. None are to know my name. Should word get out of who I am, I fear the possible consequences."

The shock of the attack over, Kero identified the healing magic from his liege and the abatement of the pain. This was an important event. His master had remained nameless his entire life. Now, though he finally had the answer, he must forever keep it a secret. It disappointed him that it must be so. "I do not understand, but I will obey your wish."

His liege wheeled toward Brumaine. "And you. Kero I can trust to keep a secret, but in you, I can place no such faith. I have promised the Merchant's Guild no harm would befall any of the emissaries though right now I am sorely tested to break that promise."

Action was needed to stave off this situation, and Kero moved to stand between the two. "Do not harm him, Master. Earlier this evening, he saved me from attack. It is why he was here at Rock House in the first place. From the short conversation I had with him, I believe you can trust this man to keep your secret. I stake my life on it."

Gragnishozar took one step back and crossed his arms. "You risk much tonight, Kero. Before my anger returns again, tell me of this attack and what play the Morican had in it. Much of my decision will ride on what I hear."

He pointed at Hiss. "That vile creature attacked me on the pier. If not for the intervention of Brumaine, I fear my life would have been lost. It gripped my head, and I could feel my energy slipping away. I thought I was done for."

His master looked first to the imp. "Is this true? You attacked my ward?"

Small as it was, the creature cringed farther down. "Hiss hungry. Only want mana. Boy have much. Hiss feed. No harm boy."

A heavy sigh emanated from Gragnishozar. "You were in no danger, Kero. This demon can draw mana from a human as food. Nothing more. You have probably never felt what it was like to be drained of your magic before. I suppose it might have seemed as if your life was slipping away. That was a while ago. Your body regenerates your mana over time. Tell me, when first released from the demon's grip, did you find your powers gone? And now, have they recovered?"

Turning his hands to view them front and back, he tried to summon his magic and discovered what his tutor said was, in fact, true. His power was back. Maybe not yet at the level he was accustomed to, but strong enough to conduct a spell should he so desire. "I-I am embarrassed. I did not comprehend what was happening to me. At the moment, I thought I was dying." He glanced at Brumaine. "Still, this does not change anything. This man would also not know what was happening. All he would have seen was the beast on my head and me on the ground. He acted without hesitation. In his mind, he was coming to my rescue. Such conduct is not from one whose word is untrustworthy."

Gragnishozar waited a moment then turned and opened the door leading back into the main room. "Go. Take the Morican home. Come back immediately and return to your chores. I must attend to the injuries Hiss has endured from the Morican's actions."

The conversation with Frollence resurged in his mind. "I thought demons were immune to magic?"

"Not mine. Now go."

He and Brumaine stepped back into the tavern and endured the stares of many who were nearby. The table had been reset, his spilled dinner cleaned away.

The big Piaxian stood nearby. "Ah, Brumaine, you're still well I see. When I learned the lord of this tavern took you into that back room, I feared you might come out the worse for wear. Come, let me buy you a pitcher of wine and another meal. I owe you at least all of that. Perhaps we can entice those two ladies to join us once more."

Brumaine waved Savan off. "I've been asked to leave and think I'll wait until later to sup as I've lost my appetite for the moment. Kero here is going to guide me home."

Savan clapped a hand onto Brumaine's shoulder. "Then I shall accompany you as well. You fight well. Better than I expected. As you rely on the boy for a safe passage, so shall I rely on you." He winked.

Kero doubted Savan needed anyone's help ever, but was glad for the extra company as he feared the conversation with Brumaine he would have to face alone. He needed to act before the Morican could reject the offer. "I understand you are staying at the home of the merchant Orvest. It is on the way—not quite as far up as the Hamak palace."

Savan eyed him. "You know much, young Kero. I did not tell you where I am staying, nor, do I suspect, by the look on his face, did the Morican."

It was best he direct the attention from him. His master had always said it was wiser to let another think you the fool. "It is my master's business to know all. I am only a recipient of his knowledge. He has just told me."

A glance from Brumaine confirmed his fib was not to be exposed. He led the two men passed Stod, Lazaan, and a few other members of the guild muttering to each other, then out into the street.

Once outside, a weakness assailed his knees. When passing the assassins inside, he had tried to use his magic to pick up what surface thoughts he could. Someone in the group was focused on the idea his assassination target was leaving. Unless careless, he could not read the thoughts of another warlock as those minds were magically guarded. That left one possibility—Stod.

But who was the target? Surely, not himself. Such folly would be a death sentence. His master...Gragnishozar...he could not rid his mind of that name...would hunt down Stod and show no mercy. No, it was either Brumaine, the Morican, or Savan, the Piaxian. The death of either man would bring an uproar to the trade talks. His best course of action was to hurry the men home and do it in such a way as to not arouse suspicion on their part. "Come, walk briskly. The night mist will soon descend and with it the chill it brings. I would sooner be home and warm than freezing outside."

Leading the way up the road, he pondered the situation. Why would Stod jeopardize the talks with an assassination? It didn't make any sense. He recalled Stod's dislike of foreigners, but the man must know he would face Gragnishozar's wrath. His master might not kill him provided Stod surrendered whoever ordered the assassination, but he would surely strip Stod of his membership in the guild, putting him into a position of taking a lesser career in life like a house guard, a job that paid poorly. He liked Stod. It bothered him to think Stod would do something so rash that would bring about his own demise.

Glancing back, three men exited and turned to follow the path he led the mainlanders. In the night, he could not make out the faces, but the lesser height of one made him think of Lazaan. Time to quicken the pace. "Hurry now. It's bad enough I have to chaperone two grown men home, let alone they should walk like doddering old men."

Savan slowed and glanced back. "What's the rush, Kero? I, for one, enjoy the night air. It invigorates me." The Piaxian came to a stop and, clasping hands to his chest, took in a deep breath. "Ah! It's good to be alive." He stretched his arms as if trying to reach for both sides of the street at the same time.

Brumaine grumbled something about enough nonsense and wanting to get home, but Kero wasn't fooled. Savan had also seen the men behind. His dalliance was intentional. If a confrontation was coming he wanted to face it now, not at the choosing of others. It did not slip his notice how, when the Piaxian stretched, his right hand jostled the grip of the broadsword strapped to his back, probably to ensure it was loose in its scabbard for easy withdrawal.

There was no sense in pretending anymore. He stepped back to pull on Savan's arm. "Don't be a fool. What good is your sword against magic? Should they desire, you'll be dead from a hundred paces away."

Savan winked. "Don't be so quick to judge, young man. There's more to this than a quick killing. If that weren't so, we'd be dead by now. No, there's something they want, perhaps only one of us, perhaps something else. One cannot know for sure. Tend to Prince Brumaine there. I will take care of myself."

Tend to Brumaine. Yes, it was a spell he had never tried, but he felt confident he could do it. Grasping the Morican's wrist he concentrated and created a magical aura round the man to protect him against magical attack. It took much of his mana to do so, and the weakness he felt at the hands of the imp returned, but not so much as to diminish his own aura to the point of ineffectiveness. Granted, it would not survive a concerted attack, but he sincerely doubted he was the target.

In time, the aura placed on Brumaine would fade. By morning, perhaps, or at least until the eighth hand of night. Either way, more than long enough to ensure the Morican was safely ensconced in the Hamak estate. He glanced at Savan, recalling the exchange of grips with Regent Tarlok, more than one of brotherly love. There was a protective aura around the Piaxian as well.

Brumaine must have finally sensed that danger was present as he drew a saber from his hip. "What is it? Are we to be set upon?"

Savan now fully faced the way they had come, fists on hips. "I don't know for sure. They've stopped following. Perhaps they've turned down some side street."

The many lanes that made up this section of the city flowed through Kero's mind. No route was more direct than the one they took, but many intersected along the way. Two could play this game. "Come, we will alter our path. They will only find us by happenstance, unless they split up." He made for the nearest street to his left.

The big Piaxian broke into a grin and grabbed Brumaine's arm to pull him after Kero. "I like this lad. He's sharp-witted. Something you Morican's could use a little more of. Come. Let's keep up. This is getting fun."

The lane he entered was still too major of a one to be to his liking, so he led the two foreigners down the first alley on his right. With Derak at his side, he had patrolled these alleyways many a time and knew this one could take him several blocks before necessity forced him onto another major street.

As they passed between the back walls of homes shuttered for the night, they encountered the occasional homeowner or two sitting quietly on small porches in friendly conversation. Such gossip would stop, the people watching with a wary eye, until they passed. Those citizens he knew, Kero hailed in friendly terms, and those he did not he offered polite excuses.

As they progressed, the question of which home they should make for tumbled round in his mind. Orvest's, where the Piaxians were, was closer, but their pursuers may know that as well. If, instead, he headed for the Hamak estate, he would stand a better chance of losing them entirely.

The decision made, at the next street, he turned uphill. Right near the top of the city, above the wealthy district where Bashar lived, was the palatial grounds he sought. Once, when accompanying the accountant, he had visited the place only to be amazed at the largesse with which it was furnished. It had its own wall capped with wrought iron spikes, and inside the gate were several homes all occupied by members of the family. He had only visited one, the main one where the patriarch of the family lived. As big as Rock House, if not bigger, and adorned with expensive tapestries and artwork everywhere.

His stay was short, but the wealth of the Hamaks was not lost on him.

It did not take much longer for the estate to come into view. A certain amount of relief flooding him on seeing it. "You're almost home, Brumaine."

"Thank you. I most certainly would have lost my—"

The explosive sound of a lightning bolt hitting Brumaine square in the chest was followed by the crackling of the defense aura holding then the sound of the Morican hitting the ground. The attack had come from an alley to his right. He pointed. "Over there!"

Savan charged, drawing his sword, and Kero scampered to kneel by Brumaine's side. Though dazed, the Morican was unhurt. "Stay down. They'll think you're dead. The magical shield I placed on you has been destroyed. You would not survive another attack."

With a small nod of understanding from Brumaine, he turned his head to check on the combatants. Two more lightning flares flew from the confines of the alley, both hitting Savan squarely, neither doing anything to slow his advance. Though the assassin still in shadows, the short scream abruptly terminating at the completed swing of the Piaxian's sword was enough to tell Kero the assailant was dead.

He helped Brumaine to his feet. "Come, let us see who our attacker was."

By the time they arrived next to Savan, he was finishing wiping his blade on the clothing of the dead man. He sheathed his sword then stepped back, allowing a better view. "I suppose this one didn't get the message that we were dignitaries."

Kero cupped his hands. Yes, enough of his mana was there to

create a small orb of light. As magic was involved, he knew it could not be Stod, but the possibility of Lazaan was still there. He let it go to float over the deceased. It wasn't Lazaan. "I know this man. I have seen him before at Rock House. He is a member of the assassin's guild. What's more"—entries into the ledgers of Bashar irked him—"he is in the employ of the house of Hamak."

Brumaine leaned in. "Perhaps he was on sentry duty. He saw three men approaching the estate under the cover of night, two armed, and jumped to the conclusion we were a threat."

Savan shook his head. "No, Brumaine, you are wrong. He did not attack until after you spoke. When Kero called you by name and you answered, you identified yourself in the dark. He targeted you."

"But why would the house of Hamak wish me ill? I am their guest."

Savan turned to face the Hamak stronghold. "Methinks a dangerous game is being played here. Had your murder been successful, then fingers of accusation would be at Piaxia as only we have attended the conference with warlocks. Still, it is my blade that has slain this citizen of Riaz. I do not think our word will hold well that we were attacked. As it is, his cry may have alerted some, and soon they will come to investigate. We must be rid of this place immediately."

Brumaine took a step toward the Hamak gate. "But the manor. It is right there, my countrymen inside. They will protect me."

"I would not chance it. Even though you are a prince, you are not indispensable. I seem to recall your older brother is here to take charge of these negotiations. Where this man has failed here in the street, success may occur while you sleep. If you value your life, come away now."

Savan pulled on Brumaine's arm. He at first resisted, but then allowed the big Piaxian to lead him away. Kero paused to look once more at the estate. He could see activity inside the gate. Savan was right. People were coming.

He turned and ran to catch up with the two men, now fugitives.

CHAPTER 12

As the sun crept over the top of the mountains of Riaz, the fog filling the bay in front of Lymos dissipated.

Her arms on the rail, Darlee peered into the mist to make out what she could of the city. Stretching upward from the shoreline, it rose in blocks of structures appearing as if stacked atop one another as it climbed up the hillside. In the middle of the city, a stream flowed down, cascading over a series of small waterfalls until it reached the bay. Something about their regularity gave the appearance of being manmade, not natural.

Near the top of the city were a number of citadels. She wondered at so many, counting five. Although impressive, none had the look of the castle she'd visited on her one trip to Sechwisk, the capital city of Sechland. Did Riaz not have a single ruling family?

A call from the captain to raise anchor was the news she had been waiting for. It wouldn't take long to dock at the long pier that awaited them. Already, a host of small fishing vessels had passed by on the way out to sea. All that remained in the bay were a number of large ships, traders most, but a handful of triremes as well, all flying different colors.

A nudge at her elbow came from her foster father. "We'll be setting ashore soon. First things first. I have to get ya settled where we're staying. Once that's done, then maybe we can see the town. It'll be our only chance before the meetings start tomorrow. From that point, you'll be on your own during the day."

Where to start? She glanced again at the city. Close to the docks, she could make out the market square. "Let's go to the market first, perhaps pick up some food. Maybe we can find out what's to see from the people there. They'll know what to recommend."

"Perhaps later. I've got people to meet with this morning to prepare for the meetings tomorrow. You can get something to eat at the inn where we're staying. I would rather you wait until I get back."

In his face, his usual worry lines showed. He was probably wondering whether he had made the right decision in bringing her. He worried about her so. Best to keep him placated for now. Perhaps she would use the opportunity to get her foster father some cured meats. That would make him happy. "Okay. I'll wait. Don't be too long. There's so much I want to see."

He tousled her hair. "That's my girl. I shan't tarry. This is *my* first trip to Riaz as well. I'm just as curious to check it out."

The boat glided toward the dock, and she could see a number of people waiting on the pier for their arrival. Between the crew on board and those waiting ashore, it took little time to secure the merchant ship and lower the gangplank. Brusk led the way with her and the others immediately behind.

A fat man, sweating profusely despite the still-cool morning air, was the first to greet them. "Welcome Captain Brusk, honored Sechlanders, my name is Damaz, and our good king has sent me ahead to make the arrangements for our stay in Lymos. I've secured lodgings at Rock House, a fine establishment with good food and a close central location only scant blocks away. I'm sure you will enjoy your stay there. I can tell you from experience the rooms are clean, and the food is quite tasty."

From the stains on his clothing, the man had already broken fast. Her guardian thanked him, and introductions went all the way around. When it was her turn to greet Damaz, he took her hand and gave a short bow. "A pleasure to make the acquaintance of such a beautiful young lady."

Pleased with the high praise and deference, despite the sweaty feel of his fingers, she curtsied back. "Thank you. I'm excited to be in Riaz. Perhaps you can advise the good captain of things to do while we are here."

"Hmm. I haven't had much opportunity to learn the city, but I would be most happy to inquire for you."

Probably too busy eating. Still, his offer was a respectable one. "That would be wonderful."

She stepped aside while everyone's luggage was brought

ashore and loaded on a waiting wagon. The driver offered for her a seat on the buckboard, which she gladly accepted. From her vantage point, she was able to get a better view of the streets and the people.

First thing of note—an awful lot of the local people had red hair. Back in Sechland, no one had such a color. Black, brown, and even some blond, but red was unheard of. Were there factors to cause such an anomaly? Could it be in the food? In the water?

No. Those ideas sounded foolish. In school, she'd learned that the Karsargi who dwelled on the other side of the western mountains were a people of dark skin. If such a disparity occurred in lands far to the west of Sechland, then why shouldn't wild red hair be common in a place far to the east?

As the horses pulled the wagon up the road, she was better able to note the step-up configuration of the city. The grade up the hill was enough to put the street above some ten feet higher than the street below.

Most of the structures in this part of town were two-story frame buildings, so when they turned on the third street the three-story stone structure a block away loomed large. It must be Rock House.

Damaz, having walked, came puffing up the street to be first to the door. Sweating before, he now he looked as if someone drenched him with water. "Huh, huh, this, huh, is, huh, Rock House, huh, huh. We, huh, have the, huh, entire, huh, third floor, huh."

Climbing down, she scanned the front entrance—solid, with a wide inviting door that stood open, an aroma of fresh washing emanating from within. She liked the place. She patted the heavy man's arm. "A good job, Damaz. I'm sure our stay will be just fine."

Stepping in, the sight of a floor still wet from mopping confirmed her sense of smell. An old woman, reposing from the job with the mop still in her hand, rose from her seat to greet them.

"Welcome to Rock House. From the sight of guest Damaz with you I take it you're the people from Sechland, finally arrived."

The woman stood with a kink in her stance and a hand held to her back. It only took an instant for Darlee to realize the signs of back pain, probably from all the work it took to mop the floor. "Please, don't worry about us. Sit back down. It looks like you've been working hard."

Stepping close, she placed a hand on the woman's shoulder and summoned her magic. The temporary transference of the ache into her own body was easy enough to withstand and, in moments, it was gone, the sore muscles in the woman healed. "There, that should make you feel better."

The old woman looked into her eyes for a moment and then stood again. "My master's touch would do the same, but it is not something he is common to do. I greatly appreciate it. I did not know our new guests could wield magic."

Darlee glanced at the crowd of Sechlanders who'd entered the hall and smiled. "No, only me. The others do not have the skill. I'd rather you kept this a secret. My foster father prefers I not flaunt what I can do in front of strangers."

"You have my word. My name is Maresh. Amongst other things, I am the cook here. Check into your room then, after, come down to the kitchen that I may reward your kindness with a sweet."

Damaz led them up and pointed out which rooms were whose. The grandest of the rooms was reserved for her foster father, with hers being the one next door. Small, with but a single bed, a wash-table, and a chair...still, clean, good sheets and bedding, and with a beautiful view of the bay.

When Captain Brusk called the merchants into his room to discuss the trade mission, she decided now might be a good time to go and get that promised treat. At the far end of the hall was a second set of stairs leading down. Deciding it easier to go unnoticed that way, she made it down to the second floor undetected.

Unsure of where the stairs led to on the main level she decided to cross over to the front stairs. As she passed a door, a boy no older than her emerged from it, backing into the hall, so probably unaware of her presence.

"I'll go down and see if the way is clear, then I'll come back to get you."

That was odd. Peeking past the youth, she could see two men sitting on a single bed, and one looked very much like the young commander from Piaxia. The very one who'd led the army who defeated the other nations of the seven realms who attacked her homeland. Before she could get a better look, the young man closed the door.

"Who are you, and why are you sneaking around here!"

The verbal assault set her back on her heels, but only for a moment. "Me? I'm just passing by, but I distinctly heard you say something about seeing if the way is clear. *You're* the one who's sneaking."

His face flushed. "Now, listen to me. I live here. This is my home, and I have half a mind to...to..."

A freckled face, and, though not as red as some, a ruddy red-brown color to his hair. Only a little taller than her, not short, but not tall, she decided he was cute enough, especially with the stammering temper. "To what?"

"To...oh, never mind. Get on with wherever you were going. I've matters to attend to."

Confirmation of who was behind that door gnawed at her. She brushed past him and grasped the door handle. "Not until I see who's in there."

She managed to get it halfway open before the young man grabbed hold and slammed it shut again. In that brief instant, she managed to lock eyes with the big man and in them, she saw recognition. It was him—Commander Savan of Piaxia. She was sure of it. "Let me open this door!"

The youth tapped her shoulder, and a sparkle from a small lightning charge crackled against her shield. *Magic, is it? Two can play at this game.* She whirled and loosed her own bolt, sending the young man across the hall and onto his butt against the wall. He looked at her with a set of wide eyes and raised brows. She smiled. "Stay there like a good boy while I check this out."

Turning once more to the door, she discovered it was open. The big Piaxian smiled down at her. "My, my, my. Darlee Murdach isn't it, if I recall correctly, sister to that lad Gar who caused such a ruckus last year. What brings you to Riaz?"

His brows knitted, and he glanced up and down the hall. "Is Captain Brusk with you? Come in. Come in. We need to talk."

With a hand between her shoulder blades, he guided her into the room. The young man, having risen from the floor, followed her in then the commander pulled the door shut. The other man rose from his seat on the bed and gave a slight bow. She figured him to be a few years older than her. Dark hair and eyes and very handsome, even though he looked somewhat disheveled. She guessed he spent the night sleeping in his clothes. A second glance at Savan showed the same concern.

Something strange was up, and she intended to get to the bottom of it. "What's going on here?"

Savan placed a finger on her lips. "I must ask you to keep your voice down and your word of silence on what I am about to tell you."

She nodded, and he smiled.

"Good. There is foul play afoot in Lymos. An attempt was made last night on the life of Sire Brumaine from Morica." Savan waved a hand at the dark-haired man. "If not for young Kero here"—he tousled the hair of the boy she knocked down—"he would be dead. Until such time as we can ferret out the truth, discretion is our best course of action."

So the man was from Morica, and royalty no less. She narrowed her eyes to study him closer. The simple smile and expression gave no impression of the same kind of people who had her tortured. The memory made her lift a hand to gently touch the patch covering where her left eye had once been. Judging someone from a single glance was not her forte, but something about his stance, his demeanor, lent the impression of innocence. "What do you want from me?"

"We need eyes and ears. From what I just witnessed in the

hallway, you have your brother's gift. As I understand it, you can hear the surface thoughts of others. Help us find the players in this game. Only then can we counteract whatever plot they have begun."

Kero scrunched his nose while looking in her direction. "Do you think it wise to involve this...girl? I thought our plan was for *me* to do the scouting."

"It just changed. I know of this lass. She's got the spunk to do it. Besides, two of you can cover twice as much ground, and if she's part of the Sechlander delegation, she'll have access to the meetings that you won't. It's daytime. We've got to get Brumaine to those friends among his people he can trust and me to mine. By now, they're all wondering. Luckily, after our talk earlier, we both have a reputation for liking the ladies. The excuse of being in the clutches of some fair maidens will pass muster. Meeting at this tavern will suffice to exchange notes, even with all the assassins in attendance. Your master has made sure of our safety."

Although she understood what Savan wanted, the idea she was also helping the Morican was unsavory. Still, glancing at Prince Brumaine, her original assessment had not changed. If anything, he looked lost. "All right, I'll do it."

"One more thing. You cannot let Captain Brusk or anyone else know of this. The fewer mouths that could spread what we are up to, the less likely our search will become known."

Not let her foster father know? This was a difficult demand. She took a deep breath then nodded. "If I must. Now, if you'll excuse me, the cook promised me a treat downstairs."

Once Kero had checked, she stepped out into the empty hallway and made for the stairs.

What have I gotten myself into?

CHAPTER 13

How did I get talked into this?

Brumaine followed the others down the stairs, still befuddled over his predicament. The question of whether he should have proceeded into the Hamak estate gnawed at him. Surely, there would have been at least some who would protect him. He knew he could always count on Var.

Or could he? Thinking back to that night when his father informed him of his attendance at the talks then, assigning him the menial task of quartermaster, demeaned him. After all, like his brother Doren, he was royalty. Such a duty should have been below his station. Then there was the silence by Var as to what the meeting was to be about. His guardian had given every impression he knew the details, but held them back. Why? Like him, Var should have found such an appointment an affront to Brumaine's personage, yet he failed to react so. Did he know of a real threat to him? He certainly gave enough warning to be wary.

Though one stair in front and below, Savan was still taller. He knew already of the man's prowess in a fight and lethal skill with a sword. How did he end up with having the Commander of Piaxia as an ally in this thing? They should be sworn enemies. No less so than the young Sechlander girl he met earlier. All of it was insanity.

Leading the way was the lad Kero. In scant hands, he had gone from saving the boy to the other way around. Riaz was friendly with Morica, but a youth as his sole assistance in Lymos bespoke a more troubling allegiance than what was presumed. Was there nowhere he could be safe?

When they reached the main floor, there was no one in sight. Stepping quickly into the bright morning sun, the street was alive with people. Mostly women, they were going to and fro from the various shops on errands of a household nature. Many could be seen carrying foodstuffs from the direction of the market and others were visiting stores that filled the blocks headed toward the bay.

A quartet of old men was sitting together at an outdoor cafe, steaming mugs in hand. Whatever they were talking about, the discussion ended once all four espied Brumaine and his companions.

Following Kero once more, he turned away from the men to proceed on the path they had taken together the night before. This time there would be no diversions down alleys and narrow lanes but the straight and obvious of the main roads.

To his left, he noted two women exiting a home and headed his way. He recognized them as the girls who had shown interest in Savan. It was time he started thinking on his own. Although the Piaxian's excuse as to their absenteeism was plausible, perhaps a little additional support to it might make it all the more believable. He stepped in front of the two before they could pass. "Excuse me, ladies, but if you can spare the time, I might be interested in garnering a favor from you both. There would be a silver in it for each of you."

The one who had argued the night before, a dark redhead, scoffed. "You left us alone after we stood up for you. It ended up with both of us getting a lot of insults, and now you want to buy us like some whores down in the south end? What kind of girls do you think we are? You're out of your mind."

They started to move past him so he gently grabbed each by an arm. "Ladies, please, hear me out. I ask nothing more than for the two of you to walk me home. After that, you can go your merry way. My life depends on it."

The quiet one, a strawberry blonde, originally tugging to pull free, stopped her struggles and met his gaze. "Your life? You wouldn't be teasing me?"

The more he thought about it, the more he realized he needed these women. The question was, how much to tell them. He decided to go for broke. "I am not. These men can attest to the attempt on my life last night. As a result, I did not attend to the Hamak estate where I am a guest, for fear of another attempt. To explain my absence, I am intending to tell them I was with a couple of the local girls, and I need the two of you to play the part. Forget about the silver. A gold piece each, if you'll do it."

The redhead, her arm free, slipped it back under his. "A gold piece, you say. I've never owned one. And the Hamak estate. I've always wanted to see the place. I'm up for your game, but first, the gold."

He fished into his purse and pulled out two gold pieces then placed them into the hands of the girls. The blonde simply stared at it while the redhead held it up to the light, scratched at it then finally attempted to bite it. She smiled. "It's real enough. I put a dent with my tooth. Only real gold would be soft enough for me to do that. Come on, let's get going. I want to see that place."

Savan laughed. "I must say, Morican, you're not the dimwit I originally took you for. I'll take my leave from here and have Kero get me to merchant Orvest's place."

Brumaine wished Savan and Kero well then proceeded toward the Hamaks, chatting with the girls as they went. The redhead, he learned, was named Janina, and the blonde, Lasha. Likewise, they discovered his name and, more importantly to them, his title. Discovering he was royalty changed the way they talked to him from one of indifference to one of deep interest.

Lasha wanted to know the details of the previous night's attack. Without disclosing how Savan had killed the fellow, he gave her a thin sketch of what happened from the time they left Rock House until then. He noted how, as he related the story, her grip on his arm grew tighter.

As he neared the estate, the front gate, now wide open, gave an unimpeded view into the courtyard and standing there were a number of his countrymen, including Var. Brumaine was still thirty paces away when his guardian made eye contact and walked toward him at a quick pace.

"Sire Brumaine, there you are. We've been looking all over for you. Where have you been?"

Before he could answer, Janina poked a finger into Var's chest. "Where do you think he's been? What do I look like, a figment of your imagination? He's been with us."

The ferocity of Janina's verbal attack made him smirk, especially at the way Var shied from the girl. He also noted over Var's shoulder back at the gate entrance someone watching and listening who was not a Morican. Once Janina had finished her tirade, the man turned and made for the main home. He guessed the informant was satisfied with what he heard and was off to report to his employer.

Pleased that his ruse was working, he relaxed and breathed out a sigh of relief. "It's been a long night, and I could use some rest, Var. Can you take me to my sleeping quarters?"

"Certainly. The conference doesn't start until tomorrow. I've already sent someone to the docks to get our cargo so there's nothing for you to do until then. Follow me."

He extricated his arms from the grasp of the two women. "At this point, ladies, I wish to thank you for everything. Perhaps we shall meet again? It is my intention to visit Rock House later tonight."

As Janina complained about not getting to see the Hamak estate, Lasha grabbed hold once more. "Will you be safe?"

Var, ever alert, leaned in. "Safe?"

Such was the risk of telling too much. The girl had betrayed what he wanted to keep secret. Still, it was only Var. Deep down, he still trusted him. "I'll tell you about it when we're private."

He turned to face Lasha and placed a hand over hers. "I'll be fine. You must have faith. Till tonight?"

She grabbed his head, pulled it down, and gave him a deep kiss and then spun to go, taking Janina with her. She glanced back. "Tonight."

They strode away, and he studied them from behind, deciding only then Lasha had the better figure. There would be more than a clandestine meeting with the others that evening if he could get his way.

A tug on his arm from Var brought him out of his reverie.

"Come. You can worry about which of those you would bed tonight later. For now, you must tell me exactly what happened."

Following Var, he entered the estate and was led to one of the houses on the left. Var explained that the house had been vacated for their visit and the Moricans had free rein to use as fit.

A private bedroom had been reserved for Brumaine. Var joined him there and closed the door. "Now...why must you be safe?"

It took the better part of a hand to explain all that had happened. During it all, Var never moved, but stood with a hand on his chin and a slight tilt downward of his head. When he finished and looked at his teacher he wondered, in the silence, whether Var had listened at all.

Finally, Var moved, dropping his hand and taking a deep breath. "It is as I feared. When you were assigned to this mission, the king spoke of risks and the necessity for two members of the royal family to be present. The look exchanged between him and Commander Oberus at that moment gave me concern. Was there something they knew that wasn't disclosed? A threat? Or something more sinister? He sent me for you and bid I not disclose anything. He is my king and so I followed orders, but you are my ward. I have looked after you since you were a child—more time spent with you than with my own children. I now question if this attempt on your life was not forewarned...or planned."

This was something he would expect from Oberus, but his father? It did not make sense. True, he spent little time at the court and recalled that, as a child, it was his mother or Var who comforted him when upset. Being the fourth son and so many years younger than the oldest lent some credence to his father's dispassion, but to plot his demise? "Why would the king wish me dead? Surely the death of any member of the party would achieve the same result. Do you not think?"

"No. Only someone of your station could create the diplomatic chaos desired. For now, while you are ensconced here in the Hamak estate you should be safe. A death confined within these walls would bring questions to the Hamaks as well as our own people. You must stay within them until this conference is over. That means no trysts with those women you arrived with earlier. Do you understand?"

He did. Still, the morrow would come, and both Oberus and his brother would be at his door demanding his presence at the meetings. "Feigning illness will not work. Further, despite what you say, during the day there would be none here to ensure my safety. An empty house would still invite disaster. I would not be safe if alone."

"Then I will stay with you."

He recalled the spell placed on him by the youth Kero. It saved his life. "And what good would you be against the likes of an assassin warlock?"

"I..." Var grasped his chin once more. "I don't know, but I would try. I would lay my life down to save yours."

He rose and gave his guardian a hug then held his shoulders at arm's length. "I believe you would. It would be in vain. No, I shall attend to Rock House tonight to learn what I may. It is an unlikely accomplice I have in a Piaxian, but, for now, I trust him more than my own people."

"What then would you have me do? Join your group?"

He smiled. An idea came to him sure to confound those who wished him harm. "Join them. Tell them of the attempt on my life and see what reaction you can get. Woo them to draft you to their cause. Use your deep fealty to the king as a reason. Whatever it takes. When chance arrives, report to me what you learn. Perhaps they may let slip their plans."

"Hmm. Your plan is plausible. I shall endeavor to win them. What of today? What steps will you take for now?"

He glanced at the bed. Fine silk sheets and large pillows adorned it. "First, I'm going to get some sleep. I had little last night, and I suspect such will be the case until this ordeal is done."

CHAPTER 14

The crack of something hitting the desk woke Kero from his unintended sleep. He lifted his head to see Bashar standing over him, a long ruler in his hand.

"What's wrong with you? I did not take you on to nap instead of loading entries into the journals. What would your master say if I reported such conduct on your part? Get to work."

He rubbed at his eyes. The lack of sleep was taking its toll. "My apologies. I'll redouble my efforts."

"Huh. See that you do. There'll be no time to get these entries done in the next few days as I'll be tied up at the trade talks. You'll have plenty of time to sleep while I'm gone."

Bashar left the room, and Kero grabbed the next stack of postings. It was hard to concentrate on the reports. He sorted through to load them into the proper books. Even holding his quill was a task. Glancing outside, he noted there were still more than two hands to go before he could go home. He must have been asleep for almost a hand. Although still feeling a bit woozy from just waking, he hoped it was enough rest to stay alert the balance of the way.

More tedious notes than he would have liked lay before him. Pausing to get a drink of water before continuing, he then seized the top one to register the details.

Grabbing the journal for personal expenditures by the Hamak family, it finally registered what it was he was holding. A substantial sum of money, paid to the family of the assassin Savan had slain the night before.

Why would the Hamaks do such a thing? It could only be proof that the man had been on Hamak business and not acting independently.

Whenever he loaded an entry his next step was to file the individual note in a container where all such notes were deposited once recorded. To his knowledge, no one had ever gone through the notes to ensure they were still there. Bashar would only take the journals with him to the Hamaks for reporting purposes. Deciding it was important information, he placed the note inside his purse to share with the others later on.

There had been times before when an assassin had been conscripted for a job. They always involved a prepayment as well. Flipping back, he found the original entry. The man was hired only scant days before. His own records, of agents for the visiting countries, were with Gragnishozar, but he could recall them well enough to match the date with the time the representative for Morica first arrived. Proof of some kind of arrangement between them was staring him in the face.

Who else had been hired? Six assassins had received advance payments. As expected, both Lazaan and Stod were there. That meant there were still four others with assignments made that day. What those were was information he was not privy to. How many were given the task of killing Brumaine?

He continued to load entries. Six more hirings were among the current stack. Obviously, the loss of one man meant they also were doubling their efforts.

Eleven assassins now in the employ of the Hamaks. That was more than half of all in Lymos. Such a lopsided number would not sit well with his master. Most of these men were independents though he did espy two he knew were employed by other families. If assassins were being amassed in the employ of the Hamaks, what did it mean? Riaz had always been controlled by group management of the five major families. Something was afoot, and it smelled of trouble.

He needed to go home, but if he left early, Bashar would not only be upset, but suspicious as well, and may review more closely the entries posted that day. No, the thing to do was concentrate on his work, perhaps finish early then ask for permission to leave.

Attacking the stack of notes with gusto, leaving good penmanship behind, he raced through the records quickly. A new level of energy had seized him, propagated by the important knowledge.

Slamming closed the last journal with a sense of finality he went to look for Bashar, finding him in his own office. It was surprising to find two more assassins, Bokko and Petrius, seated with his employer. They both gave Kero a quick glance then thanked Bashar for his time. Each scooped up a small sack resonating the distinctive *chink* of coins within and headed out the door into the courtyard and the street beyond.

"Well Kero, what is it you want?"

Realizing he had been staring out the door at the departing assassins while standing in the doorway to Bashar's office he returned his focus to the chief accountant. "Sorry for the interruption, but I've finished the entries. I was hoping to leave early that I might help Maresh at Rock House. The place is filled with Sechlanders for the conference, and it will be hard enough even with my help to attend to them all."

Bashar waved toward the door. "Go then. I won't be needing you again until after the conference. Make sure you come back ready to work. No sleeping on the job!"

A quick goodbye, and he made for the door and the street beyond in a hurry to see where the two men who had just left were headed. He knew both of them worked for the Toumas family. Bashar handled some accounts for them as well, but only those that dealt with the farms—employee salaries and produce records, not business deals or assassins. There would be no reason for such men to visit him.

The men were out of sight, so he guessed they were headed downhill, not up. Racing to the next street, his suspicions warranted out as the two were headed in the direction of the market. Perhaps the extra coin in their pockets was weighing heavy.

Slowing his steps so that he was able to stay some forty paces behind, he let the two lead him to the one place he didn't want them to go—Rock House. When he entered, they had already found a seat, and Maresh was bringing them mugs of mead. It looked like the celebrating was going to start a little early.

They gave him nothing more than a passing glance as he entered. Obviously, he was of no matter. He went straight for the door to Gragnishozar's room.

Stepping in, he discovered the Sechlander girl, Darlee, sitting where his master usually did. "What are you doing in here?"

"That is none of your business."

She had neither flinched at being found out nor blurted out some kind of defensive retort justifying her actions. This surprised him. Small, with little in the way of feminine curves, and she might be cute if not for the patch over her left eye. She was obviously not one to be intimidated or frightened. He wondered how much of the brave front she put up would remain had it been his lord to discover her. "This is my master's private quarters, and you have no right to be in here."

"No matter. I am finished. Rather than berating me, you should be asking what I have learned. I thought that was the whole idea of us meeting again."

Finished what? The question raced in his mind. The ease with which she bested him in the morning implied a higher level of magic. Gragnishozar had taught him how top warlocks could summon additional power through the solid stone of the world. To his knowledge, outside of his lord, only Lazaan possessed such skill. Could it be this wisp of a girl had the same? The idea rankled his own bravado.

Perhaps it was a matter for another day. She was right in that they were supposedly on the same team and as such he should act accordingly. "Very well. What have you learned?"

She smiled. "Better. Now...there is much furor over the man killed last night. Apparently, they say whoever did it was very powerful and in possession of a broadsword. The killing wound has identified as much. Should Savan be spotted with that thing on his back, it will lead to his accusation by many. I don't doubt there will be some who will recall it from yesterday."

Could the type of weapon be identified by a wound? Maybe it was possible. "We need to warn him."

"We need to find him first. Where do you think he'll be?"

The home of Orvest the merchant sprang to his mind. "I know where to look."

Darlee rose from her seat and headed toward the door. "Great, let's go."

He put a hand on her arm, stopping her from exiting. "It's best you stay. Someone needs to be here should Brumaine arrive. I can manage this on my own. After I'm gone, wait in the common room until we return."

Using the door that emptied out into the alley, he made for Orvest's. Hopefully, the two assassins would not wonder as to why he entered his master's quarters and Darlee exited. If they did, they might imagine something of a more amorous nature than a plan to uncover whatever plot was in motion.

The idea of a romantic ruse set his mind to wondering. She *had* smiled. Maybe she liked him. Because of his situation with Gragnishozar as his guardian and his living at Rock House, most of the girls his age gave him wide berth. It would be nice to have some female companionship in his life. After all, in scant months he would be sixteen and reach the age of ascension where he would be deemed a man, not a boy.

No, that was not a reasonable possibility. As a Sechlander she would return home when the trade conference was over. He had best concentrate on the mission at hand.

The home of Orvest came into view. He noted there were guards on duty wearing the colors of Piaxia, and among them, Prattrow, who had already given him much grief. Hopefully, the old warlock would be amenable in allowing him to see Savan.

There were also a group of men in conversation with Prattrow. Based on all the red hair, they looked like citizens of Riaz. Something was up.

He stopped short of the confab and did his best to listen in without appearing to do so by looking in another direction. The men were representatives from the constable's office. He could tell because they all wore medallions indicating their station. Charged with enforcing the laws, everyone believed they simply did whatever the Merchant Guild told them to do. At the moment, they were requesting Commander Savan present himself regarding a murder the night before. Prattrow was arguing something about diplomatic immunity, but the officers were having none of it.

Finally, Prattrow and the men agreed for the questioning to be conducted right there at the gate. A guard was sent to fetch Savan.

As he paced back and forth, he noted his movement had caught the eye of the old warlock. Fortunately, none of the constables were paying him any attention.

When Savan came out of the home, Kero could see the hilt of the broadsword showing over the left shoulder of the big Piaxian. It was too late to warn him. He needed to intercede.

As the first constable asked Savan of his whereabouts the night before, Kero approached the group. "Ah, Commander Savan. There you are. Since my escort of you home last night, Rock House requested your return to atone for the treatment you received yesterday."

The lead officer turned to face Kero. "And you are...?"

He gave a short bow in the man's direction. "Kero, sir. The master of Rock House is my guardian."

"And you claim you escorted this man"—the officer nodded toward Savan—"home last night? Did anything out of the ordinary occur during this trip?"

A gentle tingling told him the man was trying to probe his surface thoughts. A warlock, then. Kero concentrated to make sure his shield was up. "Nothing that I can think of. What exactly did you mean by 'out of the ordinary'?"

"A murder."

Feigning shock by taking a half step back, Kero held a hand to his chest. "Murder? I can honestly tell you no such thing occurred. Who was killed?"

"Never mind." The man gave up his probing and looked to Savan. "It seems you have an alibi. Understand, though you are a guest of this country and here under a flag of truce, that does not relieve you from the laws of our land. Murder is punishable by death. Remember that."

After a polite agreeing by Savan, the three constables left, and the big Piaxian stepped out to join Kero. "Your timing was most fortuitous, Kero. You lied most eloquently on my behalf. I could detect no body language or nervousness in your reply."

He smiled. "That's because there was no lie. I am a representative of Rock House and extended the return request personally, not my master. As to the murder, it is only so had the man been innocent of anything. His attempt to kill both Brumaine and yourself meant his death was nothing more than self-defense, not murder. No murder was committed."

"Spoken truly. Come, let us head to Rock House. There is much to talk about."

CHAPTER 15

Darlee was pleased to see Kero enter with Savan in tow. Obviously, the Piaxian had not been arrested as Kero feared. That was good. It stalled the urge to inform Captain Brusk of the goings-on.

Seated at the back bench, the two joined her. She glanced around the room to see what eyes were watching as a couple of the Sechlanders and Damaz were seated nearby. What would they think? What would they tell her guardian? She needed to create a false image of why they were together lest other thoughts prevail. "Finally! Thank you, Kero, for bringing Commander Savan. Knowing he was in town I have wanted to meet him again. I have so much I wish to ask."

Kero did a double take between her and Savan then turned to see other people present. "At your service, miss. We here at Rock House pride ourselves on providing excellent service."

Hoping the commander also was as quick of wit, she turned her attention to him. "Now tell me, Commander, how fares my brother? You're treating him well, I hope."

A slight nod by the big Piaxian was more than enough to indicate to her he had caught her ruse. "Darlee Murdach, it is a pleasure to see you. You've blossomed some since last year's war. Nasty business, it was. It was fortunate things ended as they did. I mean, compared to his momentary death, your brother's incarceration in Lia is good fortune indeed. He is well and learning much. In fact, I am told his magic is the strongest in the land. It is a good thing he is a willing prisoner. I would hate to have him otherwise. It might lead to a darker outcome."

The willing surrender by her brother to the Piaxians had put an end to much of the conflict. Still, she wondered when would be the day they would let him free. "Sit. I would have you detail all. I miss him so. And Thunder. Does the big, invincible demon still guard him? As fearsome as he looks, my recollection is of nothing more than a monstrous, cuddly, pet cat—one gentle and caring."

Savan sat down and chuckled. "Cuddly, you say? With one claw he could shred me into pieces in a single stroke. But tame? Yes, for now. He pretends to sleep almost incessantly, but when he thinks I'm not looking, I note the slightest gleam of his eyes open a slit. And there is the ever twitch of his ears—listening, no doubt. He's a danger, that one, especially with him being impervious to manmade weapons. Should he desire to act, I think there is nothing we could do to stop him."

They talked for a while about her brother. There was nothing she hadn't already heard. The chats with Gar through the stone of the world had kept her informed. Most importantly, others in the room, and the numbers had grown, were no longer paying attention. As more voices filled the hall, it would soon be difficult for any to overhear what was said at her table.

The dark demons her brother had released from the stones came to mind. "And the others—
Dread, Pleasure, and Doom?"

"Held deep in the gaol. Only warlocks magically strong enough to resist their powers visit them. In a way, they are back in stone once more. I must admit, I can see how your brother was enticed by Pleasure. She is a vixen most extraordinary."

A redheaded young woman had entered, her blonde friend alongside and they now stood directly behind Savan. The redhead put her hands on her hips, a slight flare of pink to her cheeks. "And *who* is this vixen you speak of?"

Savan turned abruptly, his eyebrows raised. "Ah, Janina. There are none who measure up to you."

Janina's posture softened. She stroked Savan's forearm. "It's good to see you again. We never finished what we started last night."

The blonde looked back to the door. "Is Prince Brumaine coming?"

"I would imagine he will be along shortly, Lasha."

So, Lasha had eyes for the prince. Darlee thought for a moment how easy it would be to swoon for the dark-haired Morican. The equally dark brown eyes set in his handsome face were alluring, even to her. Fantasizing about being swept up in his arms was useless. She could never hope to match the good looks and figure of Lasha.

It wasn't fair. With a wave of her hand, she could snuff the life from the blonde sultress, but would never get consideration of her power as a thing of beauty. For the moment, she allowed anger at it all to cloud her mind. It was only when she heard Savan mention something about his attempted arrest that she realized she wasn't paying attention. "I'm sorry. I missed that. What happened?"

"Young Kero here provided the necessary alibi for me to avoid incarceration."

She glanced at Kero. He reddened when their eyes met. Still a boy. Neither Savan or Brumaine would so much as blink when complimented, inured as they were by their positions of military commander and prince of a realm. Smaller in stature, sporting a darker shade of red-brown hair than most citizens of Riaz, and freckled, his appearance coincided with her initial assessment, not yet a man. She smiled at Savan. "At least you're safe for now."

Janina continued her purring, attracting Savan's attention away. Scanning the room to take a measure of each male in the place, Darlee decided there were none in the room she found particularly attractive, until she noted Brumaine enter.

Framed by the daylight from the street behind, it was decided. He *was* dreamy looking. She made eye contact and he smiled as he neared their table. Was that smile for her, or just for the group as a whole? A moment's hesitation to rise and greet him was usurped by Lasha who sashayed into his path.

"Prince Brumaine, you're here. I was *so* worried about you."

He paused to give her a polite nod. "Ah, Lasha, thank you for your concern. I spent much of the day in the company of many who only have my goodwill at heart. Still, unless this matter is dealt with, I will continue to fear for my life until I am home, safe, in Morica."

As he continued toward the table, Lasha hooked her arm into his and, together, they sat directly across from her and Kero, their backs toward the door.

She re-appraised the situation. Savan to her right with Janina hanging onto him, Brumaine across, Lasha seated close, and her and Kero on the bench. Some might think it a triple date, not the clandestine meeting of conspirators looking to undo some evil plot. Perhaps it was for the best.

With the others, Darlee reviewed the details of all that had occurred throughout the day and of what steps they and their allies were taking. Savan added that he met earlier with agents from Riaz to discuss security for the coming days. All those except the man from the Hamak family were in agreement to allow armed details from each country to be stationed outside of the Merchant Guild hall where negotiations would take place starting on the morrow.

A smallish bald man came to stand behind Brumaine. "Kero, you're in my seat."

The look of distaste, and perhaps some fear, creased Kero's face. "There is no Assassins Guild meeting tonight, Lazaan. This table is only reserved for those times. These guests are welcome to sit at this table when no meeting is scheduled."

A couple of other men gathered near, throwing nervous glances at the door to the private quarters of Kero's guardian. To her knowledge, no one was in there. Would they know whether such was the case? With a door that exited out to the alley, perhaps it was occupied now.

"There *is* a meeting tonight, for I have called it, and you and your...friends...must leave."

Kero rose. "Only my master can convene a meeting of the guild. You are out of line, Lazaan."

"We shall see."

Lazaan reached a hand for Brumaine's shoulder. Assuming his intention was to pull the prince from his chair, Darlee lifted a hand and loosed a small charge, like the one she'd used on Kero that morning, to dissuade the fellow from doing so.

Her effort crackled and fizzed out against the magical shield of Lazaan. Definitely one with a greater aura than Kero.

He sneered. "So. The young whelp from Sechland would dare use magic against me." He turned to face the rest of the room.

"You all saw it. She attacked first."

He spun, both hands reached out in her direction, a massive bolt of lightning flared at her. The shock wave from the charge sent the others at the table sprawling, but Darlee held her ground. He was powerful, yes, but at a disadvantage. *She* was the one seated on the stone bench, and from it, she used the Key to draw additional power. Obviously, the light tap she'd tried earlier would be of no use. It took but a thought to blast away his shield then sent him sprawling to the floor.

Rising, with wisps of smoke emanating off his clothes, Lazaan staggered toward Darlee. Wondering what new attack he planned, she steeled her shield in preparation. He lunged for the bench, grasped hold with one hand then loosed a volume of fire from the other.

Lazaan must also have the Key, for the force of his attack was far greater than the one before. Fortunately, all but Kero had moved away from the table, and, placing a hand on his shoulder, she bolstered his defenses as well. The flame circled their bodies then spent itself against the stone of the bench and the wooden table.

The door nearby opened, and a huge man sheathed in black stepped out, grabbed Lazaan, and hurled him across the room. He raised a hand in Darlee's direction but lowered it once Kero interjected his body between them. Turning toward the fallen Lazaan, he crossed the floor and hoisted him up by the throat with one huge hand. "I spoke last that no man should break the rules of Rock House, and I find a magic battle waged in the heart of it."

With a face purpling from the stranglehold, Lazaan pawed feebly at the big man's arm. "She...struck...first."

Dropping Lazaan to the floor, Kero's master strode toward her, and, for the first time, she felt fear. She knew him to be of great magical power, yet his aura was invisible. She had no idea what level it was. Would she be able to best him?

Kero moved to intercept his guardian halfway. "Master, do her no harm. It is true she acted first, but her initial volley was hardly more than a harmless tap that had no effect on Lazaan. She is from

Sechland and would not know the rules here. Have mercy."

His master raised a fist in the air, and, in one stride, brought it down on the fire-licked table, smashing it to pieces. After a moment's pause, he looked to Kero and pointed at the wreckage. "Clean up that mess."

Exiting the main hall back into his private quarters, Kero's master closed the door with a slam that blew enough breeze to be felt by Darlee at the two paces distance she stood away.

Across the room, three men helped Lazaan to his feet and half carried him out the door. Angry glances from them and others who followed the group out did little to assuage her hope that the problem was over.

Kero bent to the task up picking up the pieces of still smoldering broken boards that once made up the table. In between each piece grasped, he would glance at her then back at what he was doing.

The comforting graze of Savan's concerned touch on her shoulder did nothing to alleviate her disappointment at the turn of events. Her focus was not on him or his kindness, but on Prince Brumaine, who stood a couple paces away, his arm round the shoulders of Lasha who held him tight.

Did he not understand it was *she* who'd protected him from Lazaan? Should it not be *her* he should be comforting?

Darlee brushed aside Savan's hand and dashed for the stairs to her room. The people in the room parted quickly in advance of her rush. More who did not sympathize, but feared her.

More who did not love her.

Taking the steps two at a time, she reached her room quickly, dropped the privacy bar in its place, and then flopped on the bed to muffle her sobs in her pillow.

CHAPTER 16

Brumaine glanced at the open door. Already, he could note softening of the daylight. Dusk soon, then night. He needed to make a decision whether he should remain past dark or head back to the Hamak estate.

A second question was what to do about Lasha. The girl clung to his arm so fiercely, he thought it would take a legion of men to pull her free. Whatever he decided, stay or go, she would be with him.

While pondering what to do, a familiar face arrived—Var, with two other soldiers.

"My prince, I have come to escort you home. There is a feast planned for tonight, and it is requested that all guests be present. I have brought with me two men I know who can be counted on to assist you."

So. His decision whether to go or not had been made for him. Remembering his journey the night before, he recollected Kero's placing a magic shield on him. "All right. Give me a moment." He turned to face the youth. "Kero, before I go, would you once more place a protective aura on me? I would feel safer walking the streets of Lymos with it."

Kero placed a hand on Brumaine's shoulder for but a moment then stepped away. "It is done. Once again, my magic is somewhat depleted from the attack by Lazaan, so I do not have the highest hopes on its durability. It's too bad Darlee is no longer here. I'm quite sure she could have wrapped you in one capable of withstanding so much more."

The thought had not occurred to him. Yes, after watching the battle between Darlee and Lazaan, he had no doubt hers was a stronger magic. With tears in her eyes, she had fled the room. "You are probably correct, but my escort waits, and I doubt the girl would welcome such a request at this time."

A quick farewell to Savan and Kero then he made his way for the door with Lasha at his side. Passing the stairwell, he glanced up in hopes of seeing the Sechland girl, but that was not to be.

Stepping out into the street, he wondered what had made Darlee so distraught. Clearly, she had bested the warlock. She'd never wavered when confronted by Kero's master. Even he found the huge guardian, covered in black head to toe as he was, a fearsome individual. There was no doubt as to the magical skill level either. Being frozen in place, as so many others were, was not an experience he was soon to forget.

A squeeze on his biceps reminded him of the fair-haired woman clinging to his arm. A possibility surfaced. Could it be? In the three years since his day of ascension to manhood, Brumaine had been the quarry of many a lady. To date, none had been interested in anything more than his station as royalty. There had been young women who had shown some infatuation, but most knew their station in relation to his and realized the ridiculousness of such a notion. He was a prince of Morica. They were vassals.

Darlee would not think that way. Being a Sechlander, his birthright would have little meaning. If anything, he was a traditional enemy. After all, they were at war only a year before. The idea was silly. She was what...fifteen? Not even old enough to legally wed. It could be nothing more than a passing crush. She would soon forget it.

Scoffing at the notion, his thoughts turned again to the buxom blonde clinging to his arm. Although she was not a Morican, regardless, he still saw in her the recognition of his title. Sighing, he resigned himself to the fact she would be his company for the night. Still, regardless of her intentions, it should make for a pleasurable experience.

With Lasha clinging to his right arm, Var strode along on his left. The two Morican soldiers followed. He noted both warily scanning the street, their heads pivoting constantly left and right. They were being more than attentive. He gave his tutor a sidelong glance. "Are you expecting trouble?"

Var focused on the road ahead. "I have surmised they would never strike during daylight. For the assassin to be identified would ruin their plans. It is why I am hurrying you back to the estate."

Var's personal attendance bespoke another problem. "How went your attempts to follow our plans?"

"Not good. When I hinted to your brother, he seemed oblivious to what I was talking about. Oberus, on the other hand, immediately dismissed me, obviously having no intention to bring me within his circle. I have since done my best to determine who amongst those from Morica would follow our lead. These are the only two I can trust."

Not exactly the best news. Not including himself, Var, Doren, and Oberus, forty-five men attended with them as crew of the trireme, merchant vessel, and honor guard. One would expect a fealty to both his brother and the commander, but one would also expect an even greater fealty to his country, king, and honor above all. He supposed there was only so much Var could reveal when interviewing the troops. Two loyal men would have to do. "What are your plans for the evening, then?"

"Enjoy the meal, feign congeniality with all those present, and then ensconce you tightly in your quarters with a guard rotation through the night."

When he arrived at the Hamak estate, everyone was already seated. His group was forced to take a table farthest from the head one. He received a hard glare from his brother that continued throughout the evening.

The meal itself was sumptuous. Expensive foods and free-flowing wine made the event raucous as men overindulged and became loud in their commentary. Fearing intoxication, Brumaine drank little. Of course, Var drank none. Lasha, on the other hand, imbibed to the point where her tongue loosed, and she rambled on incessantly about trivial things. Her hands roamed over him below the table. Perhaps it was time to retire to his quarters. With a gentle tug on her arm, he urged Lasha to stand then nodded toward Var. "I'll take my leave of these festivities. I'm not in a celebratory mood."

Var started to rise. "I shall accompany you."

He placed a staying hand on his teacher's shoulder. "Stay. See what else arises in my absence. It is but a short walk across the courtyard to the building where we are housed. I should be fine."

Var turned to the man nearest him, the bigger of the two. "Escort the prince to his room then station yourself outside the door."

The big fellow rose then saluted sharply. "Yes, Lieutenant."

Stepping out into the yard, he guessed it to be the second hand of night as the moon lay low on the horizon. A quick glance at the gate confirmed a couple of Hamak men guarded it.

Inside the residence reserved for him and his fellow Moricans, only one oil lamp burned in the main room and one in the second-floor hallway. The place was deserted as everyone was over at the main hall. All the better. He preferred the quiet. Leaving the soldier to lounge in the common room, he escorted Lasha upstairs into his private chamber.

No sooner was the door closed and the bar in place than Lasha wrapped her arms round his neck and kissed him deeply. "I've finally got you alone."

The curves of her body pressed against him roused his sleeping libido. Perhaps the night might be enjoyable after all. "Yes, you do. And what are your intentions from here?"

She spun free from his embrace, winked, and pulled her dress over her head, exposing her naked body. "To please you."

As she climbed onto the bed, Brumaine worked at the buttons of his doublet. He had always suspected the girl to be well figured, and without her clothes, his suspicions proved to be true.

A hard rapping at the door stopped him from undressing. Why did the guard not halt any visitor? "Who is there?"

"Open the door, Brumaine. It is your brother, Doren."

Doren? What would he be doing here? He hesitated for a moment as a number of possibilities raced through his mind. Was he required to return to the feast? Had his departure insulted some dignitary? Or was the intent of the visit more malevolent? Lifting the privacy bar, he opened the door to find his brother standing solitary in the hallway. "What *is* it, Doren?"

His sibling swept past him into the room, gave it a perfunctory once-over glance then scowled at Lasha, who had covered her body with the blanket. "Get out of here."

"I'm sorry, my lord. I am naked."

Doren grabbed her dress from the floor and threw it at her. "Naked or not, you must go."

Brumaine was not going to let his brother send her away. "She's staying. She's my guest. Now, what do you want?"

Scowling still, Doren faced him. "What is going on, Brumaine? I have reports you are fraternizing with Sechlanders and Piaxians alike, no less than that big oaf who knocked me down on the pier. What is wrong with you? These people are our mortal enemies."

The memory of Doren bowled over by Savan brought a hint of a smile to his lips. Knowing his brother would disapprove, he quickly ceased.

Apparently, not quick enough. Doren raised a hand as if to strike him and then dropped it. "Your insolence is unbearable. Why you are here is beyond my understanding."

Because I am to be sacrificed. "You *know* why I am here."

Doren's brows knit as he squinted at Brumaine. "What mystery are you hinting at? Today, Lieutenant Varamanthu also implied some clandestine goings-on. Were he not in such favor with both you and the king, I would have had him lashed for insubordination."

Did his brother truly not know? If not, should he tell him? How much should he disclose? "Did you not hear of the death that occurred last night, right outside the gates to this estate?"

The squint disappeared, as did the knitted brows. "How do you know of this? You weren't even here last night. It has been suggested the man was killed by that big Piaxian friend of yours. The one with the broadsword. Apparently, he had an alibi, and they could not arrest him for it."

He needed to take things slowly. Perhaps by revealing the details by increments, he might find out what his brother knew. "The man killed was an assassin. He had a high-profile target within this estate."

It was in his brother's face—the look of complete

befuddlement. There was little doubt Doren had no idea of what was going on.

"You speak like you know more than you are telling. Who was this target? Me?"

There was some noise emanating from the hallway. Brumaine could hear voices coming from downstairs, though what was said was unintelligible. No matter. Doren was waiting for his answer. "No, Doren, it wasn't you. It was me."

"You? Who would want you dead? The Piaxians? If so, I will have every one of them put to the sword before I leave this island."

Now was the time to tell all. "No, Doren, it wasn't the Piaxians. In fact, it was Savan, the big oaf as you say, who slew that man to save my life. It had me thinking it was you who wanted me dead."

Doren moved to stand close and placed his hands on Brumaine's shoulders. "Why would I want you dead? You're my brother. Yes, you anger me incessantly because you fail to live up to your title as a prince. Instead, you waste it in taverns and brothels with things such as this." He waved a hand at Lasha.

There was some truth in what Doren said. Over the years, he had done little to act princely, but there was also a reason for it. His father had never entrusted him with the duties of a prince. Thoughts of it did nothing more than make him angry.

Brumaine could hear the sound of footfalls on the staircase. People were coming. He needed to wrap things up and get his brother out before anyone looked in. "My life is what it is because no one has placed any faith in me. Since my ascension, what duties have I been given? I'll tell you, none. No...wait...there is one. Stay out of the throne room. So, for now, stay out of mine."

The sound of people approaching had stopped outside the door, and he and Doren both looked to see who was there. Standing in the doorway was a man dressed in black with purple piping on his sleeves and cloak, the cowl pulled over his head to mask his identity, only his clean-shaven chin showing.

"He's here."

A second man, dressed similarly, but with a heavy beard,

stepped behind him. "Kill him now."

Doren reached for his sword. "Piaxians!"

The first one held out a hand toward Brumaine, and a bolt of lightning issued forth striking him dead center. Like the night before, it knocked him down.

The warlock looked to his companion. "No good. He's shielded."

"Then kill the other one. It matters not."

As Brumaine struggled to his elbows, Doren, sword drawn, charged at the two. In the second flash of lightning, his brother flew backward to land on top of the bed, smoke issuing from his chest. Lasha screamed.

Groggy, he managed to get to one knee as the two cloaked men fled. There must be others in the house to intercept the assassins. The soldier Var had sent must still be downstairs. "Stop them!"

His wits recovered, Brumaine went to the bed and tried to rouse Doren without success. The smoke stopped, and he placed his ear to his brother's chest. Nothing. Straightening, he looked down into his brother's face showing eyes wide open. A tremor overtook him as the realization his brother was dead hit home. He stumbled backward until he hit the door frame and half stepped into the hallway. There was no sight of the intruders. Pulling his sword, he dashed down the stairs. The soldier sent to guard him lay on the floor, probably dead. He did not pause to check but instead charged into the courtyard and toward the estate gate where the two Hamak men also lay cold on the ground. Scanning the street beyond, he could see no sign of those he chased.

He sheathed his weapon then made for the main hall. How could the Piaxians be so bold as to kill his brother? Why? Had not Commander Savan defended him from attack the night before? It made no sense. Who was the enemy and who was a friend? Perhaps there were factions within the Piaxian group who had alternate plans.

He slammed the door open with a crash. Many in the room looked his way. When he was certain the noise level was low enough so that all could hear, he looked to Commander Oberus, seated next to Alban Hamak. "The heir to Morica is dead. We are at war once more."

CHAPTER 17

The night had provided a much-needed rest for Kero. Feeling refreshed, in the pre-dawn, he made his way down the back stairs to the kitchen. The room was dark. Maresh had probably not yet risen to begin her cooking.

No matter. A haunch of cooked pork lay in the larder, and he carved off a piece to break his fast. With a mug of weak beer to wash it down, he entered the main hall to sit and enjoy his repast.

Hungry from having eaten little the night before, he recollected the evening while stuffing his mouth. After Brumaine had left, Darlee reappeared, attended by her foster father, Captain Brusk. Together, they ate in the company of other Sechlanders, and she never looked once in the direction where he and Savan still sat. Eventually, they finished and she retired to her room without a word spoken. Those who had witnessed her earlier display of power kept their distance, and the whispers grew with the resumption of her absence.

Paying attention to the customers was all that was left for Kero to do. Savan's attention was totally absorbed by Janina, who eventually dragged him away out of Rock House. With no company to enjoy, he had made himself useful by clearing tables until the crowd dispersed.

He wondered what the day would bring. The talks were to begin that morning, and both Brumaine and Savan would be tied up in them at the Merchant Guild hall. That only left him and Darlee to work on finding out more details of the plot to kill the prince. Considering her abrupt abandonment of the meeting after her confrontation with Lazaan, and her cold shoulder later, he doubted she would be a willing compatriot during the day.

The sound of his master's door opening caused him to turn his head. Gragnishozar stood in the doorway. "Kero, I would have a word with you."

What did his master want? "Coming."

Taking his food and drink with him, he entered the private

quarters and noted the demon imp in the room. Once the door was closed, he turned to his lord. "What is *he* doing here?"

His guardian pointed to a chair. "Sit. There is a tale to be heard. There is no better spy than Hiss here. He has been out all night and has much news to report. Likewise, when he is done, I need to know what is going on with you and your friends. I fear much conflict in the days to come and need to be prepared on how I should go forward."

There was no arguing with Gragnishozar. He recognized the tone as not one of a request, but a demand. He would sit and listen then report what he could.

The imp clambered up onto the table next to Kero's laden plate. He sneered at it then glanced back and forth between Kero and his master. "Saw it, I did. Two men garb Piaxian warlocks. Kill many. Run away. Chase them, young Morican prince. No catch. They gone. I sneak. See who die. Prince Doren. Much noise, main hall, Hamak. Hiss run. Sniff mana. Catch up warlocks. Go, they did, house."

Brumaine's older brother dead? This was horrid news. The Moricans would demand blood for the loss. Why would Commander Savan allow that to happen? Surely, he would have not instructed such a heinous act. Kero thought of his delegate list. "To which house did they go? Orvest the merchant's? It's a light bluish stucco one with a red tile roof."

"No there. They go old wood house, many blocks south from here."

The old part of town. Not exactly the best part, either. Perhaps, with Derak's help, he could find it. "Describe it to me."

"Two floor. Wood. Green door. Between others. Next, red door both."

So it was in a row. There were blocks of houses like that. Plenty had green doors, and plenty more had red, but how many green doors would be between two red ones? There was a good chance he could find it. He turned to Gragnishozar. "I'll go look for it today."

"First, you will tell me all about your business with the others.

Miss no detail."

It took some time, but he imparted to his guardian all that he knew. When he finished, Gragnishozar rose first. "Before this conference begins, I shall meet with the merchants. They will not refuse me. Find these two men. Report to me later. We must hurry lest Lymos become a battleground for foreign forces. Go now."

Before he could act, Gragnishozar stepped out the back door into the alley and was gone. Kero stared at Hiss. It would have been helpful to have the imp show him the way, but such a sight in the streets would cause too much controversy. No, he would chase down Derak, and they would search together.

There was a soft glow to the demon. Remembering his first encounter with Hiss, he grabbed the creature by the wrist. "I *know* what you were doing. You were feeding, weren't you? That's what made you follow those warlocks. You attacked them, didn't you?"

Hiss squirmed. "Me hungry. Little mana from dead. Me need mana."

This was news he could use. If he hurried, the two men would be low on mana and unable to use magic against him.

He let Hiss go. It was enough these warlocks knew of the demon's presence. It would be better if no one else did. "Stay here, out of sight. My master would not want you being seen or caught."

"Me stay. Me be good."

He did not trust the imp. "You had better."

He slipped out the back door and made for Derak's house. His friend lived on the way.

Derak was outside weeding the small garden, no more than five paces wide and two deep, which composed the front yard of a two-story frame row home probably no larger than six rooms. His father worked, but with Derak having three younger siblings it was probably all they could afford to feed and clothe them all. Still, the house appeared well kept, and the homes on the narrow street all showed the same level of care.

Some other youths were playing stickball, and Kero reminisced about the times he had joined in the game. That was back a few years before when other children judged him as just one more kid to play with and not the ward of the leader of the assassin guild. How he missed those days. Now, only Derak remained close as a friend.

It was a nice neighborhood of the common people who made up the bulk of the citizens of Lymos. Many still spoke kindly to him. They just kept a little more distance than they used to.

There was no time to dawdle. "Come on, Derak. I need your help."

On his hands and knees, his friend looked up from the task at hand, clumps of uprooted vegetation in his fists. "My mother says I have to finish this before I go anywhere."

What to do? He glanced up and down the street, trying to decide whether to go without his pal, then studied the garden. There wasn't much left of the weeding. Better to help his friend finish and have his assistance than go it alone. He dropped down between the rows of young plants. "Here, let me help."

The morning dew had made the ground moist enough to make the work none too difficult. Together, they finished the weeding while he explained the job that lay ahead.

Derak grinned. "Sounds like fun. Is there a copper in it for me?"

Always looking to palm a coin. "As there are two of them, maybe two. We're finished here, so tell your mother, and let's get going."

It took Derak only a moment to dash in and inform his mother of his leaving then join Kero, and the two of them headed toward the south end. As they worked their way through the streets, the front yards disappeared, and the houses clustered close to the narrow lanes. Such was the south end. Row upon row of homes pressed tight against each other, blocking some of the morning sun making the road shadowed.

Red and green. They were the predominant colors of front doors everywhere. Sadly, he found more than one green between two reds. There were several. Which to choose? As he hesitated, the option was taken away by Derak who dashed to the first one and knocked.

The door opened, and an old woman bent with age appeared. Derak bowed so deep it looked comical. "Good day, madam. I am looking to earn coppers doing housework. Are you hiring?"

"No. Go away. I have no coppers to waste."

She closed the door, and Derak returned to Kero's side with a grin on his face. "One down."

Resisting a smile was impossible. His friend had taken the difficult task of trying to guess who was behind each door and made it simple. In such a neighborhood, youths looking to earn a copper would be commonplace. He would fit right in.

Rather than follow along and imitate his friend at other doors, he decided to watch from a discreet distance to see who answered at each one. The idea that the two men were not Piaxians but assassins of Riaz had percolated in his mind since hearing the story. After all, why would two Piaxian warlocks hide down in the south district when they were comfortably housed at the home of Orvest the merchant? No, more than likely they were men in disguise, and if they were members of the guild, he would recognize them...and they, him.

Derak continued down the street knocking on each green door between red ones. Kero had to wait for a bit when one man actually took Derak up on his offer and put him to work for a quarter hand.

At the fifth door, Kero recognized the man who answered. It was Petrius, one of the two who had met with Bashar the day past. Kero froze when the man, once finished shooing Derak away, scanned the street, and their gazes briefly met. The fellow looked away as his examination of the street continued then he closed the door.

Had he been identified? He was not sure. A greater scrutiny was required because more information needed to be identified. He waited until Derak stood near. "Did you manage to see inside?"

"Only briefly. There's another man in there, that's for sure, but I couldn't see what he looked like or much else."

The theory fit. Now he needed to verify it. "Let's go around back. Maybe we might get a better look."

They retraced their steps to the last intersection then crossed over to the narrow alley that would lead to the back of the home in question. Having counted the doors out front, Kero started the count again to ensure they ended up behind the right house. Chance was in his favor. There was no one present in the alley, and the house featured a window overlooking the back porch. The window begrimed, he could not see through it from the alley, and so, stepping onto the veranda, he made his way close to peer in.

No sooner did his nose touch the glass, than the rear door opened and Bokko exited and fired a bolt of lightning at him. His shielding held and, facing the man, he loosed his own charge striking the fellow in the chest and sending him to the deck.

Had he killed Bokko? In his haste to fight back, he had leveled the most powerful bolt he could, more as a reaction than with intention. There could be no doubt the warlock's defenses had been weak, most likely from the mana drained by Hiss.

He bent over the man to check. No, not dead. He still breathed, though unconscious. A wave of relief passed through Kero at the knowledge he had not slain someone.

He glanced through the open doorway into the home and noted the Piaxian robes draped over a chair in what must be the kitchen. His theory had been vindicated. These men had indeed posed as Piaxians in their brutal act of killing the first prince of Morica. But why? The Moricans were guests of the Hamak family and yet it was the Hamak family who had hired these men. Worse still, they had also killed a couple of servants of the Hamak household. It was all confusing.

As a shadow passed over him, Kero glanced up to see Petrius in the process of swinging a club at his head. Despite seeing it coming, there was no time to dodge the blow.

CHAPTER 18

It had been a short, fitful sleep. Brumaine rubbed at his eyelids. He needed to be fresh for the task ahead. Much of the night was spent with Commander Oberus arguing what to do.

Now, with the passage of some time since his brother's death, Brumaine's initial anger had faded. *He* was the highest ranking authority present, not Oberus. Despite that, the commander gave every impression he would act without consent. Oberus' authorization came, not from him as prince, but from his father, the king. Notwithstanding finally agreeing on a plan of action, the inferred disobedience irked him some.

His mentor, Var, stood near the door of his room as he readied. "So have you decided what you intend to do?"

It had taken him all night to realize the value of Doren's words. He needed to be more princely. He'd decided not to carry out Oberus' original wishes. "We are in a foreign country. I cannot order an assault on the residence where the Piaxians are. I shall attend the trade conference in my brother's stead. There I shall list my grievance with Piaxia. I will follow the final suggestions of Commander Oberus. It is through diplomacy I will win my brother's justice."

"It is good. Rashness leads to disaster. Your brother would have done no less had the situation been reversed."

The ease of Doren's death at the hands of the warlocks distressed him still. How he wanted to rush, sword in hand, to face those who had done it. Oberus' original suggestion had been they gather the troops of the other nations and attack last night. Part of him desired to do just that. Oh, how he wanted to. In the time they spent discussing the details, his mind had changed. Along with the suggested diplomatic plan, Doren's words set in.

He glanced at Var as Brumaine buttoned his jacket. Words such as his brother's he had heard a thousand times from his teacher. Until then, he had never taken them seriously. He had never believed there would come a time when *his* would be the authority, not with so many older siblings, not with the disdain of the court and his father. Now, everything had changed. "My brother has been properly attended to?"

"Yes. He has been wrapped and will be transported to our warship this morning. It will break King Jessop's heart when we deliver his heir in such a state."

Concern over what his father thought was far from his mind. A check out the window to determine what hand the sun lay told him he had dallied enough. The convention was waiting. "Come. Let's collect Oberus and his guard detail. Hopefully, there won't be problems when we get there."

Stepping into the courtyard, he found his commander waiting, along with six armed men and the three merchants who had accompanied them.

Oberus huffed. "About bloody time. We're going to be late."

Ignoring the exhortations of his commander, he headed for the gate. Var kept step, and Oberus jogged to catch up. Despite the glower from Oberus, he stayed focused on where he was headed. The hall was close to the city market.

He set a brisk pace. In short order, his path brought him past Rock House. He spared the inn only a glance, wondering whether the Sechlanders and Darlee still waited inside or whether they had already departed for the hall. Probably the latter.

As they neared the hall, he recognized the various troops stationed outside as being from the invited kingdoms by their colors. The purple of Piaxia drew his greatest attention. Among those were men in black, the warlocks. Three in total. He wondered which of the two had killed his brother.

Only paces away, he studied them more closely. With the hoods of their cloaks drawn back, he noted two bearded and one not. Only one of the men from the night before had facial hair. That meant the clean-shaven Piaxian was definitely one of the two.

As he passed them to enter the hall, leaving his own six-man unit outside, he was troubled by a sudden lack of certainty. He did not recognize the chin. For that matter, neither of the bearded warlocks looked exactly like the one the night before. Were they the men? They had to be. Who else wore such clothing? They *must* be. It had been a quick and traumatic moment. In the excitement, his memory may have been faulty. It was probable he did not get a good enough look at the assailants and could not for certain match them among the Piaxians outside. Nevertheless, they had to be them.

The hall was more than adequate. A large open room, it could probably host several hundred people when necessary, a thousand standing, but for the conference, it featured nine tables, three a side with the exception of only one table on the fourth, arranged in a square, all chairs lined on the outside, facing inward. Most everyone was already seated with the odd person still standing here and there. His table was positioned beside the host table of Riaz and next to those from Queensland. Directly across the floor between was Sechland flanked by Piaxia and Storburg. Set at the fourth were three men, a number of parchments spread out before them. He surmised them to be the scribes assigned to take notes of the proceedings. On either side of the scribes were tables laden with foods and refreshments and nearby stood servants to cater to the delegations.

At the host table were seated five older men, all dressed in silks and jewelry. In the middle was the Morican host, Quinto Hamak, patriarch of the Hamak family. Standing some three paces behind them, his back against the wall, was the dark owner of Rock House. His presence was disconcerting. Brumaine wondered what the powerful warlock's role was in this meeting.

When Brumaine and his group were seated at their table, Quinto rose and held out his arms. "Welcome everyone. Gathered here today are representatives from all the trading nations— Morica, Fermia, Gatway, Piaxia, Sechland, Storburg, Braxborough, Queensland, and, of course, our fair country of Riaz. Over the last year, there have been troubled times between us. Merchant ships have been raided, goods stolen, profits lost. It is hoped this gathering will iron out those differences that exist between us so that commerce can again flourish and goods can flow freely once more."

Quinto held his hands toward the other men at his table. "My fellow merchants of Riaz here, have set out what we think is a workable agenda. We would like to begin with—"

Throughout the opening remarks, Brumaine had seethed as he glared across at the Piaxians. They acted as if nothing was wrong. It incensed him. He leapt to his feet. "Hold! There is a matter that must be discussed first."

The Hamak patriarch smiled and held up one open hand. "We know of your issue, Prince of Morica. We grieve for your loss, but such a thing is not for this gathering, rather, one to be handled by our constabulary. They have been notified and will delve into the issue with all expediency. Have faith in our judicial procedures."

He was not going to be silenced, and he was not going to rely on "judicial procedures." "No, I will be heard. Last night, my brother, Prince Doren of Morica, heir to the throne, was slain by warlocks from Piaxia."

Shouts from people in the room expressing outrage filled the hall, and the entire Piaxian contingent was now standing, voicing their denial. Regent Tarlok asked for civility and urged his brother and the others at his table to sit back down. Once a measure of calm was restored, he met Brumaine's stare. "This is a significant charge you levy, young prince. My warlocks are not assassins, and I can assure you none left the compound last night to commit such a heinous deed."

Lies. They had to be. He studied the calm face of the Piaxian regent, then that of his commander seated next to him. Savan's appearance was more of one of curiosity with squinted eyes and furrowed brow. What was he wondering? If he was fabricating the whole thing? "If I had not seen it with my own eyes, then there would be some question. They say your warlocks can read a man's thoughts. Come. Read mine. You will find what I say to be true."

"Such is true. Though I can get some surface thoughts by being merely nearby, the read is best if I touch your forehead. May I have permission to do so?"

He wondered whether it might be risky. Could this warlock alter what thoughts were in his mind? Or worse, destroy it? He had gone this far with the challenge. It was up to him to see it through. "You have my leave to do so."

From behind the Riaz table, Kero's guardian stepped into the middle area. "*I* will do it, lest there be disagreement or subterfuge."

Tarlok moved to join him. "We will both do it, lest there be disagreement or subterfuge."

The big man nodded. "So be it. Together."

Brumaine stepped out from behind his table to stand before them, the memory of his brother's slaying foremost in his mind. "I am ready."

It took only a moment as both touched his forehead. The first to take his hand away was Tarlok, his lips drawn tight.

When Kero's guardian pulled away, he turned to face the group. "What he says, his memory shows to be true. Two men, dressed in the robes identical to those of Piaxian warlocks, attempted to slay him, but, failing, slew Prince Doren instead."

The outcry from the representatives of the other nations of the seven realms, not including Sechland, made it impossible for him to clearly hear anyone in particular. Things were being shouted, some involving justice, others, military action, but he failed to echo any of these. Instead, he studied the faces of the people gathered to measure their outrage then turned to Quinto.

The old man was rubbing his face, obviously distressed at the proceedings. He whispered something to the others at his table, too inaudible for Brumaine to hear. Finally, he banged a cane against his table, which quieted all those in the room. "Young prince, as I have stated before, a serious issue indeed, but this is not the forum. We will pass on this information to our constables and await their action."

This was not the answer he looked for. He had mused on what to do since rising, running through his mind the suggestion from Commander Oberus, and with the room quiet he knew now was the time to make his plan clear. "There is one thing more we can do. Embargo."

Already pallid, what little color remained in Quinto's face drained away. Once again he held a quiet conversation with the others at his table. Some of the emissaries in the room began to chant "Embargo" until Quinto rose slowly and quiet descended once more. "What you ask is a difficult thing. Very difficult. Piaxia is our largest trading partner. Such a decision would put too great a strain on our people. The whole concept of this cooperative was to bolster trade, not shutter it. I am afraid Riaz cannot agree to such a restriction. Now, if we can get back to the business at hand—"

"No!" Likewise, Oberus had predicted the response and the agreement of what next to do needed to be played out. "If you cannot agree to such terms, then not only will Piaxia be shut out, but so, too, will be Riaz. Think about it. What would you rather have? Some trade...or none at all?"

The patriarch of the Hamak family shook his head as the others at his table whispered feverishly at him. Finally, he rose. "We will adjourn to discuss this question. Please, there are refreshments to be served. My fellow merchants and I will return to propose alternatives."

Things were progressing as expected. He motioned to his group to stand. "There are no other options acceptable. We shall retire from this meeting until we hear word of your acceptance. Think wisely."

With one final glare at the Piaxian table, he led his group to the exit and out into the street beyond. Gathering his honor guard he made for the Hamak residence. There was much to be discussed there as well. Oberus had promised a receptive ear awaited them in Alban Hamak. He hoped such a promise would be kept.

CHAPTER 19

For half the morning, Darlee moped in her room. She even refused a treat from the old cook, Maresh, who had climbed the two flights despite her bad hip to bring the pastry to her.

Her foster father had left early for the treaty negotiations, leaving her alone. Rather than spend the free time exploring the city, she was wasting it acting like a petulant child. She knew it. What did she expect? That Prince Brumaine would throw himself at her, lavishing her with kisses? Despite her powers, she knew she was no match to the sexual allure of Lasha. It was time to grow up.

Entering the hallway outside her room, she found all quiet. Everyone had gone to the meeting. She made her way to the back stairwell and descended toward the kitchen. The aroma of fish cooking wafted up the stairs to her. A small hunger pang warbled through her belly. It smelled delicious.

When she stepped into the kitchen, Maresh grinned at her, putting down the pot she held.

"There you are. I thought you were going to hide in your room all day."

Returning a weak smile to the cook, she held a hand to her midsection. "I decided that was a stupid idea. Besides, the scent of your cooking has me hungry. Can I get something to eat?"

The woman hobbled over to a small table, retrieved a pastry, then held it out. "Not right now. The food isn't ready. Here, I saved this for you. It will satisfy until I can serve a proper meal."

Accepting the treat with as much grace as she could muster, she then headed out into the main room. It was empty as well, so she sat once more at the bench she and the others had occupied the night before.

While she munched on the pastry, the events from the last evening replayed in her mind. Why had that warlock challenged her? In hindsight, it made no sense. He must have recognized the level of her mana with a glance. It was a skill every lord level warlock possessed. He never had a chance. What had been his motive? To ascertain her knowledge level? Of course, it was one thing to have the mana, a totally different one to know how to wield it. It was the only thing that made sense. He was lucky she hadn't killed him.

In Rock House, there was no sign of Kero. That was fine with her. She wasn't in the mood to meet with any of the group, including Commander Savan. As far as she was concerned, her sleuthing days in Lymos were over. What she did want was some comfort. Her foster father was gone to the meetings. Rubbing her hand on the stone bench, she eyed the wall it passed through knowing it continued on the other side.

She had tried before, without success, to contact her brother. She wondered whether the additional distance had made the link impossible. Was the ocean between a factor? Of course, it mattered if Gar was also in contact with the stone of the Earth. He may have been elsewhere.

The decision made, her snack done, she got up and went to the door to the private room beyond. Her gentle knock brought no response. Good. No one was there.

Lifting the latch, Darlee pushed the door open and stepped inside. The room remained exactly as she had last seen it. The bench continuing from the main room, the small table with a tallow candle upon it, the open brazier where coals still smoldered, and the door that led out into the alley beyond.

Wasting no time, she used her magic to light the candle then centered herself on the bench, her arms resting on the table. It always took time to connect the link. Using the Key to draw additional power from the stone, she focused on her brother. "Gar. Where are you? Please talk to me."

From behind the brazier, the small form of Hiss appeared. "No here you belong. Is master's place you sit. Go you from this place."

He jumped up on the table, his talons held in a menacing way.

Darlee had knowledge of how to deal with the imp from her encounters the year past. She backhanded the demon who tumbled off the table to fall to the far end of the bench. "Leave me alone,

Hiss. I need some privacy, and this room provides it. Sit quietly until I'm finished and then you can have it all to yourself once more." She returned to concentrating on Gar.

"Gragnishozar not be pleased. He punish."

Trying to maintain her focus, part of her mind still wondered who Hiss was talking about. Was that the name of Kero's master? "Gragnishozar?"

Before her, a vision of flames appeared, and the rest of the room darkened. The hissing, snarling, growling language of the demons she had heard before pounded at her. What was happening? She wanted to sever the link, but she was being held. Who could do that? Stories of the old warlock Bron passed through her thoughts, but she doubted it could be him. As she recollected, his spirit was still embodied in a raven. No, the language was that of a demon. Which could it be? Doom? Was he not still imprisoned in Lia? Did he even have the ability to transmit through the stone of the Earth?

She was locked in an open link. She could not even struggle. "I do not understand. What do you want?"

The flames muted some. "Common tongue? Very well. Where is Gragnishozar?"

That name again. One of the few things she could do besides talk was move her eyes. Straining her view to her right, she espied Hiss curled in a ball, looking through his fingers. Obviously, the imp was frightened. By whom? Not her, so whoever she was talking with. "I do not know who Gragnishozar is."

The flames brightened. "You lie. You spoke his name."

An attack on her mind began. She tried her best to block it, but it hurt so. "I...I only repeated...what I had heard...no more."

"From who?"

The fact whoever it was needed to ask meant her mind shield was holding, but considering the pain she was in, just barely. Maybe if she spoke the truth she might get released and possibly break the link. She strained to look right once more. "From Hiss."

The vision of the flames widened, brightening the room. "So, child, it is you."

Hiss screamed in terror, dived at Darlee, and yanked her free from the bench. Together, they tumbled to the floor.

The image of the flames vanished. The room was most dark now, the coals providing what little light there was as the candle had been knocked over and gone out. There were spots before her eyes as she sought to regain her vision.

What had just happened? Who had such magical power to hold her? Why did she not see who it was instead of the flames? Who was Gragnishozar? Why did the mysterious one at the other end of the link seek him?

As she stood, righted the candle and relit it, she gazed at the imp slinking to a corner. *Why did he call you child?*

She pursued the small demon and grabbed his wrist. "Who was that, Hiss? Who was on the other end of that link?"

The imp squirmed. "No tell. Me no tell."

The strange voice must have belonged to a demon. Probably one she did not know. Why else would it call Hiss, child? With no intention of letting the little beast stay silent, she shook him hard. "You *will* tell me. If you do not, I will turn you over to the authorities here. I doubt they take kindly to a demon in their midst."

Hiss slashed sharply at her wrist with his talon nails. She released him and grasped at the cut. Blood spurted from the wound. "Why, you little—"

The door from the alley opened.

Her focused turned to it. Into the room strode the large lord of Rock House. He glanced at her, then at Hiss, and finally settled his gaze on her and her wound once more.

"What goes on here?"

Anger still roiled in her from being lacerated by Hiss. Despite how terrifying Kero's master was, she was not going to back down. "Nothing for you to be concerned with. I asked Hiss a question, and the little monster cut me."

The Rock House lord glanced once more at Hiss then stepped closer to her. "Here. Let me touch your arm. I can heal it."

She stepped back, regaining the space between them that had

existed before. "I don't need your help." Concentrating on the wound, she closed it, and soon all that remained was a slight redness. "There. All fixed."

"Impressive. I see by your mana aura you are of lord level. Stronger, I think, than any other in Riaz. It was no luck with which you bested Lazaan last night. Not only is your magic powerful, but your knowledge is as well." He closed the gap once again. "But know this. Compared to mine you are but a whisper in the wind. You have encroached on a space I consider private. Go now, before I lose my temper and make an example of you."

An urge to remain defiant lasted but a moment. She sighed. "I will go. I would know one thing first. Who is Gragnishozar?"

The huge man spun, and, with a speed she did not expect, seized Hiss by the throat and shook him. "You told her?"

"No, Master, no...me...no, I...no."

"Ever the liar." Tossing the imp into the corner, he faced Darlee. "Upon pain of death, you must promise not to repeat that name."

He could have killed her now, there was no doubt. For whatever reason, he had not. She took some courage from that fact. "Why? What harm could the repeating of a name do?"

"Because it is mine. There are those who exist who would desire the knowledge of where I am. For over a hundred years, I have remained hidden. I will not be found now."

Over one hundred years? Now some things made sense. The tale of the demon stones replayed in her mind. How, at that time, warlocks of the seven kingdoms, in an effort to discover the source of the Key, split asunder the ground and released the demons who then wreaked havoc upon the land. It was only the effort of the warlock Bron who had imprisoned the demons in the stones. Gragnishozar must have been one that got away. "Then you, like Hiss, are a demon."

"No demon am I. Cousin, yes, but different. The demons, as you call them, are the children of the gods. I am not one of those. After an age spent below the stone of the earth, the freedom of the surface is one I would not surrender. When we climbed out onto the land, it was I who vanquished the warlocks who sought to close us back in."

"Hiss scampered to cling to Gragnishozar's leg. "No, Master. You best. You free us. You our lord, not...them."

The memory of the voice behind the flames came to Darlee's mind. "Who are *them*?"

Gragnishozar shoved her toward the door to the main hall. "No more questions. I have shared with you more than any human knows."

There was no point in pushing the matter further. The briskness with which he was handling her told her so. Surrendering to leaving, she was moving on her own toward the exit when a knock on the door occurred.

The door opened and Maresh, her eyes wide and her face taut, held a boy, with a shock of bright-orange hair by his collar. "Master. This is Kero's friend, Derak. He has something important to tell you."

The lad, once freed from Maresh's grip, stepped in and bowed. "Master of Rock House, your help is needed. Kero has been taken captive."

Gragnishozar stepped in front of Darlee to stand before Derak. "Who would dare take my ward hostage?"

"The two warlocks he and I sought. We found them in a house on the south end. When Kero went to investigate closer, they pounced on him. They did not see me, and when they took him, I ran here."

Kero taken? She wondered whether such would have happened had she returned to the group and not sulked in her room. Perhaps he would have asked *her* to seek out those men, then, maybe, the results would have been different. She felt guilty.

Kero's guardian took Derak by the arm and steered him into the main room. He turned to Maresh. "I will bring him back. There are many goings-on that are greatly disturbing. I do not have time to tell you all. Secure Rock House against all entry save that of those who are our guests. We will not be long."

Sensing the seriousness of the situation, and with the guilt weighing on her conscience, she stepped to Gragnishozar's side. "I'm coming with you."

He looked at her for a moment. "Very well." He nodded toward Derak. "Lead the way."

CHAPTER 20

Where am I? Kero's eyelids felt like they were sewn shut. He could not open them. The back of his head hurt with a throbbing pain. Seeking to remedy it, he discovered his hands tied and could not reach the affected area. As he struggled, his left eyelid finally cracked open, and he peeked at the shaded surroundings.

Stilling his movements, from his prone position on the floor, he observed the two men sitting at the table, neither looking in his direction, but instead, engaged in a debate he had not paid attention to until then.

Petrius was sitting back in his chair, his eyes lidded as he pulled on a pipe, smoke from his exhales putting his features in a muted haze. "Your trouble is you worry too much. Our orders were to wait and hide out here until the end of the day. We will receive new instructions then."

Holding a mug, Bokko took a swig then wiped his mouth with his sleeve to remove the froth left on his beard. "Still, I don't like it. What with getting attacked last night by that creature and then the assassin lord's whelp showing up, it seems too many know where we are."

Hearing the reference to him, Kero closed his eye, figuring such a comment would draw their attention. Best to appear still unconscious. Perhaps he might hear something of value.

"Earlier, I'd have said you were right, but there's been no one else since. For whatever reason, young Kero there was in the street and spotted me. Everyone knows he's a spy for his master, which is probably why he decided to check out back to see what we were up to."

"Which has me wondering why we don't just kill him."

"And earn the wrath of the assassin lord? Are you crazy? By tomorrow, everything around here is going to be different. When the new order of who's in charge here in Riaz sets in, he'll have to adjust to it. We can let his ward go then, and no harm will follow. Killing him, you and I are dead."

"Ha! You're just scared of him. He can't be that tough. He's only one person."

Taking a chance the conversation had moved past him, Kero opened the one eye again.

Petrius was leaning forward, elbows on the table, pointing the end of his pipe at Bokko. "Only one person? How about, only one person who can create golems. Or the only warlock who's mana is not visible. Or maybe the simple fact he's a huge, powerful man who could toss you twenty paces with one arm. You're right I'm scared of him, and you should be, too."

Bokko hoisted his mug, spilling some. "Lazaan's not scared."

Petrius waved a hand in disgust. "Lazaan's an idiot. He couldn't even beat that wisp of a girl from Sechland."

"Ho! That was a sight to see, him being the only lord level and all. She stomped him good. It'll teach him right for the braggart that he is."

At the sound of a knock at the door, both men went silent. They rose as quietly as they could with Petrius motioning to Bokko to go open it while he took a position behind it.

Bokko readied to cast a spell. "Who's there?"

"Open the door, you fool. Would you have me standing in the street forever for all to see?"

Kero's heart sank on hearing the voice from outside. He *knew* that voice. Bokko lifted the security bar, and Stod strode into the house. As he passed Bokko, he waved a hand in front of his face and scrunched up his nose. "Bokko, you reek of drink. You need to stay sober. There is much yet to do tonight."

Petrius stepped from behind the door. "I've told him so, Stod. He doesn't listen."

Stod took another step then grabbed up the Piaxian cloaks from the back of a chair. "Obviously, not the *only* one not listening. Why haven't you destroyed these?"

Petrius grabbed them and threw them in the fireplace. Holding one hand above the cloaks, they burst into flames. "I meant to, but my magic was gone, and I could find no flint to light the fire. Thankfully, it's coming back now."

"Gone? Where did it go?"

Bokko held a hand close to the ground. "Some little bugger of a creature attacked us. All dark-grey with sharp talons. Somehow, it sucked out our mana. Before I could do anything I was powerless."

"Where is it, now? Did you kill it?"

Petrius chuckled. "Kill it? Hardly. It drained me first while Bokko watched, laughing, though I had no idea what it was doing at the time except clinging to my back. When it attacked him, he cowered in a corner. I tried magic. It was then I discovered I had none left, so I grabbed the thing and tossed it out the door. For all I know, it could be anywhere."

Stod's gaze fell on Kero, meeting the stare from his one open eye. He rushed over and hoisted him to a sitting position. "Kero, what are you doing here?" Stod looked back at the others. "Well? Why is Kero trussed up here?"

Bokko, in the process of sneaking another drink, hid it behind his back. "He was spying on us. Near killed me with a lightning bolt. After Petrius koshed him I wanted to finish him off, but instead, Petrius made me bind him...hic...something about not wanting to have Kero's lord kill us."

"At least one of you was thinking. We don't need the assassin guild master involved. Him set on the status quo, he would only muddy things up." Stod began to work at undoing the knots. "You best go before he comes looking for his ward. I'll handle things from here."

Petrius opened the back door. "Whatever you say." He nodded toward his accomplice. "'C'mon Bokko."

Bokko drained his mug before placing it down. "On my way."

Stod paused until the two men had left, and then returned to his unbinding. "This is a rotten mess you've involved yourself in, Kero. There're changes coming to Riaz. You don't need to mix yourself up in it. I'm going to let you go. I want you to promise me you'll stay out of the way."

Glancing from the business of being freed to Stod's look of concentration on the task, he tried to reconcile what was going on.

Maybe this *was* something he shouldn't be involved in. Whatever Stod was talking about was obviously much bigger than the assassination of a prince of Morica. *"Changes to Riaz,"* he had said. A number of possibilities screamed through his mind, but based on the hiring of so many assassins, foremost was the idea of a takeover by one family, the Hamaks. "Why are you doing this?"

Stod looked up. "Because I want you safe."

His, until now, friendship with Stod teetered on the edge. Would the assassin tell him the truth? "No, not about me. Why are you doing this? Why change things? Were they so bad before, a change was needed?"

The hands now untied, Stod resorted to pulling out one of his knives to cut the bonds round Kero's ankles. When he finished, he grabbed Kero by the shoulders. "Listen. Things are in motion now. There's no stopping it. You and your master need to stay out of it. In a couple of days, things will settle out."

With the last strands of rope pulled free from his legs, he and Stod rose to their feet. Though a little shorter, he did his best to look eye to eye with the muscular assassin. "In those couple of days, how many people will die?"

"If it were up to me, as few as possible...but it's not up to me. Now, before things get any worse, go home and stay there."

Kero wasn't going to surrender so easily. "Who's doing this, Stod? Quinto Hamak? He's already the richest merchant in the land. What more could he want?"

"No, not Quinto, it's—"

The front door split asunder, the shards of wood flying everywhere, causing both he and Stod to raise their arms in protection against the airborne debris. The light from the open doorway was only momentary as a number of golems now blocked the door and were forcing their way, ripping more of the front of the house apart in an effort to get their huge frames in.

Gragnishozar had come. They would not harm him, but Stod was a different matter. He turned to lead the assassin to the back door when it, too, was burst open by more golems. Unless he did something, they would make short work of Stod. Summoning his magic he fired his most potent bolt at the nearest, shattering the thing back into the globs of mud, stones, and sticks it was comprised of.

Stod, blades in both hands, slashed and cut at another, dismembering it before it could do harm.

There were too many. He needed Gragnishozar to stop them. He faced the opening where the front door had once been. Looking out into the street beyond, he could see the dark-clad form of his lord. "Master! Call your creatures back!"

Too late. A scream erupted from Stod as a trio of golems slashed at his body. Kero squirmed between the creatures and Stod's fallen form, pushing at them with his hands. "Master, no! You must stop!"

Despite his best efforts to interpose his body between Stod and the golems, they still managed to continue their attack. After a few more whimpers, Stod fell silent, blood seeping from a dozen wounds. "No! No! No! You must not kill him! Master, please! Let him be!"

Only with a deep penetration into the chest of the assassin by the stone fingers of a golem, and a rattled last breath expelled from Stod, did the golems cease their attack. They turned and filed out of the destroyed home, exiting the way they had entered.

With a wave of his hand, Gragnishozar turned the golems to lifeless mounds of mud and stones.

Kero knelt next to Stod. His eyes were still open, a look of shock on his face. There was no pulse. His friend was gone. While tears filled his eyes, he pressed on the lids of the assassin until they closed. He could no longer bear the look of terror frozen there.

As he wept over the body of his friend, a shadow fell over him. He knew it to be Gragnishozar.

"Come Kero. I would take you home. The one who has taken you against your will is no more."

A shiver ran through his body. He breathed deeply to rid the sensation. The actions of his master were what he had become accustomed to—act without mercy. "You are wrong. He was freeing me. You killed the wrong man. It was Petrius and Bokko who held me. *They* were the ones who killed Prince Doren of Morica, not Piaxians."

He looked at his hands. Both showed splotches of blood from touching the slashed body of Stod. In a panic, he wiped them feverishly against his shirt. Though his hands now somewhat clean, his shirt bore the stains. Would he never be free of the guilt he now felt?

His back still to his master, he was surprised to find a gentle tug at his elbows by small hands.

"Come Kero. Let's get out of here. You can mourn your friend all you want, but you must leave this place."

Turning, he saw the look of concern on Darlee's face, her lips tight, her brow furrowed. When did she arrive? She must have come with Gragnishozar. At his other elbow was Derak. He gave a tight-lipped smile to his pal. Wiping at his eyes with knuckle, he nodded. "You are right. Someone will come to investigate. Whether it's the constabulary or other assassins, someone will come."

He let them help him rise then went to the fireplace and managed to retrieve different pieces of the garments burning, stamping the flames out on the floor. Facing his lord, he puffed out his chest, lofted the pieces, and looked up. "My friend has died, and those responsible have gotten away. If ever there was a time for you to act on my behalf, it is now. Will you do it?"

"The summoning of golems takes a great toll, even for one as me. I could not do another summoning right now. For the time being, we must retire to Rock House. Once I have seen how the day unfolds, I can determine a fit course of action."

He recalled Stod's discussion with the other warlocks. "By the time this day is done, it will be too late."

Gragnishozar ignored the comment and instead started for home. With no other choice but to follow, Kero, flanked by Derak and Darlee, trailed his lord three paces back.

As they walked, Darlee pressed close. "What do you mean when you say it will be too late tonight?"

Being a Sechlander, he doubted she would appreciate what

was happening. After all, she lived in a monarchy. More than likely, she found the system in Riaz flawed. Besides, after the night before, he doubted she still held any real interest in the political machinations in Lymos. Stod was right. Foreigners did not belong in Lymos. "It's none of your concern, only for Derak and I. When this is all over, you'll get on your boat and go home. Only *we* will remain to deal with the new order of things."

Darlee remained silent, but he could see by her downcast eyes, the knitting of her brows, and the tightness of her lips, that she was perturbed.

Derak gave him a nudge. "You're right, Kero. It's not her problem, but you and I...we're still not at the age of ascension. Who's going to listen to us? What can we do about it?"

What were they going to do? Gragnishozar had made no promises. More than likely, his master would sit the whole thing out and pick up his life once more when the power shift was complete. After all, he was still, far and away, the most powerful person in all the land when it came to magic. None would dare fight him, would they?

Lost in thought about what the future held, he was surprised when Darlee stepped in front of him and put a staying hand on his chest. "You're wrong. I do care what happens. My foster father is here trying his best to negotiate a trade deal that would benefit our country and yours. We just went through a terrible war a year ago where, beside my left eye, I lost my parents and my grandfather. Sechland cannot afford to go to war again, and if things that happen here lead to such a thing, going home is only a temporary refuge until the enemy is pounding on the gates once more. There's plenty we can do."

He slapped her hand away. "Like what?"

She cupped her fingers, and a ball of flame appeared. "Interfere in their plans. Your guardian may be powerful, but he says I'm next, and you're not so bad yourself. We have magic."

Kero looked from her flushed face to Derak's, keen with attention, and lastly to Gragnishozar's, who had stopped to turn and face them, a gleam in his eyes. All were waiting his response.

Should he strike without his master's assistance? Could Derak and their other assorted friends aid in any way? Could he count on Darlee for however long it took and not disappear back to her homeland? He had just lamented that foreigners were no help. Would their magic be up to the task? There were a lot of ways it could all go wrong.

And then, if he did not act, there were a lot of ways it could still go wrong. He gave them a small grimace. "Let's try."

CHAPTER 21

The day passed without word from the Riaz merchant guild. Brumaine continued to play over and over in his mind everything that had happened—his brother's death, the talk of attacking the Piaxian contingent, and the ultimatum he had laid down at the meeting. Alban, Quinto's eldest, continued to assure them a resolution was at hand. All that was needed was patience.

Patience. It was something he was sorely starting to lack. When would the Lymos leaders give in? Surely, they must know what he proposed was no idle threat. Oberus had assured him things would turn out for their benefit.

The commander had disappeared after the midday meal, stating he was going to the warship to check on Doren's safekeeping. Now, with the day waning toward a close, the absence of his military commander had prevented him from making any further plans. He was starting to fret. Something must have gone wrong.

He rose from the table where he and Var waited. "Come. Let us go down to the pier and find out what keeps Oberus so long. This abhorrent waiting is driving me crazy."

"I agree. He and those who went with Doren's body should have returned hands ago. Something is amiss."

Before they could exit the building, Alban stopped them. "Prince Brumaine, where are you going? Supper will be served soon."

Something about the man bothered him. When they had returned from the morning session at the merchant hall, Alban was waiting. Expecting to hear words and promises of support, he instead offered platitudes of, "Don't worry, everything will turn out right." He then smiled in a way that made Brumaine believe perhaps the man withheld some secret from the Moricans. "I would check on things at the wharf and the securing of my brother aboard our warship. Do not worry, I shan't be long."

Not to let the son of Quinto Hamak delay him further, he

stepped past the man and out into the courtyard of the estate.

No sooner were they outside when Var nudged him and pointed. "Look, Sire, smoke. There is a fire in the city."

Indeed, dark smoke billowed up from somewhere not more than a couple of blocks away. Curiosity gnawed at him to know the cause of the fire, but his initial plan of action would have to wait if he followed that urge. "It is not our concern. Our mission right now is to find Oberus and bring him and our troops back to the Hamak compound."

He set a brisk pace as they strode down to the docks. Only as they stepped onto the pier did Var stop him. "It may be my imagination, but there is a youth with a shock of bright-red hair following us."

He looked back to see the youth in question fidgeting around some shipping crates. Although now engaged in a discussion with a fisherman, Brumaine noted how the boy glanced in their direction every now and then. "I see him. I cannot recall whether I have seen him before. How long has he been trailing after us?"

"Ever since we left the Hamak estate. He is unarmed, and, I suspect, no threat. Still, he is monitoring our movements. If you like, I can apprehend him for you. Perhaps he might yield who he is working for."

Turning to once more face the Morican boats, he shook his head. "Leave him be. I am already concerned that we have arrived at our destination yet still see no sign of Oberus or our troops."

Striding down the pier, he kept his focus on the deck of the trireme. There was no sign of anyone. Not even the guard was visible. Where was everybody?

He took the plank quickly and stepped onto the deck of the warship. Seated on a bench, eyes closed, was one of the merchants who had accompanied them. As he neared, it was obvious the man was fast asleep. He grasped the fellow by the shoulders and shook hard. "What are you doing here? Where is the guard?"

The man, startled, soon regained composure. "My prince, I was asked by your commander to keep an eye on things for today. He and his men left several hands ago."

Left? To go where? Leaving the merchant, he checked below deck. There, stowed carefully, was his brother. The wax-soaked wrap on his body was still sealed, and no smells emanated from it. At least this detail had been taken care of. He patted his brother's shoulder. "Things are unraveling here, Doren. I am unsure of what to do. Oberus is ignoring my commands, the men are as well, and I am left with only Lieutenant Varamanthu to set things right. The negotiations are without resolution. If only you were still here, I would not be burdened with this task."

The only response he received was a quiet creaking as the boat rocked slightly and rubbed against the dock in the waters of the bay. Despite his wishes, Doren would not rise from the dead and assume command. He made for the exit and emerged back on deck. "Come Var. Our only choice is to retreat to the estate and await Oberus' return. The fact our vessels are left not properly guarded and our troops unaccounted for is disturbing. Whatever the commander's explanation, I doubt it will suffice."

They headed back toward the Hamak estate. He glanced at the sun. In less than a hand, it would be dusk. Then he noted a second column of dark smoke rising to the south-east. "Take note, Var. A second fire. This one farther south, but still near the top of the town. I do not like the look of this."

"Let us run. Perhaps we will discover more if we hurry."

Despite the hilly nature of Lymos that required him to run uphill the entire way, the many hours of training under the auspices of Var shone through as he stayed in step with his mentor. As they ran, he made note of the people in the town. Many were standing round in whisper circles rather than going to the aid of those whose homes were under siege by the blazes. Why was no one going to go assist in dousing the flames? Did they not fear the fires spreading? He pointed to one large group. "They are just standing there—none moving to help."

"I noticed as well. I suspect these fires are not accidental. You and I are obviously unaware of what is going on in the city, but no doubt word has spread of whatever it is."

When they rounded the final corner and the fire came into

view, they found more than burning buildings to be concerned about. Four corpses littered the street—men cut down by sword and arrow. Brumaine knelt by the first dead man he reached and examined the body. "Run through by more than one blade. He wears on a chain a medallion of some sort."

Var knelt beside him and hefted the medallion, examining the insignia. "An emblem of authority, I suspect. This must be one of their constabularies."

Brumaine stood and stared at the fire. It would not spread easily. The blaze was contained to a great manor home in the middle of a walled estate. It reminded him of the Hamak compound, though not quite as large. "This must be the home of another one of the major merchants who rule this city. I can see more dead in the courtyard."

Var stood as well and looked north toward the other fire. "My guess is such is the case of the other one. The city is being purged of its leaders. We'd best get back to the Hamak estate as quickly as possible."

Once more he broke into a run as they headed north. On the way, they passed the first fire they had seen. As expected, it, too, was an estate, though fewer dead lay about and the fire was smaller. He could see a few people attempting to douse the flames using buckets. By the cut of the clothes they wore, he suspected they were servants and not members of whatever family lived there.

He dared not tarry to find out. It wasn't until he could see the gate to the Hamak compound that he slowed his pace. It wasn't the reason he was back, it was the fact the grounds teemed with men.

Var put a staying hand on his arm. "Do we risk entry? They are most likely the men who have pilloried the other merchants."

Pausing, he noted no violence going on. If anything, things appeared somewhat congenial. He spotted a few of his own men mixed in the crowd as well as a couple of servants busily pouring wine into waiting cups. "I think we will be safe enough. My guess, Commander Oberus is somewhere in there. Our question as to his whereabouts has been answered. The only thing left is why."

As he strode into the courtyard he noted, by their colors, not only were there men of Morica there, but Queensland and Braxborough as well. So, some of their allies had assisted in the raids. He didn't expect to find anyone from Fermia as they had once again claimed neutral status, but also absent were those from Gatway.

There were also many men who must be citizens of Riaz. They wore no colors, instead dressed as common citizens. Indeed, he even recognized two—the man who first assaulted him two nights before in Rock House, and the small bald man who had lost a magic battle to Darlee. If his recollection was correct, the fellow was named Lazaan, and he was, as most likely many of the others were, a warlock and a member of the assassin guild.

One of the Hamak guards stepped in front of him. "Prince Brumaine, your presence is requested inside. Please follow me."

He, along with Var, entered, not the main hall, but one of the smaller houses on the grounds. Inside, he found not only his wayward commander, but military men from the allies out in the courtyard. In the middle of the group sat the Hamak patriarch, Quinto, with his eldest, Alban, standing near. From the sound of raised voices through the door an obvious heated debate had been going on, but all stopped talking upon their entry.

Alban moved to greet him. "Prince Brumaine, I'm glad you have returned. You are about to be witness to the agreement you sought, an embargo. Please, take a seat."

He noted only Quinto sat. The old man never met his gaze, but instead hung his head, rubbing at his face in a worried way. "I think, like the rest of you, I shall stand." He stepped past Alban to be closer to Quinto. "Is what your son states to be true?"

The old man looked up. "What my sons says...what my son has done...is insanity. He fails to understand the complexity of his actions. This takeover of the other houses, this embargo, is doom for Riaz."

Alban tugged gently on Brumaine's arm in an obvious effort to pull him away from Quinto. "My father is somewhat addled in his old age. This house now rules in Lymos and soon, all of Riaz.

In thanks for your assistance, we will honor the embargo.

He shrugged free. The comments made by this elder merchant intrigued him. All things taken into consideration, Quinto was effectively king of Riaz. "Why is it doom? You now rule. The word of the house of Hamak is now law. What could go wrong?"

"Because the balance is lost. While five houses ruled this island there was an understanding among the citizenry that no one house would rule, and as such, no one house was held accountable for things. They trusted the disparity between us would result in us keeping each other in check. Where one house might gain an upper hand, the other houses would ensure such advantage did not last long. As such, we treated each other as equals, and the people flourished in the détente. There was no royalty to lay blame on, no one person to fault, no reason to fear hardship from a monarch.

"And other nations gave us space. We were no threat. No army. No military armada, just trading ships and fishermen. We are simply a central trading post between those nations gathered here and a few others across the Great Sea. We offer little military value for conquest.

But now, the trade will change. No longer will other countries be able to negotiate between different houses for the best deals. Instead, there will be only one, us. Doubt will set in on whether we offer a fair deal. This doubt will develop into angst and from there, the possibility of invasion becomes very real."

As Quinto fell silent, Brumaine scanned the faces of those gathered there. In Alban, he saw nervousness, in Oberus, anger, in the others, suspicion. He wondered which of these allies, or possibly, even his own father, might take advantage of this situation and attempt a takeover of the island. Expecting a fight from both the warlocks and the local citizens, it would take at least two thousand men, an impossibility to ship in a single trip across the Great Sea, as no country supported such a navy. He did not believe the island need fear an invasion any time soon. Of course, there was always the possibility of alliances.

He needed to focus on the matter at hand. His people, under the direction of his commander, had assisted, along with

Queensland and Braxborough, in a coup that transferred the power of the island into the hands of one family. An embargo, as requested, was now available to him. First and foremost was what would best serve his country, Morica. His thoughts returned once more to the cold body that lay in the hold of the trireme. The desire for vengeance had not left his mind, it was only subdued by the delinquency of his commander. He would rebuke Oberus later. For now, a decision was needed. "I understand your concerns, merchant Quinto, but the actions you feared have already occurred. Will you accede and grant the embargo requested?"

Quinto sighed heavily and then rose, holding tight to his cane. "I am tired and too old for all of this. Though I have great fear about what lies in store for my homeland, I fear I will not live long enough to see my predictions come to fruition. What I state now shall be fact from here on. I hereby relinquish my role as leader of the Hamak family to my son Alban and shall retire to my villa on the south end of the island to spend my last days in solitude."

He walked toward the door, waving a hand at everyone to step out of the way. "It is a long trip, and I will need my rest before I take my leave in the morning. Good night to you all, and may the gods have mercy."

Everyone watched as the old man exited the house. Brumaine could not help but feel a certain amount of sorrow for the old man forced into such a decision. He, along with the others, turned to Alban—an exultant glow on the man's face. "Well, merchant Alban, sovereign of the Hamak family, what say you?"

"Tomorrow morning, at the resumption of the trade talks, I, as the sole legal representative of Riaz, shall endorse the embargo."

CHAPTER 22

When they got back to Rock House, Kero had sent Derak off to tell all their friends to meet in the market one hand before dark and after that see what Prince Brumaine was up to.

With little time until the meeting, he ate a special supper prepared by Maresh. For the Sechlanders, the fare that night was rabbit stew. For him—steak. It was a real treat. There were only a handful of animals on the island, and none for slaughter, but strictly for milk and working the small farms here and there. The hilly and mountainous countryside was not conducive to raising cattle. As a result, the few cows that did arrive were often bought by the wealthy and rarely by local butchers.

As he ate, Maresh fussed around him constantly. "How is the steak? Is it cooked enough? Too much? Are you feeling all right? Is your head where you were hit okay? Do you have any dizziness? Are you—"

Kero understood her concern, but her incessant nattering was driving him crazy. "Don't worry, Maresh. The food is fine. I'm fine. Ev-er-y-thing-is-fine."

She shook her head. "I don't understand why the master puts you at risk so. You're just a boy. Sending you out on all those foolish errands. He'll get you killed is what he'll do."

In all his years, Maresh had never fussed so much. As she continued to mutter about all males being stupid, he sighed and returned to eating, ignoring her until she went back to the kitchen.

With Maresh's nagging no longer distracting him, he was able to focus on the discussions going on elsewhere in the room, most notably, from the table where Darlee sat with her foster father. It was easy enough to listen in as the conversation became heated. Darlee was arguing about having permission to go out at dusk. Her guardian would have none of it.

Finally, Captain Brusk rose from the table and went to pound on Gragnishozar's door. This would be interesting. No one pounded on his master's door. They knocked politely, if at all. Most wouldn't try.

In the meantime, Darlee had joined Kero at his table. "He's off to talk to Gragnishozar. He thinks if your master makes you stay home, then I have no reason to leave."

Hearing her call his master by his name surprised Kero. That was supposedly a guarded secret. Not even Maresh knew it. "How do you know my master's name?"

"Hiss told me. I know I'm not supposed to tell anyone, but I figured, as his ward, you must know."

The demon imp. That's how he'd learned it as well. He had no doubt that little creature would get them all into trouble one day. "Just remember to keep it a secret. I don't know why, but he's insistent on it."

"I know why."

He gaped while wondering how she knew, but then turned his head at the sound of his master's door being flung open.

Filling the door with his massive frame, Gragnishozar glared at Captain Brusk. "Who dares disturb me so?"

Kero had to give Darlee's foster father credit. He never flinched.

"I am Captain Brusk, emissary of Sechland, and your guest here at this fine establishment called Rock House. I would have a word with you about a matter of some importance regarding those under our care, my stepdaughter, Darlee, and your ward, Kero."

Gragnishozar glanced at Kero and Darlee, then moved to tower over Brusk, staring down at him. "There is nothing to discuss. I have taught Kero all I can. There is a soft streak in him that I have not been able to weed out. It is in his nature to care. Whatever he does or will do is no longer possible for me to change. As to your stepdaughter, do not ask me to intercede for you. I have taken the measure of the girl and consider her more than capable to take care of herself."

His master slammed the door shut, leaving the captain blinking. It took everything not to smirk when Darlee's foster father turned to face them, took a deep breath, and then approached the table. "May I sit?"

Kero held an open hand toward an empty chair. "Please."

Captain Brusk settled into the chair with a thud. He glanced around the room first then returned his attention to Kero. "I am concerned, young man, you are leading my stepdaughter into great danger. She is adamant on going, and outside of tying her up, I see no way of preventing her. I hope you can persuade her otherwise."

It was nearly the time to go. His meal finished, Kero rose. "I'm afraid I can be of no help. You heard my guardian. In his mind, I'm a rogue. My country is at risk. I need all the help I can get. If she decides to join me, I will not refuse."

Darlee also stood. "I'm going. Have faith in me. I won't do anything so stupid as to get killed."

The captain shook his head, rose, gave her a hug, and then clasped forearms with Kero. "Be careful. May the gods be with you."

***

Word had spread fast. Kero and his friends were gathered in the city market, now empty of any citizens of Lymos. Once word had come of the attack on two of the estates of top merchants, the vendors had all quickly packed up their wares and abandoned their stalls. Some, in such a hurry, left behind many of the perishable goods, making a grab for free food a veritable skirmish amongst the city's poor as they had tussled over the stuffs until there was nothing left. Even he and his mates had managed to grab a morsel or two of breads and such to eat while watching the mayhem around them.

Now, there were only the seven of them and Darlee. From the top of the city, two of his mates had reported that one of the other families had deserted their home and fled the city. At least they would not be put to the sword. None had survived in the other two. One other family remained—the Jindos, their gate closed and signs of a significant defense corps within their grounds.

The delegates from Gatway, guests at the estate fled, were

now relocated in another inn, the same as held those from Fermia. He doubted the inn could hold so many, and it was possible Rock House could have accommodated them, but sharing space with the Sechlanders was probably more than the Gatwayans were prepared to chance.

Like all the people in town, the other delegations were holed up as well, waiting out the political storm that had enveloped the city. What they thought of the usurpation of power by the Hamak family must have them wondering where the trade negotiations would go.

Of his friends, Derak had been the last to arrive and be questioned. "What news from the Hamak camp and the Moricans?"

"I followed Prince Brumaine to the dock and then back through town past the two burning homes until he got back to the Hamak estate. The place was swarming with armed men. Not just his people, but those from a couple of the other delegations and just about every man who visits Rock House. It's a small army there. Right now, they're whooping it up, drinking and laughing."

He turned to Darlee. "It looks like the prince has teamed up with the Hamaks. To think I saved his life. How does he repay me...by massacring innocent families and turning my island upside down."

"He doesn't know the truth. We've got to tell him somehow."

Even in the limited light of dusk, Kero could still make out the rising plumes of smoke from the two fires. He didn't know those who had died, just that they had. It angered him. "Know or not, his men have killed Riazians. What kind of man orders such atrocities? Whose side are you on, anyway?"

Darlee's cheeks flushed. "Okay then, what do you propose we do? So far, outside of standing around in an empty city market picking at abandoned food, we've done nothing. We must do something besides talk."

She was right. He had agreed to attempt to thwart the plans of the Hamaks. Now he had to decide how. "The Jindo family. I figure the only reason they're still untouched is they're defended too well. Most likely, they'll be attacked come dark when night makes things easier to do so. We can help them."

Derak chuckled. "Hey, I'm willing to help any way I can, but unlike you two, the rest of us have no magic and none of us are armed. What good would we be against soldiers and warlock assassins?"

Kero could see among his friends the ashen cheeks, the gaping mouths, of those frightened at such an idea. Only Derak appeared nonplussed. This was going to require some strategy. Knowing who was inside the Jindo walls, there was some good news. "No assassins will be there. The Jindos have hired two of their own. Assassins don't kill assassins. It's one of the codes of the guild. Lazaan and his compatriots won't break that rule. They know my master would take exception to such a breach of conduct. It will be strictly up to the soldiers and mercenaries to do the fighting.

"So you're saying I won't get fried with lightning or set ablaze with fire, but only run through with a sword. Not my kind of fun."

Putting together that ledger for Gragnishozar of all the foreigners and where they were staying was about to come in handy. "Nothing of the sort. We're going to use fire to our advantage. Let me show you."

Grabbing a stick, he used his magic to char the end of it. On the cobbles that covered the market, he etched a simple map of the city. He marked the locations of the Jindo estate, the Hamak estate, and the inns housing both the Queensland and Braxborough contingents. "All we need are distractions at the right times. In half a hand, it will be dark." He placed the tip of the stick where he knew Prince Brumaine to be. "At that time, the troops at the Hamaks' will make their move." Moving the stick, he scratched a path. "They will move down these streets. From this point, they will have a distant view of the inn where the Queenslanders are staying. After some of you start a fire there, a shout from one that the inn is on fire will draw those troops away from the conflict." He scratched the path farther. "At this point, it's the view of the inn housing Braxborough. Same program, same results."

Derak grinned. "I always disliked the first inn. I want to start *that* fire."

Kero clapped his friend's shoulder. "The honor is yours. Now all that's left is to draw up the teams from all of you for each inn. Grab some empty crates from the market here and head to your respective locations. Keep this in mind. Once the call goes out—run home. I don't want any of you getting caught."

"What about you? What are you going to do?"

He turned to look at the Sechlander, the girl with a patch over one eye, the girl small in stature, the girl who looked even younger than her fifteen years, but the girl with enough magic to beat any warlock in the land. She gave a gentle nod. Maybe, just maybe, she would make a real difference. "Darlee and I are heading for the Jindo's."

CHAPTER 23

It was a difficult footrace to keep up on the slanted roads of Lymos. Building a city on a hillside would create such inclinations and no doubt Kero was used to them. He was already several strides ahead of her. In the gathering darkness, she might get lost. Darlee was also getting a stitch in her side from the exertion. "Slow down! You're going to lose me."

He stopped and waited until she caught up. "I want to make sure we get there before they do. We're going to need someplace to hide once we do."

Hiding made sense. They did not want to confront those troops from Morica and any others who might arrive. "What did you have in mind?"

Walking again, he pointed toward a dark alley. "In there. At the other end, we should be able to see what happens out in front of the Jindo estate."

Narrow, with no moonlight entering it, only the odd window illuminated by candlelight from within provided any visibility to the passageway. "How far from the gate will we be?"

"About forty paces. It's my hope we will be completely behind them when the attack begins."

Although a better neighborhood, the alley still bore a putrid smell of refuse. Apparently, those people who did the menial job of carrying away such trash had not serviced the lane in some days. There was no time for her to be offended by the odor. Resolutely, she followed Kero to the end where he led her to hide behind a hedge.

Their timing could not have been any later. A glance down the road north showed the distant approach of torchlight.

Over the rooftops, back the way they came, the orange glow of fire lit the sky.

The voice of Kero's friend rang through the night. "There's a fire at the Seaman's Inn!"

Kero chuckled. "Derak. Right on cue."

It was hard to be sure, but Darlee thought she could see at least two, if not three people, break off from the approaching group and head toward the fire. Not the numbers Kero had hoped for, but every man drawn away was one less with which to contend.

She turned to look toward the Jindo gate. There was activity there. She could see men moving, and a couple of them posted atop the wall that surrounded the estate. They must have seen the coming attack force and were readying to defend. Unless they had a lot of people out of sight, they were sorely outnumbered. She nudged Kero to look. "They'll be slaughtered."

"There's still the second fire. Hopefully, it will draw more of them away."

A second flame appeared in the skyline, and another voice rang out of the fire. This time, only one man left the oncoming group to investigate.

"Your plan isn't really working."

"It doesn't look good. You stay here. I'm going to go set up in a different spot."

Kero crossed the street and hid behind a low wall. She was still unsure of what she should do. They had discussed options, but she doubted they would make that much of a difference.

As the men neared, they doused their torches and were approaching in the near dark of the street where only the moon and stars shed any light at all. It was as Kero had expected—an assault under cover of night. She glanced at the Jindo compound. Nights where her foster father, Captain Brusk, told her tales of battles in previous wars reminded her of what was wrong. Clearly, the Jindos had no one of military knowledge to advise them. They were foolish as their compound was illuminated, making them visible while the attackers were not.

As the men passed, she crouched tight against a bush by which she hid. It would take someone to investigate it to find her. She hoped such a thing did not occur. She could render such a person unconscious, but then she would have no choice except to retreat back down the alley and leave the Jindos to their own defenses.

Only when the men had all passed did she finally breathe

normally. None had looked in either alley where she or Kero hid. Instead, they were now arrayed in front of the gate to the Jindo estate.

From his hiding place, Kero emerged and, raising his arms in the air, conjured two large globes of light that he set to float over the attackers illuminating them clearly for the defenders to see. Cries rang out from those in the street and those within the walls. The battle began in earnest with arrows flying and, more surprisingly, magical attacks from both sides. Kero had been wrong! Warlocks were indeed among those assaulting the Jindos.

She studied the road. There...a stretch of open stone lay not four paces away. She hurried to it. As she did, she saw Kero fall to the ground, hit by both an arrow and a bolt of lightning. She felt relief to see him stir—wounded, but not dead. Still, in such a state he would not be able to flee. Stepping onto the granite, she summoned the Key. The sheer sense of power always excited her when she did so.

There were too many for her to target individuals. Kero's light globes had extinguished when he fell so she could no longer identify who might be a warlock and who wasn't. There was enough room on the open stone to step just in front of where Kero lay. Doing so, she drew heavily on her mana and created a wall of flame that stretched from one side of the street to the other. Without hesitation, she sent it forward.

For the warlocks it passed over, their magical shields crackled and held, leaving them unharmed. For all of the others, where they were exposed and not having others stand before them, it ignited clothes, hair, and singed exposed skin. Not fatal, but painful enough to have them drop weapons, cry out in pain, and for many, crumple to the ground to writhe while they struggled to douse flames.

The flame wall vanished a handful of paces past the men, and the street plunged back into darkness. Reaching down, she helped Kero to his feet and turned to retreat the way they had come. She doubted any would dare follow, but after a couple of steps, she looked ahead and discovered two others standing a few paces away. They must have stayed back when the attack began.

Although her powers sorely diminished, she had enough to create a flame ball in her hand to hurl. In what light it shed, the faces of those two in the dark became visible. One was Prince Brumaine. The other she did not know, based on his uniform a lieutenant of some sort. The sight of the prince gave her a moment's pause. Was Kero's summation that Brumaine had joined sides with the Hamaks correct? Why else would he attend such an act of aggression? "Stand aside, or else I will use this on you."

The lieutenant started to draw his sword, and Darlee drew back her arm to throw. Before she did, Brumaine reached over and put a staying hand on the lieutenant's arm. "Hold, Var. I would see them pass unharmed."

The lieutenant sheathed his weapon. "As you wish, my liege."

With Kero holding on, she edged past the men. "Good. We'll be on our way then."

Brumaine took one step toward her, but when she lifted the flame ball again, he stopped. "Darlee, things are out of my control. This coup was not my doing."

She changed the flame ball into an orb of light and set it to float above them. There was something about his look, the downturn of his mouth, the half-lidded eyes, which gave her an impression of sorrow. Was he distressed about the deaths that had occurred that day, or the ones yet to happen? Perhaps. "You are a prince. You can order your troops to stand back. You can convince your allies of the same. Yet, you do not do so. Why?"

He looked down at his feet then met her gaze. "Because I have lost a brother."

Memory of those lost in the past close to her flashed across her mind. Her parents. Her grandfather. All gone. "War takes the lives of many. You are not the only one who grieves. Every life lost leaves behind loved ones who miss them. Husbands. Wives. Children. It takes courage to accept those losses and move forward. Where is yours?"

He sighed and looked away. "I guess I haven't any."

She was torn between feeling pity for him and anger. Though

she knew him to be four years older, he was acting as a child.

Noise from the street where the battle yet raged caused her to glance back. Light orbs hovered over the scene, and warlocks were moving from man to man, healing them. It would be not long before they bested the Jindo defenses. She and Kero had failed to stop the slaughter—only delayed it. It was best they left as soon as possible.

Like her, Brumaine and Var were staring at the carnage as it occurred. For the moment, she and Kero were forgotten. Rather than remind the prince of their proximity, she moved to the deep shadows of the alley and led Kero away. There was no point in continuing a fruitless conversation.

Kero was mumbling—the words not quite understandable. "What did you say?"

"You...didn't tell...treachery."

That was right. She hadn't told Brumaine. Should she go back? Let him know that assassin guild warlocks had committed the murder? Would it change his mind? Put an end to the conflict?

Kero dropped to a knee, almost pulling her to the ground. No, her priorities had changed. "We'll have to tell him another time. Right now I've got to get you home and get that arrow out of you. I can't perform a healing with it still in there."

She pulled as he struggled back to his feet, and together they stumbled down the alleys and streets until they reached the back door to Rock House, the one that entered into Gragnishozar's room.

Both he and Hiss were there when they entered. She held Kero out before her. "Help me." Though the demon skittered about, Gragnishozar, standing near the brazier, never moved.

She laid Kero on the bench with some effort then collapsed beside him. The physical exertion had spent her. Only when she'd managed to catch her breath did she bend over Kero to check on him. He was unconscious, his breathing shallow. She needed to heal him quickly. She looked at Gragnishozar. "Don't just stand there. Earlier today, you went out to save him. Now you do nothing."

Gragnishozar folded his arms across his chest. "This morning, he was taken prisoner against his will while doing an errand of my bidding. Tonight, he acted on his own, knowing full well I would not approve. He must suffer the consequences of his own actions."

She rose to confront Kero's guardian. "Does that include dying?"

When she received no response, she opened the door to the main hall and went in search of her foster father. As a military man, he would know what to do. Fortune had it. He was enjoying a repast nearby. She did not want to alert the other Sechlanders who dined with him. "Come. Kero is in need of your professional opinion."

Captain Brusk looked up. "It can wait until I finish."

As Brusk resumed eating, she pondered how to urge him. Maresh passed the table and arched an eyebrow that asked Darlee, *"What's happened?"* She nudged her foster father. "I'd like you to come now, *Father.*"

The captain tilted his head and looked at her with one eye squinted. After a pause, he put down his fork and rose. "Right. Take me to the lad."

She led him to the private room where Kero lay. Brusk kneeled over him and examined the wound.

Maresh entered as well. "Is Kero hurt bad?"

The captain stood up. "That arrow's lodged in a bad spot. No doubt a lung is punctured. If I try and pull it out, he'll die in seconds. I'll have to cut him open to get it free. That arrow is barbed."

It would require a quick heal to prevent Kero dying. She wondered if she still had enough mana to do so. Worried she needed more, she snatched the imp by the wrist. "Hiss, give me your mana. Now!"

The demon squirmed and struggled to get free. "No give. Me need."

He slashed her arm with his free hand, causing Darlee to release him. She balled her fists. "You give me that mana or I'll beat it out of you!"

Maresh put a staying grip on her arm then stepped up to Gragnishozar. She stared into his face a moment then slapped it hard. "For years, I've worked hard to keep this place going. I've had to mother this boy when you ignored him. He is your ward. You *will* heal him. Otherwise, I will leave this place and, when he dies, you will be all alone."

Gragnishozar unfolded his arms and raised an open hand as if to strike, but then dropped it. "I will do it."

Moving to Kero's side, he placed a hand on the youth's chest and with the other, slowly pulled the arrow back. Darlee watched in amazement as the flesh around the arrow undulated to allow the easy passage of the barb. That was definitely a skill far beyond her ability. His previous boast of being vastly superior showed true. As he handed the arrow to the captain, the wound closed and disappeared, only a slight redness remaining. Straightening, Gragnishozar faced Maresh. "It is done. The boy will live."

Maresh gave him one last scowl, patted Kero's cheek, and then left the room.

Brusk rotated the arrow in his hands. "Morican design. I can tell by the barb."

The speed with which Gragnishozar snatched the arrow then stared at it closely surprised her. There was fury in that action, she knew it. "So what do we do from here?"

Gragnishozar glanced from the arrow to Kero. "Let him sleep. Come morning, I shall bring him with me to the resumption of the trade talks where the truthful revelations he provides will determine the future course of everything. As for tonight, there is something for my minions to attend to.

He opened the door to the alley behind then exited, Darlee and Brusk close behind. She followed as he walked to an empty lot nearby and held out his arms. There was a noise emanating from the ground out there, like a slurping sound, but she could see nothing. She created a light orb and sent it out to illuminate the area.

The earth swirled and roiled, sticks and stones in the mix. It looked like a churning burned stew, all black and lumpy. She watched as the stuff gathered into separate piles.

From the ground, some fifteen or so golems rose. The creatures, monstrous in size, standing some ten to twelve hands taller than their summoner, moved into a semi-circle near Gragnishozar. He turned to the captain. "Stand by me and hold out your hand."

Brusk did as asked. Kero's guardian held out the arrow. "On this arrow is the scent of three men. Ignore the one whose blood on the tip matches and that of the man who stands beside me. It is the third you must identify."

The golems shuffled by, each sniffing at the captain's hand and at the arrow. When all were done, Gragnishozar broke the arrow. "Go. Find that third man. His life is forfeit."

The things sniffed the air. Then, as one, they turned northeast. Darlee's foster father moved to stand by her side. "Where are they going?"

She watched for a moment longer. She had not gone where she suspected they were going, but she had no doubt where it was. "They're headed toward the Hamaks."

CHAPTER 24

The battle over, Brumaine turned away from the carnage that remained of the Jindo estate. With the other family having fled the city, the Hamak plan to wrest complete control of Lymos was complete.

He, along with Var, trailed several blocks behind those returning to the Hamak estate—a combination of Moricans and a few Riaz assassins. The others who aided, men from Queensland and Braxborough, along with the majority of warlocks, had all gone their separate ways to retire to their various lodgings.

Despite the frightening flame magic of Darlee, things had gone well. The sheer number advantage had been too much for those defending. In the end, only one man from Morica was lost and two from Queensland. The warlocks had healed all those wounded, though it would be some time until hair grew back or pink flesh tanned to match those areas not burnt.

The surprise attack by the young lass from Sechland was another matter altogether. No one had expected it, and it had been fairly obvious none could have prevented it. The girl was very powerful. Commander Oberus suggested they attack Rock House in retribution, but he had countermanded that. The girl, along with the Kero lad, had acted alone. No troops from Sechland were present.

As they walked, he glanced at Var. Perhaps he might have some answers. "What should we do about the young Sechland girl Darlee and the boy from Rock House?"

"It was your command to let them pass unharmed. Is there reason you now doubt that decision?"

Why had he decided that? The question gnawed at him. "I suppose I owed the boy a life for he once saved mine."

Var put a staying hand on his arm and turned to face him directly. "Or might it have been when she insulted your honor?"

Even in the dark, he could make out the gaze of his mentor. Along with Var's body posture, hands on hips, Brumaine was being challenged. For the briefest of moments, anger passed through him, but then he recalled the many teachings and realized what Var was trying to do. "My honor is intact. There was no possibility I could allow the death of my brother to go un-avenged. He was beloved by the men. I'd sooner cut my own throat than resist their lust for vengeance. It is this path toward embargo that best serves my country. Attacking the Piaxians would only lead to war, something I would hope to avoid."

The lines in Var's face softened, and he reached out to clap Brumaine's shoulder. "Well said. There may be a statesman in you yet." Var turned toward the Hamaks and wrapped an arm across Brumaine's back, urging him to continue their journey. "Come. A good night's rest will bring the morning where your plan will come to fruition. Then we can board ship and get home. The confinement of this city burdens me. I yearn to once again ride horses in the Morican countryside."

The words of Var supplicated him, though some doubts still nagged at his mind. Perhaps it was best to try and forget them until morning. No more could happen that night to alter what the morrow would bring.

They entered the avenue, home to the Hamak estate. Before reaching the gate twenty paces away, Var gripped Brumaine's arm. "Hold. There is something strange going on in the street to the south of us. It is not clear, but I see much movement."

Indeed, in the direction Var pointed, the dark seethed. "I do not like the look of that. What could it be?"

Var pulled on his arm. "Come, let us get inside the gate. I fear the worst."

He followed his mentor into the estate where Var stopped to take a torch from a wall sconce, step back into the street, and heave it in the direction of the approaching darkness. As the torch dropped to the ground, what moved in the light was a horror beyond Brumaine's expectation. A large number of huge grotesque creatures lumbered closer. They appeared to be composed of the very ground one trod upon—earth, stones, and whatever matter that would lie on it such as sticks, grass, and more. "By the gods!

What are they?"

"I know not. Some evil spawn of the dark. Whatever they are, they are a danger to you and all others whom their paths cross. At this moment, your protection is my utmost concern. Let's get you inside."

A guard for the compound turned and ran. "Doom is upon us! The assassin lord's golems approach."

So they were golems, a term he was unfamiliar with. Now, it was one he would never forget. As men rushed to close the gate, he retreated with Var to the stoop of the main house then turned to watch.

From the house, Commander Oberus emerged with Alban Hamak at his side. "What is happening?"

Both men were wide-eyed, but while he read confusion in the face of his officer, Alban's showed fear. "It appears we are about to be set upon by the minions of the assassin lord, monstrous constructs of his."

Oberus grabbed hold of Alban and shook him. "How do we counter these things? Can they be killed?"

Alban shook his head. "You cannot kill what is not truly alive. Whenever they move through the streets, people lock their doors and pray they are not the target of whatever dark mission they are on."

The things had reached the gate and were in the process of battering it down. It would only be moments before they entered the courtyard. Practically all of Alban's people had abandoned the area. Only his Morican troops stood in the way. Some fired arrows at the creatures. They either bounced off or penetrated without any effect.

Oberus drew his blade and stepped off the porch to join his troops. "Swords. Draw your weapons. Arrows are useless. Our only hope is to hack them to pieces."

The last of the gate crashed to the ground and the golems swarmed in. His own troops, including Oberus and Var, who joined the fighting, counted twenty-eight. The golems numbered fifteen, an almost two to one ratio. Despite the number advantage, he didn't like the odds. If body mass were to be used to calculate, his own forces would be badly outnumbered. Each golem must be three or four times the mass of a single man. They also benefitted from a greater reach by several hands. His men were having a difficult time getting close enough to effectively attack the behemoths. Then there was the injury factor. When one of his soldiers got raked by the stone claws of the golems, he retreated to staunch his wound. The monsters continued despite the damages they suffered.

Too many of his troops were wounded. Although Oberus' tactic to dismember the golems was working to some degree, the attrition rate was not in his favor. Brumaine noted a pattern in the golem advance. They were ignoring attacks from left and right and focused on moving toward one of the men in the rear. From the battle earlier at the Jindo estate he recognized who this man was. "Oberus! Call your men back before you lose them all."

The commander glared at him. "Are you mad? They'll decimate us."

There was no time to argue with his officer who was still the higher authority. Brumaine stepped into the fray and pulled men away from the golems. "Step back. That's an order. Let them through."

It took a moment, but he managed to achieve the result he desired and the golems, no longer pressed, descended quickly on the one soldier, tearing him to shreds. Only when the fellow was surely dead did they turn and leave the courtyard and back the way they had come.

When the last one faded into the darkness Var approached. "How did you know what they would do?"

He went to kneel over the fallen man, whose body and face were slashed to a bloody mess. Both Var and Oberus followed. "This is the man who shot the assassin lord's ward. Something Alban said rang in my mind. *People lock their doors and pray they are not the target of whatever dark mission they are on.* I recognized that mission as one of retribution against the man who attempted to kill Kero. Once their warped sense of justice was done, they had no cause left to complete."

The commander grabbed him by the arm. "You sacrificed one of our own!"

He shook free. "To save the rest? Absolutely. I would do it again. In the future, you will obey my orders. Fewer would be injured if you had, and...*in the future*...you will never lay a hand on me again."

"Why, you spoiled little whelp. I take my commands from your father, not you."

Oberus, his face flushed, balled his fists, lifting one to waist level.

Var interceded and grasped the commander's wrist. "Let's not allow our emotions to get away with us. Striking a member of the royal family is treason and carries the death penalty."

Oberus put his arm down. "I wasn't going to hit him. You take your station too far, Special Second Lieutenant. That night in the king's courtroom you agreed to the goals of this mission. Do not interfere in the plan. Your action is insubordination to a superior officer." The commander turned to face the soldiers nearest by. "Take Lieutenant Varamanthu prisoner. He is to be held in detention until such time as I can convene a military court."

"I agreed to the concept of the plan. I was never provided details such as attacking a member of the royal family."

What plan was Var speaking of? There was no time to ponder such a question. It mattered not. Should Brumaine lose Var, there would be none he could trust. He stepped between his tutor and those men. "You will not do that. I forbid it."

The men looked at each other, confusion obvious. Finally, one turned to Oberus. "Commander, he is the prince. We cannot disobey him."

Oberus scowled. "I do not dispute the authority of a prince. Such matters can be attended to when the time is appropriate." He turned and stomped off toward the main house, entering it with Alban Hamak joining him.

Var sighed. "My liege, you have made a grave enemy in the commander. I have served with him long enough to know his temperament, and it is not a forgetful one. He will pursue this issue when circumstances favor him."

He knew he was not his father's favorite but doubted the king would side with a vassal, regardless of rank, over a member of the royal family. "Phft! Oberus has never liked me anyway. I have nothing to be concerned about. You, on the other hand, do. It may be difficult to protect you."

Var waved a hand in dismissal. "It is of no consequence. Should my career be forfeit, I am ready for it. My children are all grown, and my wife would be glad to have my company at home once more."

Brumaine turned to study the men as they bound each other's wounds. None were life-threatening but some severe enough to make those men ineffective in combat until they healed. Earlier in the night, he'd witnessed the warlocks attend to those very men when they suffered burns from the flame wall Darlee had conjured. At the time, such a skill proved invaluable in the conquest of the Jindo estate. It was at wonders such as the one he now examined where he doubted the decision of the six realms, including his homeland, where magic was outlawed.

Var nudged him and pointed to the man decimated by the golems. "What shall we do with him?"

The fellow was a mess. Slashed and stabbed innumerable times, his torso looked more like the remnants on a butcher's block than that of a human. "Wrap him as best as you can and place in him the hold next to my brother. I'm sure he has family who would appreciate the return of his body."

"As you wish." Var ordered two of the uninjured men to assist him and together the soldiers gathered up the man, carting him into the main house.

While the others filed indoors by ones and twos, Brumaine stepped back into the street to look the way the golems had come. The street was littered with parts of them. Globs of mud, stones, and sticks beset the cobbles.

Thoughts of the dead man joining Doren in the hold of the trireme reminded him that justice was yet to be served. If all did not go as planned at the meeting in the morning, what steps would he find necessary to take? The idea of combat against the enemy, Piaxia and Sechland, fought in the streets of Lymos daunted him. Should the assassin lord take a side, he would be a most formidable foe.

Most formidable indeed.

CHAPTER 25

Kero awoke, parched and weak, in his own bed. How did he get there? The last he remembered was lying on the bench in his master's quarters.

The arrow! He clasped a hand to the point in his chest the missile had pierced. Not only was it gone, but the wound healed, without a scar remaining. Someone had mended it, perhaps Darlee. After all, she had assisted him home.

Rising, he dressed quickly and headed down to the kitchen to find Maresh working on the midday's meal. "Good morning, Maresh. Is it possible I could get something to eat and drink? I'm real thirsty."

She glared at him then turned away, resuming her work. He'd seen that look before, usually when he broke something or made a mess she had to clean. He had done neither so the obvious reason was his attempt the night before to interfere in the Hamak plans. Hanging his head, he shuffled closer. "I'm sorry."

Slamming a knife onto the table, she glared at him again then went to the larder, retrieved hunks of bread and cheese along with a large mug of weak beer, and placed them before him. "Here. Eat. The master is expecting you to join him soon. You are to accompany him to the talks this morning."

Sitting on a rickety old chair at a small table in one corner of the kitchen, a spot Maresh would often rest, he drank first before beginning on the bread and cheese. He watched Maresh hack away at the fish on the table, her strokes harsh and sloppy. Every now and then she scowled in his direction. Finally, she turned to face him, wagging the knife his way. "You could have died!"

The realization had never hit him. "But I didn't."

She slammed the knife down again. "Just like a boy. Too stupid to know. In a couple of months, you reach the age of ascension. There's going to be nobody to advise you then, or protect you. The next time you take a foolish action like that one, you'll be dead, and no one will care because the decision was your right as an adult."

Unable to respond, he forced the food down in a hurry to leave the kitchen. He drained his beer, hiccupping into it and spilling some on his shirt. Putting the empty mug down, he wiped his mouth with his sleeve and dashed into the main room.

Some of the Sechland contingent gathered there, including Captain Brusk. As Kero moved across the room, the captain never took his gaze off him. There was no sign of Darlee. He would have to thank her later.

Reaching Gragnishozar's door, Kero knocked once then stepped back.

The door opened, and his master stepped into the main hall. "Are you ready, Kero?"

No *"how are you?"* No questions about what transpired the night before? This was exactly what he expected—unmoved and unconcerned. "I'm ready."

"Then attend. The meeting awaits and there are facts that must be disseminated to those gathered."

Gragnishozar strode toward the front door, and Kero did his best to keep step. Before they could exit, Captain Brusk blocked the way.

"Good host, would it be all right if me and my companions walk with you?"

His master looked at him and the other Sechlanders. "Walk with me, if you must. But understand, I am not your guardian. Should you encounter trouble along the way do not look to me to intercede on your behalf."

Brusk nodded. "Understood. Nevertheless, I believe your presence will be enough to discourage anyone looking to waylay us."

Gragnishozar paused to stare at the captain and then brushed past him to lead the way out into the street and the morning sunshine. While a pace behind, Brusk fell into step beside Kero. The captain scanned him.

"Your shirt is stained."

Kero looked down to verify the comment. It was true. A

significant stain showed across his chest. "I...hic...know...hic."

Brusk smirked. "Come on, lad. Spit it out." He gave Kero a very hard slap across the back.

It worked. Though his back hurt, his hiccups were gone. He wondered if he was bruised.

"My apologies. I was in a rush this morning."

"That much I mustered. I guess it goes hand in hand. Eating too quickly and acting too quickly without thinking. My stepdaughter has informed me of the night's events. It is fortunate for you she was there. You put both her and you at great risk. It is my hope you have learned your lesson and will not lead Darlee on such a dangerous mission ever again. It is not something an intelligent man would do."

Hadn't he just heard that speech? Was there some kind of collusion between the captain and Maresh to scold him? True, he had some misgivings over how the events of the night unfolded. Knowing his very life had been endangered was more than enough to entrench a more careful approach to whatever he did next. Still, unlike so many others in the city, he was not going to do nothing. "There are times when intelligence loses to passion, such as the passion I have for my country. If it were Sechland so endangered, would you do less?"

Brusk remained quiet for a moment, took a heavy breath through his nose and met Kero's gaze. "I suppose you have a point. The question is whether or not you could make an actual difference. If you can't, don't try."

Kero nodded. "I'll keep that in mind."

They trod in silence until reaching the hall. Once again, there were a number of troops from the various countries stationed outside. A few of them gave him a dark glare, especially those whose skin was mottled from being burned then healed. He did his best to keep his expression calm and face forward, not meeting the stares of those he passed.

Inside, all of the tables save one were filled. The Sechland group occupied that last table. Everyone who was to be present was there.

Gragnishozar moved to stand against a wall. Kero joined him. "What now?"

Gragnishozar folded his arms across his chest. "Be silent until I call for you."

Seated at the table in front of him were Alban Hamak, two of his siblings, and Lazaan. Since when was the assassin a member of the Hamak family? Once the Sechlanders were properly seated, Alban called the meeting to order.

Alban rose. "To the gathered representatives of all invited, thank you for your patience. Yesterday, the Merchant's Guild of Riaz was requested to consider a motion for an embargo against Piaxia. Since that request, there has been a reordering of power within the guild. I stand before you now to inform you that we are prepared to render our decision with a vote."

Gragnishozar unfolded his arms and took one step forward. "Hold." He moved quickly to the center of the room. "Yesterday, it was necessary for me to read the thoughts of Prince Brumaine of Morica to verify the details of the death of his brother. I have new evidence to bring forward."

Kero's master indicated he should join him. Taking a deep breath, Kero stepped boldly to stand next to the assassin lord.

Gragnishozar put a hand on Kero's shoulder. "My ward has proof of the base actions by two of my guild to disguise themselves as Piaxians and commit the dark deed of assassinating Prince Doren. I have read these thoughts and know them to be true."

Color rose in the cheeks of Alban as he looked wildly about the room. "This is out of order. You were not called upon to provide anything."

"Nevertheless, I have."

"It is only your word. What tangible proof do you have that what you say is true?"

No one ever challenged his master's word. Kero cringed a little, expecting his lord to use his power and make an example of the Hamak house leader.

Instead, Gragnishozar folded his arms once more. "You have at your side one skilled in the arts. Let him and the Piaxian regent read the lad's thoughts and ascertain what I say to be true."

No. Not Lazaan! The idea of the assassin entering his mind was most abhorrent. "Master, is there not some other way?"

"You will let your guard down, Kero. It is the surest way."

He nodded, and as the two men approached, he focused on lowering his magical guard protecting his mind from intrusion. This was always a skill he had trouble with, both putting it up as well as down. He hoped to stay calm and obey the direction. He focused on the events from the morning before and the conversation between Petrius and Bokko.

Tarlok approached first. The Piaxian regent let his fingers rest lightly on Kero's brow. Would he feel anything? Recognizing his thoughts were straying, he focused once more on the two assassins.

After a moment, Tarlok lifted his hand away, a taut smile on his face. "Thank you."

Relieved there had been no sensation of invasion he turned to face a scowling Lazaan. The assassin hesitated before approaching, but then dashed the last few steps to slam his palm against Kero's forehead. Initially, his shield went back up. He did his best to calm down and drop the shield once more. When he did, he felt a searing pain and immediately pulled his head away.

Lazaan pursued Kero's brow with his hand. "Stay still!"

Despite trying his best, the returned pain was too much to bear. He threw his shield back up and swatted Lazaan's hand away. "No!"

Lazaan, while pointing at Kero, scanned the room, obviously trying to get everyone's attention. "See! It is a lie. The boy will not let me read his thoughts."

Tarlok paused in his retreat to his seat and likewise met everyone's gaze, attempting to counteract the assassin. "I had no such trouble. The vision of the two men, Petrius and Bokko I believe, discussing their complicity was clear."

The small assassin went to stand toe to toe with the Piaxian, a somewhat comical sight as he was so many hands shorter, the top of his head below the regent's chin. "You are fabricating a story just to defend yourself."

"If I am, then how do I know the names of those involved? It is you, I believe, who is acting falsely."

Lazaan stormed away and plopped back into his chair next to Alban. "They've rehearsed this. I'm sure of it. I read nothing of the assassins Petrius and Bokko."

Tarlok smiled and bowed in Lazaan's direction. "Ah, so you admit these men exist...and assassins, no less. You reveal the truth, whether you admit it or not."

Still obviously flustered, Alban banged his table. "Enough of this. It is time to decide. I shall call for the vote."

Along with Gragnishozar, Kero had returned to stand against the wall. He watched as the hands were slowly raised and took count. Those for the embargo were Riaz, Morica, Queensland, and Braxborough. Those against—Piaxia, Sechland, Storburg, and Fermia.

All faced the Gatway contingent. Its lead representative, an old man Kero knew to be an uncle to the king, looked lost in thought.

Alban stood. "Well? What says Gatway? The vote is tied, and your decision is needed."

The old man took his time to stand and brush his clothing straight. Only when there was nothing left to sweep at did he look toward Alban. "My nephew instructed me to avoid conflict. Should I side with you, then dealings with Piaxia and perhaps the others who sided with them will cease. Should I side with them, then Morica and its allies will consider us traitors. I am left with no choice but to abstain."

From the Piaxian delegation, Savan slapped his table and laughed heartily. "So that's it, then. Morica's motion for an embargo is dead." He rose and grabbed a number of scrolls that lay in front of Tarlok. Striding around the room, he deposited one on each table. "Here is our proposal for trade and security rules on the Great Sea. Take some time to read it. After you do, we will be happy to discuss and negotiate the terms."

Rather than open it, Brumaine squeezed it in one hand, crumpling the parchment. He rose and turned to those at his table.

"Come. We're leaving."

Savan grabbed hold of Brumaine's arm. "Why are you leaving? You heard the assassin lord. Our people are innocent. There is business to be done."

Brumaine shook his arm free. "It is only his word. Last night he sent his minions to attack my men. I have no reason to accept his version. He has proven to be an enemy of Morica."

Savan shrugged. "This petulance will serve no purpose. Let us be friends again. Nothing will bring your brother back." He held out an open hand.

This moment would define everything that happened next. Would Brumaine capitulate and sit down once more to hammer out the trade deal? Or would it all come to a crashing end with the sides permanently split? He held his breath in anticipation of the answer.

The prince stared at the offered hand. All in the room were doing the same. Finally, Brumaine met Savan's gaze. "We shall see." He turned and left, the others from Morica trailing after him.

Around the room, the sound of chairs being moved announced what else was to come. The delegates from Queensland, Braxborough, and Riaz all rose and followed the Moricans out the door. Kero looked at Gragnishozar. "What do we do now?"

"Nothing. The conference is at an end. I have my own issues to deal with within the assassin's guild. It is time for us to go home."

As Gragnishozar headed for the door, Kero paused to scan the room. The balance of the delegates were looking at each other in obvious dismay. He caught Savan's eye and the Piaxian commander sighed then shook his head. It was a sign of resignation.

Hastening to catch up with his lord, he wondered what Brumaine had in mind. Would the prince do something foolish? Something divisive?

Whatever the prince did, Kero realized just how bad things were spiraling toward more conflict.

CHAPTER 26

As he marched back toward the Hamak compound, Brumaine wrestled with the dilemma before him. The idea of an embargo had failed. Failed! Sure, Morica, along with those nations who sided with it, could still impose their own, but with so many other nations unwilling to participate, such an action would be fruitless.

No, a new plan of action was needed—one that involved all the other countries and still punished Piaxia in some form or another. The only question was...what?

Keeping pace was his mentor, Var. "What now, my liege? Unless you are willing to negotiate a trade deal akin to the one proposed, this conference is technically at an end. Shall we quit this country and head home?"

He shook his head. "I think not. There must be another course I can take. I just need time to think of it. Who knows? Maybe one of our allies might come up with the answer for us."

Upon entering the grounds, he retired to his room to contemplate. Perhaps some solitude might help in his thought process. It was at such times he rued his tacit banishment from the court back home. He was unused to the mechanics of diplomacy. Even his knowledge of existing treaties was limited to what Var had taught him of their final composition, not the actual process on how the document had been negotiated or the silent loopholes that existed.

Concentrate. Maybe he could still make things work through the conference. Lying on the bed was the scroll with the proposal from Piaxia, still crumpled from his crushing it. He sat and unfurled it, being careful to smooth it out lest it tear.

Reading through, despite his hopes to the contrary, he found the terms fairly reasonable. It was not something he could turn against the Piaxians as being unfair. Perhaps there was a way to contort the clauses to benefit Morica.

The sound of Commander Oberus yelling outside brought Brumaine from his concentration to look out the window. In the courtyard, the commander was having men attach notes to pigeons. Who was he messaging? This needed investigating.

Stepping into the courtyard, he approached the group. "Hold there. What messages are you sending and to whom?"

Oberus blocked Brumaine's path to the men handling the pigeons. "It is no longer your concern."

More arrogance. Though still morning, the idea of having another verbal sparring with his commander tired him. "Everything is my concern. I am in charge. You will show me those messages."

From inside his uniform, Oberus produced a document. Opening it, he held it high, opened toward him. "It reads: *By special decree, I, King Jessop of Morica, do hereby give Commander Oberus special authority to manage all affairs in the matter of the trade conference to Riaz.*" The commander held it out toward Brumaine. "Read it, if you like. You will note it is in his own hand, and his seal is affixed to it. I am in charge now. While we are in Riaz, you will obey my orders from here on."

This could not be. He glanced at the document. It was true his father's seal was upon it. Still, it must be a forgery. It was inconceivable his father would surrender control to Oberus. How the commander had managed to gain access to the king's seal was a question easily answered. Oberus was always near the king and present when decrees were signed. Was it possible he had slipped one in without his father's notice? "You lie. My father never would have done such a thing."

He tried to swipe the document from Oberus' hand, but the commander was too quick and pulled it away.

"Not even a prince is free to refuse the orders of the king." Oberus pointed to two men. "Take Prince Brumaine prisoner. He is to be held until we return to Morica."

Again, as the day before, the men hesitated. From the main hall, Var emerged. "What goes on here?"

Oberus turned to face the challenge. "Ah, Lieutenant. Your arrival is most fortuitous. You may yet spare yourself a court-martial. Verify this document."

The commander showed the missive to Var, who studied it carefully. He eventually nodded. "There is no doubt as to its authenticity. I recognize both the king's hand and his seal. Commander Oberus is now in charge."

"Very good, Varamanthu. You can return to your duties." Oberus nodded toward the two men. "Take the prince to his quarters and lock him in there."

The soldier to his left showed some respect and held out a hand toward the guest house. "Prince Brumaine, please go peacefully."

After giving Oberus one last defiant look he nodded toward the soldier then, after they took his sword, head held high, preceded the two men to his quarters. Once he was ensconced inside, the polite one stated he would return with something to eat and drink.

When the man left, Brumaine closed the door and sat. The startling revelation his father had granted Oberus control still shook him. He needed to calm down and rationalize his way through it. It was what Var had always tried to impart on him. Stop and think. Use his brains. Reason it out. He took and exhaled a deep breath. "Okay, tutor, let's see if your teachings have paid off."

He counted on his fingers. First of all, the decree didn't appear out of thin air. The commander must have had it since they left Morence. He had held it in reserve until now. What had changed since? The trade negotiations. With the failure of the embargo, Oberus must have seen things going awry from whatever design was expected.

And what was the real plan? It must never have been to negotiate a peaceful deal such as the one proposed by Piaxia. All along, the commander had pressed for drastic action. The only possibility...to scuttle the trade deal and get Riaz and as many of the seven realms to align against Piaxia as possible, although it was never possible to convince Sechland of such a deal. After all, Piaxia and Sechland were allies.

He sat up straight, his back pressed hard against the cane of the chair. If the plan had always been to disrupt the conference, then the assassination of Doren had also been planned. No, not Doren. Him. Only the shielding placed by Kero had spared his life and left his brother as the target. His death was supposed to be the catalyst to drive the other states to Morica's banner.

He recalled the words of the assassin when the magical bolt leveled at him had failed. *"Then, kill the other one. It matters not."* The plan had always involved the death of a prince. Perhaps both. That made little sense. Doren was father's favorite and legal heir.

A moment of clarity was muddled again. He dropped his head into his hands and rubbed at his eyes with his palms.

A knock at the door urged him to stand. "Come in."

It was Var carrying a tray of food and drink. "When I overheard the guard stating he was bringing you refreshments I volunteered to carry it. He knows we are close and agreed as long as I surrendered my weapons. How do you fare?"

He grabbed Var by the shoulders and directed him to sit. "I've been sitting here trying to figure out what Oberus is up to. I've come to the conclusion he was behind the assassination attempt on me, but I cannot figure out why Doren had to be killed."

Var pursed his lips for a moment then pointed to the bed. "Sit. I shall do my best to elucidate." Var waited until Brumaine settled on the edge of the bed. "Now...here are the details. When word of the conference reached the king, and was heard by all those in the court, there was much decrying of such an agreement, most notably by Oberus and your father. Doren volunteered to come and negotiate this treaty. He argued that failure to be part of the process would result in Morica being left out of any deal and economic hardship would befall the kingdom. Though your father is king, the Merchant's League is powerful and urged the mission be done. Prince Doren was their champion. It sealed his fate."

It was clear now. "So Doren was always a target."

"Yes. I feared as much, but until I saw the missive today, I had doubts. I do not believe your father would have wanted his death, though I have no doubt he was willing to sacrifice your life. This is

Oberus' doing. I'm sorry for that. Had I acted sooner, I might have prevented the loss of your brother."

The thought of his brother being killed only because of his popularity with the merchants was most disturbing. Did his father fear a coup? He supposed such an idea may have been considered. Why else such harsh action? "Why am I still alive? Why hasn't Oberus had me killed as well?"

"Isn't it obvious? The men. Should he kill you in their presence, he would have faced a revolt. No, I suspect your demise is still required, just not yet. He had hoped to play you to complete his mission for him. When that failed, Oberus must have decided it was time to take charge. For you, it is only a matter of time. That is why I have come. We must get you out of here—now."

What Var said made absolute sense. But how? "We have no weapons."

Var stood and, with a swift kick, shattered the chair he once sat upon. From the pieces, he grabbed two legs, one for each hand. "We improvise. Grab the sheet from that bed and throw it on the first man. It is all the advantage I will need."

Indeed, a man was calling from the hall, wondering about the loud noise. When the door opened, Brumaine did as he was instructed and tossed the sheet in the fellow's direction. It tangled him only for a moment, but in that instant, Var struck, hitting the man on both the head and the wrist, resulting in the soldier collapsing to the ground and dropping his sword.

Before the second guard could pounce, Var had already scooped up the fallen weapon and parried the man's attack. It took his trainer only a moment to win the duel and run the fellow through. As he did so, Var leaned close. "My apologies. You were a good man. Your death is no pleasure to me, but the prince is in grave danger, and I must do what I must to protect him."

During it all, Brumaine had watched the man's face. It was the soldier who had been kind to him. Before he died, he gave the slightest nod. He had accepted his fate and the reasons therefore. It saddened him to see such a good man die.

With the other guard unconscious and he and Var out in the

hall gathering their weapons, he looked to the lieutenant for direction. "What now?"

"Up. In examining this structure, I noted it possible to vault from the roof to the wall. From there, we can climb down on the other side."

A ladder built into the wall at the end of the hall led to a hatch that opened on the roof. It was a bit of a hop to the wall, but Var made it look easy. When Brumaine jumped, he needed his mentor's steadying hand to prevent him from falling to the ground.

Lowering himself down from the top of the wall left only a short drop, which he handled well enough. They were out of the Hamak estate! "Which way?"

"To the wharf. I doubt Oberus has yet to notify the skeleton crew on board the trireme of his usurpation of command. If we hurry, we might be able to board and quit the city by ordering the ship to take sail. Once we return to Morica, we can tell the king of all that has occurred. It is our only hope for clemency."

Keeping pace with his trainer, he raced through the streets of Lymos. When they passed Rock House, Brumaine glanced at the open door, wondering who he might see, but the moment was too short and the interior not lit well enough to make out any faces.

Var pulled up short. "It can't be!"

Pausing beside Var, catching his breath, he glanced around, expecting some nearby threat, but none was visible. "What?"

"Come. I must be sure."

Var tore off again. He had no choice but to follow. His mentor once more halted when he reached the top of the road that sloped down to the wharf. From there, the harbor was in full view with a number of boats moored and one docked at the pier. "It's gone."

Brumaine scanned every boat. Var was right. The Morican trireme was nowhere in sight. Without it, there was no escaping the island. What to do? Eventually, Oberus would send out search parties. Between his troops, those aligned with Morica, and the assassins of Riaz, it would only be a matter of time until they were found.

Who would hide them? Surely, not the other delegations of the seven realms, or the Piaxians. With the Sechlanders housed at Rock House, not even Kero and his master could shelter them. Besides, it would be the first place the assassins would look. What would work as a place to hide? He remembered the many nights Var had searched for him without success back in Morence. "Come, Var. I may know of one place where we might hide for now."

CHAPTER 27

With her head propped on her hand and elbow on the windowsill, Darlee had watched the boats moving about in the bay. A number of the big boats that had been moored in place the last several days had vacated the harbor. Though fairly far away, it looked to her like at least one of them was the Morican trireme.

Why would that boat have left? Her foster father was at a meeting the Moricans were attending. Surely, the trade conference wasn't over that early. She could see the Sechland contingent returning to Rock House, at least a full hand since the boat departures.

Then again, Kero, with Gragnishozar, had returned some time ago. Perhaps the conference had ended earlier. She had thought to go down and question him but decided against it. He had almost died the night before. She felt some guilt at her hesitation to act when he had been first to expose himself from hiding and had taken the brunt of the attack as a result. Had she led instead of followed, things might have been different.

When Kero had lain on the stone bench in Gragnishozar's quarters, she had feared greatly he would die. His facial features, soft and pale, took away from the boyish good looks he normally shared.

Though somewhat cute, he was no match for the handsome dark-haired brown-eyed Prince Brumaine. Why did her meeting the prince have to be surrounded by so much discord and conflict? In a simpler setting, without intrusions, she would gladly have fallen into his arms and been swept away like a princess.

Princess. Ha! She was far from that. More like a peasant girl suited for the likes of Jango, who no doubt still pined after her despite her every attempt to convince him otherwise.

She sighed. Finding love was going to be a hard thing for her. Who wanted a skinny underdeveloped stick of a girl missing one eye yet possessed of power that could kill in an instant? All good men would be either dissuaded by her looks or fearful of her magic.

She could hear the voice of her foster father booming from downstairs a request for food and drink for him and the others. The position of the sun was close enough to midday when meals were often served. Perhaps she should go downstairs and join them in a repast. Some food might improve her mood.

As she straightened, she noticed Prince Brumaine and the lieutenant he called Var moving erratically down the road. There was something peculiar about their movements. They stayed close to the structures on the other side of the road, moving in and out of doorways and glancing up and down the street as they went. They were trying not to be seen!

Who were they hiding from? *Why* were they hiding? Perhaps he needed help. She dashed for the door and down the stairs into the main room. Spotting Kero, she moved to his side. "Something's up with Prince Brumaine. Come with me."

Kero, holding a couple of plates of stew, set them in front of the two nearest Sechlanders. "I'm ready."

She started for the door, but her foster father blocked the way and grabbed Kero by the arm. "I thought I asked you not to lead my daughter on any more dangerous adventures."

"She's leading me!"

Brusk's face brows went up and his eyes widened. He let Kero go. When he joined her by the door, she raced out into the street in the direction she had seen Brumaine go.

Kero paced her. "Where are we headed?"

She glanced his way. Perhaps it may have been wrong to take him away from his duties, but she needed his knowledge of the city. "I'm not sure. All I know is Brumaine was creeping this way with his lieutenant. It was obvious to me they didn't want to get caught doing so. I think he's in trouble. Maybe you know where they were going. Think. What's ahead that would attract them?"

With his gaze on the road ahead, he squinted. "All I can think of is the Hamak estate."

She shook her head. "I doubt that's it. They wouldn't be sneaking the way they did if they were going home. No, they're up to something."

It didn't take long for her and Kero to catch up enough to spot the two men moving stealthily ahead. Pulling Kero to one side, they followed the pair's example by staying out of sight as much as possible while keeping pace.

Finally, Brumaine reached a door and rapped quickly upon it. Huddling close to the building, he scanned the street up and down in a wild manner, as if afraid to be spotted. Darlee no longer retained any doubts as to the furtive motive of the prince.

When the door opened, the blonde hair of the woman inside was the quick tell of whom the occupant was. Lasha. He was visiting that woman! A hurried word between Brumaine and the hussy occurred, and then Brumaine and his lieutenant slipped inside and Lasha closed the door.

What a fool she was. Thinking Prince Brumaine was in some sort of trouble based on his actions when, in fact, it was only a clandestine meeting with the tavern girl with the large breasts. It infuriated her that she had been so easily duped. Why did men like the prince always succumb to women such as Lasha? There was so much more to a woman than her curves—like intelligence, for instance. She was quite sure that blonde had mush for brains.

Or power. Sure, she didn't have the kind of power a prince wielded, but hers was something not to be so easily dismissed. It might be the kind of thing to scare off the average person, but why shouldn't that be attractive to a man accustomed to power?

Kero grabbed her elbow. "Come on, Darlee. Let's go back to Rock House."

"In a moment. I'm thinking." She felt her cheeks flush at the embarrassment of leading Kero on a false mission. Most likely, the Riaz boy was thinking she was just as much an empty head as Lasha. Maybe worse. At the moment, the only thing she could think of was a desire to get even. How could she discredit the prince?

While she contemplated what to do, five men rounded the corner at the end of the block, headed in her direction. Four were dressed in the uniform of Morica, while the fifth dressed in the common clothes of any citizen. Perhaps here was her chance at retribution. Informing the soldiers of the unsavory location of their prince would serve as the justice she sought.

She started toward the men, but Kero pulled her back. "Where are you going? Those are Morican soldiers, and that's the assassin warlock Petrius with them."

She shrugged free. "I *know* who they are. You don't need to tell me." In fact, she didn't know the one called Petrius, but she wasn't going to tell Kero that. Still, rather than continue her progress, she followed Kero deep into the seclusion of a nearby doorway. The instant conclusion she arrived at was the men were looking for the prince. Petrius must be their guide just as Kero was hers. "Do you think they know where he is?"

Kero kept silent and, as she watched, the Morican men broke into pairs and took opposite sides of the street, knocking on the doors. Not every one was answered and those without a response they broke into. For people who were home, it was obvious the soldiers were questioning them. Heads shook and doors closed, but not before one of the soldiers peeked inside. It was a house-by-house search.

Kero nudged her. "We'd better get going. It won't take them long to get to where we are."

The men were still two houses from Lasha's home. "Hang on. I want to see what happens."

The men would be close, but Darlee figured she and Kero could still leave unnoticed because the soldiers focused on the houses they approached. Only Petrius, who stood in the middle of the street, might espy them, but his attention was also on the soldiers.

Those on Lasha's side of the street were now only one door away. Would she answer the door? Would the soldiers force a peek in? Would Brumaine be discovered? Did she want him discovered? The question swirled in her mind, looking for an answer. She didn't know whether she wanted the prince found or not. What if her assumption of a tryst was incorrect? After all, would he bring his lieutenant with him if that was the case? Doubtful. What if he was really in hiding? It was still possible for her to intervene and prevent the search.

She grabbed Kero by the arm and shoved him out into the street. "Go. Tell them to stop. This is your town. They shouldn't be doing what they're doing."

Kero knitted his brows as he glared at her but he proceeded out into the street. "Petrius, why are you allowing these foreigners to break into the homes of our citizens?"

Everyone stopped what they were doing to look in Kero's direction. Petrius blubbered for a moment then pointed at Kero. "This is none of your business. Go home to your master, lap dog, or I'll make an example of you."

Darlee joined Kero at his side. "If you try, then *I* shall make an example of *you*."

Petrius stepped back and glanced left and right at the soldiers. She followed his gaze and noted none of the men making any type of move toward her and Kero. They were all afraid. The fire wall she had summoned had probably made a good impression on all of them.

After a moment of the standoff, Petrius waved to the men to back away. "We'll be back, and next time you won't scare us off so easily. You can be sure of that." He turned and trudged off in the direction he'd come.

Once sure of the retreat of the Moricans and Petrius, she realized she had been holding her breath and exhaled in relief. Although sure she could best Petrius in a magical fight, dispatching the four soldiers might have been a different issue as she could not find any bare bedrock in the road nearby to use the Key. Still, she had successfully forced the retreat of the men. For now, Prince Brumaine's location would remain secret, although she still did not know why she did it.

Kero, without a word, turned and headed back toward Rock House at a brisk pace. She hurried to catch up. "Kero...wait!"

He stopped to glare at her. "Why? You lead me on a crazy wild chase to see where Brumaine was going, discover it was to a woman's place, get all angry over it...don't deny it, I could see it in your face...then make me take an unwarranted risk in facing down another warlock accompanied by four soldiers. Do you believe I'm stupid? Don't you think I know you're infatuated with the prince? I don't need to be insulted anymore. I'm going home."

He spun on his heel and marched off, leaving Darlee in the middle of the street. Throughout his entire tirade, she had stood there, agape, unable to respond. Were her actions so transparent?

She glanced back at Lasha's place. The blonde was peeking out at the retreating men, then at her before closing the door.

She pondered whether to run and catch up to Kero, the distance between them growing rapidly. Instead, she opted to walk slowly. She had made a fool of herself once more.

There was no stopping the tears. Was it so bad to want love so much?

CHAPTER 28

When Kero reached the front door to Rock House, rather than enter, he continued walking. No doubt, Darlee would return as well and, at the moment, he did not want to face her again.

The girl was a fool. Why was she wasting her time chasing after a prince? Especially one from a country hers had just been to war with. It made no sense. Her infatuation with Brumaine reminded him of his own failure at relationships. When it came to finding a girl who welcomed his company, success eluded him.

In life, he was alone.

Maybe not totally alone. Changing direction, he made for Derak's house. His friend, with all his wild antics, always cheered him. Further, Kero had yet to speak to him since the events of the night before. Derak would not know what happened at the Jindo estate, or, for that matter, Kero's own near demise. Besides, he wanted to find out whether Derak had managed to exact any retribution against the inn where he had lit a fire.

There was no time to worry about a silly girl, no matter whether she struck his interest or not. His city was still undergoing an upheaval.

Picking up his pace, he covered the distance to Derak's quickly and found his friend playing stickball in the street with the other youths of the area. Kero waited until a break in the game then called his friend to join him.

Sauntering over in a slow fashion, Derak glanced now and then at his house. "Hi, Kero, did you want to play?"

His friend knew he no longer played with the others. They had shunned him over the last couple of years. "No. I came to get you to walk with me."

Derak glanced home once more. "I don't know. I'm supposed to stay close to home. My parents found out about what happened last night and warned me to stay away from you. They don't want any trouble."

What? Now his best friend couldn't accept his company? It

was all sounding so incredibly unfair. While Derak stared at the ground and kicked at a small stone lying there, Kero glanced at his friend's home. From the lone window, Derak's mother stared out with a most disapproving scowl on her face.

He wanted to be angry. Don't the people in town know what was happening? Didn't they understand the prospect of what was to come? He figured they would have thought it wise to join in the resistance to the change, not accept it.

He returned his focus to Derak who was looking at him from under his eyebrows. Perhaps acceptance was too strong a term. Surrender was a better definition. After one last look at Derak's mother, he sighed and offered his hand. "I understand. This is not their fight, and hence, not yours. As long as I can still call you my friend, that is all that matters."

Derak accepted the hand. "You bet. Any other time you want to do the kind of stuff we used to do is all right with me—just not today."

He exchanged a smile with Derak then turned away to head for the market. Before he managed five steps, Derak's shout for attention made him turn back. "What is it?"

The silly grin Derak often wore returned. "You should have seen the fire in front of the inn where the Queenslanders are staying. It charred the whole front of the place."

He nodded. "I'm glad for that. It'll give them something to think about before housing any more foreigners wishing the demise of our country."

Derak ran to rejoin the stickball game. Kero watched for a moment then resumed his journey toward the city market.

The few blocks passed quietly. Unlike a normal day when people would be out and about, tending gardens, going to and fro from the market, and generally living their normal lives, hardly any people were doing those things.

In the city square, the number of active stalls was significantly fewer than normal. Clearly, the entire city was in some kind of panic with only the brave few willing to go about business as usual. How long would such a mindset last? Days? Weeks?

Months? Most likely, not until some kind of new order was established that people acclimated to.

A hunger pang motivated him to find one of the food vendors still operating. The aroma of food cooking led him to one not too far from where he stood. Fishcakes served with flatbread. Not his favorite, but he was hungry. Producing a copper from his pouch, he offered it to the operator who plopped two fishcakes on the flatbread.

Kero stared at the food for a moment then the seller. "Two? I thought the going rate was three for a copper."

"Not anymore. The Merchant League raised rates for market stalls today. I have to eat as well and have a family to feed. If you're unhappy, I suggest you take it up with them."

The vendor pointed out a group of three men walking from stall to stall some twenty paces away, one a member of the Hamak family, another the assassin Petrius as well. Not looking for any kind of confrontation, he shook his head toward the stall operator. "No thanks. I'll make do with this."

The seller grunted and returned to his cooking. Kero decided to go down to the wharf and watch the boats. He wanted to see how many fishermen were working.

It appeared the fishermen had gone out to sea as the empty berths on the island side of the pier testified. On the ocean side, there were currently no large trading ships docked. Not surprising, as that was often the case, but when he looked out into the bay what was surprising was the mooring of only two vessels, the Piaxian trireme, and the Piaxian merchant vessel the Sechlanders arrived on. Where were all the other boats? Each of the visiting delegations had arrived on one, the Moricans...two.

He selected a pier post to perch upon and watch the harbor entrance for a sign of ships. The sun high, the sky clear, only the caws of drafting seagulls disturbed the tranquility as he ate.

What was he going to do? Riaz had no army to put down the takeover. The constabulary was small and many dead already. Not including his master, the assassin guild had joined the ranks of the usurper. The presence of troops from Morica, along with those from countries who supported the Moricans, was more than a match for the paltry force of Piaxians and the few Sechlanders who might stand up to them. Despite their numbers, the citizens of Lymos were content to wait it out and not involve themselves. His ragtag band of friends was of no help as evidenced by Derak.

There must be others who were unhappy with the current situation—the market vendors, for instance. The fellow selling the fish cakes did not exactly seem happy about the change. Perhaps what was needed was a clandestine ground swell insurgency. If he could gather enough people, then maybe a revolt could be staged.

Ha. The idea the people of Lymos would follow him was laughable. What was he? A warlock who had not yet reached the age of ascension. Despite it being only two months away, none would take him seriously as an adult without it. The people needed a leader, and he wasn't it. Gragnishozar could do it if he wanted to, but Kero knew his lord too well. His was a position of self-benefit, not one for the betterment of others. Commander Savan of Piaxia was charismatic, but a foreigner. There were none he could think of to take on the mantle.

A cry from the Piaxian trireme made Kero look in the vessel's direction. There was a flurry of activity on its deck. Men were hauling up the anchor. They must be planning on leaving as well. What was going on that every ship must leave port?

He looked out to sea. Three vessels were bearing down on the entry to the harbor—all triremes, all Morican. He hadn't recognized it before, but now he could hear the steady beat of drums. The hurried rise and fall of oars combined with the drumbeat told Kero one thing. The ships were attacking.

The Piaxian vessel had managed to turn so that its ram faced the oncoming vessels, but they shipped their oars. Kero could only guess they had determined escape was impossible and instead were readying for a fight.

The twang of catapults releasing their loads from the Morican vessels was followed by the arced flight of flaming balls aimed at the Piaxians. Two missed, and the third only hit the prow, glancing off into the water. The Piaxians had already lit their own and fired a return volley that crashed directly on the deck of the middle trireme. Whatever the catapult had launched shattered and splashed out fire. Men screamed and, as oar strokes became haphazard rather than in unison, the ship slowed.

The other two surged on continuing their barrage of flaming balls, one now scoring a direct hit on the rear deck of the Piaxian trireme.

The vessels were close enough Kero could make out individuals and recognized a man in black among the Piaxians standing near the prow. From his fingers flew a lightning bolt that flew true to hit the man holding the tiller of the left Morican ship. The craft veered off course, missing the Piaxian ship, but the one on the right didn't and rammed the trireme hard. As it was mostly prow to prow, both ships suffered damage from each other's ram.

Soldiers from the Morican boat leapt onto the deck and hand-to-hand combat ensued. Kero saw the warlock striking down two more men with lightning, and it appeared as if the Piaxians had the upper hand, but then the ship that had lagged behind due to the fire on deck arrived and its additional troops swarmed the remaining Piaxians. One man jumped in the water and attempted to swim for shore, but archers managed to shoot him. Kero saw him sink and never resurface.

As for the warlock, after killing five of the Moricans, his mana must have run out, and he was forced to draw a sword like the rest of his troops. He was eventually run through.

The two damaged triremes were sinking. Those men still alive were clambering aboard the remaining Morican ships. They moved toward the pier. It wouldn't take them long to dock. The last thing Kero wanted to be was a welcoming committee. Deciding it was time to move on was the prudent thing to do.

As he hurried up the hill into the town, one thing was for sure. Any pretense of peace between Morica and Piaxia was over. The two countries were once more at war.

Tracking back through the market again, he noted those few vendors who had opened for business were now closed. The sound of the battle was enough to scare everyone away.

It was understandable for those in the market to hear the noise of conflict, perhaps even glimpse it, but would it carry to the top of the city where the wealthy lived? There were a lot of men on those boats and, with the Piaxian trireme attacked, it only made sense the delegates would be targeted next.

Kero set off at a run toward the home of Orvest, the merchant, where the Piaxian delegation stayed. Commander Savan and his brother, Regent Tarlok, needed warning.

CHAPTER 29

"We can't stay here."

Brumaine knew Var was right. If not for the intervention of Darlee and Kero, they would have been discovered. "We are strangers in a foreign country. There are none who know us as friends, save Lasha here. What would you suggest?"

"Make for another town. Did I not hear Quinto Hamak state he had a home on the south side of the island? Perhaps there is a port there. We could purchase passage on a ship to Morica."

He looked to Lasha. "Is that possible? Are there other places besides Lymos where ships dock?"

She shook her head. "No. Riaz is quite mountainous everywhere right to the water's edge. The only major port is here in Lymos. It has the only protected harbor. Waters around the island can be quite treacherous. The only thing you would find elsewhere are small fishing boats that they drag on shore every night."

So there was no other port where he could purchase passage back to Morica. Still, if there were small boats there may still be a way. Perhaps a merchant captain could be bribed to pick him and Var up at sea. It would require Lasha to do the bribing. Would she be up to such a task? The look of plight on her face with her wide-open eyes and open mouth combined with her hand-wringing made him doubt it. No, if there was anyone capable of such subterfuge it would be Lasha's friend Janina. The redhead was enjoying the state of affairs, a smile on her face despite the gravity of the situation.

He pulled his purse free from his hip to examine the contents—fourteen gold pieces and numerous silvers and coppers. More than enough. "Janina, do you think you could bribe one of the foreign merchant captains to provide the lieutenant and I passage to Morica?"

Her eyes widened as she focused on the purse in his hands. "I could try. It's not like I don't know them all, the scurves. More times than I can count, one captain or another has tried to bed me, flashing a silver or two in hopes of enticing me. I let them buy me drinks, that's all. At night, they find me attractive enough as I dress the part, but pass by without greeting me when I'm cleaning fish near the wharf and in my work clothes. I know which ones run contraband. What's in it for me?"

He held up a gold coin. "One of these. I'm going to give you two. One is for the captain you choose. Make arrangements with him to pick us up near one of the small towns dotting the coastline, and he'll get four more."

She snatched the coin from his hand. "Done. What town will you be at, and when?"

This is where part of his plan needed help. "I have no idea. I overheard Quinto Hamak mention a town on the south coast. Perhaps that may be the place to go. All I need is a guide to get there." He turned toward Lasha. "Will you guide me there?"

Lasha looked at the floor. "I...I've never left the city. I don't even know how to get anywhere."

He was surprised at her answer. Was she lying to avoid going? "You described the island earlier. I would have thought you had some knowledge of the lay of the land."

"That's all I could remember from years ago when I went to school. There was a map of Riaz which we studied, but I cannot recall the towns nor the roads leading to them. I...I wasn't the best student."

Janina held up her hands in surrender. "Don't look at me. I hardly went to school at all. My parents had me working the fish yard from the time I was ten. My father is a fisherman. He still goes out at dawn every morning and brings in his catch mid-afternoon. He used to bring me with him. Now, I just help him bring his catch in. I need to head down there soon, meet him at the dock, unload, clean, and crate his fish. After that, Lasha and I'll be serving today's catch and drinks at The Fisherman's Friend near the docks. That's where the seamen congregate."

Var had returned to the window to check the street. "The way is clear right now. Perhaps it might be a good time to change locales. You saw the empty bay. It may be some days before another trading ship arrives. Regardless of your plan, we cannot stay here."

The decision of what to do, whether to stay or leave, was a difficult one. Should he stay, the possibility of being discovered was more than he originally expected when seeking refuge with Lasha. The idea a house-to-house search would be done was beyond expectation. Still, leaving without a map, without knowledge of how long the journey would take, introduced a lot of unsavory variables. "I say we take our chances leaving town. There must be roads. All we need to do is follow the ones headed south. The island is not that large. It cannot be more than a few days' travel. Janina can make the arrangements for a fortnight from now."

Var shook his head. "Coordinating a rendezvous offshore from a town we know not where, sounds unlikely at best. Far greater is the possibility we get lost, without food or shelter, or worse, captured. This plan of yours is unworkable. Our only hope to succor passage is from here, in Lymos."

Perhaps Var was right. He nodded in surrender. "Janina, go now to your duties and look for a merchant vessel in port. Find its captain and make the arrangements. In the meantime, with Lasha's help, Var and I will find a more secretive location to wait out my plan."

Janina exchanged a nervous glance with Lasha then exited the home.

The ordeal so far had tired him. He could feel the strength in his legs wane as the stress of the situation became too great a burden for him to remain standing. Brumaine sat down at a table while Var returned once more to watching the street. Lasha pulled a chair next to him, and sitting, cuddled against him. He stroked her hair. "What say you, pretty lady? I am already deep in your debt for taking me in while my countrymen wreak havoc in your city. And yet, I have more to ask of you. I need you to think of where my comrade and I can hide without discovery."

She snuggled closer. "I don't want you to go anywhere. I want you to stay here with me."

Back in Morica, when a similar situation arose and a woman wanted to keep him around, that was his signal it was time to go. He never wanted to give anyone the idea that he was catchable. *"Stay with me"* translated in his mind into *"You're mine."*

Now, with death threatening, the idea of accepting such a request no longer seemed so reprehensible. Comfort and concern for him were things he wanted.

The sudden return of Janina surprised him. Had she already secured passage? No, by the dour look on her face, something was wrong. "What happened?"

"The bay is all but empty of ships save triremes from Morica. Apparently, three of them charged into the bay and, in a battle, destroyed the Piaxian trireme while losing one of their own."

Three triremes? Sinking the Piaxian vessel meant war. Had everyone gone crazy? "We arrived on only one. Where did the other two come from?"

Var rubbed at his face in contemplation. "They were nearby. It is six days to Morica. Such attendance was planned ahead. Commander Oberus is not alone in this. This confrontation has the consent of your father, though how they arrived today of all days is a mystery."

The earlier event in the Hamak courtyard returned to mind. "No mystery. Oberus contacted them by pigeon. Prior to my arrest, he released numerous birds with messages. Some must have been to the ships. Others, I imagine, are still winging their way home to Morence."

"Ah. I did not witness that. Had I, I would have known their intended flights...even estimated what messages they conveyed."

The sound of loud voices outside sent Var to the window. After glancing into the street, he stepped away, letting the curtain fall into place to block any view. "My liege, we are out of time. The men from Morica have returned, and in greater numbers. When last time we contemplated, if discovered, fighting our way, such a decision is no longer realistic. We must make a run for it."

Moving Lasha aside, he rose and strode to the window to

confirm Var's report. "To where?"

"If I knew where the Fermians were staying, I would suggest them, as their neutrality would give Oberus pause. We must search for them, failing which, no other alternative save your suggestion to leave town comes to mind. That is a plan I am most uncomfortable with."

Brumaine returned to Lasha and gripped her shoulders. "Think, Lasha. Where can we hide?"

She shook her head. "I don't know. As a child, we would often hide from our parents in the alleys beneath porches, but that was only for hands, not days."

Perhaps hands were all they needed. "I must admit, such childhood ploys were not something I experienced. Something I may have enjoyed, though. Such was the life of a prince, but if such a ruse worked well enough for you, then it should suffice for Var and I until night when we could return here under the cover of dark."

He turned to his lieutenant. "Come Var. We shall play in the alleys as Lasha once did." He led the way to the back door and opened it into the narrow alley that traversed the space between the back of the houses. Indeed, many of the homes featured the exact thing Lasha had described—small porches made of wood with enough space under for a child to crawl into, but were there any large enough to fit two grown men?

Fortune was with them. There were no citizens around to espy their concealment. They located two porches diagonally opposite each other where Brumaine fit under one while Var hid under the other.

The smell in his hideaway was not the most pleasant. Not only was there some rubbish that he needed to move aside, but the remains of a dead rat—mostly fur and bones with maggots crawling over it. Nevertheless, he chuckled at Var who needed to evict a live rat from his hiding place and cursed while doing so.

How ridiculous was his position? There he was, a prince of Morica, hiding in the filth below the porch of some commoner in Riaz. Prior to leaving Morence, the idea of being in such a predicament would have been beyond his wildest imagining. He felt abased by the act. Would no smidgen of his honor be preserved?

There was no time for self-pity. The sound of men in the alley approaching his position required his entire focus. Peeking between boards, he could see the men, both in the uniform of Moricans, as they neared. One looked in his direction. Panic set in. If he could see the man, then perhaps the man could see him. In an effort to better hide, he moved away from his viewing spot and deeper into the shadows below the porch.

The exclamation by the man that he had seen something move chilled Brumaine. What a fool he had been. The man had not seen him, but his movement had alerted him. He should have trusted his hiding place.

The sound of swords being drawn posed a new dilemma. Should he draw his own? There was still the possibility the men might not investigate to the level necessary to see him by getting down on hands and knees to enter his hideaway. Pulling his sword from his scabbard would be a clear enough signal an armed man waited below the porch.

The two men now stood immediately outside. Neither knelt. Instead, they stepped up on the porch, and a blade plunged down between the boards, missing him by several hands. The sword withdrew then plunged again in a different location. He was trapped! It was only a matter of time before one of the attempts would strike. He grasped the hilt of his sword and positioned his body to best quit his hiding place, though the struggle it took to get in would be hard to limit on the way out.

There was more noise coming from above. One of the men cried out, and he could hear the sound of swords clashing. Were the men fighting? No, it must be Var. Brumaine squirmed through the opening and rose as quickly as he could while drawing his sword. It mattered not. The battle was over.

Var wiped his blade on one man's tunic then returned it to his scabbard. He descended from the porch and grabbed Brumaine by the elbow. "Come, Sire, we must be away. If not the sound of battle, the mere absence of the men will soon draw others to investigate."

He glanced up and down the narrow lane that comprised the alley. "Which way, and to where?"

Var dropped to a knee, a hand to his side, a grunt escaping him. It was only then that Brumaine noticed the red stain above Var's hip. He bent to investigate. "You're injured."

Var took a deep breath then straightened. "It is nothing. I will recover. What matters most is getting out of sight."

Blood continued to seep through Var's fingers. The wound certainly wasn't *nothing*. His friend needed help—immediately. There was no longer any choice. He gripped his tutor under the arm. "Come. We will go to Rock House. Either Darlee or Kero can heal that wound."

"But what of the Sechland delegation? With how you left things at the conference this morning, I doubt they would be pleased to see you and be willing to take us in."

He thought back to those moments when Darlee and Kero faced down the soldiers in the street earlier in the day. Hidden by the curtain and watching from the window, he had noted all that transpired. There was more communicated to him than the challenge to the usurpation of authority in town by the youths. They must have known he was hiding at Lasha's, perhaps followed him there. However they became aware, their action was one of protection, not just confrontation. Of this, he was sure. Why…that was a different matter. As difficult as such an assumption might be, there was one possibility brewing in his thoughts. The girl had feelings for him.

He had never given the girl a second look—too young, on the short side…gangly, and, with the eye patch, not exactly attractive. No, not what he would pursue. Still, he and Var needed protection. Despite the unsavory aspect of such an action, if giving Darlee a modicum of attention might lead to their safety, then he would have to do so. "Come. They *will* take us in."

CHAPTER 30

It took a circuitous route for Kero to reach the home of Orvest the merchant as roving bands of assassins, Morican troops, and Hamak people were nearly the only people in the streets. Otherwise, the streets were empty of citizenry. He chanced upon one group of older men sitting quietly, drinking tea. One asked him what all the clamor was about, but he ignored the fellow and kept going.

As before, there were guards at the gate, and this time one called out asking what his business was when Kero was still twenty paces away.

There was no time for formalities. "Stand aside. I must speak with Commander Savan of the Piaxians immediately."

The guard hefted a bow with an arrow notched and aimed at Kero's chest. "My orders are no one enters without permission. Go away."

Not looking to get shot, he slowed his progress, but edged closer, hands held high. "Tell the commander his life and that of all of those inside are in danger. A force of Moricans have arrived and sunken the Piaxian trireme."

The two men exchanged words Kero could not hear, but although the man with the bow remained steadfast, the other took off at a run for the house. While the guard was gone, Kero tried to lower his hands, but the remaining guard hefted the bow higher so he followed the tacit instruction and raised them again. This man was deadly serious, and it was not worth the risk. His only hope was that Savan would come out to speak with him.

The front door to the home opened, and not only did the commander appear, but his brother, the regent, as well, followed by Orvest and the warlock Prattrow. They conversed in whispers as they approached the gate, and Orvest bade the guard to lower his bow. "Young Kero, what is this news you bring? Surely, you must be mistaken. Is this some trick to panic my guests?"

"No trick." He recalled the gentle touch of Tarlok at the

merchant hall. "Regent, as you did this morning, I implore you to read my thoughts to know what I say to be true."

Tarlok glanced at Savan, who nodded. He returned the nod and stepped tight to the gate. "Come close that I may do so."

Kero closed the gap and stood directly opposite, with the gate between them. Tarlok reached through the bars and placed a hand on Kero's forehead. He focused on the memories of all that had happened in the bay. Like before, he felt nothing, and like before, Tarlok withdrew his hand and turned to the others.

"The lad speaks the truth. A contingent of over two hundred men has landed at the wharf. Our trireme is lost along with one of their ships. War between our two nations is once again upon us. One can only conclude that it is but a matter of time before they come here."

Savan glanced around the estate. "This position is not defensible. If we stay, we will end up the same as the other merchants—all dead and the home burned to the ground."

The regent turned to Orvest. "Gather your people. We will together quit this location immediately. Forget valuables. Time is of essence."

"To where?"

Tarlok smiled at Kero. "Why, to Rock House. Together, with the Sechland contingent and the shelter being offered by this lad here, under the protection of his guardian, we should be safe."

Offering shelter at Rock House had never been his intention. He had hastened to merely provide warning, nothing more. "I am unsure whether my master will be so accommodating."

Tarlok chuckled. "Fear not, young Kero. I am a good judge of people, and though my encounters with your lord have been brief, I think he will be."

The commander clapped one hand on Tarlok's back. "I hope you're right, little brother. My own interactions with the head of Riaz's assassin guild have been less than friendly."

Save Kero and Tarlok, all scattered throughout the compound to hasten everyone out. The regent unlocked the gate and opened it wide. "While we are alone, I need confess something to you. Your allowing my touch created a conduit for me to gather more information than just what you wanted me to know. For example, I know your master's name—Gragnishozar. I also know he is not human, but some type of demon. Now, have no fear. I have revealed none of this to any save my brother, Commander Savan. His fealty is sacrosanct, and he would never breach the trust I place in him. Your secrets are safe. This extra information furthers my opinion of how we will be accepted. My apologies for the intrusion."

The initial shock of how more than just the required memories were taken tongue-tied him. What should he say? Should he accuse the regent of breaching his trust? The man had apologized. Was such a simple confession acceptable? He looked into the smiling face of Piaxia's second-highest-ranking official, next to only their queen, Tarlok's wife. How old could he be? He looked no older than Prince Brumaine, yet he exhibited a demeanor one expected from an elder statesman, not one still in his late teens. Was such a professional appearance the result of having to handle the affairs of state or from a different upbringing? In the background, he could see Savan returning to the gate. Somewhere in his mid-twenties, the commander exhibited a sharp wit, but also a certain loose latitude when in the company of others, especially women. No, one's station did make a difference. Perhaps, thrust into such a predicament, Prince Brumaine might also demonstrate the cool intellect the regent of Piaxia bore.

He extended his hand. "Apology accepted."

The regent accepted the hand in a firm, steady grip. "There is much good in you Kero. I have seen it. Know this…Piaxia shall always be your friend."

Savan arrived and knit his brows when looking at the handshake. "What's this all about."

Tarlok released the grip and faced his brother. "A matter of honor."

"Oh…honor…I thought the two of you had come up with some grand master plan to defeat the Moricans. I guess, like usual, it'll be up to me to think of it."

The regent grinned widely. "And you had better, or else I'll have to have a chat with the queen about your position as commander. I *do* have a certain amount of influence you know."

Savan grabbed Tarlok with an arm round the neck and with his free hand rubbed the regent's head with ferocity. "Don't worry, little brother. I'll take care of you. The queen may have married you, but she likes me better."

Such casual cavorting in the face of dire adversity surprised Kero, but then again, he'd never had a brother. Perhaps such frivolity was the norm. As he thought about it, the relationship he carried with Derak had some similarity, though not so much the roughhousing.

Many others gathered, and it did not take long until both Tarlok and Orvest had announced all were present. A gray-haired servant in Orvest's household had decided to stay to watch over the premises. Despite pleas from his benefactor for him to leave, the fellow refused, stating as he was an old man, he would come to no harm.

Orvest joined Tarlok at the front of the group. "All right, then. Let us be off. It is many blocks to Rock House."

Kero tried his best to walk near the front with Orvest and the regent, but both Savan and Prattrow blocked him from doing so. He settled for being in the middle of the group, behind the leaders. From that position, he could still see the path ahead and, to some degree, hear the conversation between the leaders.

Barely had they gone two blocks when they came across one of the groups of men Kero had avoided earlier when approaching the Orvest estate. Cries of recognition exuded from the men, but rather than block Kero's group, they scattered. Obviously, they felt they were too few to confront the Piaxians. Still, though the Moricans were now out of sight, Kero could hear them calling out for assistance. How long until they gathered sufficient numbers to be a real threat?

Tarlok glanced back at all who followed. "Haste is necessary. We must jog the rest of the way. Young help the old. This will not be easy."

Though so far they had only walked the portly merchant to his left was already wheezing with the exertion. Whether it was from a total lack of fitness or the stress of the situation, he doubted the man would last more than fifty paces before collapsing on the street. "Let me help you." He moved near and draped the man's arm over his own shoulder.

"Many thanks. I daresay I haven't run in many a year. This is insanity."

The man leaned on him heavily. Despite his best efforts to keep pace, he and the man were slowly dropping back in the pack. It was not long until they trailed the others.

It wasn't far now. Two blocks, and he would be home. All his concentration was on watching his footing and preventing the man holding on from falling down. Twice now, he had been forced to stop when the fellow went to one knee. Unlike the others' pace, theirs was barely more than a fast shuffling of feet.

Only the screams ahead made Kero look up to see what was going on. A cadre of ten Morican archers had set up down a side street and were raining arrows on the group as it passed the intersection. Several people were hit while a few others armed with bows returned fire.

Savan led a charge of Piaxian soldiers toward the archers, holding the shield he normally wore on his back as a block against attack. They were few against many, but drew all fire, allowing Orvest's people and the remaining Piaxians to aid those injured to escape the intersection. Even the stout fellow Kero had been helping suddenly found renewed energy to cross the open area unaided.

The open door to Rock House was within sight, and many of those in their party already struggling inside. They would be all right. He returned his attention to the fight down the side street. Perhaps he could help. With two of the four men who accompanied Savan on his charge down, he wondered if his help would be enough as eight of the Moricans, now holding swords, engaged the Piaxians.

Drawing on his mana, he discharged a bolt at the man farthest from the Piaxians and struck a direct hit, knocking the soldier to the ground. While summoning up a second bolt, he held off as, to the surprise of everyone, Prince Brumaine and his lieutenant arrived at the scene from behind the Moricans and slew two. Savan and his men eliminated two more, and then the rest broke and ran.

With nothing more he could do, Kero made for Rock House. When he got inside, the main room was crowded with not only those who had fled from Orvest's, but the Sechland contingent as well.

Many were wounded. The Morican arrows had been unkind and without specific target. Among those injured were several women and a child. Already, the warlocks and Regent Tarlok were conducting healings.

Commander Savan entered with his two soldiers, Prince Brumaine, and his lieutenant Var. Savan and Var were injured, but while the commander's wound appeared superficial, a shallow cut on his arm, blood was dripping from between the lieutenant's fingers to the floor.

Kero had never tried a healing. He knew what to do, but was tentative to try when there were so many already in the room who were practiced at it. He waited for a moment, but when none of the warlocks went to attend Var, it occurred to him that the lieutenant's Morican uniform may be the reason.

It was time he tried. Brumaine and Var had moved to sit in a corner, away from the majority of people. He knelt in front of the lieutenant. "I need you to move your hand out of the way."

Var nodded, but the slowness with which he withdrew his hand, and the erratic manner in which it shook, told Kero the wound in the lieutenant's hip was more severe than he'd anticipated. He hesitated for only a moment, then, borrowing a knife from the man, cut the tunic away so that he could place his hand freely on the injury without cloth interfering. Blood flowed more freely and Var, leaning back, passed out. He must be near death!

Placing his hand on the wound, he concentrated, his magic flowing. A terrible wrenching pain burned in his hip, the identical location as the one on Var. The desire to withdraw his touch came, but he knew the routine. For him, there was no wound, only the transference of the pain. Still, he could not resist checking his own hip with his free hand to determine his assumption to be correct.

The pain continued, but slowly abated as the wound below his touch sealed. The flesh must be joined throughout the depth and breadth of the cut to make the healing complete and, in his mind, he could see mending as it occurred. His brow was now soaked with perspiration and he wiped at it as the dripping sweat stung his eyes. The pain was almost gone, only a little longer. Someone was yelling at him, but he dared not stop before the job was done or Var would die from internal bleeding.

It was over. The pain gone. Only redness remained where the wound had been. He looked to Brumaine. "He's lost a lot of blood. Give him plenty of water."

Before Brumaine could reply, rough hands grabbed and turned Kero to face the owner, Captain Brusk, shaking him heartily.

"Where is she, lad?"

The healing had drained him, and he felt woozy, the shaking making it worse. It was hard to concentrate. "Who?"

Brusk rose, hauling Kero up with him. "Darlee. You left together, but she is yet to return."

CHAPTER 31

Darlee could not contain her surprise when she had noted Kero walking past Rock House. She had decided to follow him. Not only did she witness the naval battle in the bay, but unlike Kero, from her vantage point in the street above the wharf, she paid heed to the landing of the Morican soldiers and their eventual march into the city.

It was when a group of men, the warlock assassin Lazaan among them, appeared at the other end of the street did she realize her predicament. She was trapped between enemy forces.

She needed a refuge and dashed into the only open door nearby, an inn named The Fisherman's Friend. Inside the squat, two-floor wooden structure, an aroma, a mix of both fish and some other pungent scent reminiscent of burning leaves, assaulted her senses. Not only did the smell invade her nostrils, but her eyes watered a little at the sting associated with the smoke wafting everywhere.

Despite the bright day outside, the interior bordered on gloomy as there were few windows, and those featured louvered shutters limiting the amount of light entering. Unlike Rock House where the tables were set up individually with four chairs at each, the layout inside the tavern was three rows of long tables lined with sixteen chairs a side. The middle row was mostly occupied by a number of men, perhaps twenty in all. Many held a carved wooden item in their mouths, glowing embers in the ends farthest from their lips. Smoke billowed from both their exhales and the devices, creating the dark cloud that clung to the low ceiling of the place. Despite various ages, there was a similarity to them in both look and attire. Faces, many with a few days' growth of beard, were ruddy and creased. It was a look unseen in her homeland, but remembrance of those faces she had seen in Dun, the port city of Piaxia from which she had departed, bore a striking resemblance. Fishermen. It made sense. The constant days of traveling the Great Sea, in the face of salty spray from wind-swept waters, in search of a daily catch, must cause such a complexion.

Near the back corner, four women of various ages were seated, two also with the same devices in their mouths as the men, and all with the same ruddy look. An easy guess—the women also plied the ocean in the fish trade. This surprised her some. The fact women engaged in the same trade as men was not practiced in Sechland.

Darlee made her way past the four women and took the seat farthest from the door, the women serving as a screen. Although they all looked at her, taking time to examine her from head to toe, none spoke to her. Instead, they returned to the poses they'd held when she entered—silent, save the odd soft whisper between them then nodding in complicity.

Though she did her best to be inconspicuous, it mattered not to the old man behind the bar whose gaze was firmly upon her. Eventually, he came to stand before Darlee. "What are ya having?"

The man expected her to order something. What was she having? She clutched momentarily at the coin purse by her hip, ensuring it was still there and sensing the coins inside through the cloth. She had money. Though she had never partaken of alcohol, considering the mood she was in, the idea of trying it now did not seem outlandish. "I'll have a drink."

"Drink? What kind of drink? You don't look old enough ta drink here. I think instead what I should do is turn ya out into the street."

This was not going well. The laws in Riaz must be the same at home where sixteen is the law where one reaches the age of ascension and is considered an adult. Drinking alcohol falls under the purview of adults, not youths and her birthday was still a few months away. She had no idea whether the street was now clear and did not wish to be evicted. Before she could summon the words necessary for a rebuttal, a red-haired woman she recognized arrived and pushed the old man back a step.

"Leave the girl alone, Mudge. She's fine by me."

The man scowled. "Don't be telling me what ta do in my place. Besides, Janina, you're late. If ya had been on time, I wouldn't have ta be minding the customers. Where's Lasha?"

The buxom blonde nudged in, making her presence known. "I'm here."

Mudge glared at the women. "You're both late. Get to work. I have half a mind to dock ya each a copper."

Janina patted his cheek. "Don't be silly. You like us too much. Besides, with what's going on in this town, you're lucky we made it at all. And don't you go pretending you don't know."

The older man returned to the bar, waving a hand of rejection at Janina who turned to Lasha. "Get to the kitchen and start the stew. I'll be along shortly."

Lasha nodded and left, but not before a parting glance at Darlee.

Janina leaned on the table. "Darlee, isn't it? What are you doing in this part of town? It may only be a few blocks, but there's a big difference between the crowd that comes here and the one at Rock House. These are my people—none too wealthy or too friendly either."

She glanced at the open door. "I'm hiding. There are men in the street I don't want to cross paths with."

Janina stared at the doorway. "I seen them. Assassins. Their kind aren't welcome in here. Too many of the regulars would be afraid they're a target. Don't worry. They won't come in. You stay put. I'll get you something to drink. You do drink, don't you?"

Not looking to disagree, Darlee nodded. "Yes."

With a smile on her lips, Janina went behind the bar and returned with a small ewer and mug. After filling the mug halfway, she pushed it toward Darlee. "Riaz red. I understand they charge plenty for this stuff overseas, but it's the cheapest stuff here, and good, too. It will warm your innards until I can get you something to eat. The fish stew doesn't take long, and we make a mean one."

Reaching out, Darlee caught Janina's sleeve before she could walk away. "I don't know how to thank you."

"Don't worry about that. We girls have to stick together. I hope you have coin to pay Mudge, otherwise, I'll have to."

She produced her purse and showed Janina the contents. "I

do."

"Good." The redhead turned to the group of women sitting close by. "Keep an eye on this one. She's a friend."

The four nodded, gave Darlee one more look over, and then returned to their conversation.

Once no longer the object of everyone's attention, Darlee lifted the mug to her nose. Fruity, though pungent, the smell hinted at a flavor similar to the juices she'd enjoyed in the past. Taking a gulp, she choked for a moment and was seized by a short coughing fit. No wonder drinking was forbidden until the age required. Still, Janina was right. There was a warm feeling resulting from the drink. She liked it.

She allowed a small smile to crease her face. Janina was helping her break the law. Seeking the redhead out, she spotted her serving drinks to some of the men at the middle table. Being cautious, she sipped at the wine until the mug was empty. Grasping the ewer, she refilled the mug to the lip and started in once more.

While she sipped at the wine, she studied Lasha as she moved from the kitchen to the main hall, delivering plates of food to customers. The woman swayed in a provocative way, even while burdened. Sashayed might be the better definition. It was a method of walking she had seen her mother, Silk, practice with perfection. She giggled with pride when seeing a display that made men stare and women jealous. It pleased her that such a skill belonged to someone she cared for who was a loving partner to her father, Captain Brusk.

Now, seeing the `style of movement being used by the blonde was infuriating. Although the fishermen were a placid group, a few focused on Lasha's behind as she walked. How dare the woman be so provocative? Such exhibition should be reserved for her partner, not any man who happened to be nearby.

She picked up the pace with which she sipped the wine and finished the second mug. Filling it once more, she could sense the effect of the alcohol in a flushing of her cheeks and warmth to her person. It was understandable why adults enjoyed it. The feeling was enjoyable.

No longer focused on Lasha's movements, she was surprised when the woman placed a steaming bowl of fish stew before her, along with a hunk of bread, and took the seat opposite.

"I wanted to thank you for doing what you did for me today."

For her? Darlee had done nothing for *her*. The nerve of the woman to think she was the focus of Darlee's actions. If anything, she was the one who almost caused Darlee to do nothing. "Don't...thank me."

She patted Darlee's hand. "Of course I need to thank you. You saved my Prince Brumaine's life."

Pulling her hand away, Darlee glared at Lasha. "*Your* Prince Brumaine?"

"Of course, my..." Lasha tilted her head slightly as her brow knit. She blushed. "Oh...you don't think...oh my..."

Rising quickly, Lasha left the table. Good. Darlee didn't want her near anyway. She finished the wine in her mug then poured the last of the ewer into it. Staring into the thing and seeing it less than half full she wondered if she should order more. When she placed it on the table, it slopped some, and a small red puddle formed. Tilting the cup to peer in again and determine what was left, she decided, yes, she would order more.

After lifting her head to scan the room in hopes of hailing Janina, a lightheaded sensation caused her to blink. It passed and she spotted the redhead in conversation with Lasha, both glancing her way.

Whatever they were discussing must be about her. It would be just like the foolish blonde to go whining to her friend. How despicable. Maybe she just might teach the hussy a thing or two.

Janina left the conversation and came to stand before her. Darlee offered the ewer. "Can I get more wine?"

Taking the pitcher, Janina looked inside then at Darlee. "I think you've had enough." She sat down. "What's with this silly talk about that shallow prince?"

Now Janina? Darlee had thought of her as a new friend. "Don't call him that."

Janina guffawed. "Seriously? His kind are all the same. Sure, we have no princes here in Riaz, but there are plenty of powerful people who think of themselves like a prince. People like Lasha and I are playthings—nothing more. I'm a few years older than Lasha, and much older than you. I've seen it time and again. He's using her. She doesn't see it. I have yet to convince her of his misleading, but I'm still trying. As for you, forget about him. He'll only break your heart. It's what princes do. Go home and find some nice young man who isn't a pretentious fool. Trust me, you'll be happier in the long run."

Darlee didn't want to hear this talk anymore. If she wasn't going to get any more wine, then she might as well leave. Surely, the men in the street must be gone by now. It was getting dark outside.

She rose to leave but staggered and plopped back into her seat. The lightheaded feeling of earlier returned with a fury. As she gathered her senses, Janina pushed the bowl of still steaming fish stew toward her.

"Here. You better eat this. You're drunk. It will help. Trust me." The redhead glanced round the room. "It looks like the crowd is thinning. This place empties early. Fishermen get out to sea before dawn. When you're finished, I'll walk you home."

The wooziness was not enjoyable. If she was drunk, then perhaps eating was a good idea. Dipping the wooden spoon into the stew, she stirred it to see what was in it. One thing for sure, it smelled good. Besides the large chunks of fish, there were a number of identifiable root vegetables and some green stuff she did not recognize. Tentatively placing the first spoonful in her mouth, she was surprised at the delightful flavor. She tried a bite of the bread. Though coarse, it also tasted good, and she set into the food with as much gusto as she could manage, considering her state.

By the time she finished and her plate had been taken to the kitchen, it was dark out and only a few men remained at the center table, the women next to her all gone. Janina returned and waved for Darlee to follow. "I've asked Mudge to let us go early. Let's get you back to Rock House. It's on the way for Lasha and I."

Her step was a little unsteady, but once she exited the tavern and reached the street, the fresh air cleared her senses enough to walk with some semblance of normalcy. Flanked by the two women, she could hardly wait to get back to her room and some rest.

As they walked in near darkness with only a little light from the stars and the odd shuttered window, Darlee thought she heard whispered voices ahead. From some thirty paces away, a light globe appeared and sailed in their direction to stop immediately overhead. Whoever was in their path included at least one warlock.

Lasha stepped behind Darlee and grabbed Janina's arm. "What do we do?"

The redhead stopped walking and reached out to halt Darlee as well. "Can you also send a light ahead so that we can see who awaits us?"

Why hadn't she thought of that? Her mind must be really muddled. "Certainly." She lifted one hand high, and a glowing orb appeared above it then drifted off in the direction whence the other came. It illuminated Lazaan and four Morican soldiers creeping their way.

Once the light betrayed their covert movements, Lazaan stopped and pointed toward Darlee. "Shoot her."

Only two of the Moricans carried readied bows, and both fired immediately. One arrow streaked just over Darlee's shoulder, the other missing to her right. She was under attack! A lesson from her magical trainer, Daphora, sprang to mind. Summoning the wind, she created a current of air blowing out and away. The archers fired two more arrows, both careening wildly off course before reaching her. It was time to strike back. From each hand she loosed a bolt of lightning striking the left and right archers and sending them hurtling back and to the ground.

Lazaan fired successive bolts at her, but her defensive aura held with ease. With the section of road she walked exposed bedrock, drawing on the Key was no difficulty. The other two soldiers, despite drawn swords, turned and ran. Lazaan, scowling, followed suit. Darlee pursued them with the light globe until they turned down another street and were out of sight.

Calming, she summoned the light globe to be overhead as Lazaan's had dissipated. Turning, she sought out the two women to tell them it was safe to continue, but to her surprise, discovered Janina kneeling down over a sprawled and thrashing Lasha. Blood spewed from a gaping wound on the girl's neck where an arrow must have passed directly through.

Janina was white with fear. "Save her!"

Dropping to her knees beside Lasha, she placed a hand on the wound and summoned her magic in hopes of healing. Before she could truly begin, Lasha's thrashing stopped. It was too late. She turned to Janina. "I'm sorry. Her life force is gone. There is nothing I can do."

CHAPTER 32

So far, Brumaine had gone relatively unnoticed, huddled in a corner with a recovering Var. Captain Brusk had led a team of Sechlanders outside, taking Kero along with him to retrace the lad's movements when he had been with Darlee. They had just returned with the girl and the redhead, Janina. Both women glanced his way then whispered together. Had something happened regarding him? He needed to know.

After checking with Var that his lieutenant was fine to be left by himself, Brumaine approached Darlee. Although Janina was present, it was good Lasha was not as he now had the unsavory duty of wooing the young Sechlander to ensure protection for both him and Var. Lasha's presence would have made it impossible. As it was, he needed to separate Darlee from Janina. "Darlee, may I speak with you for a moment."

The girl broke into tears. How could his simple question elicit such a reaction? "What? What's the matter?"

"La...La...Lasha. I couldn't save her."

The realization there may be a serious reason as to the lack of presence of the blonde tingled in the back of his mind. "What about Lasha? Where is she?"

Janina put an arm around Darlee. "Lasha is dead. She was killed by Moricans on our way here. An arrow through her throat."

Lasha? Dead? What should he do? What was expected of him...to grieve? He had liked the girl, true, but with all women who had tried to be part of his life he had maintained a certain detachment in his mind, something being a prince had bred into him. As a result, affection was not an entanglement he suffered. He never loved. He also had never seen a woman who may have adored him die from such a thing. It shook him deeply.

It was not true he never loved. Like all good sons, he loved his mother, respected his father. Though he battled constantly with his siblings, the death of his brother Doren confirmed he still cared for them all. He glanced over to the resting Lieutenant Varamanthu, a mentor figure in his life. In a different way, he loved that man as well.

Love was a difficult thing to deal with. Even when he did not feel affection for others, he failed to take into account they might love him. Such had been the case with Lasha, and now she was dead. How much of that death could he lay at his own feet? He met the stares of both Darlee and Janina, one with tears, the other, set in a stern expression. He could withstand neither. "I'm sorry for that."

He stumbled away, back to the corner where Var was. Making a false play for Darlee no longer interested him. He could not mislead another where death threatened. Let the Piaxians and the Sechlanders do what they would. He would abide by their decision.

The Piaxians were settled down after having dealt with the number of injuries at the hands of the Moricans. Once more, he marveled at the healing skill of the warlocks and how such an art was truly missing in Morica. Not only had they healed their own people, but those citizens of Riaz from the merchant Orvest's household who also had come under fire.

Obviously spent from using their magic, the warlocks lazed more than those who had been injured, but others, unharmed, argued amongst themselves on what to do next. Among them was Savan, and the commander, his face flushed, confronted Brumaine. Regent Tarlok accompanied him.

"It is time, young prince, you disclose to us *all* of Morica's end game. Do not lie, for my brother will know whether you speak the truth. A sizeable force of troops from your country threatens us, and they move about, uncontested by the Hamak family who now basically rule in Lymos. Alban, the fool, does not yet realize he has surrendered control of Riaz to a foreign power."

Brumaine looked from one brother to another, both men staring hard at him. It was possible that his father had planned all that happened, but he had no actual knowledge, just hints. "I tell you, I know naught of what plans Morica has, either from my father, King Jessop, or Commander Oberus. Since I have been here I have suffered two assassination attempts, been imprisoned by my own people, attacked by my own soldiers, and had to fight them to get here. If I was part of some vast plot to overthrow Riaz, do you think I would have suffered so much?"

Savan turned to his brother. "Well, Tarlok? Does he speak the truth?"

The regent's eyes were closed. He opened them and sighed. "Prince Brumaine speaks the truth, but"—he turned and pointed at Var—"he knows."

A gamut of emotions ran through him—surprise at what he just heard, shock at the content, anger at what it meant, disappointment at how it was revealed, and finally...betrayal. "I don't understand. Tell him Var, no...tell *me*, what do you know?"

His lieutenant, his guardian, his tutor, his friend, hung his head for a moment then met the gaze of the others, and then him. "It is true. I was aware of a plan to capture Riaz. Such an achievement would fill the coffers of Morica to overflowing. Understand, I am a loyal citizen of our country. If the conquest of this island state could be achieved without major conflict, then such a plan was a good one. But know this...at no point was I made aware of any part of the plan that involved the murder of you, Prince Brumaine, or your brother, Prince Doren. I was only informed something would happen to create a united front against Piaxia, nothing more. I suspect the king and Commander Oberus, knowing my attachment to you, withheld such a detail in fear of my revolting against the plan. Regardless, I had my suspicions and counseled you to be careful."

He recalled that early conversation. Still, interpretation of his most recent discussion with Var suddenly changed. The lieutenant had spoken in a matter-of-fact way as one knowledgeable of the details, not one surmising them. Yesterday, there had been a mention of a plan, which Brumaine had summarily forgotten until now. "So what is to happen next?"

"The complete invasion. My guess is within the fortnight. The balance of Morica's navy awaits instruction to sail for Riaz. They will be mostly transport ships as a third of the triremes we have are here already. It is the land troops, and the shoreline defenses necessary to protect the island, once taken, who will arrive."

A murmuring buzz filled the air with many speculating as to potential scenarios upon the arrival of such a force. There was a palpable fear in the room. There was no denying it.

Savan glanced around then leaned close to his brother in an obvious attempt to not be overheard. "Our only hope is to quit the city. We must take all of these people with us. Any who stay behind will be slaughtered."

Tarlok squinted and stroked his chin. "Tell me, brother, how long would we have before they arrive?"

"Hmm. Assuming they sent that merchant ship to inform their navy, eleven days. Six for the merchant to get there, but the attack force could probably arrive in five."

"I suspected something along those lines. That means we must get our own forces here in ten days or less."

"Impossible. Even if we could somehow commandeer a ship to Piaxia, the Moricans have almost a full day's head start on us. Add to that they're ready and waiting to pounce while we would need a couple of days to martial the necessary forces."

Tarlok looked around the room and focused on Darlee, still being consoled by Janina and Captain Brusk. "Maybe not. There *is* a way to beat them here. Fetch the young Sechlander girl. We must talk to her."

Savan crossed the room and returned with Darlee, Brusk following. Her tears had dried, but she still wore an expression of despair with her mouth downturned and a white pallor to her cheeks. The captain, a hand on her shoulder, faced the Piaxian regent. "What is it you want from my daughter?"

Tarlok crouched to eye level with the girl. "I need your help. I know you can contact your brother through the stone of the world. I've seen him speaking with you. This is a skill beyond my ability. Can you do it from here?"

She glanced at her foster father who had a puzzled look on his face. Obviously, this was something he was unaware of. She returned her gaze to the regent, closed her eyes for a moment, and then nodded. "I believe so. I do not think distance is the issue. The only requirement is that he is touching stone to use the Key as well."

Tarlok straightened. "Then let us hope that is the case. Knowing his living quarters provide him such, I need you to get a message to him that he can pass on to the queen. My brother has told me of how you bested the warlock here in this room. I suspect that bench over there"—he nodded to the far corner—"is your conduit. Let's sit you down so that you can conduct the necessary spell."

He led her across the room, and Brumaine, along with Brusk, Var, and Savan, followed. The room went quiet as the others gathered there all turned to watch the procession. Brumaine guessed everyone was wondering what was happening. They weren't alone. He, too, was unsure of what magic was about to occur. Was it possible to talk through stone? It was certainly something he had never heard of.

Once Savan and Tarlok moved the table out of the way, Darlee settled in the middle of the bench, her hands clasped in her lap. Her stare was intense but not at any one person. Rather, she seemed focused on the air directly in front of her.

It started as a mist from out of nowhere. Some people gasped, but a glance at Tarlok was enough reassurance for Brumaine as the regent smiled. A darkness formed in the middle of the mist and slowly congealed into the shape of a person, waist up. Finally, the image of a young man hung in the air, smiling at Darlee.

"Hey sis, how have you been? I've tried to contact you for days! I was starting to worry, figuring I might need to break out of here and come looking for you."

Darlee smiled in return. "Hi, Gar. I didn't have a chance to tell you. I took a trip with Captain Brusk. I'm in Lymos, the capital city of Riaz."

"Actually, I heard. Silk and Daphora have come to visit. How's the trip?"

She shook her head. "Listen. I don't have time to palaver. We're in trouble here, and Regent Tarlok has asked me to get a message to the queen of Piaxia."

"Queen Tessia? What's the message?"

Tarlok moved to enter Gar's field of vision. "I'm here, Gar. Tell the queen she must send the entire navy immediately."

"The na—"

The image of Gar vanished, replaced by a wall of flame. Much brighter than the light from the oil lamps, it lit the entire room with a red glow, though no heat could be felt from it.

"There you are. I have waited for you to attempt another communication and have watched for it. The last time I was too slow to fathom your location. I shall not fail this time. Where is Gragnishozar?"

The brightness of the blaze intensified, and though Brumaine could not tell visually, something gave him the sensation that it was looking everywhere throughout the room. He looked at Darlee who she sat wide-eyed, as if in a trance. He knew nothing of magic, but his first instinct told him, like the time when he stood frozen near that very spot, she was being held by some mystical force projecting from the flame.

The fire grew brighter still. "Gragnishozar! Where are you?"

The voice speaking was one Brumaine would never forget. Deep, rumbling, and with a snarling tone, it reminded him somewhat of the assassin lord, though not as smooth. It chilled him.

The door to Gragnishozar's chamber opened, and Kero's guardian stepped into the room. "What goes..." The assassin lord stopped, took in Darlee, everyone close by, and the room, with one sweeping glance, then stared at the flame. "Leave her be."

Darlee slumped in her seat. Tarlok, being closest, was the first to her side. The brightness of the blaze quieted. "At last. Long have I looked for you. Did you think you were forgotten?"

"Forgotten? No. But wish it? Yes. Leave *me* be."

"That is not permissible. I am coming."

The flame winked out of existence, and it took a moment for his eyesight to re-acclimate to the normal light of the oil lamps hung from stanchions interspersed throughout the hall. Fear flowed around him. People huddled together in whisper circles, and what snippets he could overhear all involved what they perceived as a great danger.

Gragnishozar returned to his room, closing the door. He must know what was going on. Barging past those gathered round Darlee, he entered the private chamber and confronted Kero's guardian, now seated on his own bench, the imp Hiss at his feet. "What was that about?"

"It does not concern you. Leave my quarters."

He was not about to be put off. Recalling that Hiss had revealed Gragnishozar's name before, he suspected the imp knew the answer and snatched up the little demon. "*Who* is coming?"

"Hiss must run. Must hide."

He shook the creature hard. "Tell me! Who?"

"A god."

CHAPTER 33

Kero had felt bad when Darlee had failed to return to Rock House. He'd walked away from her after the confrontation in front of the house where Prince Brumaine hid.

Now, as he watched her faint when released by the link with the fire vision, he was concerned for her once more. He moved to stand beside Tarlok as the regent held one hand to Darlee's forehead and placed the other one above her heart. "What's wrong with her? Is she injured?"

Silent for a moment, he then gave a small smile. "You care for her. I *know* how much. It is not any kind of a physical injury. She is catatonic. Whoever was the entity behind that flame had ripped into her mind against her will. I must attempt to restore her consciousness. This is a difficult task. She could become an invalid, never to reason again. This is something I must approach with care and not before consulting with my fellow warlocks."

He studied Tarlok's face. After that initial reassuring smile, the man's countenance has turned to one of consternation with knit brows and taut cheeks. "But you can do it...right?"

"I don't know. I fear it may be something beyond my skill level or of that of any of my compatriots. My hope lies in Darlee's own mental will. Hers is very strong. No doubt she is fighting from within while I attempt to solve her dilemma from without. Perhaps together we will free her from this trauma."

Darlee brain damaged? The thought was almost inconceivable. She was so much more powerful than he, or any warlock in Riaz, as proven by her battle with Lazaan.

Other Piaxian warlocks were crowding in, and Kero stepped aside to give them access. Besides, he knew what should be done and who should do it. His guardian. None were more powerful than the assassin master.

The door to Gragnishozar's private quarters was ajar. That was never the case. He tentatively pushed the door open further to see Prince Brumaine facing off with his lord, the imp Hiss in the prince's grip. Fearing Gragnishozar would strike the prince dead, he stepped in quickly and closed the door behind him. "Brumaine, put Hiss down. I would speak with my guardian alone."

The prince dropped the demon and laughed. "You want to talk to Gragnishozar?" He stepped out of the way and opened a hand toward the assassin lord in a gesture of invitation. "Be my guest. No matter how hard I pry he refuses to answer. Only Hiss has been willing to divulge information, despite the gravity of what is coming."

He glared at the prince and the impudence the man was expressing. If not for the urgency of his request, he would have admonished Brumaine for his disrespect.

Hurrying before Gragnishozar, he knelt to be eye to eye with his guardian. "My lord, I have a boon to ask. The girl Darlee has been struck down by whoever was in the flame. Regent Tarlok says her mind has been corrupted and fears he may not be able to heal it. I know you have the power to do so. I beg you to aid the Sechlander."

Gragnishozar placed one of his massive hands on Kero's shoulder and gave a gentle squeeze. "Kero, long have I tried to denude you of the human virtues you so often display, and failed. It will be your failing someday. I will not help the girl. Despite your kindness, she has wrought the ruination of all—this city, your friends, and all that you love."

How? Darlee was the one who suffered. Why was she guilty of so much? "I don't understand."

"Nor should you. Simply understand that, despite all my years here, there is nothing for us in Riaz anymore. I will take leave of this country and invite you and Maresh, both of whom I consider my wards, to quit this city in search of a new home before disaster falls."

Prince Brumaine guffawed. "See? Still he refuses to explain what fate awaits. Only the lowly creature Hiss has revealed the information that should make everyone fear for their lives."

Kero sought out the imp and spotted him cowering in a corner. "What is he talking about?"

The demon skittered to hide behind the legs of the brazier, but, despite his small size, he was too large to hide there. He made some kind of screeching keen then hugged the brazier. "He comes! The god comes!"

Brumaine stood with his arms folded and shrugged his shoulders. "That's all I could get as well. Gragnishozar won't elaborate."

He looked at his guardian. "Master?"

Gragnishozar beckoned to Hiss to come to him. The demon scampered across the floor and leapt into his lap. "Have no fear, little one. Despite how much trouble you always cause, I will not abandon you. I freed you a hundred years ago. I will not let him take you back."

There was much Kero wanted to ask. Was a god really coming? In school, they were taught of the gods in an existential way. Where did humanity and, for that matter, everything in the world, come from? All things without knowledge were sourced from the gods. It was always gods, in plural. No exact count had ever been given as to how many gods there were. For that matter, it seemed that no two gods were alike. There were gods of the air, the sea, the land, and yes, of fire. Was the being Darlee contacted through the stone one of those?

His intention to inquire was cut short by a pounding on the door. Brumaine opened it and Commander Savan stepped in.

"Come quick, everyone. Rock House is about to come under attack."

Gragnishozar roared to his feet and shove Savan out of the way. "None would dare attack my home!"

Following his lord out into the main room, Kero noted everyone gathered had moved away from the main entrance to the back of the main room save Captain Brusk who was peering out into the street. "They're amassing out there. I'm guessing a good two hundred. Maybe more."

Savan joined Brusk. "Any siege machines?"

"No. But pitch arrows. My guess is they intend to burn us out."

Pitch arrows? Warlocks could better send fire within. "Are there any Riaz people out there?"

Brusk chanced a quick step out then back inside. "None I can see. All wear the colors of Morica."

"Then there are no assassins with them."

Savan chuckled. "Aye. It levels the odds some, but not exactly much in our favor. Now we're only outmanned twenty to one."

Brusk yelled a warning and yanked Savan away from the open doorway. The twang of multiple bowstrings could be heard, and a number of the flaming bolts entered. Brusk returned to slam the doors shut and dropped the dead bar across it. The thud of arrows hitting echoed in the room. "That won't hold long. They'll burn through soon enough."

The few arrows that had made it into the room were snuffed out. Brusk cocked an ear to the staircase. "They're firing into the rooms upstairs as well. With all the bedding and such, it won't be long until this place is an inferno."

Gragnishozar moved to the bench Darlee occupied. "Clear the middle of the room. Stand against the walls."

Kero moved to stand beside his lord while the Sechlanders, Piaxians and members of Orvest's household crowded against the walls. Gragnishozar held out his hands.

It started slow. A clicking and clacking as the paving stones that made up the floor began to jump up and down in place. Kero had always wondered about the odd design. Had Gragnishozar laid the stones out in their existing pattern when Rock House was built?

There were four large open areas in the room and in each the stones moved toward the middle, jostling and upending furniture as they did. At first, they appeared as nothing more than jumbled piles, but, eventually, they gathered form.

He had seen the creation of his master's minions a number of times before, each time they were comprised of the same things— sticks, stones, but most of all, mud. What formed before his eyes was something new. Stone golems. Squat and massive, the four creatures turned to face their creator.

Kero wondered whether such monsters were impervious to

harm. No sword or ax could cut through their thick limbs. Perhaps hammers might have some effect, but what soldier carried a hammer? Only an army of blacksmiths might have any chance at all.

When the golems looked complete, Gragnishozar dropped his arms. "Our home is under attack. Go. The enemy is outside. Kill all you can. Leave none alive. Show no mercy."

The creatures turned and proceeded to the door, the one closest shattering it open wide with a single blow.

Gragnishozar bent toward Kero. "Take the people through my quarters and out the back. They must leave the city. Ask Orvest for directions. Like all the senior merchants, he owns a villa in the south. Go there."

His lord started to follow his creations. Kero tugged on his arm. "Master? What of you? Will you come with us?"

The assassin master cupped his own chin. "My freedom is forfeit. You heard the flames. Although I originally thought of flight, there is nowhere to go. I will defend my home, and, if I survive, await my fate when the other comes."

Gragnishozar freed his arm and continued into the street where the cries of men now emanated. Kero spun to scan the room and found the merchant. "Orvest. My master says you must lead these people to your villa in the south. Come. I will show you the way out."

He realized there may be enemy soldiers circling the building and some in the back alley. He tagged Commander Savan. "Stay close. We might need to fight our way."

Nodding, Savan moved to the front, with Captain Brusk close behind. He led them into Gragnishozar's quarters and opened the back door. As Kero expected, men from Morica waited, and a hail of arrows thudded into the door when he had barely opened it.

Savan rushed out, holding his shield in front of him. "The fools have hurried their shots. Quickly, rush them before they can take aim again."

The soldiers and warlocks of Piaxia charged into the alley and fought with the Moricans. Prince Brumaine and Lieutenant Var, whom Regent Tarlok promised safe passage, followed. Orvest, now at the door, turned to face those crowded behind. "We must go while the others fight. Stay close. It is many blocks to the top of the city, and a very long walk from there."

Kero stayed where he was, holding the door, as all the people passed. Regent Tarlok carried Darlee, still unconscious from her encounter with the god. When the last had gone, he realized one was missing. Maresh. Where was she?

He dashed back into the main hall and not seeing her, made for the kitchen. "Maresh! Where are you? We're leaving!"

From the back stairs, he could hear coughing. Dashing up two steps at a time he then hurried down the hallway. Flames were emitting from a number of the bedrooms that faced the street. Despite the heat, he looked into each room in search of her. There was no sign of her.

She must be on the third floor. Now closer to the front stairs, he climbed the last flight and found her in one of the rooms trying to put out the flames with a wet towel, but to no avail. "Come on, Maresh. There's nothing you can do here. The fire is too great. We need to get out."

She continued to swat at the flames. "This is my home. I'm not going anywhere. Help me put out these fires."

He stepped back into the hallway. Every room at the front of the building was on fire. The smoke was heavy, and his lungs burned from breathing the hot air. Fighting the fire was foolish. They needed to leave immediately. A crash from the room Maresh was in put a chill in his heart. He dashed to the doorway, but could go no farther. The floor had collapsed, and Maresh was nowhere in sight.

Running down the stairs he tried to enter the room directly below, but the fire was so intense, he shied back, dizzy from the heat and smoke. A groan through the building hinted at impending disaster. There was more crashing as other floors fell through including much of the hallway. Maresh! He was overcome with weakness and fell to his knees. As much as he wanted to get to her, he couldn't even walk. Crawling, he made it back to the front stairs and tumbled down them to the main floor.

Everything ached from the fall, but after a quick check he believed nothing was broken. Glancing around, he made note of the flames already coming through the ceiling. It would only be moments before the entire building caved in. He got to his feet and stumbled out into the street, just in time as another crash behind him was the second floor collapsing down to the first. A blast of heat sent him sprawling again.

He lay in the street for a moment, regaining his breath. When he turned over and sat up, he watched the flames roaring inside and wondered whether the outside walls would collapse as well. He needed to move farther away in case they did. Tears streamed down his face as he lamented the loss of Maresh. Though she'd never wanted the job, she was the closest thing to a mother he'd ever had.

When he finally rose to his feet, he looked around. The light from the fire was enough to illuminate the street for a block in either direction. Dead Morican soldiers numbered in the dozens, but the balance were gone as was Gragnishozar and his golems. He could only surmise the enemy troops had fled and his master was pursuing them. Though he was unsure how long the assassin master could maintain the magic to keep his golems alive, he knew sooner or later his lord's mana would wane and the golems return to what they once were.

He weighed his options. Should he race after Orvest and the group he was leading out of town, or should he follow Gragnishozar and assist him in whatever manner he could? He concluded it be best to check whether the others had got away safely before deciding anything.

He circled the building. The alley, though darker, still was lit enough to espy a half dozen dead Moricans, Commander Savan's handiwork prevalent based on the massive sword cuts many had suffered. There was one of the Sechlanders down as well. He bent over the man to check for a pulse. The man was dead. His healing skills would serve no purpose.

The crunch of gravel urged Kero to spin and see who was

near, but before he could, he suffered a blow to the back of his head and collapsed, consciousness leaving him.

CHAPTER 34

Brumaine stuck close to the leader, Orvest. Some of the merchant's personal retinue had splintered off to return to family homes, so the group consisted mostly of Sechlanders and Piaxians, none of whom knew where they were. Two of the Piaxians dropped behind to serve as some kind of rear guard.

He was surprised at the ease with which they had escaped. Even now, many, many blocks away, the fire illuminated the night sky enough to aid in their flight up the streets of Lymos but exposed them to anyone looking. Because of the city being built on a hillside, he could still see the stone walls of Rock House and the flames shooting up from where the roof had once been. He hoped the walls held and the fire did not spread through the city. Many would lose their homes should the flames escape their confinement.

Var stayed close on his right. He checked on him to see how the lieutenant fared. The near-death of his tutor had shaken him deeply. The possibility of life without Var was not a thing he liked to think about. Though the wound was healed, how would the loss of blood affect his energy level? At the moment, he showed no weakness. Brumaine hoped Var's strength held up. A long trip lay ahead of them. "It seems my original plan to quit the city is what we, in the end, are following."

"And as before, I believe this plan is faulty."

Brumaine took in the number of soldiers and warlocks who walked with them. "How so? Before, we would have been alone. Now, we are accompanied by a sizable number of people who can assist and protect us."

"True, but we are still too few to combat a force such as the one that assailed Rock House tonight."

He decided to do an exact count. "Including both the Piaxian regent and, should she recover, the young girl Darlee, there are five warlocks in our midst. Adding in Savan and Captain Brusk, and the fourteen soldiers they collectively command, plus you, we total twenty-three fighting men. Considering Oberus must keep the majority of his troops in town, I think we would be safe outside its confines."

"Our numbers will be useless when the bulk of the invasion force arrives. It is a temporary reprieve, if anything. We must strive to find an alternative to hiding in the hills."

Brumaine glanced round once more. Something wasn't right. "Where is Kero?"

Var scanned those nearby. "I do not see him. Perhaps he stayed behind to help his master?"

He grabbed the lieutenant by the arm to arrest his progress. "No. He was there at the door to the alley." Turning, he faced the lower part of the city and the burning Rock House. "He saved my life twice. Should we go look for him?"

"A noble idea, but where would we look? We don't even know the city. I fear such an attempt would only lead to our capture. Come. The group is still moving, and we are falling behind. Until we can formulate a proper plan it is best we keep with the others."

He decided to stay where he was for a moment more, the two Piaxians passing by, giving him a glance. The flames had subsided some. It appeared the walls to the inn would hold. As for Kero, there was no sign. Had the lad indeed gone in search of Gragnishozar? Such an idea would be foolish, but there was no doubt as to the youth's loyalty. He just may have done so. If such was the case, more than likely he would be slain by Oberus' men. It grieved him to think thus.

He sighed and looked to his tutor, waiting patiently. "You are right. Let us run to catch up with the group."

It only took a block for him and Var to catch up those fleeing the city. Captain Brusk eyed Brumaine as they paced side by side. "I thought we was done with ya."

He could understand the Sechlander's viewpoint. Running from a superior force of Morican soldiers intent on their demise and having two Moricans, one a prince no less, running with them. "I was looking for Kero. He must have stayed behind."

"Good riddance. The lad has been nothing but trouble, leading my daughter into one peril after another. I've fought two wars against you Morican bastards and seen too many good men put into the ground because of it. If Darlee dies, I swear, by the gods, I'll kill you both despite the safe passage Piaxia has given ya."

Although he knew Var to be a superb swordsman, judging by the girth of Brusk's arms and the visible battle scars, he didn't think the threat idle. If the gods pleased it, such a thing as what the captain promised was possible. He then recalled what Hiss had said, and chuckled. Where was that troublesome imp anyway?

Brusk stepped sideways and tripped Brumaine to the ground. As he scrambled to sit up, the captain drew his sword and held it pointed toward Brumaine's chest. "Why do ya laugh? I should run you through right now."

Var's sword flashed to knock Brusk's point away. As Brumaine got to his feet, Tarlok and Savan stepped between him and the captain.

"I laughed, not at you but recalling what I heard from the demon Hiss when I barged into Gragnishozar's quarters. If what he said is true, then we are all soon to be subject to the whim of the gods."

It was Brusk's turn to guffaw. "And you would listen to the words of such a vile creature as Hiss. What did the imp have to say? I could use a good laugh."

Brumaine had never believed in the existence of the gods. Yet using them in the lexicon of everyday speech was common practice, even by him. Var had taught him the gods were the crutch of the common people to explain what they could not. Fear of such deities was used by leaders to help keep the masses in check. Even the troops in the army paid a certain amount of homage prior to battle, in hopes such beings would assist them in their victory. *"May the gods be with you"* was a common mantra in society. Perhaps the captain was one of those who believed in the gods and held them in high regard. "When I questioned him who was behind the flame and asked who was coming, Hiss stated it was a god. Considering how much he trembles, I have reason to believe him."

Both Var and Captain Brusk still held their swords at the ready. Savan reached out to touch both tips. "Cooler heads are needed here. My brother has promised the Moricans safe passage with us. Now I, for one, put no faith in the gods, but who am I to deny their existence? Too many of those who serve under me do. If it is really a god who is coming, then it is Gragnishozar's problem, not ours. We have lost valuable time dallying here. Let us continue our journey and make our escape before being found. If it really is a god, I would prefer not to be in his way."

As Var and Brusk sheathed their swords, Brumaine nodded. "I agree. We are wasting time." He met the captain's angry gaze. "If my outburst caused you insult, I am sorry. I appreciate how important Darlee is to you." He held out his hand. "Please accept my apology."

Brusk snorted but accepted the offer, gripping Brumaine at the wrist in a military style. They shook briefly, and then Brumaine withdrew his hand, but not before the captain had nearly squeezed the life out of his wrist.

They proceeded upward. He was not sure how much farther until they reached the top and exited the city. It couldn't be far. What awaited him once outside the walls? Days of hiding? Running again at the first hint of troops? Var's assessment of what lay ahead was correct. Eventually, they would find him.

Like the Hamak estate, those homes nearby were all well to do, which indicated to him he was among the wealthy of Lymos who occupied the top part of the city. It was only when they passed under an arch did Brumaine come to recognize there were no longer houses on either side of the street. What lay before him was open road. Behind him, an archway with an open wooden gate that looked like it hadn't been closed in years, almost to the point of being unserviceable. Such were the signs of peace. If only all gates could look so.

No sooner did he and the others exit the city by some twenty paces than Tarlok called for a moment of rest. Many of the people were showing the strain of the hastened climb through the city. The regent laid Darlee down on top of a roadside rock outcrop.

Brumaine had forgotten the man had carried the girl the entire way. Savan announced he would carry Darlee from there. The big Piaxian would have a far easier time at it.

He looked at the girl, still unconscious. He hoped she would recover, though the uncertainty expressed by Tarlok as to his ability to conduct the proper healing gave Brumaine pause as to the likelihood of Darlee's recovery.

With the short break over, Savan picked up the Sechlander girl, and the group continued their procession down the road, away from Lymos.

Brumaine returned to the gateway to look back at the city.

Var pulled up beside him. "What is it, sire? Why aren't you following?"

He met his mentor's gaze. "I've come to a conclusion, Var. I'm a coward. Since this morning, I've done nothing but run and hide. And now I'm doing it again."

Var looked over his shoulder, squinted, and then dragged Brumaine behind a city arch pillar. "Shush. Someone is coming."

From behind him, he could hear someone approach. He turned to see Regent Tarlok at his elbow.

"Prince Brumaine, what is it? Why do you crouch here in the dark?"

He held a finger to his lips then pointed toward the road. "Someone is coming. We should see who it is. Perhaps we are being followed. Escaping the city will be useless if they know where we are headed."

The regent nodded. "I shall bring reinforcements. Stay here."

Tarlok dashed off, and Brumaine focused on the gateway opening. He had not seen the person. "How long until he reaches us?"

"Another moment or two. Be still."

Brumaine kept his breathing shallow. What should he and Var do if the others do not return in time? Should they confront the individual? Attack him? Wait until he passed and surprise him from behind? He glanced at Var. The lieutenant had his hand on the pommel of his sword, but the weapon still undrawn. That was smart. It was best not to alert the person with the sound of the sword being drawn from its sheath.

When the individual finally cleared the opening, Brumaine identified the warlock assassin Lazaan. What action to take was decided for him by Var as the lieutenant put a staying hand on Brumaine's chest.

Lazaan plodded by. Upon his back, he carried a bundle. Clothing? Personal items? Was Lazaan quitting the city as well?

Var removed his hand and motioned for Brumaine to follow. Along with the lieutenant, they stayed some dozen paces behind Lazaan. When the assassin reached the outcrop, Regent Tarlok and a number of his people sprang from various hiding places. The Regent stepped directly in Lazaan's path and created a light orb to glow directly overhead. "Hold. For what reason are you on the road at this late hour?"

Lazaan held up his hands. Flames flickered on the tips of his fingers. "Stand aside. I go where I will. At the moment, I have no desire to kill you, but make no mistake, though I see your magical aura, I can still do so."

Tarlok waved at the others. "I am not the only warlock who blocks your way. I doubt you can kill all of us. Answer my question."

From behind the boulder, the merchant Orvest appeared. He stepped into the open circle between Lazaan and the Piaxians. "Hold everyone. I know this man. He is Lazaan, one of the most powerful warlock assassins in the land and held in very high esteem amongst his peers. Threats do not loose his tongue. Only coin will do so." He faced Lazaan. "How much for the answer the regent of Piaxia asks?"

Lazaan lowered his hands, the flames flickering out. He turned to view everyone, including Var and Brumaine. After obviously assessing his situation, he looked to Orvest. "One silver piece."

The merchant fished a hand under his robe and produced the coin. "Here." He flipped it to the assassin. "You are paid. What is your answer?"

After a quick examination of the coin, Lazaan stuffed it into his pouch then faced Tarlok. "My service to Alban is complete. He has control of the city. I have, like many of us, been released from my contract. As difficult as this may be to believe, I no longer wish to watch what occurs. I have lost my best friend in Stod. Like him, I abhor the presence of foreigners. Morican troops run rampant in the streets, raping women and stealing from all. Until order is restored, I would be free of the turmoil."

The regent nodded. "Then you are free for hire." He turned to look behind him, and waved for someone to approach. From the dark, Savan became visible, the girl Darlee still slung over his shoulder. Tarlok returned his attention to Lazaan. "Her mind has been corrupted. You may have the power to correct it. What is your price?"

Lazaan spat on the ground. "For that witch? Not for ten gold pieces would I do such a thing."

Orvest produced his coin pouch and fished through. He looked up. "Will you do it for twenty-seven?"

Lazaan's posture slumped. "Twenty-seven?"

Orvest tossed the bag and Lazaan, after grabbing it, peered inside. He clutched the bag and nodded. "We have a contract. Place the girl on the rock."

Savan did as requested, and as the assassin warlock approached, the commander grabbed him by the arm. "If the girl dies, then you will never live to spend those coins."

Lazaan shook his arm free. "Excepting her and that freakish creature who was head of my guild, there are none more magically capable than me. I have accepted the contract. I will do the job."

The big Piaxian stepped aside, and the assassin placed one hand on the rock and the other on Darlee's forehead. "Now then, troublesome girl, let's see what's wrong so I can fix it."

CHAPTER 35

The situation he now faced was similar to one Kero had seen before. There *were* some differences. Unlike the first time, instead of some low tenement, the room was opulent. In place of a wood fireplace, a shiny wood stove occupied one wall. Beneath him were not the worn planks of a wood floor, but rich ceramic tiles and a plush, woven mat. Still, the most important things were the same. He lay on the floor of a room, his hands tied behind his back, the assassins Petrius and Bokko sitting guard.

The two were once more engaged in conversation and not paying attention to him. And, as usual, Bokko was drinking. Kero wondered if the fellow was ever sober.

Petrius scowled at his potbellied cohort. "That's the trouble with you. All you care about is where to get your next drink, no matter where it comes from."

Bokko stared into his mug. "What are you complaining about? This is top-of-the-line Riaz red. Our hosts are generous, if anything."

"That's just it. Who exactly are 'our hosts'?"

"Pllb! You know who they are. We're here in the Hamak estate. That means Alban and his family, of course."

Petrius poked Bokko in the shoulder. "That's where you're wrong. It's the Moricans who are in charge now, not the Hamaks. I don't know about you, but I'm none too happy about that."

Bokko waved a hand in dismissal. "Ah, you're just sounding like Lazaan now. The pay is good. Why should we give it up because there are a few Moricans around? Once they leave, we'll be running things here."

Kero wondered at what he had just heard. Had Lazaan quit working for the Hamaks? Obviously, Petrius was having second thoughts about his contract. Perhaps he could play to the assassin's patriotism. He sat up, drawing the attention of the two men. "Who says the Moricans ever intend to leave? From what I've heard, they're staying for good."

Bokko shook a fist at him. "Shut up, you! You're lucky to still be alive. If I had my way, you'd be dead by now."

Why was he still alive? There must be a reason they took him captive. The time before they hadn't wanted to antagonize his master. With Gragnishozar on the attack, that couldn't be the reason now. "Once my master finds you and sees you holding me captive, you'll wish that it was you who was already dead. You always were a lousy warlock, Bokko. What chance do you think you'll have without Lazaan?"

The fat assassin slammed his mug down, spilling half the contents. He rose and took a step toward Kero. "I'm good enough to finish you off. And when I'm done, there won't be anything for your master to find."

Bokko raised his hands and Kero clenched against the pending spell, but Petrius jumped up and slapped Bokko's hands down. "Don't be a fool. He's insurance—you know that. As long as Kero is alive, his master will be hesitant to attack again."

After grumbling, Bokko sat down and refilled his cup then glared over its rim at Kero while Petrius moved to kneel close by. "What have you heard, Kero? What makes you think the Moricans are here to stay?"

The expression on Petrius was with close-drawn brows and a clenched jaw. Perhaps it was possible to win the assassin over. "The Morican plans were disclosed in full by Lieutenant Var, the personal guard to Prince Brumaine. He detailed the steps including the invasion fleet now on its way for the conquest of Riaz."

As the eyes of Petrius went wide, Bokko choked on his wine. Wiping his face with his sleeve, the fat man rose once more. "You lie! You're just saying that to confuse Petrius."

Clearly, Bokko liked the new arrangement giving him more authority and power than he had ever enjoyed before. "If you doubt me, read my mind. I will not block you."

Bokko stared into his wine cup. "I...I never learned that."

Petrius edged closer. "Then allow me. I would know the truth."

Kero nodded and waited as Petrius placed a hand on his

forehead. He concentrated on the revelation by Var, recalling every word and expression by the lieutenant. He also recalled the surprise, not just from those present, but from Prince Brumaine.

After a moment or two, Petrius removed his hand, stood, and returned to his seat, drawing a hand across his face. Bokko's gaze followed every movement. Kero could feel the tension in the air...Petrius silent, and Bokko perplexed.

The fat man put down his mug. "Well?"

Petrius took a deep breath. Once the breath expelled, he glanced from Kero to his comrade. "He speaks the truth. An invasion fleet is on its way."

"I...I don't believe you. I think you're just saying that because you want to quit your contract. Well, do what you want. Even if it's true, whether the Moricans or the Hamaks, I'm staying."

Before Petrius could respond, the door banged open and Commander Oberus entered, Alban Hamak immediately behind. "Where is he?" He scanned the room until his gaze locked with Kero's. "Ah, there you are."

In two long strides, the Morican crossed the room and struck Kero across the mouth with the back of his hand. Collapsing to the mat, Kero could taste the copper of his blood. The blow must have cut the inside of his cheek.

Alban stepped between him and the commander. "Now Oberus, we agreed it was better to keep the lad alive. My estate cannot survive another attack from those stone golems."

"No one said I couldn't rough him up. I want some answers." Oberus pushed past Alban and, seizing Kero by the shoulders, raised him to a sitting position, and shook hard." How do we defeat your lord? You know him better than any other. What is his weakness? Out with it or I'll do far worse than a mere slap across the cheek."

He licked at a drop of blood on his lip. His cheek hurt and he wondered just how much pain he could withstand. The commander was not going to like his answer. "There is no way. Eventually, he will kill you all."

The Morican reared back and punched Kero in the eye with

great force. It knocked him down again, the back of his head hitting the floor and his vision blurring. His left eye flared with pain.

Oberus kicked him in the side. "Tell me!"

With his hands tied behind his back, he could not grasp at the injury and instead tucked his knees up tight as he curled into a ball. "May...the gods...curse you."

Oberus turned away and face the others. "I want the answer from him. If anyone knows it, he does. I saw Regent Tarlok from Piaxia do some trick where he read the lad's mind. I want the two of you to do the same thing. Find out from inside his head how we defeat his lord."

Petrius knelt and placed a hand on Kero's forehead. Unlike before, despite the pain, Kero kept his defenses up, refusing access. When Petrius finally stopped trying and stood, Kero knew his shield had held.

The assassin faced Oberus. "It's no good. Kero has his guard up, and I cannot penetrate it."

The Morican turned to Bokko. "What about you? Can you get the answer I'm looking for?"

Bokko shook his head. "If Petrius cannot do it, then there is no hope that I could. He read Kero's mind earlier, but that was for a different reason."

"What?" Oberus spun to face Petrius. "What reason?"

"I was trying to verify a statement made by the boy that a Morican invasion was imminent."

Alban paled. "An invasion?"

Oberus unballed his fists and let his shoulders droop. "A crock of lies. What exactly did he show you?"

"I saw a Lieutenant Var describe the plans to conquer Riaz and the planning for an invasion fleet to arrive within the fortnight, possibly eleven days."

"Ha! First Lieutenant Varamanthu? You would believe the words of a traitor? He killed two of my men when he freed that failure of a royal son, Prince Brumaine, from my holding. He would say anything to win the support of the Piaxians to his cause.

There is no invasion fleet. We are here at the request of Alban Hamak, a long-time friend of Morica, to assist in his takeover of the merchant guild in Riaz. Nothing more."

The commander turned to Alban. "I've had enough of this nonsense. Let us retire for the night. I'm told Kero's master will need a day to recover before initiating any further attacks by his minions. We have much planning to do to prepare for it."

The two men left Bokko and Petrius staring at each other. Petrius knelt once more beside Kero. "Hold still."

Petrius placed a hand on Kero's hip. Until then, his breathing had come in rasps as a result of the kick, but, as he breathed, it eased until the pain was no more. The assassin had healed him. Once the same process was followed for his eye and cheek, Kero sat up again. "Thank you. To what do I owe the kindness?"

"I'm your jailer, not your torturer. If what you say comes true and your master kills us all, perhaps he might spare me with a quick, painless death rather than being torn to shreds by his golems."

How much more would it take to win the assassin over completely? "I hear your plea, but will my lord? I lie bound, helpless to further your cause and pass on word of your compassion. More than just a quick death, I may be able to have your life spared should you simply free me."

Petrius crossed to a window then looked out and down. He returned to his seat. "Escape is impossible. Even if I were to undo your bonds, the grounds are filled with Morican troops. You would get no further than the bottom stair."

So, even with the use of magic, there was nowhere to run. Another plan was needed. "Then you must go. Approach my master with caution, but approach him you must. As you are a long-time member of the assassin guild, he may give you audience before acting. Tell him all you can. He will not begrudge you for exercising your profession."

"I agree. As much as I enjoy the gold, I don't think I'm ready to surrender my life for it."

Petrius picked up his cloak, but as he put it on, the door

opened and Alban Hamak entered. His brows knit, he stared at Petrius. "Where are you going?"

"I...I was just going home. I wanted to check on it to make sure it wasn't being plundered by the Moricans."

"Hmm. I'm not ready to allow you to leave just yet. You are under contract to me. I need to ask you a few more questions."

Petrius took off his cloak and sat down. "What do you need to know?"

Alban pointed at Kero. "When you read his mind, did you believe it?"

The assassin pivoted in his seat to meet Kero's gaze. Would he say yes or no? If he said yes, would Alban take issue, or would he believe him? If he said no, would the Hamak leader accept it or question the validity? No doubt, Petrius feared to answer wrong.

Kero needed to sway the issue. "There is more to show."

Alban and Petrius exchanged glances then Alban nodded toward Kero. "Well...go."

Once again Petrius knelt close and held a hand to Kero's forehead. Kero concentrated on the memory of Regent Tarlok reading the mind of Var and confirming the truthfulness of the lieutenant's statement.

Taking his hand away, Petrius rose and relayed all he had seen in Kero's mind.

Alban paced for a moment then grasped the assassin's cloak. He proffered it to Petrius. "Go. Consult with the assassin master. Win him to our side. I no longer require the Moricans. The city is mine. Strike a deal—Kero's safety and benign assistance by me against the Moricans in exchange for amnesty for me and my family. Make it happen."

The assassin donned his cloak quickly and sped out the door. Bokko rose from his seat. Alban looked at him. "And where are *you* going?"

"I thought...I thought..."

"You thought nothing. Sit here and guard the prisoner. Until such time that your partner returns with news of a contract, things are still as they were. He's insurance against further attacks."

A scowl was written on Bokko's face, he plopped down on his seat and scowled at no one in particular. It was not that look which bothered Kero so much as the one given to him by Alban before he exited the room. It was one of malevolence. Kero knew too much. He doubted he would ever leave the Hamak estate alive.

CHAPTER 36

Everywhere Darlee looked, all she could see was white. If she walked one way, it would fade to darkness. If she backtracked and walked the other, the same thing would happen. It mattered not which way she went, outside her circle of white light there was nothing but pitch black.

Her head hurt. She wondered whether she was suffering from drinking too much wine. Once, her foster father had complained mightily about a bad headache after imbibing in too much wine the night before. Maybe she was suffering from the same thing.

Though unsure how long she had been in the small white world, it seemed like a very long time. She wondered how she would ever get out. It was all very confusing. The last thing she remembered was talking to her brother through the stone when she hurled into the nothing. Had something happened when she connected with Gar?

One thing that caught her attention was the ever so slowly shrinking of the circle of light. Where before she could pace three steps in any direction before entering the dark, her range was now down to two. How long would it be until she was completely in the dark?

It was hard to understand what was going on. If the last thing she remembered was talking with her brother, then maybe she was still connected to him. Maybe this was something Gar had control of. "Gar! Can you hear me? I'm trapped in some weird kind of place with nothing but a white light and dark all around. Can you get me out of here?"

Though she was unable to tell from what direction, there was a murmur reaching her. Was Gar saying something? She spun around, looking and listening in all directions. "Where are you? I can't see you."

More murmuring. Nothing could be made out of anything being said. "Talk louder. I can't hear you."

The sound changed in tone. It was deeper, but still not quite identifiable. Definitely words, but she couldn't make them out. "What are you saying? I can't understand it."

The circle closed in some more. Now, no more than a pace all around. Panic seized her. The light shrank faster. "Gar! Get me out of here! I'm scared!"

"I...tr...ing...ge...ou."

Almost. She could almost understand it. But the voice was different. It wasn't Gar's. "Who...who is this?"

"L...an."

Lan? She didn't know anyone named Lan. It mattered not. If Lan could help her get out of the mess she was in, then so be it. "Help me, Lan. The dark is almost upon me."

"Not Lan. Lazaan."

The assassin? No. It could not be. It just couldn't be. What happened to Gar? Why was Lazaan there? The light was only a handbreadth thick now. In a moment, there would be none left and it would be totally black.

Two hands suddenly emerged from the dark and grabbed her shoulders, and then the light was gone.

"I've got you."

She closed her eyes and screamed.

The hands were shaking her—hard. She struggled to knock them away. "No, no, no, no, no!"

"Darlee, open your eyes. You're safe now."

She ceased her struggles and pried one eye open then the other. The warlock assassin Lazaan, his brow soaked in sweat, was indeed the one who had been holding her, but crowded around were Regent Tarlok, Commander Savan, Prince Brumaine, and, most importantly, her foster father, Captain Brusk. She dove into his arms. "I was so scared."

Brusk stoked her hair and repeatedly kissed the top of her head. "There there. It's over. You're okay. Thank the gods, you're all right."

Tilting her head, she looked up into his face. There were tears in his eyes and streaming down his cheeks. "What happened?"

"That thing! That thing behind the flames messed with yer

mind. The regent here"—he nodded at Tarlok—" was worried ya couldn't be helped, but this fellah"—the captain now nodded at Lazaan—"fixed ya. Everything's better now. Ya'r well."

Darlee recalled her previous encounter with the being behind the flames. It had locked her physically, but her mental shield had held up. When Hiss tackled her, she broke free of the magical hold.

Whoever it was, must have captured her mind when she was talking to Gar. Obviously, her resistance to his control failed completely. She wondered why, but then recalled the wine. It must have weakened her. And she still had that headache. She would be more careful about imbibing again.

When Brusk finally released her, she faced Lazaan. "I guess I owe you my thanks."

"Humph. I guess you do, but I only did it because I got paid. You're still someone I hold ill feelings toward. I doubt anything can change that."

Recalling how she'd embarrassed him in their magical battle at Rock House, she doubted he ever would. Still, she had to make the effort. She held out her hand. "Maybe not, but there's no harm in trying."

Lazaan looked at the proffered hand, quickly scanned the faces of those gathered, and then accepted it. "I'll agree to that much."

The exchange was short, but it still gave Darlee a small sense of relief that perhaps Lazaan was no longer a sworn enemy.

The circle of people around her eased back some, and for the first time she was able to take in her surroundings. To her left, the road led to a wall with an open archway. To her right, it stretched off into the night. In the darkness, she could make out the steep-hilled countryside and the black shape of mountains against the starlit sky. "Where are we?"

Regent Tarlok stepped closer. "We are outside the walls of the city of Lymos. If I may, I would like to touch you to check the healing."

With a nervous glance at Lazaan, she nodded. Tarlok touched her forehead and knit his brows in concentration. Lifting his fingers, he smiled. "I sense no distress in your mind. Lazaan has done a very commendable job."

Lazaan snorted. "When I take a contract, I fulfill it. I find your checking an insult to my skills."

The regent faced him. "My apologies. No insult was meant, merely a concern for the girl, but now that you are once more free of any obligation, I would hire you as well."

"To do what? At the moment, my mana is sorely drained. I doubt I could do anything."

"It is not your magical skills I desire, but, as merchant Orvest has put it, your esteem amongst your compatriots in the Riaz assassin guild."

"My esteem? What of it.?"

"I want you to gather all of the assassins to rid the city of the Moricans. Tell every one of them I will pay them a sum of fifty gold pieces each, and for you—two hundred."

"That's...that's five times what Alban Hamak paid. Are you good for it?"

"You have it on my honor as regent of Piaxia. To show good faith, I will give you one hundred gold pieces now. The rest I will pay when you have collected all of your comrades."

Lazaan grinned then slapped his hands together. "You have a contract. Meet us tomorrow night at the merchant hall. Be sure to bring the gold with you. As for now, I will take that up-front payment."

Tarlok waved a hand at one of his warlocks. "Prattrow, bring me your purse."

A warlock, much grey in his beard, produced a coin belt from under his robe. "My regent, here it is."

He handed it to Tarlok, who withdrew from it the necessary coins to pay Lazaan. Darlee could not help but notice how empty the wallet was after the assassin had been paid. How would the regent ever obtain the balance in one day?

After recounting the coins, Lazaan hefted his pack. "I'd best get back down into the city. Until tomorrow night then, one hand after the sun sets."

Tarlok smiled. "Until then."

She watched as the assassin entered the city and disappeared from sight in the dark. Gathered near Tarlok were his brother and merchant Orvest. Savan put a hand on Tarlok's shoulder. "Well, little brother. You've given away all our gold and promised to pay more with gold you do not have. Just how do you intend to come up with all that coin?"

"There is always a way." He turned to the merchant. "Tell me, Orvest. Who is the money lender in town?"

"Bashar, the accountant. He handles all the small loans for the big merchants, even me. His recordkeeping is impeccable, and his honesty is down to the smallest copper. I daresay, he must have at least a couple hundred in gold held for me, but that won't be enough."

Tarlok waved a hand in dismissal. "No, you've done your part. At this point, you need to continue and get your people to safety along with those of my retinue and the Sechlanders as well. I only need instructions to this Bashar's house and I shall procure the necessary loan tonight."

"What if he won't give it to you?"

The regent slapped his brother on the back. "Then I shall bring this big oaf along to help me persuade him. Either legitimately or not, I will return with the funds."

Orvest scratched the side of his head. "Hmm. I suspect the two of you will not be enough to convince him. There are at least two guards on duty all the time, and then there is his house retinue as well. You might find yourself outnumbered."

"I shall bring two warlocks with me and a couple of soldiers. I'll leave Prattrow and the rest with you. He knows what to do. Get to safety. Whether I succeed or not, you can no longer make a difference. If Darlee's message got through, then you need only wait out the storm until relief comes from Piaxia. If she failed, then once the Morican invasion fleet arrives, there is no safety for any of us."

Orvest detailed the directions to the estate of the accountant then Tarlok and his team entered the city. As she watched them go and the others get up, ready to continue their journey inland, she noted Prince Brumaine and Lieutenant Var dallying near the gate. What were they up to? Despite a call from her foster father to hurry up and follow, she made for the two men. "Why aren't you joining the others?"

Brumaine smiled at her. "It's Kero. I owe him my life...twice. Somehow, he got left behind. I've decided I'm going back to look for him. It's the least I can do."

Kero. She had forgotten about him as well. She considered the handsome face of the prince and then recalled the disappointed one of the Riazian. Did he care for her? Or was he just upset about her infatuation with Brumaine? Looking at the prince again, was there ever any hope? Perhaps it was time she looked out for her own interests, whether the boy or the man. "If you're going, then I'm coming with you."

When she felt a tug on her upper arm, she turned to see Captain Brusk. "Come on, Darlee. Leave these Morican trash alone. I just got ya back from near death. I'll not lose you again."

The prince nodded. "For once, I'm in agreement with your foster father. This is dangerous business. There's a good chance we may be killed in this endeavor. Despite your magical skills, this is not the kind of thing for a young girl to get involved in. You nearly died scant hands ago."

One other thing gnawed at her. Lasha. She had failed to protect and save the girl. Even allowing for the influence of the wine, her actions had caused the girl's death. Had she not sought refuge in The Fisherman's Friend, Lasha would still be alive. Then there was Janina. Something needed to be done to turn back the Morican takeover. "If I cannot go with you, then I will go on my own."

She'd started toward the gate when Brusk grabbed her from behind and threw her over his shoulder. "Ya'll not be going, even if I have to carry ya all the way."

He probably meant it. Knowing the captain the way she did there was no doubting the headstrong attitude. Since he took her in, she had come to love him as much as any child would their own father, so what she was about to do was something akin to treason. She touched his neck and released a small lightning shock.

Together, they fell to the ground, but she was first to recover. "Forgive me, Father, but this is something I must do."

Brusk sat up and rubbed his neck while looking at her. "That stung, it did. Ya got Silk's independent attitude, that's for sure."

She took his hand and pulled hard to help him stand. "Maybe a little, but I think there's more in me of what's good in you."

"Well, then." He brushed off his leggings then straightened. "If that's the case, I guess I can't stop ya."

She hugged him. "I guess not." She kissed his cheek. "I'll be careful. I promise."

"I suppose that's possible, but just to be sure, I'm going to tag along. Ya might need a good sword."

She smiled, and her eyes moistened. How she had come to love him. "All right, as long as it's understood I'm in charge."

He rubbed his neck once more. "I figured that."

She started for the gate, her foster father at her side. Pausing beside Brumaine and Var, she nodded toward the city. "Are you coming or not?"

The two exchanged glances then the prince smiled. "Lead the way."

She took a deep breath. Her first military foray and her with a prince, a lieutenant, and a captain under her command. She intended to succeed.

The sky broke, and it started to rain. It mattered not.

She walked through the gate.

CHAPTER 37

Though he smiled, everything that had just occurred spun the thoughts in Brumaine's mind. How had things gone from a quick escape from the city to not just one but three separate incursions back in?

The conversion of the assassin Lazaan to their cause, albeit with much gold involved, had been a piece of luck. If he could indeed marshal the warlock assassins into using their skills to eradicate Commander Oberus' forces, then much was possible.

Of course, the success of such a plan was contingent upon the achievement of the regent of Piaxia's mission to secure the necessary gold to placate the assassins.

Still, there was the problem of the invasion force. He doubted the number of assassins available was a match for an army of thousands. Even if the message by Darlee to her brother had properly gotten through, would he be able to convince the queen of Piaxia to send sufficient forces to stem the invasion, and would they arrive in time? Even if they did send enough, should the Moricans get to Riaz first then the defense of the island would be much easier than the conquest of it. Var had taught enough military tactics to understand what kind of advantage defending had compared to an assault.

Such a question was one only time could answer. No one asked, but it was easy to assume the bad idea of asking Darlee to attempt contacting her brother once again being beyond question. The possibility of her suffering at the will of the one behind the flames was too great a risk.

There was nothing to do but concentrate on the mission at hand—find Kero. Darlee did not know the way, but Var retraced every step of their way up the city. The lieutenant took the lead on the way back down.

The moon had already traversed most of the sky. In a couple of hands, it would be dawn. Being cold, wet, and tired was something he could ill afford. Should action be required, he would need all of his wits and reflexes. What he was feeling did not show in the others. Both Var and Brusk looked not only alert but even tense in anticipation of danger. He could only assume their lifelong military training had prepared them for it. Darlee, on the other hand, was as fresh as someone at the start of the day. He wondered if the healing done by Lazaan had something to do with her energy. If it had, it was something he could use right then. He would have to struggle through his weariness and hope it wasn't a hindrance.

As they neared the remains of Rock House it surprised him they had yet to see a single patrol of Morican troops. In fact, they had seen absolutely no one in the streets, though the hour would prevent the average local citizen from being out.

A mild glow still emanated from above the top of the remaining walls of the inn, indicating fire still burned despite the entire night having passed. Considering the steady rain since they began their descent into the city, it surprised him.

When they reached the back of the building, Var pointed. "Look. Someone is inside."

Through the open back door, he could see shadows moving. "The building yet burns and must be unsafe. Who would chance such a thing?"

Brusk withdrew his sword. "Must be that lord of Kero's. I got a feeling he's immune to fire."

Var shook his head. "No, there's more than one shadow. If it is the assassin master, he has company."

Darlee knelt in front of Var. "It must be Hiss. The imp always stayed close to Gragnishozar."

That made sense. After all, there had been no sight of the demon when they fled the building. Still, something didn't seem right. "The shadows are too large for either to be Hiss."

Their voices reached his ears. Though he couldn't make out the words, Brumaine recognized the tenor of the assassin lord, and the second voice was not the imp's. They needed to get closer to discover who was visiting. "Come. Let us enter. Whoever is with Gragnishozar, it is only one person. We are in no danger. Kero's guardian will cause us no harm and, most likely, prevent harm from coming to us."

He strode purposefully to the open door, the others scrambling to keep pace. Stepping into the room he noticed the many timbers that had collapsed into the room from above had been shoved to one side. Surprisingly, there was nothing that remained of the fire that had consumed Rock House, but the brazier, badly bent and straightened, had been reset in a place somewhat protected from the rain and lit. The odd drop would sizzle against the burning coals.

Gragnishozar was face to face with another man, one who Brumaine thought he had seen before. Yes, now he remembered. It was the warlock assassin who had scoured the street when he and Var had hidden in the home of Lasha. The sudden memory of the girl, now dead, saddened him for the moment, but there was no time to mourn. He needed to confront the two. "Gragnishozar, some of us have returned. We would know the status of things."

The big assassin master glared in his direction then waved a hand in dismissal. "Though it is good to see the girl has recovered, there is nothing for you to know. For hands, *this* fool, Petrius, has harassed me in an effort to barter on behalf of house Hamak. I barter with no one. He should leave my home...now. I would be at peace while I restore my strength. Tomorrow, I will finish punishing those who have destroyed my home."

The assassin sighed. "Indeed, I have tried for too long to convince you. I shall leave, but these foreigners block my way."

Brumaine checked quickly as to where his compatriots stood then moved to fill the gap that would allow Petrius exit. "Before you go, there are questions we would have answered. Foremost, where is Kero?"

Petrius glanced behind him, but the main hall was an impassable mound of burnt timbers offering no escape. He held out open hands. "I am not here to fight, but to deliver a message. Kero is held hostage at the Hamak estate. Alban wishes to barter the lad's safe return in exchange for the assassin lord's promise of no retribution against him or his family. In fact, he is prepared to assist in any way he can with the removal of the Morican forces. They have overstayed their welcome."

At least Kero was still alive. Prisoner, yes, but alive. That was welcome news, as was the fact that Alban was ready to evict the Moricans. "So the Hamaks are ready to openly defy Commander Oberus?"

Petrius smiled and shook his head. "Nothing so dramatic. His will be a passive resistance, obscure in nature. He is not wishing to terminate his friendship, merely to act in such a manner as to expedite their exit. I doubt the commander would even be able to recognize the subterfuge. I believe the terminology he used was *benign*."

He stifled a laugh. Benign? "In other words, he will do nothing."

"Exactly, but the act of doing nothing is still better than doing something where that something is helpful to the Moricans. It is all a matter of perspective."

His comrades all gave signals of helplessness through shrugs, rolled eyes, and smirks. Gragnishozar was facing his brazier, paying no attention to anyone. Facing Petrius once more, he read the man's expectant posture as Brumaine awaited a response. Should he tell the assassin of Lazaan's mission? There were still questions that needed answering before he did. "So you have been unable to make an arrangement with the assassin lord. What is your next step? Will you be returning to Alban Hamak to report?"

"Although the temptation to disappear into the night is there, I will return. At this time, I do not wish to make Alban Hamak an enemy. Besides, I have agreed to a contract. It is not yet fulfilled. Finally, there is Bokko. Though he is an adult and responsible for his own actions, he is not the best at fathoming what to do. He needs my help and guidance. After all, he is my friend."

Loyalty. It was something he could respect. He edged sideways to open a corridor to the door. "Go then. Make your report. Know this. I expect you to safeguard the life of Kero. Should I hear of his demise, there is nowhere you will be safe in Riaz."

Petrius nodded. "I understand." He stepped between Brumaine and the others and exited out into the night.

Darlee moved closer to Gragnishozar. "What about you? What are you going to do? Kero is your ward."

The big assassin lord turned and towered over the girl. When he dropped his massive hands on Darlee's shoulders, the girl's upper body disappeared beneath his fingers. Should Gragnishozar wish it, he could snap the girl's body in half in an instant. Brumaine had come to the conclusion Kero's lord was unpredictable. What would he do?

Fearing the worst, he was relieved to see the giant of a man crouch to eye level with Darlee.

"There is much power in you. I respect that. But you lack experience. Compassion is a curse. In time, you will come to understand such a statement. Kero knew the risks. His actions have led to his situation. He will have to accept whatever outcome he faces as a result of those actions."

Surprisingly, Darlee slipped from Gragnishozar's grip and hugged him round the neck. "I feel sorry for you. You have surrendered one of the most important things to learn in life. Love. Not only does Kero respect you, he loves you. One should never give up on love."

She kissed his cheek then backed away. Gragnishozar rose, touched the spot on his cheek where Darlee's lips had brushed then turned his back to the girl and faced the brazier once more. "Enough of human sentiment. It is time for you and your party to leave. I will only ask once."

Darlee sighed, turned, and headed out the door. He and the others followed. Brusk looked into the sky. "It will be morning soon. We must find shelter before Morican troops discover us."

There was movement in the street. When Brumaine looked farther, he noted several small groups of people headed toward the wharf.

Darlee smiled. "Come. I know just where to go."

When they stepped into the street, those people they espied paused only a moment to glance at them then continued on their way. A number of them held some kind of small light in their hands, glowing embers really, what light they shed being negligible. He wondered at their use. Not one but two of them held the things to their mouths. The embers glowed brighter, and then the individuals withdrew the devices and exhaled a plume of smoke. He had no idea what the purpose of it was.

Darlee, in the meantime, had caught up with four women, two with the glowing devices. She nodded to those in the group, who nodded back. No words were exchanged, but by their demeanor, Brumaine assumed they had accepted her presence amongst them. Darlee motioned for him and the others to follow.

When they reached the last street before the docks, Darlee turned in, the four following. All the other people out and about continued on down the hill to the wharf and were boarding the many small fishing vessels that occupied the inner part of the pier. Fishermen. They must start early.

Like Darlee and the women, he, Var, and Brusk entered a dingy tavern. The sign above the entrance called it The Fishermen's Friend. Mostly dark inside, the only light was from a single candle set on the bar at the far end. A portly fellow, several days unshaven, and, Brumaine suspected from the smell of body stink, as many days unwashed, was cleaning mugs.

Darlee placed her hands on the bar. "Good morning, Mudge. My friends and I need rooms."

The fellow scowled, looked from one woman to another of those who stood beside Darlee, then put down the mug he was holding. "All right. I'll rent them the rooms."

The four women nodded at Darlee and left. Brusk let out a low chuckle. "I recognized the look those women gave. My Silk gives that one to me now and then. Despite being a demoness, she's still a woman, and they tend ta stick together."

Mudge led them to a narrow staircase at the left side of the building. Upstairs were a number of small rooms. The one Brumaine got was barely large enough to stand in and close the door. He was crammed in with a single bed and a small table.

The early morning light before sunrise was lightening the sky.

He closed the shutters and flopped on the bed. The bed was straw stuffed and lumpy. Still, as tired as he felt, it was sorely welcome. He would be asleep in moments.

CHAPTER 38

The day had passed somewhat uneventfully. Petrius had returned sometime in the early morning and he and Bokko whispered together, with Kero unable to hear much save that no deal had been struck with Gragnishozar.

Both men had slept the morning away until such time food was brought by one of Alban's servants when the sun was high. Only then did they undo Kero's bonds to allow him to eat. It took him some time to rub life back into his wrists. The tight ropes had cut his circulation severely. Eventually, he had tried a healing, with some success. Bokko, despite already imbibing once more, had kept a close eye on him to make sure he dared not attempt magic for any other purpose.

Now, he watched out the window as the day waned, Bokko dozed, and Petrius alert. Kero's reverie was broken when shouting could be heard out in the yard and a hornet's nest of activity stirred in the room. Petrius roused Bokko, but before the fat man could get out of his chair, Commander Oberus, with two soldiers in his wake, burst in and pointed at Kero.

"Bring him...now!"

The two soldiers hustled over and hoisted him by the elbows then hauled him out the door. The assassins trailed behind as Kero was unceremoniously dragged down the stairs, his feet unable to do more than bang on each step as his ankles were tied together.

Rushing out the open front door of the house, Oberus brought everyone to halt with a raised hand. Kero glanced around. Quite a number of Morican troops were scattered across the courtyard, all brandishing weapons and collectively staring at the estate gate. Following their gaze, he looked out into the street and spotted what drew their attention—a dozen golems of the more usual earth, sticks, and stones design headed directly their way.

When two lieutenants drew near, asking Oberus for instructions, he strained to listen in. The commander studied the oncoming behemoths for a moment. "We've tangled with these things before. Arrows are useless. Swords can cut, but you have to get too close. Those things may be slow, but they've got the reach. Only a halberd has the blade and length needed to do the job and we have only a handful. Far too few.

No, I think we'll rely on our hostage here. In the midst of those monsters you can see the assassin lord in his black clothing. Let's get this brat out in the open where he can be seen. Take him there and call out a threat to make the lad's guardian take notice and halt his advance."

Kero believed their attempt to use him as a hostage to deter Gragnishozar was useless. He knew his lord well. Whatever happened to Kero would be a result of his own actions. Such was the mindset of the assassin master. He steeled his mind against the worst—a painful death.

One of the lieutenants grabbed Kero and pulled him toward the gate. Producing a dagger, he waved it in the air toward Gragnishozar. "Hold there or else"—the soldier moved to hold the blade near Kero's throat—"your ward di—"

Gragnishozar pointed at the lieutenant. The man froze in place. Then, slowly, the lieutenant moved the blade away from Kero and turned the point toward his own chest. Kero could see the eyes of the man as wide as could be. The officer's face etched in horror as his other hand joined with the first to grip the handle then plunge the blade into his own chest. With a spurt of blood, the lieutenant's eyes fluttered closed, his hands went slack, and he dropped to the ground.

Gragnishozar had acted to save him. The surprise of such an action momentarily froze Kero. He was unattended. Kero glanced quickly at Oberus, but the commander was focused on his lord. Should he try and escape? The golems hammered at the gate. It would fall soon. Men backed farther away. Perhaps there was a chance.

With his hands tied behind his back and his ankles tied together, he could hardly move or conduct magic. Hopping, he positioned his backside toward the fallen soldier. First crouching, he then fell onto the man and searched for the dagger with his fingers. If only he could cut his bonds, then escape would be so much easier.

A cry from Oberus made Kero turn to see the two soldiers who had brought him outside rushing toward him. When they were halfway, both men burst into flames and fell screaming to the ground. Kero spared only a moment more to watch them flop and roll before resuming his search for the grip on the dagger. Found it! Leaning forward, he struggled and pulled the weapon partway from the lieutenant's chest. Now he only need guide the leather strap tying his wrists onto the exposed blade.

Glancing once more in the direction of the commander, he panicked at the sight of the second lieutenant, with two more soldiers, leading the charge his way. In a flash, a bolt of lightning arced into the lead Morican trooper who flew backward to land dead, smoke wafting up from his blasted chest.

A second bolt killed the other soldier in a similar fashion, but the third bolt only knocked the lieutenant down. Was Gragnishozar's mana waning? It took much to create the golems. It was possible. As the man struggled to rise, Kero hurried the pace with which he rubbed the binding against the blade. Pulling hard, he could feel the straps parting as the edge of the dagger cut through. His arms were free!

Twisting, he grasped the hilt of the weapon and finished wrenching it free from the torso of the dead lieutenant. Now, he needed to cut those bonds wrapping his ankles. Checking on the progress of the second lieutenant, he noted the man now up and bearing down on him. No new bolt from Gragnishozar appeared. There was no time. He needed to act. Summoning his own magic, he fired his strongest lightning strike at close range into the man's chest as the fellow was mere hands away. Not only did the man's chest explode, showering Kero in blood and gore, but the lieutenant flew backward several paces.

He wiped at the blood, spattered across his eyelids, to clear his vision. In the shock of being bombarded by human flesh pieces, he had dropped the dagger. Where was it? He scanned around him without success when a searing sharp pain struck him in the back near his left shoulder. Turning, he discovered Oberus standing behind him, a glare of pure menace on his face with bared teeth and a scowl. The commander's right hand was behind Kero, and as Oberus' arm twitched, another wave of pain flooded through Kero from the same spot in his back. The dagger he had dropped was embedded in him, and the commander had twisted it to further the damage. His vision clouded, and he bent forward in a futile attempt to escape the dagger.

Oberus waved to Gragnishozar. "Cease your attack, or, with one more twist, this lad dies."

The hammering at the gate stopped. The golems had stopped their assault. They swayed gently where they stood, arms slack. Gragnishozar walked forward until he stood at the gate. "I will make you a contract. You will ensure the safety and life of my ward, and I will retreat."

"Not good enough. What is to stop you from assaulting again tomorrow? Here's my deal. You promise never to attack again, and I will guarantee no harm shall ever come to Kero."

This was a lousy deal. First of all, he doubted Oberus' word, and without Gragnishozar's help, he doubted there would ever be a way to rid Lymos of the Moricans. Such a deal would doom Riaz. "No, master, don't agree. I can accept my fate. You must save our country from these usurpers."

Gragnishozar bowed his head. Calm settled over the area. All stood silent in anticipation of his answer.

His lord lifted his head. "Countries come and go, as do the lives of people. In another hundred years, much will have changed, but I will still be here. I have recently been reminded of what is, in fact, one quality I lack. I shall not forget it. To know that for the rest of my eternal life I must bear the burden of your death when I have already failed to defend Maresh's, both of whom I have agreed as my wards, is more than I can accept."

Gragnishozar faced Oberus. "Morican, you have a contract. Do not test it. My fury will chase and kill you to the ends of the world."

The assassin lord turned and strode away. As he did, the

golems collapsed into piles of what they were comprised of—mud, sticks, and stones.

Kero stared in disbelief at the retreating figure of his lord. This was not like the unyielding figure he had come to know. What would happen to his homeland? Had Gragnishozar doomed it to Morican rule? The thought shook him and brought a tear to stream down his cheek and splash in the dust of the courtyard.

Beneath the roar of approval by the Morican soldiers, he could make out the sound of fast-approaching steps.

Petrius knelt beside him. "Hold still Kero. Once Oberus removes the blade, I will heal you."

Petrius nodded at the commander who, with a jerk, pulled the dagger out. Kero almost fainted as he reeled and was caught by Petrius. The assassin placed a hand on the wound and immediately began the healing process.

In the time it took for the magical heal to complete, Kero considered what future lay in store for him. At best, he would forever be a prisoner of the Moricans. Coupled with that were beatings, torture, starvation, and jailing in some dark hole. He expected nothing less.

Oberus was marshaling his troops. "All right, first things first. Let's move those slag heaps away from the estate. I don't want them to spring alive once again when they are so close. Once that is done, we begin tomorrow in earnest in taming the rest of this city. It's time to show these Riazians who's in charge around here."

From the front step of his manor, Alban Hamak stepped into the courtyard. "That would be me. Do not forget our deal, Commander. You are here by my good graces. No ruffian presence will make the citizens of Riaz provide the goods and services you would seek. Only my merchant guild can do that, and I am now in sole control of such. It is time not for further flagrant aggravation, but gentle coercion into acceptance of the new order."

Oberus moved to stand next to Alban then squinted at the sky. "It will be dark soon. With the end of this day comes the end of our deal. In the morning, there will indeed be a new order, but not the one you envisioned. On behalf of King Jessop, I will be laying claim to this island as part of the realm of Morica."

"Then you will find no help from me or the merchant guild. Without my support, the guild will resist, and you will have achieved nothing."

"I don't need your support. Their resistance will be temporary. Once a few get put to the sword, the rest will fall in line." The commander still held the dagger he had pulled from Kero's back. He shifted his grip on the weapon. "Starting with you." With ferocity, he plunged it into Alban. The head of the Hamak family went limp and fell to the ground.

The commander turned to his troops. "Purge the compound. Not a single Hamak must live. Women, children, kill them all. I will not have any insurgency started by survivors."

Soldiers charged into the three homes. With horror, Kero could hear the shrieks of women and children as they fell to the swords of the Moricans. He exchanged a look with Petrius. In the eyes of the assassin, he could detect nothing but sorrow. Based on Gragnishozar's actions, there was no doubt the proposed deal Petrius was charged to make the night before had failed. No assassin lord, no Hamak family and the merchant guild, who was left to resist the Moricans?

CHAPTER 39

Having slept a good part of the day Brumaine chafed at being confined to the small room until dark.

He wasn't alone in this. Brusk also was relegated to wait. Darlee never left the building, but did visit the main room to obtain food and drink for him and the captain. He agreed she was the least likely to draw attention in the tavern.

Lieutenant Var, on the other hand, had exited The Fisherman's Friend. With his uniform, he would have free rein throughout the city as long as he avoided other Morican troops. The local citizens would give the officer a wide berth, afraid of repercussions should they in any way interfere with whatever business he was on.

With night having fallen, the plan was to gather together, hear what Var had to report, then make their way to the merchant guild hall in hopes of finding the Piaxians and the assassins. The hall was a scant block away with the pre-set meeting time one hand after dark. They would need to leave soon.

Rather than exit through the building, he and the others climbed out a window, scrambled down the exterior wall, and dropped into the alley behind.

Var waited at the bottom. Brumaine welcomed his mentor with a military clasping of wrists. "What can you tell us is happening in the town?"

"As expected, Kero's lord assaulted the Hamak estate. I followed at a safe distance. It's bad news. Not only did he withdraw from the fight, he promised never to attack again in exchange for a promise of his ward's safety."

Considering how Gragnishozar spoke the night before, Brumaine found the news surprising. He believed the assassin lord could have, over time, single-handedly wiped out Oberus and his troops. Had Darlee's simple kiss and statement affected him so? With his amazing powers no longer in play, the success of the Piaxian regent's plan was now paramount. "Then we best get to the hall and hope Tarlok was able to secure the funds to pay the assassins."

"The news gets even worse. After the battle, I could hear the screams of women and children from the Hamak estate. I fear the worst...the commander has put all of the Hamaks to death."

Women and children? Had Oberus no morals at all? "If so, he is a monster. No severe demise can be too harsh for him. Alban Hamak was too late in wishing the Moricans gone. He has paid the ultimate price."

Var led the way, and Brumaine walked beside Darlee as Brusk trailed one pace behind. "With Kero still held by Oberus and surrounded by hundreds of troops, it appears our wish to free him is impossible."

"Not impossible, merely more difficult. You are the one who vowed to rescue him. I concurred. Do not give up so easily. There must be a way. We have simply yet to find it. At least we can rest assured no harm has or will come to him until we discover how to retrieve him from their grasp."

Had he given up? What she said was true. His whole intent had been to do whatever it took to find the lad, even if it meant putting his own life in danger. Had such an altruistic goal fled him so quickly? No, he did not believe that. He just didn't know how to achieve the result desired. "Perhaps you are right. If all things go well tonight, we may yet ascertain a method by which we can rescue Kero."

She smiled. "I know we can."

In truth, the young girl amazed him. Of slight frame, with a patch over one eye, one would think her frame of mind would be one of avoidance of trouble, not of embracing it. Yes, there was her powerful level of magic to consider, but from what he knew of magic, it didn't fully manifest until puberty. What had occurred in her childhood to give her such strength of character? Nothing now fazed her—fighting against vastly superior numbers, confronting all powerful warlocks, swaying the mind of the assassin lord, and, yes, seeking the love of a foreign prince. He had not forgotten her interest in him.

He still considered her physical beauty to be somewhat less

than what he was accustomed to, but not as bad as he, at first, had judged. There was a fieriness about her that he found attractive. Perhaps a union with her was not such a bad idea after all. She would be a formidable ally, and the possibility of his offspring gaining her magical prowess was nothing to sneer at.

He glanced behind at the trailing Brusk. Such a marriage *would* have its consequences. His only hope would be the captain did not kill him first.

They arrived at the hall without encountering anyone save two men guarding the door—one a member of the assassin guild, and the other, one of the Piaxian soldiers. It was the latter who identified them and allowed them entry.

The last time in that hall he was convinced the Piaxians were behind his brother's murder. How things had changed. Bit by bit, he learned the awful truth of the plot engineered by Commander Oberus at the least, and, quite possibly, his father, King Jessop as well.

In the center of the hall were the Piaxians, Lazaan, and a number of rough-looking characters Brumaine could only assume were the members of the assassin guild. One individual who stood out was a portly fellow who stood close to Tarlok as he was dressed in finery.

The regent acknowledged their arrival with a nod then faced the well-fed man. "Bashar, welcome the balance of our retinue...Darlee Murdach and her foster father Captain Brusk from Sechland, Prince Brumaine, and Lieutenant Var from Morica."

When the man offered his hand in welcome, Brumaine made note of the ink stains on his fingers. They denoted him as a scribe. The man must be the money lender the Piaxians had sought out. "Greetings, Bashar. Are you here to preside over this transaction?"

The man gave a gleeful chuckle. "Most assuredly. I must tell you I was surprised to find the regent of Piaxia at my doorstep in the middle of the night, and accompanied by force I might add, but once he described his need, and my being a man of business, I welcomed him into my home and negotiated terms most favorable."

He wondered who the "terms most favorable" benefited. No doubt the accountant would come out the winner. "It is good to hear that friendly terms have been worked out. I worried the regent would fail in acquiring the funds needed and this meeting would be less than friendly."

Bashar chuckled once more. "Friendly indeed, and gathered here are all friends of mine. I know each and every one of these fine gentlemen on a personal basis. In fact, I handle the financial affairs of several."

Fine gentlemen. Assassins all. He allowed a small smile at the comment, but withheld the snide remark that percolated in his head for fear of the gathered *gentlemen* taking offense.

Lazaan moved to take the center floor between Brumaine, Bashar, and Tarlok. "Enough of the pleasantries. There is a contract to finalize. Did you bring the gold?"

Without any aplomb, Savan dropped a large sack on the nearest table, it landing with a loud thud and the chink of coins inside. "The gold is here, but so far we only have your word, not the ones of your comrades. How do we know they will uphold the contract?"

The steely glare from Lazaan at those gathered told volumes. "If any man here breaches the contract, then they will have to deal with me."

Since arriving, Brumaine had done a count of the assassins. Including Lazaan, there were eleven in the room. To his surprise, he noted Petrius standing in the back. Was not the man under contract to Oberus? How did it work when contracts competed? "Explain to me how assassins serve two masters? I see one here I know to be in service to the Morican commander." He pointed toward Petrius.

Everyone turned to look at the man, with those closest to him edging away. Lazaan moved to stand before him. "Explain yourself."

Petrius held up his hands in surrender. "I have come here unsure of what to do. When our original contract expired, Bokko and I signed on for another. Last night, after visiting with the assassin lord, I ran into another member who told me of this meeting. Today, I witnessed something more foul than I could have imagined...the wanton murder of young children. Even babes. Our creed prevents me from breaching my contract, yet I have the strongest desire to do so."

Lazaan stepped close and placed a hand on Petrius' shoulder. "You know the rules on a broken contract."

The assassin sighed. "Yes, death, though seeing the bodies of innocent newborns thrown into a pyre with all the rest slain was a sight worse than death."

Lazaan shook his head. "Regardless, you cannot be offered a contract here tonight. A contract can be canceled, but it cannot be broken by a guild member. Should the awarder of the contract commit a breach, then you would be free of it. Has such a thing occurred?"

"Not yet, though I searched today for such a thing. Believe me, when such an event occurs, I will be quick to void the balance."

"Go then. Heed your contract, but be watchful. You may yet get your wish."

Petrius nodded and left the hall. Once he was gone, Bashar doled out the gold to the guild members present. When he finished, there was still a fair amount of coin in the sack. Brumaine learned there were twenty members to the guild, but with Petrius and Bokko still under contract elsewhere, the assassin lord with his own contract of promised inaction and the death of a member named Stod, combined with five members who refused to participate, only eleven remained to be paid.

A troubling thought kept recurring in Brumaine's mind. Yes, he hated Commander Oberus but the rest of his countrymen, although guilty of the crimes just committed, were merely foot soldiers following orders. None would dare not follow a command.

Now, he was watching as the Piaxians and the Riaz assassins plotted the demise of each and every one of them. The plan was for the guild members to do what they did best, kill discreetly. This was a difficult thing to simply stand by and allow it to happen.

"Tarlok, is it not possible to spare the lives of these men? Surely, there must be a way to get at Oberus?"

The regent broke away from the conversation he was holding with Lazaan and faced him. "Assuming such a thing was possible, and Oberus was caught out in the open, something I am told he has yet to do, then what?"

He glanced at Var, who shrugged. When it came to the answer, he was on his own. "I am still a prince of the land. With Oberus, eliminated I should be able to retake command."

"I consider that highly unlikely. Most probably, whoever is second in command will take over and resume the mission. You are an outcast, responsible for the death of Morican troops. Any fealty would be dismissed by now. Your return to their encampment would most certainly mean imprisonment and, in all likelihood, your death."

Var put a hand on his shoulder. "My liege, the regent is correct. There is no chance of reconciliation with the troops currently here. Your only hope lies at home in Morica."

Savan guffawed. "You think there's hope for him there? You're dreaming. He won't be able to set one foot in Morence before being arrested and disappearing forever. If you ask me, your only hope is the death of your king. Possibly the rest of your family, too."

Brumaine balled his fists as the sensation of reddened cheeks flushed upward. "You would suggest I succumb to the same baseless crime as Oberus? What kind of person do you think I am?"

"Definitely not your father's son. *He* wouldn't hesitate."

It was one insult too far. He reached for his sword, but once he grasped the hilt, Var's hand closed over his. "No Sire, the Piaxian commander is goading you. You must reason through this, not react rashly."

Savan had already drawn his own massive blade. "Aw, Lieutenant, you spoiled all the fun." He returned his weapon to its sheath on his back.

Tarlok stepped in front of his brother. "Forgive this big oaf. It is his way. Still, you must remember your place, Prince. You are safe at my acquiescence. Outside of your faithful Lieutenant Var, none in this room would grant you leniency. Concoct what plans you must for your return home. If possible, without returning to war between our two countries, I will assist in any way I can. If it comes to it, I am prepared to offer you sanctuary in Piaxia, but until then, do not try my patience here."

Though a rebuttal was in his mind and his mouth open to utter it, he snapped his jaw shut. He had been put in his place. Perhaps the best path did lie with the regent's suggestion—devise a safe means of return that would not result in a confrontation with the court.

No, a better plan was required. He needed to return to Morica aboard whatever flagship led the invasion fleet, and not as a criminal, but a hero. The question remained, how would that be possible?

One thing for sure, he needed to devise a way to save what Morican troops he could before Riazian assassins killed them all. "Regent Tarlok, if the opportunity arises, will you spare my people?"

The Piaxian pawed at his chin. "Only *if*...the opportunity arises."

CHAPTER 40

Five days had passed since the last attack by Kero's lord and though the camp was much quieter ever since, not so the streets of Lymos.

When Oberus sent ten men to the market to collect stall fees and inform all the merchants of who now was in charge, four did not return. When Kero learned they all died from magical attacks, there were only a handful of possibilities. Either his lord had decided to kill Moricans in the street, which would, in a debatable way, not void his contract—something highly unlikely knowing Gragnishozar's applied value to one's solemn word, or the Piaxians had not fled the city and were still in town sowing mayhem where they could.

Six more were killed on the second day. By the third day, the group that left the camp was at least forty men strong, including many archers, bows at the ready. Only five returned.

No Morican left after that point. Still, supplies were scarce, and meals had consisted only of porridge the day before last, and yesterday...none, just water.

They let Kero out a couple of times a day to use the latrine and stretch his legs. The misery that filled the camp was obvious. The men gave him angry stares and grumbled.

There was also the small possibility it was Darlee, but such wanton killing was unlike her, or at least as much as he had gathered of her character in their few times together. She had twice, in his presence, restrained from attacking the Moricans with the intent to kill. Surely, she had not undergone such a change of persona since then.

One more explanation floated in his mind. He turned to his two jailers. "Petrius, you know what's going on out there. Are your fellow members of the assassin guild behind these attacks?"

The man glared at him then faced away and returned to the conversation he was having with Bokko.

So, it *was* the assassins. Were they acting on their own, or had someone hired them to do so? He had spied on enough meetings of the guild to know the rules well enough. Never breach a contract. Had Oberus breached first?

No, not Oberus...Alban Hamak. Kero recalled some of the hirings in the home of Bashar. Such dealings would have been on Alban's behalf. With his death, the contracts all became immediately void. Thinking back, over the past number of days he had noted no other guild member within the estate. They must be free agents again.

So why were Petrius and Bokko still working? Either they were unaware of what was happening outside the gate...unlikely, or Oberus offered them new contracts and they were bound. Considering Oberus needed warlocks to guard him, Kero suspected the latter as the only real possibility.

Petrius often left the grounds to accompany Morican troops. He must know what was going on. How much conflict must be in his mind regarding the situation? Based on his reaction to Kero's question, the assassin must be disappointed with the current predicament.

But what of Bokko? The fat oaf, always with a drink in hand and often food in mouth, was as happy as could be. Getting paid to watch a bound fifteen-year-old with limited warlock skills was a perfect job for him.

The two men were close friends. That much was obvious. Could he drive a wedge between them? Despite having the attention of either man, he was going to try. "It must be tough to sit here all day when your fellow assassins are terrorizing the Moricans."

Bokko took the bait and looked his way. "Those fools took the wrong side. Morica will rule this island, make no mistake about that. Petrius and I will be lords when that happens." He nudged the other assassin. "Right?"

After a quick glance at Kero, Petrius looked at his feet. "Maybe."

This was the opening Kero was looking for. "Petrius is not such a fool as you, Bokko, to think the Moricans will grant you such status. After all, you're still Riazians. Blood always trumps loyalty. You don't have the right kind of blood in you."

Bokko rose from his seat and took a step in Kero's direction. "Why you liar. I'll tea—"

Noise from the courtyard cut through to the room, and both assassins went to the window. The sound of footsteps rushing up the steps preceded the door bursting open and four soldiers entered, one pointing at Kero. "Bring him. Oberus wants both of you and the lad outside. We're under attack."

Petrius was first to move. "Golems? The assassin lord?"

"No. Warlocks. They've already killed the watch guard."

"You have a couple hundred men. Fight them off."

"There's only thirty-five in the camp. Oberus sent out the rest to get food. They must have been counting us."

Petrius and Bokko hoisted Kero from his chair and dragged him from the room to the top of the stairs. Kero looked into the fat man's face, wide-eyed and breathing heavily. "Will you fight against the guild if ordered?"

The assassin let go, causing Kero to stumble, forcing Petrius to grab him to halt his descent.

"You idiot. He almost fell down the stairs. It might have killed him."

"If Lazaan's out there, I'm not fighting." Bokko turned and fled back into the room, slamming the door shut.

The four soldiers, who were halfway down the steps, turned and rushed back up and into the room. There was some yelling until Kero heard a scream, then a strangled sound.

Kero glanced at Petrius. "So much for his lordship."

The four Moricans exited the room, one wiping then sheathing a bloody sword, and passed Kero and Petrius on the stair once more, the leader pausing to stare into the assassin's face. "Don't make the same mistake. Bring the boy."

Petrius hesitated long enough for the soldiers to be out of earshot then leaned close to Kero's ear. "We must keep each other alive." He bent to cut the leather strap that bound Kero's ankles.

Kero nodded. The assassin was right. Surviving the attack was all that mattered now. "Cut my wrist bonds. I can do nothing with my hands tied behind my back."

He shook his head. "Not now. I'll do it when it won't be noticed."

Free to walk, he descended the stairs and exited into the courtyard to see Morican archers firing arrows at men beyond the gate some thirty paces away. Walking at the forefront was Lazaan, his hands and fingers spread wide. When arrows neared, instead of following their trajectory, they veered high and over the advancing men.

He knew how magic worked. One never missed a stationary target. In the time it took for the Moricans to fire a round of arrows, six bolts of lightning flashed in from the assassins, and six archers fell with only one showing signs of life after hitting the ground.

From the open doorway of the main home, Oberus waved inward. "Everyone inside. We need to take this fight to close quarters."

At Petrius' urging, he broke into a run and joined the crush of men jamming through the open door. He glanced toward the gate the assassins had reached. Hacking at it were both Savan and Brusk. The Piaxians and the Sechlanders were aiding in the attack! He could even see Darlee standing close by. She must have recovered from her catatonic state. Even Brumaine and Var were at hand. It appeared everyone had gathered to bring the fight to the Moricans.

Once inside the compound, they found the door to the villa was closed and barred. What archers remained took up positions to fire at both the doorway and the shuttered windows.

Oberus grabbed Kero and pulled him close. "I noticed they stopped their damned magic when you were among the troops." He pulled a dagger and held it close to Kero's throat.

The room, at first a beehive of men drawing weapons and crowding toward the middle, grew quiet as they waited. Kero did a quick count—twenty-one, including Oberus. Their numbers were already thinned.

A hammering began at the door. The commander took a half step toward it. "Hear me out there. Quit this compound, or I'll kill the boy."

The attack on the door stopped, followed by a succession of three knocks.

"This is Lazaan, the new master of the assassins. I have accepted a contract on behalf of all in my guild to eliminate every Morican in this estate. Kero is no friend of mine. Ask him, or ask Petrius. Either will confirm I speak the truth. Those who have contracted me have given me the option to offer mercy to any soldier who surrenders. I will give you a quarter hand to do so."

A quarter hand. That wasn't long. Murmurs filled the room as those farthest from the commander whispered to soldiers nearby. The fear in the room was palpable. The men did not want to die, but none dared challenge their commander.

There was more shuffling outside the door.

"This is Prince Brumaine, your rightful liege. Those men inside loyal to our country, listen to me. You have been deceived. Commander Oberus has lied to you. He engineered the death of Prince Doren. The assassins hired to do such a deed are still with you. I can prove this claim. Surrender now, re-pledge your loyalty, and hear me out. The quarter hand is running down."

Kero watched Oberus but felt someone behind him, cutting the bonds at his wrist. He turned his head to find Petrius. "Hurry. Things will get out of hand any moment."

The commander turned and made eye contact with Kero. He drew his sword. "You killed Doren." He spun to face the men. "Kill the assassin!"

Kero's hands were free, and he tossed a weak bolt at Oberus. The man fell down, and the soldiers who had begun to move on Petrius froze to look at their fallen commander. Kero had kept the bolt light in power. Oberus, now on his hands and knees, was shaking his head, probably trying to clear his mind. Kero pointed at the downed Morican officer. "What Brumaine says is true. Yes, Petrius and Bokko committed the murder, though they did so at the command of Oberus through Alban Hamak. He is the criminal.

Arrest Petrius and me if you must, but Oberus, too. Open the doors and submit to your true leader, Prince Brumaine."

A man from behind Petrius dove at him and plunged a sword into his hip. "You killed the prince!"

Kero fired a more powerful bolt at the man, killing him where he stood. Men started yelling—some saying, "Listen to the prince," others demanding loyalty to the commander. The door broke open in a shower of wood fragments, and many backed away from those entering.

Kero grabbed hold of Petrius. There was so much blood issuing from the wound! He placed a hand on it and summoned his magic to heal, but he was all but drained, having used most to stun Oberus and kill the other man. Normally, he would have enough in reserve, but the starvation diet of the last few days must have had an effect. "I need a warlock to save this man. He's dying!"

He returned his concentration to Petrius. Concern for the fallen man now consumed him. He no longer considered the man an enemy. Instead, a protector. Despite how he pressed, the blood still flowed. The assassin's eyes were now closed. He must have slipped into unconsciousness. He feared the man would be dead at any moment.

Around him, men dropped their weapons, and some knelt in submission. Brumaine's plea had won out. Kero searched those gathered in the room for a warlock to aid Petrius.

A small hand joined his. It was Darlee. He was amazed to see how fast the wound closed. The girl continued to concentrate on Petrius. After a while, she let up and smiled. "He'll live. The wound was deep, but I've mended everything. It felt good not to be too late as I was with Lasha."

He was pleased Petrius would live. Even better, the man began to stir and wake. Kero rose and then offered the assassin a hand in standing as well. The act of pulling the man to his feet hurt his wrist. Looking at it, his wrist was badly chafed and bruised from the lengthy time the bonds had been on. The other wrist was the same.

Darlee grabbed his wrists. "You're hurt as well. Let me heal those for you."

He waited patiently as she applied her magic to heal him. The softness of her hands and the gentleness of her touch made him think once more of his interest in the girl. While her gaze was fixed on his wrists, he studied her face. He tried to imagine what it would look like without the eye patch. The leather strap across her forehead and cheek creased her flesh and prevented a true picture of the girl. It didn't matter. He realized it wasn't her looks that mattered now, it was her demeanor. She was a caring person, neither selfish, nor arrogant, attributes anyone would find attractive.

She let go of his wrists and smiled. "All done."

He flexed both. There was no pain. "Thank you."

Everyone filed into the courtyard. Oberus, now bound as Kero had once been, was led out by Var. With Darlee at his side, he followed the procession to see what would happen next.

Prince Brumaine was standing to one side, surrounded by the Morican troops. A number of assassins and Piaxians stood outside that circle, keeping guard. The prince was detailing all that had occurred.

Oberus was once more on his knees. He must still be woozy. Lazaan and Tarlok were conversing, more than likely confirming the completion of the contract. Savan and Brusk were also having a private conversation. To Kero, it was a good sight. The control of his city by the Moricans was over. Perhaps things could return to normal.

In the midst of all this, a pigeon fluttered down from the sky to land beside Oberus. Var reached down to scoop up the bird. From its leg, he retrieved a scrap of vellum tied there. As he read the message, Oberus started to chuckle. What did the commander find so funny? Kero stepped close to the lieutenant. "What does it say?"

Before Var could reply, Oberus struggled to his feet. "I'll tell you what it says. The invasion fleet has arrived. Your efforts have been useless. Riaz will belong to Morica."

CHAPTER 41

Var pointed at the most westerly house. "Go inside to the second floor. There's a ladder to the roof. From there, you should have a clear view of the bay."

Darlee, along with Kero, Savan, and Brusk followed the instructions the lieutenant had given. When she stepped on the roof, the vista toward the Great Sea would have been beautiful if not for the large flotilla of boats just entering the harbor. It was as Oberus had claimed. The Morican invasion had arrived. She looked to her foster father. "What do we do?"

"We watch." He pointed farther out to sea. "Look...on the horizon...a second fleet."

She shaded her eyes to get a better look. Yes, it was true. Though still quite distant, a second fleet was bearing their way. It could only be the Piaxians. Her message had gotten through. "How long before they get here?"

"Hmm. I reckon it'll take them at least a hand or more to arrive. We'll have to survive until then."

Commander Savan moved quickly from one end of the roof to the other, pausing at all four corners and looking down. "The walls to this estate are sound. Provided we lock up the Moricans here, it may be possible to defend it until my people win through."

Brusk nodded. "Aye, that's a thought, but hightailing it out of here's a good one too."

Savan chuckled and slapped the captain on the shoulder. "Come now. You've been bristling for a fight for the past six days. Don't tell me you Sechlanders get squeamish when the time is upon you?"

"I'm not afraid, just not a fool either. If we had some reinforcements, yer plan might be a good one."

Reinforcements. It was an excellent idea, and she knew just where to get some. She grabbed Kero by the arm. "Come on. We've got to go get help."

Her foster father held out a hand to block her way. "Where're ya off to?"

Grinning, she pulled Kero tight. "To get his guardian. With Kero free, the contract binding Gragnishozar is ended. If anyone can bolster our forces, he can."

Brusk glanced out at the harbor and the entering boats. "It'll be a footrace to Rock House. You stay. I'll go."

She stepped in to give him a quick hug then separated. "He won't listen to you. Only Kero, and I might have some influence as well. You need to stay here with Commander Savan. Together, the two of you will best know how to defend this estate."

Savan tugged gently at Brusk. "She's right. Neither you nor I would have any sway with the assassin lord. Time is wasting. Let her go."

She smiled then dashed down the ladder, the stairs, into the courtyard and out of the estate with Kero at her side. The one nice thing she faced...the run was all downhill, not up. She would not get winded.

A block into the city, she glanced at Kero. "Maybe you'd better lead the way. You might know a faster route than me."

"Okay. Follow me."

Kero stayed on the main street for another block, but then he cut through an empty lot of mud, rocks, and weeds. She wondered if it was the one where Gragnishozar created the golems that night. After that, he led the way down an angled alley. When they emerged from it, Rock House, or what was left of it with the roof and part of one wall caved in at the third floor, was within a thirty pace dash.

Until this point, their luck had held, but as they began to cross the open stretch to the back door of Gragnishozar's private quarters, a squad of Morican soldiers marched up the street. One yelled for them to hold, but they kept running. The door was ajar, and Kero put his shoulder into it, forcing it the rest of the way open. He disappeared inside. Hopefully, the assassin lord waited there because if he didn't, then they would be trapped when the soldiers reached the building.

When she stepped inside, it warmed her to see Kero in the

embrace of his guardian. What didn't please her was finding Hiss in the room as well. The little demon was always a sign of trouble. No doubt the arrival of so many troops must have ferreted the imp from whatever hiding place he was holed up in.

One thing about Hiss, he was a great spy. Yes, he could run and hide better than anyone, but he also could sneak about and see much. She snatched him up. "Quick. How many troops have landed so far?"

"Too many. Too many. Maybe two...three thousand."

She dropped the imp and turned to Gragnishozar. "The time for greetings is over. We need you to come with us and defend our and your people."

The big assassin lord released Kero and moved to tower over her. "No one makes demands of me. I am grateful for the return of my ward, but that does not mean I will work without a contract."

A contract? He wanted to be paid? She shook her head. Understanding Gragnishozar was impossible. He was an enigma. She searched in her coin purse. It was almost empty. She held out the few meager coins. "I only have four coppers. I'm quite sure Regent Tarlok would be prepared to match whatever handsome price you require."

Gragnishozar grabbed Darlee's wrist and tilted her hand to empty the coins into one of his. "Four coppers will suffice. We have a contract."

Noise from the doorway caused her to turn her head and see. Two Morican soldiers stood in the entrance, one with a notched arrow in his bow and the other holding his unsheathed sword. The swordsman motioned with his weapon. "Come outside, all of you. Two of you have run from us, and we would know why."

Gragnishozar held out an open palm at the men. "None enter my private quarters without permission. The men flew backward to land on their backs in the alley. The assassin lord slammed the door shut and then dropped the privacy bar in place. He then proceeded to the open doorway to the main hall. The room was still filled with the half-burnt timbers that once comprised the upper floors.

Climbing onto the stone bench, he held out his hands. The timbers rattled and shook, many breaking apart. In time, they formed into an army of golems. "There are intruders in our city. They are to be repulsed. Drive them back to the sea."

The golems turned as one and headed out the door, leaving the main hall empty. That was one way to clear the room of debris. She took a moment to glance at the shell that remained of Rock House. Yes, rebuilding was possible. The exterior walls, many hands thick, were still solid save one patch on the third floor.

As she stepped into the street, the battle was already on. The golems were setting upon Morican troops in all directions. Many of the soldiers ran at the sight of the creatures, but some were putting up a fight. Even as she watched, they were able to hack one of the golems to pieces and, obviously emboldened by their success, were now assailing another.

Gragnishozar turned to her. "My minions need help, and my magic is spent. It is within you to aid them. Set them all afire. It will make attacking them that much more difficult."

On fire. What a wicked idea. Concentrating, she created a steady stream of fireballs she sent careening toward the golems, one at a time. They would hit with a splash and envelope the creatures in flame. Any soldiers nearby shied away or were burned.

Waving his arm for her and Gragnishozar to follow, Kero started uphill. "Come. The golems will eventually fail. Hopefully, they will stall the Moricans long enough for the Piaxians to get here. In the meantime, we need to join the others at the Hamak estate."

Gragnishozar paused to grab hold of a cowering Hiss. "Come, little one. I may be in need of your specific talent." Hoisting the imp up onto his shoulder he set out after Kero.

Following him, she paused for only a moment to glance back at the battle. Two more of the golems had succumbed to attack, but the number of dead soldiers had risen, and many were still fleeing instead of fighting. Perhaps Kero was right. From the street, she could still see the entrance to the harbor. The other fleet was much closer. They would be engaging the Morican fleet very soon.

From a more southern direction, a number of smaller boats also headed in. The Riazian fish boats! How would they get past?

There was no time to ponder the question. Both Kero and his lord were several paces ahead. She ran to catch up.

As she climbed the city, she paused now and then to look back. At times, her view was partially blocked by buildings. She could see one fleet, or two, but never all three. What was happening? It was only when she neared the gate to the Hamak estate that she could see all three once more. The Piaxians and the Moricans were engaged! Mixed among the warring triremes were the fishing boats. It was too far to clearly differentiate one boat from another as they were all so close and some were on fire. Further, the sky above the boats was filled with flaming balls fired by catapults.

When she entered the compound, she was surprised to see so many soldiers there. Apparently, while she was gone, a number of the troops already on the island had returned to the estate. There was no sign of further fighting, only the meek submission of these new arrivals. Prince Brumaine and Lieutenant Var were busy walking amongst them and talking. Regent Tarlok, his own warlocks and troops, Lazaan, the members of the assassin guild— all were all still present and keeping a wary guard on the Moricans.

After taking in the situation on the ground she made straight for the rooftop where she had stood before, leaving Kero, Gragnishozar and Hiss in the courtyard. Climbing the ladder, she joined Savan and Brusk, both still there, watching the carnage occurring in the bay. "What's happening? Are the Piaxians winning?"

Her foster father glanced her way then resumed watching the sea battle. "I thought it would be a tough call. The Moricans have the larger navy, but the Piaxians are being assisted by the Riaz fishermen. Those small boats get in the way of the oars and prevent those triremes from gaining ramming speed. At the rate they're either sinking or set afire, I figure by nightfall Piaxia might rule the sea."

Savan pointed. "Look. Even now, one of my country's ships is breaking for shore."

Brusk nodded. "Aye. They need to establish a beachhead before it gets too dark. Otherwise, they'll be stuck in the bay till morn. Considering how the day is waning, it seems unlikely they'll get the chance."

"And by tomorrow, the Moricans will be able to set up defenses, making landfall almost impossible."

"Exactly, but can one shipload of yer people be enough to take the dock and hold it until the others arrive?"

"I don't know."

Listening while the two men argued over the merits of the battle, she focused on the incoming ship. The pier was already crowded with a number of Morican transports—merchant ships really, unable to fight. The trireme rammed into the one farthest down the pier, and she could see people scampering over the rails of the Piaxian vessel and onto the deck of the merchant vessel then down to the wharf.

A large number of troops awaited them, and they set loose a hail of arrows at the first to arrive, cutting them down as they set foot on the dock. Others followed with some archers as well, returning the volley at those crowded on the pier. With the Moricans so tightly packed, hitting targets would be no difficulty.

Some of the Piaxians fired magical attacks at those on the wharf. Between the soldiers, archers, and warlocks, they managed to clear an area where the Piaxians could get a foothold.

Sadly, it was a numbers game. Despite some success, they were simply too few. The Moricans, after retreating some, surged again at the Piaxians and beat them back onto their boat. Only a handful managed to climb back aboard the trireme before the boat pulled away from the dock. Along with its departure was the last of the day's light.

Brusk sighed. "That's it, then. There'll be no land assault tonight. By morning, more than likely, the Moricans will have that pier so locked down a wharf rat won't get in."

Fires still burned in the bay. While her foster father and Savan decided to descend to the ground, she chose to wait and watch a little while longer.

She wondered as to the fate of the Riazian fishermen. She could not recall any of the small fishing vessels making it to the inside docks reserved for them. Had they all perished in the bay? Tears formed in her eyes as she thought of the four women who protected her. The possibility they took sides might have been because of that relationship. Had her taking advantage of their kindness resulted in their death? It was a hard thing to swallow.

In the darkness, she scanned the countryside left to right. Though she could see nothing, the memory of her arrival was enough to envision the steep cliff walls that formed the land's edge for the island on either side of the bay. As both Brusk and Savan had postulated, she could see little difficulty in defending the shore from any assault if given time to set up defenses. It may be true that Piaxia now ruled the sea, but without somewhere to land, what good would that be? Eventually, they would have to return home. Riaz now belonged to Morica.

CHAPTER 42

"My liege, what are your plans?"

The sense of despair at his situation made Brumaine nervous. Here he was, surrounded by almost two hundred soldiers of his realm, Commander Oberus in chains, and all of them collectively prisoner to the assassin guild of Riaz and the Piaxians, yet outside the walls of the compound, thousands of troops, loyal to Morica, roamed the streets of Lymos. It was untenable.

Lieutenant Varamanthu waited patiently for his answer, one he did not have. He glanced at the others gathered. Regent Tarlok certainly had a cool head for things, but asking advice of someone recognized as a sworn enemy would be pure folly. His men would note it and doubt his loyalty. That immediately ruled out Commander Savan and Captain Brusk as well.

Loyalty. It was all he had at this point—loyalty to his lineage as a prince. In many, he could see the turmoil as they tried to reconcile which allegiance they should follow—him, as a member of the royal family, or Oberus, as their supreme commander.

Normally, royal blood overruled any military position, but with all that had occurred, Doren's death, the two guards Var killed to help Brumaine escape his imprisonment by Oberus, it was easy to understand how confusing it must all seem to the average foot soldier.

He studied the commander, whose wrists were tied behind his back. The man was every day as old as his father, King Jessop. The two had been boyhood friends. Despite graying in his hair and beard, he did not look his age. Fit, less than average in height, but chin held high, there was a certain amount of arrogant bearing in the man's posture, despite the bonds. Brumaine estimated the man to be a full hand shorter than he and probably two stones in weight more.

The option roiling through his mind was a difficult one to choose. Should it succeed, it would solidify the loyalty he desired, but should it fail...well, there was no future if it did.

Noise from his left proved to be Savan and Brusk exiting the house where they watched the events in the bay from the rooftop. He intercepted them as they stepped into the courtyard. "What is there to report?"

Brusk glared at him. "Yar people hold the city and the wharf. There'll be no rescue by the Piaxians tonight. Maybe never."

Clapping a hand onto Brusk's shoulder, Savan smiled. "I wouldn't be so quick to make that determination. It's true the Moricans hold the shore, making a landing by my people impossible tonight, and difficult tomorrow, but never say never. They control the sea. All that is necessary is to find another point where they can land. It's a big island. Not every part of it can be defended. Given time, they're sure to do just that."

The captain chuckled. "Aye. Time. A luxury we don't have. How long before this estate gets overrun? One day? Two? At most? We have to defend it from outside *and* deal with those within." His gaze shifted to the Morican troops seated on the ground, under guard by the assassins.

Brusk was right. The men would not sit quietly forever. Likewise, how long would the warlocks remain? They were mercenaries, not loyalists. He doubted valor was in their creed, only gold. How many would abandon the estate during the night?

Standing near the gate were Kero and Gragnishozar. The lad's guardian was staring through the entry into the street. Obviously, his focus was against any attack from without. The courtyard was lit by a number of torches, but outside the compound the night obscured much. Could Gragnishozar see in the dark? Brumaine had seen the assassin lord exhibit amazing powers, but even he had a limit. Counting on Gragnishozar as the sole defense against attack was folly.

Such optimism was obvious in Kero. He stood proudly beside his master, beaming confidence. Brumaine admired him. How one still not a man could have done what he had done so far since the entire sordid affair had begun was impressive. Should they survive and Riaz fall back into the hands of its citizens, then Kero could easily grow into someone to lead his people. Considering how the country was previously governed, they needed someone to take charge who wasn't a member of the merchant's guild. A political system based on wealth was not a good one.

There was a growing buzz among his countrymen. News of the current military status in the city had them grumbling. Though none, save Oberus, were bound, they had all been relieved of their weapons. Still, he feared they might do something foolish and attempt to rush their captors. Many would die, and he doubted their success.

He wasn't the only one to note the disquiet among the men. Oberus, as well, had keyed into it. He stepped toward Tarlok. "Well, Piaxian, what are your plans? You have us at your mercy, for now. Do you think holding us hostage will win your freedom? I think not. Your only chance lies in freeing me. If you do so, I will give you my word you will get safe passage off the island."

The regent faced the commander. "Your word? Is this the same word you gave the Hamaks? I don't think there is much value in *your word*."

"Perhaps...or perhaps not. Either way, I don't think you have much choice."

Tarlok did not answer. Instead, he turned away to go speak with his brother, but not before giving Brumaine a glance that spoke volumes. Whether the regent was thinking the same thing was a debate he could have at a later date. For now, one thing was clear—he was stalling on the decision he had already made sometime before.

From the doorway where Brusk and Savan emerged, Darlee appeared. There was another of surprising fortitude, much like Kero. Was this a trait amongst all fifteen-year-olds? Altruism? He was only four years older than the pair, yet he could not recall having embodied such behavior. It embarrassed him. Unlike Kero, her expression was one of concern and worry with her head down and a frown upon her face. Yet, when their gaze met, she straightened and smiled. She would not remain dour, no matter the circumstances.

Still at his side was Var, his ever faithful mentor and guardian.

The man's gaze was intense as he still waited for an answer to the question posed so long ago. Everyone in the army claimed Var was unmatched in skill with the sword. It was time to discover whether, as a teacher, he had imparted enough of those skills. Taking the lieutenant's wrist in a military style, he smiled. "I have decided. Honor it. Wish me well."

He turned to the Piaxian regent. "Tarlok, release Commander Oberus. There is a matter to be resolved."

The regent stared at him for a moment and then nodded to his soldiers who undid the bonds holding Oberus.

Facing the commander, Brumaine freed his sword from its scabbard. "Pick up your weapon. It is time to establish who truly is in command here."

Once freed, Oberus stretched and rotated his arms. He chuckled. "An honor match, is it? I accept." He retrieved his sword from where it lay on the ground. "You are a fool, Brumaine. Soon, you will be lying in the dust, dying, and the honor will be mine. I shall be swift."

Var grabbed his arm and leaned close. "He favors the right, but can use either hand. He is strong, but you have both a height and reach advantage."

Memory of the many lessons in the training ring played through Brumaine's mind. He had always been bested by Var. What moves did he have that could win? Oberus circled him. He held at ready and rotated to always face the commander. Watching the man's steps, he looked for a moment when the legs would be in an awkward position, something that would allow a quick attack, but it never happened. At no point did the commander move one leg to cross his body, but instead shuffled in a way to always keep one foot forward and the other back. Brumaine could not see an opening to attack. Var's lessons resonated in his mind. *"When your opponent is sure-footed, sometimes it is better to wait for the attack when such stance must give way to movement."*

"What's the matter, Prince? Unsure of what to do? Here, let me show you."

Oberus lunged forward. Even though Brumaine thought he

was ready, the speed of the attack surprised him. Not only did it take quick moves to deflect the blade, but a dangerous step backward to avoid one thrust. Moving backward made attack impossible. His only hope was to survive the commander's initial flurry.

Brumaine's retreat allowed him to reset and prepare to go on offense, but Oberus relented and resumed his circling. "So. You must have learned a thing or two at least. You're still alive. No matter. I'll sort you out soon enough."

While talking, the commander changed the grip on his weapon and now attacked left-handed. In his training with Var, the lieutenant had fought that way on occasion. He recalled one lesson vividly. *"Not every person you confront will be right-handed. You must learn to fight against both."* Now he appreciated such classes as he adjusted his own stance to face a left-handed enemy. Unlike the first flurry, in this one he held his ground.

The commander stepped back once more, returning the sword to his right hand, his face—flushed. Obviously, Oberus had not expected Brumaine to have lasted so long. *"Anger is your enemy. It makes you rash. Control it.'* Maybe now was the time to try his assault. He started with an overhand attack, hoping to force the commander to retreat and, in doing so, provide an opening.

It was a mistake that nearly cost his life. Oberus parried his sword up then rushed in to attack at close quarters. Brumaine was barely able to get his sword between his body and that of the commander's weapon. Oberus pushed hard, and Brumaine staggered back, doing his best not to lose his footing. While doing so, the commander's blade slashed across his thigh, opening a cut. Swinging his own blade, he scored a wound on the right shoulder.

"The end is coming for you, Prince. How long before that wound drains you?"

Circling once more, Oberus had switched to the left hand again. The wound on the commander's shoulder did not look as severe as the one in his own leg, yet the hand switch implied a more serious aspect than was visible. He had yet to return the taunts. Perhaps now was a fitting time. "Spoken by the one-armed man. When I injure the other, with what will you hold your sword?"

Oberus charged. *"Beware the sorely injured man. He has nothing to lose and will sacrifice all to take you with him."* Brumaine stepped to the side, allowing the headlong rush by the commander to take the man too far and open him up for attack. Easily deflecting the commander's blade, he caught the man with a heavy blow across his back, sending him sprawling. *"Never give your enemy a second chance. Finish him when he is down."*

As Oberus scrambled to rise, Brumaine struck a lethal hit to the commander's throat, nearly severing his head. In a spray of blood, the commander flopped down and lay still.

As he stood there, panting, staring at the fallen man, Var came to his side and put an arm round him. "My liege, you are injured. Let me help you."

Sheathing his sword, Brumaine smiled then gently pushed free from the lieutenant. "Not now. There are yet things to do."

In the fighting, he had somewhat lost his bearings. He turned to locate Tarlok. The regent waited some five paces away. While stepping toward the man, the wound in his leg hurt to the point where he almost collapsed. Blood still streamed from it. No matter. He had duties to perform. "Regent Tarlok, I have established my right as commander of my people. As one of them, I submit to you." He undid the belt that tied his sheath and handed it and the weapon over. "I surrender and will join my men as one of your hostages. I wait to hear what fate you decide for me and my people in hopes you will be honorable."

"I accept your terms." Tarlok handed the belt and sword to Savan who was standing nearby.

The big Piaxian examined the sword. "What a small blade. No wonder he was able to knock it away." He grinned. "Nevertheless, well played."

Brumaine turned to his lieutenant. "Var. Drop your weapons. Come stand with me now."

Var did as commanded and rushed to Brumaine's side. "You need to have that leg attended to."

With the help of his lieutenant, he struggled to where his countrymen were, finally sitting in their midst. To the man, they saluted with a fist to the chest. There would be no more controversy over where their loyalty lay.

As his men settled down once more, Darlee approached and knelt by his wounded leg. "That was very brave of you. Foolish...but brave. He could have killed you. Hold still and I will fix that leg."

Resting on one elbow, he more than watched the Sechlander girl work her magic. He felt it. The blood stopped flowing, the wound closed up, and the throbbing ebbed away. In a matter of moments, his leg was whole again. During the process, he noted a moment where the girl grimaced. Did she feel what he did? Was that part of the process? Why would she endure the agony when any one of Tarlok's warlocks, or the regent himself, could heal the wound?

"There. All done." She rose and began to walk away, but paused to glance at him before proceeding onward to Brusk's side. She wasn't a young girl. She was an amazing woman.

Regardless of Darlee's ministrations, he was dreadfully tired. After accepting a long drink of water, he lay back and stared up at the stars. It was said they were jewels placed by the gods to decorate the night. Whatever they were, their twinkling was soothing to his mind. It was always best when the sky was clear of clouds, and such a night as this, the sky could be viewed in all its beauty. It comforted him as sleep beckoned. Knowing the morning might bring his ruin, he would take what solace he could find.

CHAPTER 43

Kero had slept at the feet of his master. The gentle shaking he now received woke him to the dull grey of pre-dawn and a light fog.

Gragnishozar, seeing him alert, straightened. "Time to get up, Kero. Morning comes. I suspect a difficult day ahead."

Rubbing sand from his eyes, he looked about the camp. Although a couple of men had roused, most of the Moricans still slept. A few of the Piaxians were still on guard, but the number of assassins in the courtyard could be counted on one finger. Lazaan still remained. All the others were absent. "They're all gone?"

"Yes, most left when the moon was at its highest. I suppose whatever light it afforded gave them enough comfort to travel the streets and see whether any enemy lay before them. The rest waited until the moon set, obviously counting on the darkest part of night to mask their movements."

It was what he expected. The first loyalty of guild members was to the gold they were paid. Once their contract was fulfilled, any further efforts on their part did not exist. They were mercenaries, pure and simple.

As to why Lazaan yet remained was a mystery. Rising, Kero brushed off the dust that clung to him with the morning dew. His limbs ached some as a result of the sleep on hard ground, but he knew they would limber from the warmth of the rising sun. Making his way past the reposed bodies littering the ground, he approached the assassin. "I see all of your comrades have fled. The contract has been fulfilled. All those Morican troops who were on the island prior to the invasion force have been either killed or captured. Why do you yet remain?"

Lazaan gave him a sidelong glance. "Do not test me, Kero. I will interpret my contract in my own way."

He studied the assassin as Lazaan stretched and yawned. Based on the bags under his eyes, the man must have stayed awake all night, keeping guard. Why? The others had left. Until now, his opinion of the man was of one only concerned with his own self-interests. Perhaps that opinion needed revision. Perhaps he was more than just a warlock mercenary. Perhaps he was a Riazian loyalist.

The door to the main hall opened and both Tarlok and Savan emerging into the courtyard. They must have slept in beds once belonging to the original occupants of the estate. There were no more Hamaks. Oberus had made sure of that.

Studying Lazaan one more time, he finally understood. It was Alban who had hired him. When the assassin had last been present, the leader of the Hamak family still lived. There may be another aspect of things that motivated him. Guilt. Combined with those of the other guild members, his actions had led to the death of his number one benefactor, probably someone with whom he had established more than a contractual relationship, but rather amity. How far would one go to right a wrong in the name of friendship?

He had misjudged the man. Not only had Lazaan lost Alban, but in thinking on the issue, Stod as well. The two had been inseparable. Stod was the one assassin whom Kero had liked best and missed the big man as well. When Lazaan lost Stod, it would have been the same as Kero losing Derak.

Despite the history of friction between them, the only thing he felt now was compassion. There had been no knowing what actions Oberus would have taken. He reached out to touch the assassin's shoulder. "It's not your fault."

Lazaan gently lifted Kero's hand away. "Kind words. As often as I have derided you, they are words I did not expect." He turned to face the morning sun beginning its crest over the mountaintops. "No, there is fault, though perhaps not the fault you may be thinking of. The fault I speak of is not in one, such as myself, but in all." He turned again to face Kero. "The fault is greed. Greed is natural in people. I have my own level of greed, perhaps higher than most. I accept it." He looked out at the men from Morica as more stirred to wakefulness. "War is upon us. There is no fault in war. Only casualties. War is begat by greed, and one cannot blame greed. There are consequences to war. I must accept them."

The assassin moved to greet the Piaxians. "So what is the plan?"

After whispering something to Lazaan, Tarlok, with Savan right behind, edged past the assassin, nodded at Kero, then proceeded to confront a now risen Brumaine. "Yesterday, I received an offer from your once commander. Knowing his word as worthless, such offer was not acceptable. I have it from my brother that yours may be. What say you?"

The prince glanced at Var, then at his men, before bowing to the regent. "On behalf of my men and my country, I promise my word is my bond. Before I can honor your request, I must know the state of affairs as they currently lie."

"Savan and I have just come from the rooftop and assessed the situation. It is simple. Your people have taken the city and hold the shore. It appears all of their transport ships and one trireme remain undamaged and docked at the wharf. Beyond the bay, Piaxian warships patrol the entrance. How many, I cannot determine, but let us say in significant numbers to state they control the sea."

"Then we are at somewhat of a stalemate. Oberus' offer to grant you safe passage off the island is currently impossible. There are no Piaxian ships docked for you to board, and any Morican ship attempting to sail will suffer swift destruction. It may be possible to parlay with your fleet, but before I could ever consider such a course I would first need to establish control over the invasion force. They stand between us and the harbor."

Could Brumaine do it? Could he walk outside the gate and take command? It might be possible with him being royal blood, but if there were another member of the royal family out there, one sure to outrank the prince, him being the youngest, then such a prospect would be highly unlikely. Kero watched as the two stood in silence, and then parted to each hold private conversations, Tarlok with Savan, Brumaine with Var.

The prince finished first and returned to the spot where he waited for the regent. It was then his sweeping gaze met Kero's, and Brumaine's mouth showed the hint of a smile, if ever so shortly, before returning to a taut line.

Could the prince be trusted? Tarlok was correct that Oberus would have acted in bad faith. Kero tried to remember each moment where trust of the prince was required. As he recalled the events, the trust was usually the other way where Brumaine trusted either him, or Savan, or whoever. Even the night before, it was in the regent's trust that the prince put things. What was Morican culture really like? True, they talked the same, dressed similar, and looked alike, save the red hair common to Kero's people. They were almost all of black hair and olive skin tone. Those differences weren't enough to justify a unique mindset.

There were some hard facts to take into consideration. Morica had just finished a war against both Piaxia and Sechland. In fact, it was with Sechland that the conflict was a constant. Any acquiescence Brumaine made to Tarlok would have to be extended to Brusk and Darlee. Would that be too much for the other Moricans to bear?

Whatever might be the case, it was out of his hands. The Piaxians were now returning to the discussion, and only time would tell as to what would be done.

Tarlok stopped before Brumaine. "What is needed is a truce until the matter can be better resolved. I suggest you allow us to remain in this estate, unmolested, until the conflict is decided or you are able to take full command. We will take no further action on our part to interfere."

"A reasonable request. I can abide by those terms."

"Our people will not have free movement within the city for the purpose of obtaining provisions. I must ask you to provide for us until that changes."

Brumaine held a hand to his chin. He glanced around, spied Kero once more, smiled, and then waved for him to come near.

Kero hesitated, but only for a moment. Whatever plan the prince had in mind involved him. As he moved to stand near both Brumaine and Tarlok, Var and Savan circled him. "What do you want from me?"

"There is a task that requires your special skill set. Of all those gathered here, none know the city as you do. Do you think you could gather victuals for those who stay here, and do it in such a way as not to interfere with my people?"

He considered all the locations outside of the market where foods could be purchased. Provided he had enough coin, it might be possible. "Maybe, but if the Piaxians cannot be seen in the city, why would I be allowed?"

Brumaine pointed toward Gragnishozar. "Because of him. Once the rest of my countrymen learn should any harm befall you, they'll be subject to the assassin lord's wrath. It should be enough to give you fairly free rein."

Tarlok nodded. "Provided the lad is willing, it should suffice. Further, he could convey messages and keep us updated as to the status of affairs."

Savan chuckled and dropped a hand onto Kero's shoulder. "Well, young man, what'll it be? Will you do this for us? Once the Moricans are gone, it's only my brother and I, our two soldiers, two warlocks, Captain Brusk, Darlee, Lazaan, you, and your lord. Though, considering his size, he must eat like a horse."

Shaking his head, he glanced at his master. "He does not eat, not like you and I, anyway. I will need to chase down his brazier, though. He is loath to be without it."

The regent held out his hand. "We have an agreement, then. May the gods grant this ends peaceably and without further loss of life."

Brumaine grasped Tarlok's wrist. "You have my word."

Savan stepped into the house and came out carrying some weapons. He handed them to Brumaine and Var. "Your swords. The rest that belong to your men are in the main hall. Gather them and be on your way. The sun is now fully risen. It's best you find your people before they come here looking to find you."

Once his sword belt was safely secured, Brumaine instructed Var to lead his men into the main hall to retrieve their weapons. As they emerged back into the courtyard, despite the pact, Kero could sense the rise in tension. With approximately two hundred armed men, despite the presence of Gragnishozar, the odds were strictly in favor of the Moricans. This would be the first real test of

Brumaine's honor. Once the men had all re-armed, he ordered Var to lead them out the gate. Kero noted he wasn't the only one who had been holding his breath in anticipation. Not only did Savan exhale heavily, so did the prince. The men following orders provided a real confirmation Brumaine was in command.

Var marshaled the men into ranks. Yelling instructions, he marched them to the gate and out into the street. Once the last had exited, Brumaine bowed slightly to the regent. "I take my leave. Wish me well."

Tarlok nodded. "Until then."

The prince tapped Kero on the arm. "Come. I must introduce you. All will be well, trust me."

There it was again. Acceptance of Brumaine's trust. Why did he have misgivings? Too much of what was agreed lay subject to this trust. Once outside the gate he could be held hostage again and all terms forgotten.

There was no choice. He had already committed. To fail to follow through would be a breach of his honor and trust. He started for the gate.

Before he could take three steps, Gragnishozar barred Brumaine's way. "Hear my word. If any harm befalls my ward, I will travel the Great Sea and kill every man, woman, and child in your family. There will be none left in the royal family of Morica. This I promise."

The prince paled. "I believe you. None shall harm him. I will sacrifice my own life before allowing that to happen." He stepped past the assassin lord and exited the estate, joining his men who waited outside.

Kero followed. When he walked into the street, two Piaxian soldiers closed the gate behind him. Things were in motion now. There was no turning back.

The prince pointed down the road. "Let us proceed toward the wharf. It is either there, or the city market on the way, where we should find our people and whoever is in charge."

No sooner had they walked one block when they came across a patrol. The officer in charge directed them to The Fisherman's

Friend where headquarters had been set up. Kero knew the way and ensured Brumaine got there.

The street where the inn lay was filled with war machines. Catapults, aimed at the bay, lined the lane. As it was the closest lane to the wharf, he could understand why they picked it as the best position to set up defenses.

Men, mostly officers, were coming and going from the front door. Brumaine knew some of them, Var almost all, and together they greeted those soldiers. In the bustle, Kero had failed to listen closely, but whatever one officer had said to the prince showed in his scowl.

After stepping inside, he noted the tables had been moved aside save one large one where an elegantly dressed man sat. He rose and, after moving round the table, gave Brumaine a tight hug Kero recognized the similarity—the same chin, shape of his nose and dark brown eyes. The man could only be the prince's brother.

"Brumaine, I feared for you. You can understand my dread when I was told Doren lies wrapped in the hold of our last trireme. I feared you lost as well. How many of you survived?"

"There are still over two hundred of us left. We were held in the Hamak estate at the top of the city until this morning. Only through a deal I made did I win the release of me and the men."

The man turned to Var. "It is good to see you, Lieutenant. I suspect you have done well to keep my brother from harm."

Var saluted with a thump to the chest. "Prince Cassan, such laurels are more than I deserve. Your brother has acquitted himself most admirably."

Prince Cassan raised one eyebrow. "Truthfully?"

Var nodded. "Indeed."

The prince turned to Brumaine. "Well brother, I look forward to hearing of your exploits."

The man now stared at Kero. "And who is this?"

Brumaine put an arm across Kero's back. "This is Kero. He is Riazian. I have vouched safe conduct for him anywhere within the city."

"Have you now. We shall have to see about that. Why would I

endorse such an order?"

"Because his guardian is the assassin warlock lord who can create those monstrous golems. You do not wish to induce his wrath."

A captain entered and whispered something into Cassan's ear. The prince's eyes went wide then he dismissed the man. "Is it true you killed Commander Oberus?"

"Yes, in an honor fight. It was necessary. He was responsible for Doren's death and almost mine."

"This complicates matters. I think it best you stay here until I can sort things out." He turned to face Kero. "As for you, how old are you, lad?"

This was not going well. It sounded like Brumaine was about to be put under house arrest. So much for the plan of the prince taking control of the invasion force. "Fifteen, sir."

"Fifteen." He looked behind him. Where is that fellow who owns this place? I need to speak with him."

A soldier in the back disappeared into the kitchen and returned, pulling Mudge by the elbow. Cassan pointed at Kero. "This youth claims to be fifteen. Can you verify that?"

Mudge looked haggard. Not that he didn't always appear that way, but at the moment he looked worse than ever. The pudgy barkeeper nodded. "Aye. Fifteen. I've had to shoo him out of here more than once."

Cassan sighed. "I don't take youths prisoner. Begone from here. Should you return I would have no choice but to put you in irons."

Kero glanced at Brumaine. If he was cast out, there was no way he could convey messages.

The prince nodded. "You best go, Kero. Once I have told all to my brother, things may change. For now, stay out of harm's way."

"I'm going."

He exited the inn and headed for the Hamak estate. The regent would not like this report. He would have to hope that Brumaine could convince his brother, but even if he did, would that be enough to terminate the invasion? Unlikely. This was war, and the

spoils of war were not so readily ceded without a fight.
He set off at a trot.

CHAPTER 44

Four days.

For four whole days, they had been holed up in the Hamak estate and Darlee was getting tired of sitting around doing nothing.

No one had bothered them. At least no forces tried to storm their position. Instead, the Moricans had set up a blockade of some sort more than a block away. Gragnishozar stood guard at the gate the entire time. He never slept. On occasion, he would hover over the brazier Kero rescued from Rock House, but always with an eye on the street.

Kero, throughout the days, would appear now and then with an armload of foodstuffs. No one bothered him. He came and went as he pleased.

It wasn't fair. She wanted to go see what was going on. Why hadn't Brumaine managed to get the same exemption for her that Kero received?

There was no point in lamenting over it. Bored, she climbed the ladder to join the vigil both Savan and her foster father held on the roof overlooking the bay before the sun set. "Anything new?"

Brusk nodded. "Aye. The commander here has noted something interesting."

Savan pointed out, past the bay, to a Piaxian trireme patrolling across the opening. "It's one of our ships. Even at this distance, I can note differences between them. As commander, part of my job is to know every boat in our fleet. The triremes keep crossing outside the bay, ready to attack anything that tries to exit."

That made perfect sense to her. One would expect the Piaxians to bottle up the harbor. "So what's so interesting?"

"There are only three boats doing the patrolling. The rest of the fleet has not shown itself since the battle. My guess is they're elsewhere."

Elsewhere, as in where? She knew almost nothing of the island save it featured high cliffs most of the way around. This was the only large bay sheltered from rough seas that could allow for a significant port. "So where do you think they went? Home?"

"No, not home. To the only other port this island has down on the south shore. It's for small fishing boats only, but it's enough to land troops."

The implication rang clear. A military force would come across land to attack the city. Recalling the gate she'd entered a number of nights before, she suspected it, too, would be guarded, as well as the wall that encircled the city. "How many troops do you think?"

"Hard to say. Considering how many triremes we have, my guess is five hundred at most, probably four."

There were thousands of Moricans occupying Lymos. "It's not enough. You've already told me it's easier to defend than attack. They've got numbers *and* the wall on their side."

"Who knows what they'll do. They may try and starve them out. There's already a blockade at sea. Another one at the gate would make things uncomfortable."

Thinking of the food Kero would bring, she wondered, not just for herself, but the people in the city. "They'll starve everyone."

Her foster father patted her arm. "Not fer a while. That kinda thing can take months. Back in Visk, knowing war with Morica was always something that could happen at any time, I always maintained emergency supplies. I'm betting there's some here, too. Folks know better than to keep an empty larder."

Sometimes she wondered about the simple acceptance those men in power took toward war. They acted like it was part of the natural order of the world. Before leaving the estate, Lazaan preached to her about greed as the culprit. She had a different opinion. Shaking her head, she glared at the two men. "This is insane. War is insane. All of it is insane. All kinds of innocent people will die. Why? I can only figure it is because some people are insane, and those people are often the ones making the decisions. Simple folk don't care about war. They just want to live their lives. We need to do something before things around here go insane."

Savan sighed and folded his arms. "What would you have us

do?"

She stepped to the edge of the roof and looked down toward the bottom of the city, knowing full well the bulk of the Morican forces were entrenched there. "We need to go down there and talk with this Prince Cassan. Strike some kind of agreement. Kero says he's not like Oberus at all, but more like Brumaine. If one prince can see reason, why not both?"

"He's also has his brother under house arrest since he went down there. I'm not so sure how much alike they are."

She spun and faced him. "Maybe, but he's also abided by Brumaine's deal with your brother. We've been left alone, and Kero goes about without harassment. There must be some honor in him."

Her foster father chuckled. "Yer right about that part. There just might be a chance to negotiate something. What say you, Savan?"

"I say we sit tight and wait. My brother has already agreed to one set of terms. Negotiating a new one will only invalidate the first. I'm off to inform the others of my findings." He made for the ladder and descended into the house.

She looked to her foster father. He waved her off. "The decision's made."

Leaving Brusk on the rooftop, she made her way toward the large hall in the main home. She would do it herself. What she needed was a way to get there. As Kero had free movement in the city, he was the logical choice to serve as her companion. The Moricans might ignore her because she accompanied him. They might think them nothing more than a young couple out for a walk.

She entered the room, located Kero, and told him of her idea to go talk to Cassan.

"I don't know. The last thing he said to me was, should I return, I'd be arrested. We should wait until Tarlok says so."

He was helping prepare dinner. She noted the vegetables he chopped were near spoiled. "How goes the food situation out there?"

He paused to stare at the diced vegetables and then faced her.

"The prices are rising daily. From my talk with people, there might be enough for a fortnight before rationing becomes severe."

The idea of waiting until the Piaxian regent ordered otherwise was ridiculous. It's not that she didn't like the man, but he wasn't a Riazian and his best interests were not necessarily theirs. Not that her Sechlander birth gave her any statutory high ground, only her moral beliefs. She snorted. "Huh. And you want to wait until when...everyone has starved?"

Kero reddened and dropped his knife. "Do you think I don't care? That I want my people to suffer? Before you walked in here, Savan announced the possibility of a Piaxian army attacking from inland. He said that could happen any day. Why would you want to risk going out there when you're safe in here?"

It was her turn to anger. "Did he also tell you they may lay siege instead of attacking? Based on the look on your face, I think not."

"If that happens, then I'll gladly go with you. Until then, I'm staying."

Needing a moment to let her anger cool, she stepped away and took in the room. Save Gragnishozar, everyone was there—Tarlok, Savan, and Lazaan at one table, two Piaxian soldiers and two warlocks at another. They would look her way then continue in whatever private discussions they were engaged in. Were they talking about her?

Her foster father must have entered when she was speaking to Kero as he stood by the door, watching her closely. She glanced back at Kero, who, despite cutting vegetables, also was watching her between knife strokes.

Everyone was tracking her. It was clear none would help. Would they try and stop her if she proceeded on her own? Let them try. She had made her decision.

She marched toward the door. Brusk edged her way. "Where are you going?"

Not looking at him, she stepped past. "Outside. I need some fresh air."

He didn't stop her, but followed as she continued into the

courtyard and toward Gragnishozar. The assassin lord turned her way when she was a couple steps from his side.

"Young witch, is there a reason you disrupt my vigil?"

Peeking, she noted her foster father had ceased his pursuit some ten paces back. She hoped Brusk was far enough away not to hear her conversation. To be sure, she leaned close. "I have decided to attempt a negotiation with the Moricans. I'm going out there now and would prefer none follow. Will you assist me?"

Gragnishozar looked over her head then met her gaze. "What of the love you spoke of before? Your guardian would probably not wish to lose you."

That was true, but staying would not be right. "There are things that can outweigh such love, such as the lives of thousands. War is about to descend on this city, and whether it is combat in the streets or a starvation siege, either way, the innocents will die. I must do what I can to prevent this."

"Your will is most strong and impresses me. What you speak holds truths. Go. None will follow. You have my word."

She nodded and started for the gate. The sound of fast approaching footsteps was followed by a strangled noise. Turning, she discovered her foster father in a frozen pose of running. Gragnishozar's work. "It has to be done, Father. I'm going out there."

"Not without me, ya aren't. If yer convinced in carrying out this scatterbrained idea, I'm coming with ya."

She shook her head. "No, you're not. You have to stay here. First of all, you're a Sechlander captain. Our two countries have been at war since long before I was born. They'll hate you right from the start. Then there's the Piaxians. I'll need you to keep them busy while I'm gone."

"If it wasn't for that blasted assassin lord, I'd be taking you back into the hall, shocks by ya or not. Tarlok and Savan will not be happy when they hear of this. Keep them busy. Ha! And just how do ya think I'm going to do that?"

She smiled. "Challenge them at something you're good at—drinking games."

"You've got me at a disadvantage. I don't have much choice. As to the drinking games...I don't think so. Sooner or later, I'll get out of here and come looking for ya."

She stepped close to kiss him on the cheek. "I intend to end this war. Wish me luck."

Spinning on her heel, she made quick steps to the gate. Not until she had opened it, stepped through, and closed it behind her and taken a dozen more paces did she dare to look back. Brusk unfroze at that moment, finished his step in her direction, stumbled, straightened, shook his head then turned toward the main hall and trudged that way.

Knowing he would follow her wishes, she took a deep breath and continued her mission by walking toward the Morican post at the end of the block. She expected a difficult time passing the blockade meant to keep her and the others in, not to let them pass.

As she neared, she noted much activity in the small camp. Men were donning armor, and gathering weapons. Were they planning to attack her? No. None were paying her any attention Only when she stepped into the light from their torches did one finally notice her.

He held a loaded bow and pointed it in her direction. "Hold where you are. What business brings you?"

She held up her hands in surrender. "I would ask you to take me down to see Prince Cassan. I have something important to discuss with him."

A lieutenant stepped to the fore. "I've seen you in the Hamak estate. You're that witch. Why would I bring you to the prince where, with your magic, you might kill him?"

She flicked a finger at the archer, shocking him enough to drop his weapon, and then took one step closer to the lieutenant. "Because we need to stop this war and save countless lives, including yours."

She had to give credit to the man. He never blanched, unlike his men who panicked and bristled weapons in her direction. He waved her forward. "If you want to save my life, then come with us." He ordered his men up the street. They obeyed, though keeping an eye on her.

She glanced down, toward the bay. "You're going the wrong way. The prince is by the wharf."

"Possibly, but a Piaxian army approaches the gate. We've been ordered to aid in its defense. If you truly want to stop the fighting, now is your chance. Dawdling here serves no purpose. We must hurry. I'm told the battle is about to begin."

She moved to his side and together they followed his troop toward the city gate. In truth, she was surprised at the easy acceptance by the officer. What had changed? Only one answer made any sense. Brumaine. The prince must have convinced his countrymen of the truth. Perhaps a new treaty was not so impossible after all.

A distant boom sounded, and the lieutenant ordered his men to a run. Darlee did her best to keep pace.

Short of breath, she arrived at the scene, heightened action showing men trying desperately to reinforce the gate as the booms continued and the old wooden thing shuddered with every one. It would burst any moment. How many Piaxians would come spewing through that opening when it was breached? She surveyed the Moricans. There could be no more than three or four hundred present. The rest must be either still at the waterfront or, at best, on the way. It would take time to march up through the city. The men here wouldn't have that long.

A question faced her...when the fighting began, what should she do?

CHAPTER 45

Though still not fully in his brother's confidence, there had been enough corroboration of the details by Brumaine to convince Cassan that he was not an enemy of the state and still loyal to Morica. Fealty to their father was a different issue and one they had argued over the days.

Now, as he rode beside his brother for the city's high gate on the only two horses found in Lymos, none of that mattered. Those forces stationed there were under attack, and the bulk of the troops were rushing to aid them, while he and Cassan rode ahead to take command of the situation.

Why would the Piaxians force a fight? Yes, they had the element of surprise, but only for a short while. The troops are at the gate should be able to contain them until reinforcements arrived. At that point, they'd be sorely outnumbered.

The pact he'd made with Tarlok came to mind. So far, his brother had honored the deal because there was really nothing to be gained by attacking the Hamak compound and losing men in the process. Should the struggle for Riaz go to Morica, his brother suggested the regent would be worth a sizable concession as a hostage. The idea of such a reneging on his agreement bothered him. He would have to wait until the looming battle played out to decide on what he should or could do to honor the terms.

He glanced at the sky. The moon was just beginning its transit and offered some light, but night would advantage the Piaxians until they entered the city. It would be impossible for the defenders to effectively target attackers in the dark. The fight would be in the streets, he was sure of it.

Arriving at the gate, they were just in time to see it collapse in a pile of broken timbers. Regardless, the sound of catapults launching their payload continued and instead of stones hitting where the gate had been, flaming balls of pitch streamed over the wall and into the midst of the gathered troops.

Quitting his horse, he scanned the area as men scrambled to

avoid the incoming fireballs and did their best to douse what flames they could. "Have you no catapults to return fire?"

His brother dismounted as well. "None. They're all stationed to guard the bay."

Lieutenant Var, seeing their arrival, approached and saluted Cassan. "Orders, Sire?"

"Arrange your archers. They'll charge in sooner or later. I want their first volley to take out every man in the initial assault. We need to make sure they pay heavily. Don't forget to especially target their warlocks. They're usually dressed in black."

They found a stairwell attached to a house and climbed up to a landing that gave them a vantage point over the area. The main road that led out of the city was also the same one in. Wide, it ran straight through the town all the way down to the market area. Most of the troops were gathered in that street, some twenty or so paces back from the gate.

An open lane also ran all the way along beside the wall. From it, men could climb stairs to stand atop and fire at attackers below. As Brumaine scanned the wall, he could see no defenders on it. "The wall isn't guarded. Are you certain they'll come through here?"

"They have no choice. At best they would be able to climb over in twos and threes. We'd be able to pick them off from below. No, their only chance lays in a frontal assault. They'll rely on their warlocks. Those bastards can kill with their magic, but they have a limit—four or five at the most. In the end, we'll win with numbers."

Looking once more at the men gathered in the street, he estimated five hundred at most. "Let's hope they don't have more than a hundred warlocks then because if they do, every man we have here is doomed."

"By then our men from down at the wharf will have arrived, and we'll wipe them out. Have faith, brother. We've learned a thing or two about their tactics from the war last year. I think we'll be ready for them."

He hoped his brother was right. He also worried about the

position he and Cassan had taken. Elevated as they were, they were an easy target for Piaxian warlocks. "Perhaps it be best we remove ourselves from here. I've seen what those lightning bolts warlocks toss can to do a man."

"It's a risk I must take. Cowardice on my part would reflect upon the men. Courage is what is needed at this point."

Was it courage, or stupidity? He studied the men as they readied for the assault. Were they watching Cassan for leadership? No, almost to the man they were focused on the shattered gate waiting for whatever would come through it. The various fires here and there flickered shadows across their faces that gave them an image of walking dead.

Wait. Amongst the men there was one who should not be there. Easily identifiable by the patch on one eye was Darlee. What was the young Sechlander girl doing there? He needed to find out. "Brother, I'll return in a moment."

Cassan nodded at him as Var returned looking for further orders. Leaving the two to discuss strategy, he descended the steps and made his way through the men until he reached the girl. She saw him near and smiled. "Darlee, what are you doing here?"

"I've come to end this madness. Where is your brother? I would speak with him."

A lieutenant standing nearby, with a tight fist on a stiletto at Darlee's throat, saluted. "Prince Brumaine, it is I who has brought this witch. She promised to help. I intend to hold her to her word."

Considering the way in which he held his dagger, the man must have thought he could plunge it into Darlee before she took any foul action. The man could not be more mistaken. First of all, Brumaine had come to understand the honorable tenets the girl lived by, and should any attempt on her life be noticed by her, the officer would be dead in an instant, of that he was sure. "Thank you, Lieutenant. Turn her over to me. I can vouch for her word. And release that grip you have on your dagger."

The man saluted again. "Yes, Sire."

Grabbing Darlee by the arm, he pulled her toward the stair. "Look about you. These men are ready to fight to the death. Just how do you intend to stop this?"

"I don't know exactly, but I know I must try."

He glanced up the steps to where Cassan now stood alone again, Var having descended. Not once, but twice Kero had saved his life with magic. Perhaps Darlee could so the same for his brother. "If you wish to speak peace with Prince Cassan, you must keep him alive until the end. Will you do so?"

She nodded. "If you think it will help, then I will."

He pointed up the stair. "All right then. Come."

Preceding her, he caught his brother's attention. "Cassan, this is Darlee Murdach of Sechland. She is a most capable witch and has vowed to protect you. It requires her to touch you. Please let her do it."

His brother scowled at her for a moment then met Brumaine's gaze. "Are you sure of this?"

The stare they exchanged was as tense as any one he had ever experienced. He was asking his brother to accept a trust that may put him at great risk. He glanced at Darlee. She, too, was steely eyed, watching Cassan. He returned his brother's gaze once more. "On my life."

"Very well then."

Darlee reached out and grasped Cassan's wrist. It took only a moment, then she let go. As he could see no change or sign of the magic, he wondered as to how to verify the magical shield was in place. He could only hope it was so.

She turned to him. "It is done. He is shielded from any magical attack. Now, it's your turn."

Brumaine stepped away. "No. Save your magic for whatever you intend to do. I have pledged my life to my brother's safety and will see it through."

He was nudged by Cassan. "Hush now. Be ready. They come."

Turning to watch the gateway he realized the catapults had stopped and quiet had descended upon the scene. A number of pitch fires still burned in the open spaces, providing enough light to see the area clearly. The sound of bows being drawn taut emanated from the troops below.

A roar sounded from the other side of the gateway. What manner of beast made such a sound? Not a bear, it was unlike anything he had ever heard before.

The few remaining gate timbers that lay in the way were cast aside quickly by a creature rushing headlong into the street. It was terrifying. The monster was unrecognizable save one feature he had seen before—its grey skin. It was a demon like Hiss.

Many hands taller than a man, muscled, and bearing a frightening countenance full of sharp teeth, this beast cast wood beams aside like they were twigs, timbers that weighed more than any man.

The singing of released arrows filled the air, and dozens of them struck the monstrosity. It was as if they hit stone, bouncing off or breaking on contact. The demon roared one more time, its arms wide, spreading the huge claws it bore on each hand.

Darlee gasped. "It's Thunder!"

Cassan nodded. "I would agree with how it sounds, but what is it?"

"Not sounds...is. That's his name. I must go and stop him."

Darlee fled from the platform. As he watched her go, a sudden sense of defeat coursed in his mind. What was wrong with him? He felt mentally exhausted. Turning to see the demon Thunder once more, he espied someone standing a few paces behind him. It was a woman. Tall, well-figured, yet grey like the other. Another demon. She had her hands spread out. Was she casting some kind of spell?

Thunder charged. More arrows sang, some at the huge demon, others at the woman. Once again, all failed to harm their marks.

The monster plunged into the front row of soldiers who flailed their swords uselessly against the impervious hide of the demon. Nothing harmed it. The beast killed with impunity.

He tried to think. There must be some way demons could be beaten. Not with weapons, for sure. Recalling the kick he had given to Hiss and seeing the creature scamper away holding its ribs, the answer occurred to him. Only hand-to-hand, brute strength, fists, feet, nothing more. There was no way it could be killed, only subdued.

Perhaps it could be tied or chained. Scanning the men in the street, none bore ropes. Instead, panic had set in as some ran and collided with those trying to press forward.

Noise from the gateway heralded more bad news. Soldiers of Piaxia were streaming in. With the archers no longer ready, they entered unmolested. Warlocks were among them, casting bolts of death hither and yon. This was going to be a slaughter. He read the surprise on his brother's face. "Did your preparation against Piaxia include how to fight demons? They cannot be harmed with weapons. Only trapped, and you have none of the tools necessary to do so."

"What would you have me do? No one could have planned for an attack by such as these."

Brumaine returned his concentration to the battle. Through the fleeing soldiers, he could see Darlee dashing directly toward Thunder. The behemoth stopped his attack, scooped her up, turned his back on the Moricans, and retreated to the woman, now joined by a tall warlock and a blonde female. Even from where he watched, he could hear her yelling for them to stop the attack.

Inside, he knew this was the window of opportunity to cease the hostilities. The situation on the field spoke otherwise. He grabbed Cassan by the upper arm. "Come. We must go down there and talk while we can. Either we will bring this to a close, or, at the very least, provide the time necessary for your troops to arrive, though I doubt even they will be capable of defeating the demons."

Leading the way, he raced down the stairs and made for the demons and Darlee. He hoped the girl would safeguard him as they approached.

His brother pulled even with him. "I must go first so the men will see. Stay close."

Nodding, he let Cassan take the lead. His brother slowed to a walk, his posture erect, arms in the air. He followed suit.

When they were five paces away, one of the warlocks cast a bolt. It hit Cassan square in the chest, knocking him to the ground.

He knelt quickly by his brother. "Stop your attack! Can you not see we come to parley? His hands were raised."

The same warlock pointed at him. "Death to the enemy."

Brumaine closed his eyes. So death would come now. All had been in vain.

At the sound of a magical bolt hitting, but feeling no pain, he opened his eyes to see the warlock fall. Standing free from the embrace of the demons was Darlee, hands held out at the Piaxians. "Enough! This stops here. I will strike anyone who attempts to harm the Morican princes. It is time for talk."

The young warlock turned to face his countrymen as well. "If my sister says stop, then we stop."

That must be Gar, Darlee's brother, the one she contacted through the stone. There was no doubt the message she had sent had successfully gotten through.

The two demons also moved to block the Piaxians, the big one growling menacingly. How swiftly the dynamics had changed on the street.

A groan from below returned his attention to his fallen brother, attempting to rise. Darlee's magic had worked. His brother was unharmed. He smiled. "Here, Cassan, let me help you. We have sudden allies that have halted the attack. Now is the time for you to be stately and negotiate the best deal you can."

A Piaxian captain stepped near. "This is an impasse. As the senior officer here, I have no authority to strike a deal with you. My orders are to rescue our people and remove you from the island. No exceptions."

Glancing behind him, Brumaine noted the surge of Morican troops arriving from the lower part of the city. If something wasn't done immediately, the fighting would resume. As his brother stood and brushed the dust from his clothes, Brumaine considered what the captain had said. "You are correct. Such a negotiation should occur between those of like rank. Regent Tarlok is safely ensconced not far from here. May I suggest that such discussions be left to him and Prince Cassan? Until then, we shall both withdraw from this conflict."

This was the moment where, whether or not, the fight renewed. He watched as the captain looked over Brumaine at the massing troops in the street, probably re-evaluating their chances as the odds changed.

Cassan took charge. "I am ready and willing to dismiss my soldiers to conduct talks. I await your answer."

Although only a moment or two, it seemed like forever before the captain finally nodded. "It is agreed. Lead me and my senior staff to the regent. There will be an armistice until the sun sets tomorrow. If an agreement cannot be reached by then, the armistice shall end."

Darlee spun to meet the gaze of everyone nearby. "I am coming, too. I intend to be part of this discussion."

Cassan smiled at her. "Considering your actions tonight, I had no doubt."

As the Piaxian captain and Cassan returned to their armies to inform them of the temporary halt to hostilities, Brumaine edged closer to Darlee. She beamed with confidence. Perhaps her plan to end the fighting would come true.

Glancing from her to her compatriots, he took the time to study the four. Despite the height difference and the thin beard, he could identify the family resemblance in the warlock. The blonde, he guessed, was somewhere in her mid-thirties. She did not look like Darlee and Gar so he doubted there was any family connection.

The other two were a dichotomy to behold. Though both demons, the female was simply stunning, perhaps the most beautiful woman he had ever seen despite her grey skin and hairless head. Both tall and voluptuous, he could describe her as nothing less than stunning, one who would make any man's knees weak. He suspected she was Brusk's mate, Silk. The captain was a lucky man.

If that was Silk, then the blonde could only be the other mentioned by Gar when Darlee spoke to him through the stone. Daphora. She was dressed like a highwayman, all in leathers, though upon closer examination he noted they were of the highest quality. She carried a bow and a number of sheathed knives were strapped to her arms and legs. A fighter. She was buxom as well, and attractive, but had not quite the beauty of Silk. He doubted any woman in the world did.

Finally, the behemoth was both a terror and a marvel to look at. Even the simplest movement by the demon exhibited muscles flowing beneath his skin. His fangs were the length of Brumaine's fingers. The rest of his teeth, pointed as well. The claws were thicker than his thumb and could probably shred a man to pieces in seconds. When he moved a step closer to Darlee, the beast growled and wrapped an arm round her. She smiled and patted at it, which brought forward something surprising. The thing was purring. Amazing.

When Cassan finished informing his troops, Brumaine turned to lead those going to the Hamak estate. At that moment, the hair on the back of his neck rose. Something fearful was in the air. Thunder began to growl, but was soon outdone by a loud rumble accompanied by the very ground shaking beneath his feet. What was happening? It continued to increase in intensity, and he soon lost his footing, falling to the earth. On his hands and knees, he scanned everywhere around him. Most people had followed suit and were now either on all fours or flat on their backs or bellies. A large crack appeared in the wall some thirty paces away, and a number of houses down the streets collapsed into rubble.

An earthquake. He had never experienced one before, but had heard of such an event. But unlike the mild tremors he had been told of, the immensity of what he was experiencing made him think there was more to this than normal.

It lasted only a few moments then quieted and was able to stand once again. What misfortune did the quake foretell?

CHAPTER 46

Kero should have gone with her.

When Brusk entered the hall and announced Darlee's departure, Kero went into the yard and stood next to his guardian. He decided to stand watch with Gragnishozar until she returned.

When the quake came, the assassin lord held him upright until it ended. The sound of destruction came from all directions. One entire wall that surrounded the compound collapsed, and the main home suffered significant damage.

Once the quake was over, the others, along with a cloud of dust, exited the hall and joined him outside.

Tarlok lofted several light globes into the sky to illuminate the courtyard further than the couple of simple torches that burned. "Is everyone all right?"

One of the soldiers had a sore shoulder where a ceiling beam had glanced off him, but, other than that, there were no injuries.

He turned to his lord. "What caused the ground to shake like that?"

Gragnishozar stared toward the east. "The mountain was woken. You cannot see it, but a black plume now rises from its crater. Volcanic activity has not happened on this island since I have been here, but it is like a resting giant that has had its sleep disturbed...awake and angry."

He tried his best to locate what his lord spoke of, but could not see past the area of illumination in the yard. "You are right, I cannot see it, but I do not doubt what you tell me. What woke it?"

His lord was quiet for a moment then turned to face him. "I cannot say for sure. There are many possibilities. It could be as simple as it was its time, nothing more. Volcanoes are unpredictable. I have my suspicions, but it would be best not to hypothesize."

Gragnishozar resumed his watch on the street. Kero knew there would be no more information drawn out of his lord. He remained quiet as he rejoined the assassin master in the vigil.

Something fluttered before his face. He watched as it drifted to the ground at his feet. It was a large black flake. Bending, he touched it and found it warm. When straightening, he discovered the air was full of them, drifting down everywhere. "What are they?"

"Volcanic ash. Tell me, was it hot?"

The possibilities of what his guardian hinted at frightened Kero. "No, but warm."

"Quick, check some more."

Bending, he ran his fingers across the ground to touch as many flakes as possible. Many were cold, some warm, but there were still a number that were hot, a couple even burning his fingers. His first reaction was to blow on the tips to cool them, and then decided to concentrate and use his magic to heal the burns. "Master, many are smoldering. What should we do?"

His lord gazed upward. "The sky is full of them, and some still glow red. Who knows how long they will continue to fall. I fear the worst."

Kero spun to see the reaction of the others to the ash. One of the warlocks was cursing how the cowl on his cloak had caught fire. Savan was patting his arms where flakes landed. Lazaan was constantly brushing at his bald head. "We need to get everyone back inside."

Gragnishozar grabbed hold of Kero. "Hold. I see people approaching."

Staring into the street, he, at first could see nothing. The falling ash had obscured nearly all light from the moon and stars. As he continued to stare, he could make out the forms of people running their way. Was it the Moricans? He looked behind him. "Quick, I think we are about to come under attack."

Savan was the first at his side, sword drawn. "Where? I see nothing."

Kero pointed. "There. Figures running in the dark our way."

Tarlok arrived and put a hand on Savan's sword. "Put it down. Can you not see by the size? The big one can be none other than Thunder. It is our rescue." He launched a light globe in the direction of those approaching.

He had no idea who Thunder was, but as they came into view, he could see the large one to be a ferocious looking creature, but in its arms was Darlee. It was with her! Alongside were both Brumaine and Cassan, and a number of others.

Tarlok opened the gate, and the group streamed in. A Piaxian captain saluted. "My regent, we have agreed to a temporary armistice in hopes of negotiating something better, but this cursed evil snow is descending, and we needed to run. Please allow us indoors."

The smell of singed hair had Kero brushing at it. A hot ash must have landed there. If the top of his head could catch fire, so could the roofs of houses. "Forget about getting indoors. If we don't do something, the city will burn tonight. We must warn the people."

Now standing freely, Darlee moved to his side. "Kero is right. We must first save Lymos. What point is there arguing over Riaz if it is destroyed by fire? You must both tell your troops to spread out through the city and fight the fires as they occur."

Gragnishozar stepped behind them, placing one hand on Kero's shoulder and another on Darlee's. "In the last few days, I have learned the value of listening to youth. Their minds are free of entrenched hatreds and limited thought. They believe anything is possible. Heed their message."

The first to react was Prince Cassan. He stood before Kero and Darlee. "I am in agreement." He turned to face the others gathered. "Which is Regent Tarlok?"

"I am, and I concur. Before any discussions on Riaz, we must do as Kero and Darlee suggest."

The two men shook hands and each turned to the officers from their respective armies, the Piaxian captain and Lieutenant Var. Kero listened as the men gathered and discussed the logistics— who would monitor which area, how water would be moved, and more. This was the kind of discussion for military people, something he could not aid in. Instead, he was drawn to the remaining people who had arrived. Notably, there was a tall, very pretty, hairless, grey-skinned woman. He suspected her to be a demon, like Hiss, and like Thunder.

The woman had gone to stand before Gragnishozar. "Your voice. It sounds familiar. I would ask that you remove the veil that I might see you."

With great surprise, he saw his master pull back the cloth to expose his face. Never before had Gragnishozar shown what he looked like to anyone besides him and Maresh. It was even more surprising when his master stepped into her embrace.

"Hello, Mother."

Mother? The demoness was his mother? He wondered how that could be. Gragnishozar was, by human standards, very old. He did not know for sure, but knew it was in excess of one hundred years. The demoness did look more than thirty. Did demons not age? He supposed anything was possible. He knew almost nothing of them, except from his exposure to Hiss.

She released him and stepped back to look him up and down. "It is good to see you are well, although I do not care for this all-covering black you wear. You should be proud of what you are, not hiding from mortals."

"It is not them I hide from. You know the truth."

"You're right. I'd forgotten."

The big demon Thunder stepped in and grabbed Gragnishozar in a bear hug and with a large pointed tongue, licked his face. As he struggled to free himself, his master laughed, a sound heard most rarely by Kero. It made him snicker. Obviously, the bond between these demons and his master was close.

All of the military people who were in the camp began to move out. It was late, and Kero was feeling a little tired, but he wasn't going to shirk his duty of helping in the fire brigade. He would help. The question was, with whom would he go?

As if in answer, he watched the rest split up. Cassan and Tarlok led one group along with Thunder, Brusk, Gar, and Lazaan. He guessed they would talk while they worked. Savan and Brumaine led the other accompanied by Silk, Daphora, and Darlee. Their joining the second group made it equal the number in the first. Besides, Darlee was in this group, and he would rather be with her.

Brumaine led the group out, but Kero was the only person who knew the city well. "Where are we going?"

"Toward the wharf. There's somewhere I need to check. Call it an obligation."

The city was designed in such a way that a number of large cisterns were positioned across the top and water flowed downhill from each through a clay tile flue all the way to the bay. Citizens would be able to draw water from small cisterns that served as collectors along the route. From the Hamak estate, they had gathered what vessels they could to use for a water brigade.

When they reached a house with a roof on fire, Brumaine stopped. "It looks like this is our first stop. Let's line up. I'll draw the water, pass to Kero, then Daphora, followed by Silk and lastly Savan, as he is tallest and can best throw the water on the roof. Darlee, you bring the empty vessels back to me."

Silk approached the door. "Count me out for now. I'm impervious to fire. I'm going in to look for people."

She dashed inside while Kero and the others stretched out their line and began the drill. The fire was small and in the time they spent putting it out, Silk returned with the family, all alive and well. Kero recognized the man. He worked in the market. As the flakes were still falling, it was best to make sure the man stayed outside and kept watch. He went and told him so.

The man looked skyward. "But what if the embers should land on me or my family?"

As if on cue, the clothing of one of his daughters caught fire, and they had to pat it out. There didn't seem to be any limit to the ash as it continued to drift down, already leaving a carpet across everything. "Keep the kids inside unless necessary. In the meantime, douse yourself with water. If you're wet, you'll be safe."

When finished, he turned to Savan. "Instead of us putting out the fires one at a time, it would be better to get everyone outside. Let's run door to door. The people can put out their own fires or help their neighbors. We can cover a lot more area that way."

The big Piaxian ruffled his hair and chuckled. "An excellent idea. Silk, Darlee, and I will take one side of the street. You, Brumaine, and Daphora take the other."

They split up and began pounding on doors. Knocking on every third one, they made great progress. Not only were the people doing as asked in wetting down their roofs, but some of the older children decided to help in the door knocking. If news continued to spread, soon the whole city would be outdoors on fire watch.

Brumaine tapped him on the shoulder. "Follow me. I still have that task to perform."

Silk and Daphora fell in behind. The blonde paced beside Kero. "Where is the prince going?"

Kero had his suspicions, but didn't want to say. "He said he has something to do."

She snorted. "Something to do, huh? I wonder."

He stayed silent but made note of the streets and with each passing the likelihood of his assumption became more and more prominent. Sure enough, the prince stopped at the door to the home of Janina. The redhead opened the door. "Brumaine, what are you doing here?"

"I've come to make sure you're all right."

She looked over his shoulder at both Silk and Daphora. "Considering your company, I'd say you're doing more than all right. If you think I'm going to be added into your covey of women as a replacement for Lasha, you're sorely mistaken. You've already got a blonde to play with."

Daphora stepped past Brumaine and grabbed Janina by the hair, yanking her into the street. "Listen carefully. If you think I consort with this young man, you're wrong. My circle includes kings and queens, not wet-behind-the-ears princes. He came here to rescue you. Accept his honor and agree."

Janina was desperately trying to pull her hair free. "Ow, ow, ow, ow, okay, ow, I agree. Just let me go."

Daphora released her grip and turned to Brumaine. "She's

yours. I hope she's worth it. Now, let's get back to work."

As Daphora started back up the street, Brumaine leaned close to Darlee. "Kings and queens? Is she serious?"

"Absolutely. She's good friends with both Queen Tessia of Piaxia and King Devron of Sechland. I wouldn't make her angry. She's also a top witch, my tutor at magic, and she can shoot your eye out with an arrow from a hundred paces. I'd say she's serious."

They started walking, checking with the growing crowd of people in the street that all fires were out. It was beginning to look like things were under control. Between discussions, Brumaine would stop to glance at Daphora. "Friends with King Devron, too? That could be valuable should Morica and Sechland ever come to terms."

Darlee giggled. "Well, maybe a little bit more than just friends."

"A consort? But I've heard he is a man in his mid-twenties. Though very attractive, she must be several years older than him."

Daphora stopped and turned to face Brumaine. "Ten, to be exact. Is there a problem?"

The prince sputtered for a moment, his jaw working, but no words coming out. Janina laughed. She stepped past Brumaine and hooked her arm into Daphora's. "I like you. You're my type of woman. Let's go."

Kero stopped to wait for the prince to move. "Brumaine? Are we going?"

A patrol of Piaxian soldiers came by, and the lead officer headed straight for the prince. "My liege, for the moment all fires are out, but the ash continues to fall and the cisterns are running dry. Soon, there will be no water to quench them. What shall we do?"

Brumaine looked to the bay. "Can we bring the water up from the sea somehow?"

"Unlikely. Perhaps we should be thinking instead of evacuating the city. If the hot ash continues and there is no water, the fires will spread quickly. Many will die."

Kero dashed to the nearest small cistern and peered in. It was already empty save the damp bottom. He looked up the street. If there was nothing draining down to where he was, then surely all those below him would be empty as well.

For those houses near the stream that ran through the center of town, there would be no problem, but much of the city was too far to access that water. He edged the soldier aside to get Brumaine's attention. "The large cisterns at the top of the city...they're the only answer. They needed to be refilled. Currently, only a portion of the stream is redirected either way into the cisterns, the rest allowed to flow freely down. We need to totally damn it to get the rest of the water."

Brumaine gazed up the street. "The stream you say. Quick, show us where it enters the cisterns."

"This way." He took the lead, Brumaine and the soldiers keeping pace, Darlee, and the others right behind them. As he ran he could overhear people crying out that there was no more water. New fires were starting everywhere. People were climbing on their roofs, working furiously to sweep the falling ash away.

He continued to climb the street as fast as he could. The ash, now the depth of almost half a hand, made hurrying treacherous, as he slipped and slid on the stuff, doing his best not to lose his balance and fall.

Breathing was becoming more difficult. The air was choked with soot floating everywhere. He was constantly coughing as did those nearby. He could feel a crust of it circling his lips and constantly had to wipe at his eyes. Braving a glance skyward, he wondered if the ash would ever stop falling.

He arrived at the small bridge crossing the stream at the top of the city. On either side were sluices directing a limited amount of water into the large cisterns. The stream was dark and muddy with ash and flowed slowly, and the water level was barely above where the sluices were. Little water was being diverted. He pointed down. "We need to damn the water to flood the system."

Brumaine scanned the area. "With what? I see nothing to use."

What would they use? Turning, he had a view of the lower part of the city with numerous houses now on fire, a patchwork of blazes dotting Lymos. Time was not on their side.

Another patrol, this time of Piaxian troops, water vessels in hand, was busy running a water brigade nearby. As he bent to cough out more of the dust, the answer came to him. "The bridge itself. It's made of stone slabs. We need to knock it over and maneuver the pieces into place."

"Brilliant." Brumaine turned to Daphora. "Quick. Get those troops to come help. We need every able-bodied man to do this."

She nodded and went to do as asked. The prince instructed his own soldiers what to do. The men began to chip away at the joints and mortars with their swords and pickaxes in an effort to loosen the pieces. He ran back to the street when spotting more Moricans passing near, to get them to assist. As they worked, more and more joined in and there were at least one hundred men from both armies hacking and pushing at the slabs.

When the first piece broke free, a small cheer went up. It slid onto its side and achieved exactly what Kero wanted—water diverting left and right of it, but it was in the wrong place. It needed to be pushed up the stream several paces to where the sluices were.

Another slab was shoved in, and men were gathering behind them, pushing with all their might against the flow of water and slightly uphill. Would they be able to do it? Brumaine jumped into the stream and joined in with the pushing. "Everyone in the water. We've got to move these slabs."

How much did the slabs weigh? Four hundred stone each? Or five? Despite as many men as could crowd around each piece, pulling and pushing, they only nudged slightly now and then. Even as he watched, men would drop away as they tired, although new ones took their place.

Darlee raced to Silk. "Please, you've got to help them. Give them the will to do it."

The demoness nodded and raised her arms. As Kero watched, the slabs moved faster. Whatever she was doing was working. What magic was she performing? Did she make the stones lighter? Perhaps levitate them some? No. Darlee had said something about will. It wasn't the slabs she was affecting, it was the men. She was giving them the will to succeed.

Brumaine's group gave one final shove and managed to get the slab in place. A huge torrent of water now turned into the sluice. The prince ran to the other side and help guide the other piece into place. "We've done it!"

Silk lowered her arms and collapsed.

Kero ran to her side as did Darlee and the prince. She smiled weakly. "I'll be all right. I'm just drained right now. Give me time to recover."

Brumaine stepped back into the creek and ordered the men to gather what smaller stones they could to place behind the slabs and ensure they didn't move.

Although the water was black with ash, Kero dunked his head to clear away as much of the soot as he could. Straightening and gasping for air, he noted many of the men following his example.

The prince was moving about them, congratulating them on their effort, both Morican and Piaxian alike. "A wonderful job of cooperation, but our work isn't done. There are still fires to put out."

The soldiers moved off to go fight the blazes where they could. Kero watched the water as it continued to be directed away, hoping it would be enough. Several larger fires were now burning in the city. He stared upward once more. Would the ash ever stop falling?

CHAPTER 47

Morning had finally come and with it, a change in the sky. No longer did the hot ash float down everywhere. Looking at the mountain, smoke still billowed up and into the atmosphere giving the morning a dull grey look, but it was a welcome sight compared to what they had been through.

Brumaine, exhaustion weary throughout every bone in his body, rested on the shovel he had been working, scraping ash off of the roof he stood upon.

From his vantage point, he could see a number of fires still raged here and there, but most had been put out or contained.

Almost half the city...that's how much appeared lost or damaged. For many of the people of Lymos, life ahead would be a struggle. He had no idea how many lives must have been lost. Hopefully, the number was less than he expected.

Climbing down to the street, his limbs shook. The one thing he wanted more than anything was sleep. Gathering his team, he started the walk toward the Hamak estate and hoped the two still-standing houses were undamaged.

Walking to his right was Janina. He gave her only the most cursory of glances...too tired to consider a dialogue. She was eyeing him. Something was on her mind. What did it matter? The woman probably hated him because of the death of Lasha. He lamented the girl's death, admitted his sorrow, and accepted what blame he could. As cold as it may be, there was nothing he could do.

"I've misjudged you."

What? That statement did not fit into his assessment. She knew the truth. He wondered if she suffered from shock. He met her gaze. "No, you haven't."

"Yes, I have. I thought you concerned only with your own well-being. Considering all you did last night, I was wrong."

He needed to correct her, return her to the mindset she had before. "One night does not define a person. I *am* a selfish man.

I've lived my life that way."

"You're correct, one average night doesn't, but last night was far from average. It was cataclysmal. Nights such as last night can define a person, not average ones."

He was too tired to debate the point. He waved a hand in dismissal. "Perhaps...perhaps not."

Upon reaching the gate, a sense of relief flooded him as he found the estate unharmed. How? Gragnishozar and Hiss still remained where they had stood when everyone had left. He could only assume the assassin lord had remained there all night. Despite his weariness, his curiosity had the better of him as he approached Kero's guardian. It was somewhat unnerving as, ever since the arrival of Silk, Kero's guardian remained unmasked, his face visible to all. Though not the same as the demons, it looked...alien. There was some similarity to the rocky features of his golem creations. "Seeing you for the first time, I recognize some of the demon that is in you. It is understandable why you kept yourself concealed."

Silk came to stand beside him and held an arm against his. "At the moment, you appear more like me than he does."

Looking down, he noted not only were his clothes covered in the dark ash, but his skin as well. Brushing at the dust, he managed to get some of his olive-colored flesh to show through the grime. "I suppose you're right. I could use a good bath."

He glanced at the houses. They stood as he remembered them, unharmed save the middle one. "What happened here? Why is there no fire damage?"

The assassin lord folded his arms across his chest. "Do not misjudge the powers I have. In a small locale such as this, it was possible for me to create enough of a wind to keep the roofs clear. Considering the knowledge that negotiations are to occur here today, I felt it best to ensure there was somewhere to meet."

He had forgotten about the talks. They were something he needed to be part of. Blinking a few times, he searched inside of him for the strength to stay awake. "Yes, a good idea. Have the others returned yet?"

Gragnishozar nodded and pointed to the house on the left. "Yes. They are engaged inside. Originally, I thought to join them, but I am not the proper person to represent this country. I have sent Lazaan in my stead. He has a different view on politics than me. Perhaps, at this time, after all that has occurred, it might be time to listen to it."

He thanked the assassin lord, instructed the others to get some sleep, though Silk declined, and then made for the home in question. Stepping inside, he made note of who was seated— Prince Cassan and Lieutenant Var, Regent Tarlok, and Commander Savan, Captain Brusk, and the assassin Lazaan. Whatever would be decided at that table would determine the future of Riaz.

Var, seeing Brumaine enter, stood and saluted. "My prince, in your absence I have been assisting your brother. Now that you are here, please, take my chair."

He acknowledged the salute. "Thank you, Var. Briefly, what has been discussed so far?"

"Both Piaxian and Morican military reports. Between the earthquake and the firestorm, almost one-third of all housing is uninhabitable. Deaths are estimated at between eight to nine hundred citizens. Both armies lost a number of men as well. Outside of the city, as far as I could see, all crops have been utterly destroyed, including the grape vines. During the sea battle, every fishing vessel was lost, though not the fishermen. Many were saved by the Piaxians. As a result, Riaz is without food, shelter, and the prime ingredient of their overseas commerce, wine. Unless action is taken, countless will starve or die of exposure. Frankly, the country is a mess."

As Brumaine sat, Cassan acknowledged his presence with a nod then turned his focus to Tarlok. "Now then, Regent, back to the matter at hand. Who will govern this land? Piaxia? I think not. They are in need of immediate assistance, we have far greater troops here already to help with the rebuilding stage, and we have the transports necessary to restock these people until they can once more be self-sufficient."

Savan pounded the table. "Not without a fight you won't."

The commander's brother put a calming hand onto his forearm. "Let's not be harsh and urge action that would result in more deaths than have been suffered throughout the night." He gave a terse smile to Cassan. "As you can see, my rambunctious sibling is itching for combat. Despite your numbers, do you think you can best us for control? I have my doubts, but such conflict would do little for the people of Riaz. What is needed is a treaty to cease all hostilities for ten fortnights until such time as the city is sound and producing their own food once more."

"And give you time to bring reinforcements? I think not. Yes, it may be possible that you could best us, but then who would be the losers? Morica? No, Riaz. You lack the manpower and resources to help these people."

Brusk guffawed. "Morican compassion? Not likely. Ya bastards have been preying on my people for decades. Even if yer father was here swearing on his life to commit to such honor, I wouldn't believe it. *Especially* him. By the gods, he had yer brother killed. How can he be trusted for anything?"

Cassan reddened. "There is no proof of that claim. Only the actions of Commander Oberus have been verified, and he lies dead for that treason. My brother can testify to that." He turned to face Brumaine. "Am I right?"

For the past number of days, he had debated this question with his brother. The question remained unresolved. Now, Cassan was trapping him into denying the possibility. Perhaps he should have taken the advice he had given the others to go to bed and get some rest. From all that he had heard and seen, his intuition told him their father was implicit in the death of Doren. It was originally supposed to be his death, but others, especially Kero, had intervened. If it was up to the young Riazian or Darlee, he had no doubt what path they would choose.

He was torn on what to do—support his brother, or implicate his father. He studied the faces of all those gathered as they looked to him for a response. He knew they were waiting, and his hesitation on answering was probably swaying opinion regardless of what he said.

What would Doren have done had the roles been reversed and he lying dead in the hold of the trireme? Would his brother have sided with Cassan...or not? He was unsure. In retrospect, it mattered little. Doren was dead and the decision was his anyway. He needed to be the one to make it, not act on what he imagined his brother would do, but this was not the time or place for such a thing. For now, he needed to stay neutral. He would not answer it, but instead reply with a question. "I thought the point of this meeting was to discuss the future of Riaz, not revisit the past?"

The assassin Lazaan stood up. "Well put, young prince. I can no longer sit and listen to foreign countries discussing ways to divide up my homeland. The answer is simple. We want neither of you. Instead, I call on both Piaxia and Morica to withdraw their forces from Riaz and leave us be. We will manage somehow."

Savan laughed. "That's the thanks you get. You come to their help, and they throw you out. We should just let Morica have this place. They're ungrateful."

The regent shook his head for a moment then met the stare of the assassin. "Combined with the assassination of your merchant leaders, you have no government in place to restore order, to direct the rebuilding, to organize the food imports. Your crops are devastated, your fishing industry without vessels, your export industry destroyed. How will you feed and shelter your people?"

"The grape is a hearty plant. From the roots, safe below ground, they will flourish once more, as will other crops. True, the near future will be harsh, but we will rebuild this city, and it will become a gleaming gem once more. To run things, we will elect officials of high caliber and moral tenets. It shall be a government of the people. A democracy."

Tarlok stood as well. "If that is your answer, then all that is left is to negotiate the orderly fashion in which our collective troops will withdraw. If Morica intends to stay, then so will we, and the battle will resume. At the end, there will be no winners, only losers. I leave it to Prince Cassan to capitulate to your demands, as I will."

Brumaine recalled the fight at the gate and the one-sided way it progressed because of the demons at Piaxia's disposal. Unlike his brother, he did not think a victory was assured. Further, even if they should, by some chance, win, there still were the assassins to deal with, and most notably Gragnishozar. There was much to discuss with his brother. He grabbed Cassan's arm above the wrist. "Ask for time. Do not decide now."

Cassan glanced at him, raising his eyebrows as he studied Brumaine's face. He then stood. "I shall request some time to consider the proposal."

Savan stood. "Only until sunset. Those were the terms originally set by your captain. Not a moment longer."

As Brusk also rose, Brumaine realized he was the only one left seated. With how tired he felt, the idea of joining the others afoot was not what he wanted to do. Then the beginning of a tremor kept him seated, holding onto the table. "Another quake."

Tarlok pointed to the door. "Quick, everyone outside. Who knows whether this house will withstand a second one."

Those gathered rushed to the door, Brumaine at the rear. As he stepped into the courtyard, the most terrifying noise deafened him and the magnitude of the tremor greatly intensified sending everyone to the ground.

The sound had come from the mountain. As he clambered to his knees, he looked east to see a number of large chunks of rock flying into the air above the crater. The top of the mountain had blown clean off. Cassan was standing and offered a hand to help him rise while saying something, but Brumaine could not hear him, only read his lips asking if he was all right. He was deaf. "I can't hear you."

The regent placed a hand on the back of his head, and as the moment passed, the continued roar of the mountain became louder, though the tremor had passed. He nodded to Tarlok. "Thank you. I'm better."

Mesmerized, he watched as a golden-red river issued from the crater, heading north, but then inexplicably turning in their direction. Everyone gathered around, people issuing from the other house joining in. "Why does it turn this way? Will it reach the city?"

"It will."

He turned to Gragnishozar, whose voice he had recognized. The assassin lord stared intently at the lava flow. "How do you know?"

Between them was Silk, the demoness. After glancing at Brumaine, she turned to Gragnishozar. "It's him, isn't it?"

"Yes. He is coming."

Brumaine knew who *he* was. Memory of what the imp Hiss had said still in his mind. He stared at the lava in the distance. *The god comes.*

CHAPTER 48

The noise of the blast woke Darlee from a dead sleep. As she attempted to rise from the bed, the tremor knocked her to the floor. She crawled to the door then, with the assistance of Daphora, made it outside to see the spectacle issuing from the volcano.

When Gragnishozar stated it was *he* who was coming, despite the warm air, a chill went through her. How powerful was this being to split open a mountain and descend on a stream of molten rock? Memories of her encounters with the god through the stone were not good ones. Despite her shield, he froze her one time then ravaged her mind the second, all done without actual physical contact. How could he possibly be stopped?

Tarlok, after staring at the mountain, turned to Gragnishozar. "Watching how slow that lava is flowing, it seems to me it will take some time before the god gets here, perhaps a couple of hands. Do you agree?"

"Yes. Though he can, he will not likely leave the stream. He draws power from it."

"Then perhaps there is time."

Savan stopped staring at the oncoming doom to look wide-eyed at his brother. "To do what?"

"Evacuate the city. We must get these people to safety."

The regent, grabbing Cassan by the shoulder, broke the prince's concentration on the mountain. "We must work together in concert one more time. There is no knowing what havoc the god may do when he arrives. It would be best to move the citizens to somewhere safe."

For a moment, the prince stared slack-jawed at the regent. Shaking his head, he broke whatever reverie he was in. "What you ask is impossible. Where would they go? My transports in the bay are in need of repair from the firestorm, and even if they were all functional, there is no way we could transport the thousands and thousands of citizens of Lymos. It would take hundreds of vessels. I have barely enough for my own men, let alone all the people of this city."

Darlee listened in as they discussed other possibilities, but none offered a solution. In the time it would take to get people to the inland gate, the god would have arrived, putting the citizens right into the teeth of it. All the work during the night to save the city may have been for naught. A fiery god approached, and there was nothing they could do to stop him. "As I listen to the two of you bicker, I fail to hear what the only possible course is. We must stop the god from coming."

Savan laughed. "What should we do? Ask him nicely to go away? I don't think he'll listen."

There must be a way to defeat him. There had to be. She tried to remember some of the childhood tales of encounters with gods and whether any involved them being bested, but the only times a person got the upper hand was through trickery—outsmarting them. And those were just stories. Most likely fabrications and none of them true. She doubted the god would fall for some simple ruse.

If anyone might know how, it would be Gragnishozar. She moved to stand beside Kero's guardian. No longer wearing the veil, his appearance was somewhat fearsome with his skin looking like mottled stone, but she preferred it. Talking to someone with their face covered was never a pleasant thing. You could not read their eyes to determine whether they spoke truth or lies. "Is there a way the god can be beaten?"

"With the help of another god, yes, but there is not one available."

She grabbed one of his hands and turned it in hers to study it. She examined the texture of the skin—it felt like warm stone—and the size of his fingers—each nearly half the thickness of her wrist. He was the son of the god who came. That made him a demigod. "You are powerful. Maybe, with your golems, *you* can defeat him."

Gragnishozar smiled. "I am honored you think me worthy, but, alas, from experience I know he will outmatch me."

Thunder moved to stand nearby and growled at the oncoming

lava stream. Gragnishozar pushed him away. "This is not your fight. You and the others must go. It is possible he does not know you are here. Should I succumb, then perhaps he will simply leave without looking farther."

Silk grabbed onto the assassin lord's arm. "No, Thunder is right. It is time we stood our ground. Maybe he will see the error of his ways and leave us be. I, too, shall remain by your side during this trial and help in any way I can."

Seeing the resolution in Silk, the possibility of losing her had become real. Though Silk was only her foster mother for the past year, the idea was not one Darlee was willing to accept. In the war against the other realms she had lost both her real father and mother. Could she suffer such a loss once more? Not if she could prevent it. She looked into Gragnishozar's eyes. "What are you going to do?"

"There is little choice. He knows I am here. If I run, he will raze every inch of Riaz until he finds me. Furthermore, there are the demons. I helped them escape from his control a hundred years ago. He will wish to bind them once more to his will."

Despite his stubborn ways, she had grown fond of the assassin lord. Considering that Silk was his biological mother, that made him family. "Silk is my foster mother. That makes you my stepbrother. If you intend to fight, then I intend to fight with you. I'm not exactly without my own powers."

She looked for Gar amongst the others. Spotting him, she waved for him to be by her side. "Come Gar. You have a new brother to care for as you care for me. Your friend Thunder stands with him, will not you also?"

His brother separated from those he stood nearby and joined her. "I'm here, Sis. I promised you before. I'll never let you come to harm."

Hearing her brother's words swelled the pride she felt inside. They were the two most powerful warlocks in any of the seven realms or Piaxia. If anyone could make a difference, it must be them. With Thunder and Silk, together they would stand with Gragnishozar against the god. The thought brought a large smile to her face. Look at us. We are unafraid.

From the other group, Kero moved to stand in front of his master. "My magic isn't that powerful, but you have been, for a very long time, my father. I must help in any way I can."

Gragnishozar attempted to shove his ward back the way he came. "No. The risk is too great. I will not see you die."

Kero pushed back. "It is my choice. You have always said I am accountable for my own actions. I want to do this. You cannot stop me."

The assassin lord ceased his attempt to evict Kero from the group. "It is true. That is what I have said. What is important is whether you have reasoned out your decision before making it or whether you are acting on impulse. Be wise."

Kero moved to stand once more in front of Gragnishozar. "Okay, I've thought about it. I'm staying with you."

Kero then met her gaze and nodded. In the short time she had been on the island, she had definitely made a friend in the young Riazian, perhaps even more. She did not know to what level he had feelings for her, but it was there. She also didn't know whether she could reciprocate those feelings. With so much danger and conflict since her arrival, she wondered whether such a bond would have developed without the situation having thrust them together so closely.

It was a difficult question she could ill afford the time to consider. What happened in the next few hands would affect everyone. Her possible love interests would have to wait until later.

She needed to concentrate on how she could help defeat the god. He couldn't be all-powerful because she had resisted him that first time, although only partially. Her body had frozen, but her mind remained shielded. If she could achieve that single small victory, then perhaps, combined, it could be done. When Lazaan extended his hand to Gragnishozar, stating he must help defend his homeland, the number of lord level warlocks now stood at three. Surely, there must be a level that surpassed the breaking point. She could only hope they had reached it.

From behind, Darlee felt a tug on her arm. Turning, she came face to face with her foster father, Brusk. He was red in the face, obviously angered.

"Here now. This is insanity. Ya don't think you can defeat a god, do ya? Come away from there and listen to me fer once. I love you like I was your real father, not just yer step one. I don't want to lose ya." He looked to Silk. "Or you. I haven't had a woman in my life for many a year, and for the last one I've been blessed with ya as my partner. Come away."

Silk stepped to Brusk and kissed his cheek. "You know my skill. I can sense in Darlee her will in this is very strong. I intend to do whatever I can to strengthen it further, along with those who would help. If I fail and am taken again, I will miss you, with all my heart, but do not attempt to prevent me from protecting my son, nor Darlee her brother."

"Huh. You're all nuts, the lot of ya. Fighting against a god...crazy, that's what it is. Simply crazy." He grabbed Silk round the waist, pulled her tight, and kissed her hard. "All right, then. Where do I sign up for this crazy outfit? I'll not be standing by when the fighting begins."

Daphora hooked an arm into Brusk's free one. "Count me in as one of the crazies. My brother's been calling me that for years."

Darlee joined them in a group hug. She was so proud. When Brusk released her, she cast a magical shield on him. "Thank you, Father. This shield should help, but it's not as strong as my own. I don't know for sure how well mine will stand up against the god's magic, so do your best and try not to be in the direct line of his attack."

"Aye, girl, I'll be careful, but if I can get in one good hit, I'm taking it."

Savan chuckled. "I bet you will." He turned to Tarlok. "Well, little brother, it seems it's just us and the Moricans left. We can't evacuate the city, just us. Any idea what you want to do?"

The regent was pacing, stopping every now and then to glance at Cassan or Brumaine. When he finally came to stop, he squared up in front of the older Morican prince. "Prince Cassan, I doubt this is wise, but I believe our only hope is to fight. Whether the god can be beaten is debatable, but we don't have a lot of other choices."

Before the prince could answer, Brumaine placed a hand on his brother's shoulder. "You must fight, Cassan. If the god is not stopped and he razes the city, all will have been for naught. Think if you make the difference and victory is achieved. The songs they will sing of you back home will become as immortal as the gods themselves."

"Do you really believe that?"

"With every bone in my body."

Cassan broke into a wide grin. "Then I guess we are fighting a god!" He turned to Var. "Lieutenant, quick. Gather the men and bring all of those catapults and ballistas up to the gate. Find every loose stone of size for ammunition. Time is short."

As the lieutenant dashed off, Gragnishozar made for the street. "There are some stones I prefer not collected. I best get to them before the Morican troops do. I will meet you at the gate."

Along with Lazaan, all the Moricans and the Piaxians dispersed in different directions, intent on marshaling their forces and preparing in whatever way possible for what seemed impossible—defeating a god.

Darlee walked toward the gate with her brother, Kero on her other side, Daphora, Brusk, Silk, and Thunder immediately behind them. "If only there was some way we could channel all our magic together instead of using it separately. I bet that would be enough."

"Only the staff of Bron could do that, and it's not here. We'll have to fight as best we can."

Silk tapped her on the shoulder. "There is another way. Hiss. He has the ability to absorb and transfer mana. When I arrived at your camp, he was with Gragnishozar, but I have not seen him since. Do you know where he is?"

Where did that little imp go? "Quick, we need to find him."

Thunder stuck his nose in the air, sniffed, and then hurried off south, toward the wharf. Gar chuckled. "If anyone can find Hiss, it's Thunder. That nose of his is more sensitive than anything. I've seen him in action before. My guess is Hiss is looking for a ride off the island before the god gets here. He's always been a coward."

While walking, Darlee would peek every now and then toward the mountain. The city wall blocked from view the front edge of the lava flow. How close was it? Was there time to prepare a defense? She nudged her brother. "Let's hurry. I can no longer see the god coming."

Gar glanced toward the mountain then nodded. "You're right. Shall we run? You were always the slow one in the fields back home."

Home, somewhere she and her brother planted crops and vegetables to maintain a simple existence. Home, the simple two-story frame house with the big central room and its stone fireplace, now burnt to the ground a year past. Home, where two graves—their mother and father, killed by her own countrymen—rested in the garden. It was no longer home. Home was with Captain Brusk, the demoness Silk, and, at times, her magical instructor Daphora, lived more happily than she ever remembered the old house to be. "No. Save your strength. Let's make sure everyone is there at the same time to confront the god."

Arriving at the gate, a number of Piaxian troops were already present, the two catapults they had brought with them already inside the wall. Commander Savan was busy instructing the men on how he wanted them placed to face the mountain.

She stepped out of the gate to locate the lava stream and determine how close it was. Considering how much time had passed since it first appeared and how far it had flowed. It was also her first chance to see the devastation of the crops.

She glanced at Kero, who stood solemnly to her left. Since the start of the conflict, he had lost his home, his friend Stod, and the woman Maresh who'd helped care for him. Unlike her, he had no new home with new stepparents to go to. If things went badly, whether to the Moricans or the god, he could lose his guardian and his country. For him, there would be no home. Even should they win the day, there would be almost nothing left. She had only sympathy for him

He sighed. "Prior to the firestorm, the view from here was

beautiful. As far as the eye could see, the hills were filled with farmers' fields and vineyards. Now, save for the stream that feeds water to the city, there is nothing but black ash. It is a dark day for Riaz."

She glanced at the creek. The rivulet was improving as the ash that had floated on it was either sunk to the bottom or forced to the banks. "It will recover. Already the water runs clearer. How long until the countryside is green again? The year is still young. There is time."

The noises coming from behind the wall had increased, and she looked back to see the war machines of Morica arriving, Prince Cassan and Prince Brumaine along with them. There were an awful lot of them, and she had to believe they would make a difference. How could the god withstand the constant barrage of rocks and huge iron bolts that would be fired at it?

It took some time to get the devices all positioned, and as they neared doing so, the noise of moving them competed with a steady thumping that grew in volume.

From down the street, Gragnishozar came into view accompanied by four huge stone golems. They were a marvel to behold—twice the height of a man and almost as wide as a person tall. "They're amazing."

Kero nodded. "Yes. They are the ones made from the floor of Rock House. My master can only keep them alive for a couple of hands. After that, his mana will wane, and they will collapse back into the pile of stones they once were."

She turned to look at the river of lava. It was getting close, and striding down it some fifty or so paces from the leading edge was a man—tall, but no more so than her brother, muscular, yet not the thickness of her foster father. Even from the distance, she could see he was incredibly handsome. In a normal circumstance, he would make any woman swoon. Whatever the raiment he was dressed in, it showed gold in color, making him look resplendent and regal. Atop his head, instead of hair, a crown of golden-red fire burned. He looked every part the god he was.

She checked behind her to see how close Gragnishozar and his golems were. Only paces away. Behind him, she could see Prince Cassan, his arm raised in the air.

He dropped it.

"Fire!"

CHAPTER 49

The god stopped and held out his hands. In front of him, a wall of molten rock rose from the river of lava. Into the barrier thudded a number of the projectiles, while many sailed wide, high or short. To Kero, it looked like someone dropping stones into mud. There was a splatter at the point of impact with chunks of lava flying out in a circular way, but the rock or spear then simply stuck where they hit.

The lava flowed over the projectiles, and as the wall continued forward, every trace vanished save licks of flame where they had hit. He wondered whether they melted and simply added to the mass that constituted the flow or were buried under it.

Behind him, Prince Cassan kept up the barrage while the god resumed his approach. The barrier before him was contorting as it moved. It was changing...defining into...something...something huge...a monstrous lava golem.

Once fully formed, the creature hurled a ball of molten rock. It soared directly over Kero's head. Even though the projectile was at such a height as to clear the city archway, he still felt the heat emanating as it passed. From his position under the arch, he watched it all the way through its trajectory until it splashed down among the Moricans, sending torrents of flaming lava in all directions.

Two catapults caught in the wake immediately burst into flames, but more sickening were the number of men also hit by globs of lava. They screamed and fell to the ground, some dying almost instantly, others in the kind of pain one could hardly imagine.

Piaxian warlocks raced to the injured, doing what they could to heal those who still lived. Even that was difficult as more than one warlock fell away from the man they attempted to heal, the job undone. Such was the one curse of the healing magic. The warlock suffered the pain of the patient while the healing process occurred. For some, it must be too difficult.

Nevertheless, despite the damage, Cassan continued to urge his troops to carry on the assault. Prince Brumaine had formed a water brigade whose members were doing what they could to quickly quench the lava where it lay.

Kero turned to look at the god once more. Behind him, another giant lava golem was forming. When one seemed impossible to harm and stop, what could they possibly do against a second?

From a few steps away, Darlee hurled lightning bolts at the god. She was fearless, standing fully exposed on an open granite face. He knew she was using the Key to draw power from the stone of the world. Would it be enough?

The bolts sizzled and died against the god's defensive shield. Perhaps the god was the wrong target. Summoning his own magic, he hurled his at the still-forming lava golem. It struck and sent a splatter of material from the shoulder of the thing. Success! The golems, like Gragnishozar's, had no defensive aura. "Darlee! Aim at the golems."

She nodded and changed her attack. He resumed his own. Her first bolt severed the thing's right arm. His next damaged a leg. Her second tore the head of the monster clean off. Firing once more at the damaged leg, he managed to sever it at the knee. Followed by a shot from Darlee that ripped through the huge chest, it collapsed in a heap.

He wanted to cheer for joy, but it caught in his throat. Rising from the heap, the creature began to form anew. Darlee continued to attack, but Kero's mana level was already woefully weak.

Never in his life had he felt such a sense of utter despair and uselessness. What harm could he do? The feeling of impotence had him wondering whether the original plan of Tarlok to run and hide may have indeed been the better option.

The second golem, now fully formed, stepped from the lava stream toward Darlee. She would be crushed. He would be next. Panic seized him as he dashed to Darlee's side to pull her away. "Come on. You're not safe out here."

"This is open stone. I need it. I'm not leaving."

Silk and Daphora had also moved to be near. He assumed they

also wanted Darlee to withdraw, but instead, Silk placed a hand on the girl. When the demoness also touched him, he changed his mind about running. He suddenly felt like they could win. Why couldn't they defeat the golem? No longer on the lava stream, it would have no source to replenish itself.

He renewed his attack, as did Darlee, with Daphora throwing bolts as well. With each step the lava monster took toward them they continued to chip at the creature until, finally, mere paces away, it collapsed into a slag pile of steaming molten rock. A victory, but Kero was now totally spent. No more magic could he perform today. "I'm out of mana."

Silk gave him a gentle shove toward the city. "Get behind the wall and help there any way you can. I'll continue to feed these two with will until either they or I run dry."

He nodded and hurried toward Brumaine. Perhaps he could help with the water brigade. It would be none too soon as another huge ball of lava crashed into the Moricans.

He glanced at the god and the giant golem that protected it. They were definitely getting closer as the lava stream continued to flow toward the city. If it entered Lymos, the city would be doomed. They needed to stop him somehow.

He needed to step to the side as Gragnishozar and the four stone golems thundered past. His master was going to confront the god. Despite his original plan of going to help the prince, he remained transfixed to watch the oncoming battle. Could his lord win? So far, the god had shown extraordinary power in what he had done. Besides the golems, what did it take to direct a flow of lava the way you wanted? Was it possible for the god to tire and run out of mana? Maybe, just maybe. He could only hope.

Despite the massive size of the stone golems, the lava golem was more than twice the size of one. When the first of his lord's creations reached the behemoth, it swatted the stone giant with the back of its hand and the golem tumbled into a pile of the rocks that comprised it.

Still, he came to understand the sacrifice as the other three tackled the monster, grabbing arms and a leg. Whether it could be brought down was yet to be seen, but it was, for the moment immobilized. No more flaming balls of molten rock would sail into the city.

Gragnishozar sped past the battling golems to engage the god directly. As he stepped into the lava flow, his clothes flashed into flame and were nothing but ashes by the time he threw the punch at the god's face.

Considering the size difference, his master being so much larger, he expected the blow to send the god sprawling, but it had little effect, merely turning the god's head before he faced Gragnishozar once more. He then threw his own blow to his master's midsection, causing his lord to drop to one knee.

The god laughed, a deep, resonating sound that reverberated through the air. Gragnishozar and everyone gathered in the fight were mere playthings to be toyed with. Despite the influx of will he had received from Silk, the possibility his master would be vanquished and taken away was very real. He needed help.

Thunder appeared at his side and thrust Hiss into his arms then, in great strides, charged into the fray. He had always suspected his master immune to fire. There were more than enough times he had seen Gragnishozar dip his hands into the brazier unharmed. With no experience to relate to, it surprised him that Thunder was also unaffected. The huge demon tackled the god and the two fell in a heap, which gave Gragnishozar enough time to straighten.

Hiss clutched tight. "Not enough! Not enough! Thunder and Gragnishozar not enough! All lost! Not enough!"

As the sets of combatants continued their struggle, it suddenly occurred to Kero that all other attacks had stopped. He glanced at the women to see Darlee, Daphora, and Silk standing idle. They must be out of magic as well.

Turning, he looked inside the wall to check on Prince Cassan and his forces. Hundreds lay dead. Many of the soldiers had fled. Of those who remained, many were busy removing the wounded from the area to a triage established down the street by Regent Tarlok and the Piaxians. The water brigade of Prince Brumaine continued to fight what looked like a losing cause. Fires burned everywhere. All the war machines were destroyed save one ballista. Cassan yet lived, and he and Savan were struggling with the last machine, trying single-handily to drag it toward the gate. Surprisingly, Captain Brusk joined them to move the thing.

He turned to watch the battle on the lava flow. The god was pummelling both Gragnishozar and Thunder, but they kept up their assault. Hiss was right. The two were no match. As to the golems, one more of the stone creatures had fallen, leaving one less to battle the lava monster.

They were quickly running out of forces to fight the god.

It would soon be over—everything. His city, his country, his people, all would be lost. The lava flow continued to edge toward the gate, not more than twenty paces away now. At that distance, he could feel the heat waft his way with every gentle breeze. If the flow reached the gate, it would speed downhill from there. The city would burn to the ground. Thousands would die. Was there no way to stop it?

The sound of many feet made Kero look for the source. Approaching at a jog was Lazaan and a large number of the members of the guild. Could fifteen warlocks turn the tide? Considering the ineffectiveness of not only his, but Darlee's and Daphora's attacks, he doubted it. What was needed was someone of the same power as the god.

He looked down. Maybe the answer was in his hands. Clinging so tight to his shirt that his claws were biting into Kero's skin was the imp Hiss. That very first encounter with the demon still weighed in his mind. He had been drained, magically, totally. Silk had said such mana could be transferred from Hiss to another.

He moved to step in front of Lazaan and block the assassin's progress. "Lazaan, you must listen to me. No individual warlock can harm the god. We've all tried...and failed, even Darlee. I have an idea on a possible way to beat him, but it requires the assistance of you and every member of the guild."

The assassin held up a hand and stopped in front of Kero, the others following suit. "Quickly, then, what is this plan? The city is about to be lost."

He lofted Hiss in the air for all to see. "This demon can transfer mana from any warlock to another. Give me all of your mana, and maybe I can do what has so far been impossible, strike the god with magic."

A murmur spread through the warlocks, and Lazaan paused to listen. He then reached out and took hold of the imp. "I think your plan has merit, but it must be me who does it, not you. Unlike you, I can access the Key to multiply my power, and I have the experience and knowledge on what best to do."

At first, Kero did not wish to release Hiss. The idea was his. The duty should be his. It wasn't fair that Lazaan should usurp it, but then he stopped to think about what the assassin had said, and it was all true. He did not know how to access the Key. He was not fully trained in the use of magic. He had no experience in such a fight.

He let go. "You are correct. Take him."

He crouched to be face to face with Hiss. "This is up to you. There is no time for any more of your fear. You must transfer all of the mana, every last bit, into Lazaan. Do not be selfish. Do not hold any back. Do you understand?"

Hiss whimpered then nodded. "Me understand."

Kero straightened and looked over Lazaan's head to the others. "All right. Everyone must step up to the imp and let him place a hand on your head. Do not fear. It will not hurt. You will only feel a weakness that, once he is finished, will pass. I am already drained, so I have none to offer. Who will be first?"

Pushing through the men was Petrius. "Me. I will go first."

As the assassin gained close access, he and Kero exchanged smiles. "Thank you,

Petrius. Bend close and hold still. It will not take long."

Petrius ducked to allow Hiss easy reach for his forehead. The demon clasped a hand across the assassin's forehead and reached up with the other hand to hold onto Lazaan's. After a moment, Hiss released Petrius and the assassin straightened. "I feel woozy, but, like you said, the sensation is passing already."

Lazaan beamed. "I can tell you, I felt the transfer and have never felt stronger before. It's working."

One by one, the other assassins took turns to be drained of mana. With each transfer, Lazaan would gasp lightly. Kero wondered whether there may be a negative side effect to what was happening, but it mattered not. At the moment, all that did matter was defeating the god.

When the last had finished, Lazaan handed Hiss back to Kero. "Thank you. I go now to fight the god. Pray that I succeed."

Normally, the response in society would be, *"may the gods be with you,"* but that wasn't appropriate. Instead, he shifted Hiss into his left arm and extended his right to take Lazaan's wrist. "You can do this."

Lazaan nodded and strode out of the gate, but instead of heading toward the god, he headed the other way. Where was he going? Kero put Hiss down who scampered to Silk. He followed the assassin, pausing to glance at the lava flow to see only one stone golem remained.

Lazaan stepped into the creek. Holding his hands in front of him, Kero watched as the water at his feet began to roil and splash, a whirlpool appearing, but instead of water draining down, it began to funnel upward. The water continued to build higher and higher, the creek all but dry toward the city. Everything flowing toward Lymos was joining into the building mountain of water.

As it continued to grow, it began to take form—arms, legs, and a head. It was a giant water golem, larger even than the lava monster. When it appeared fully formed, Kero waited for it to attack the god. Instead, it remained standing where it had been created. "What are you waiting for? Attack!"

Lazaan shook his head. "I've used everything to create it but can't control it. There's only one choice."

Lazaan closed his eyes and crossed his arms with his palms flat on his chest. In the next instant, he collapsed into the water and the behemoth began to move. Kero raced into the stream to pull Lazaan out of the water. When he got him on shore, he placed a hand in hopes of trying a healing, though he knew his mana was gone. There was no point. The assassin was dead. "Lazaan!"

The huge golem paused. "Here, Kero. I have transferred my life essence into the golem. I don't know how long I will last, but I must try." The Lazaan golem started moving once more, directly for the lava flow.

The god's golem destroyed the last of the stone ones. Would the thing Lazaan inhabited be able to defeat it?

The noise of wheels caused Kero to glance at the gate. Cassan, Savan, and Brusk had managed to get the ballista into the open and were arming it with one of the large harpoons. What was their target? So far, such weapons had proved useless.

The lava monster roared and charged Lazaan's creation. On contact, the wind from the explosion knocked Kero to the ground. Scrambling to his feet, he was pleased to see the water golem still standing, though somewhat smaller, and the lava monster exploded into hundreds of pieces.

He moved to stand beside Brusk while Cassan was stationed at the rear of the machine, his hand on the release, Savan at his side. The captain was holding a hand up toward the prince. "Wait. Let's see what happens. Maybe we'll get the chance when that thing attacks the god."

Both Gragnishozar and Thunder were down. The god stood above them. As Hiss had surmised, they were no match. Lava was flowing and hardening about his master and the demon, encasing them, but it stopped when the god spotted the water golem. He raised his hands, and a stream of lava started to mount, but the water golem was too quick and fell upon the god, absorbing him into its body. Kero could see the god struggle inside the water golem, trying to be free of the thing.

"Now!"

The captain's shout startled him, and he turned in time to see Cassan release the lock that held the ballista taut. From the war machine, the harpoon flew, straight and on target, and pierced both the water golem and the god through the body. In the next instant, the golem collapsed in a splash, landing on the lava flow. In the huge plume of steam that followed, he could not see. Was the god dead?

The men still stationed on the wall sent up a cheer. They yelled the news into the city, and a second cheer arose. They must believe the battle over and the god defeated.

Lazaan was gone, that was for sure. Near him, both Silk and Darlee began to run toward the god and the others. He joined in the charge. He had to see what happened. Behind him, he espied Brusk, Savan, and Cassan also running.

As he neared the scene, the heat from the lava flow still emanated, though the surface was black and solid in appearance. Sprawled atop it, the god lay, impaled by the harpoon, eyes closed, but he still moved, though slightly. He was still alive, but perhaps mortally wounded.

Beside him, both Thunder and Gragnishozar were struggling to free themselves from the lava that encased them. Savan and Brusk pulled their swords and began taking turns dashing in, striking at the lava encasing them then retreating before being overwhelmed by the heat. After repeated blows, Thunder was the first to break free. The huge demon rose and pounded on the stuff holding Kero's master.

It didn't take long. Once free, Gragnishozar knelt beside the god, placed a hand gently on the god's chest, and then touched the harpoon, lodged just below.

Cassan shook a fist. "Finish him!"

"No. He is a god...and my father. I will not do so. It is my hope he has learned from this. That he understands the resistance of both myself and the demons to return to his servitude. That his will is not the only one that matters. There are greater issues in the world to be concerned with."

Gragnishozar nodded to Thunder. "Remove the harpoon. I will hold his body."

Thunder grasped the front end of the weapon and pulled. As he did, the god convulsed, arching his body. As the bolt pulled free, Gragnishozar placed his hands over the entry and exit points, the blood of the god streaming through his fingers, wisps of flame with it.

His lord closed his eyes. Kero knew exactly what was happening—a healing. Was this the right thing to do? Once revived, would the god renew his attack? There were misgivings in Kero's mind as to whether saving the god was a wise thing.

What he thought mattered little. There was no stopping his guardian. As he watched and waited, Brumaine and Tarlok arrived from the city, as well as many of the assassins. The murmur of dissent could be heard in their ranks. Like him, they disagreed on what was happening.

Finally, Gragnishozar straightened. The god's eyes opened, and Kero's lord reached down to help the god rise. Silk, Hiss still in her arms, joined Gragnishozar, passing the imp to him. Along with Thunder, his lord confronted the god. "We will never submit. You must come to understand that."

The god shook his head. "You are all mine. If you truly wanted to be free, you should have let me die."

Gragnishozar sighed. "In the last number of days, I have come to appreciate the value of life." He waved a hand toward everyone gathered near. "Unlike us, these humans have short ones. I have touched you and know your magic is spent. Do not come here again and threaten them so. There will be no point. I will not be here. These people have suffered enough. I will leave to ensure they can rebuild their lives peacefully."

"No matter where you go, sooner or later, I will find you."

"Perhaps, but it took a hundred years to find me once. If another hundred years passes before that happens it will be too soon, but for these people, it will be the time they need to live out their lives without fear of a vengeful god."

For the first time, the god looked at everyone gathered. For a brief instant, his gaze locked with Kero's. It chilled him.

The god faced Gragnishozar once more. "The humans are nothing more than playthings. I do not concern myself with their well-being. If I discover they are concealing you from me, then I will sweep them aside."

"Then I will go where they are not. You will not find me. It is time you return. Can you walk?"

The god drew himself up, obviously indignant at the remark. "Yes."

His lord pointed toward the mountain. "Then go."

Waiting a moment and fixing one final glare at everyone, the god turned and began walking. After a while, everyone returned to the city. There was still much damage to attend to and people to help.

Not for Kero. He stayed where he was, watching the god walk farther and farther. As dusk fell, he could no longer see, but still he lingered. Were his people truly safe? He could only hope.

CHAPTER 50

So many dead, so much lost. Brumaine sipped from his drink and waited until Cassan dismissed Var from the room. "The invasion is over. You must return to Morica."

Cassan sighed, leaned back in his chair, and hefted his tankard taking a long draught. "In this you are right. With the Piaxians here, the army depleted, my war machines gone, I have nothing left with which to hold the island. Father will not be happy."

Father. It was a title Brumaine now felt uncomfortable using when he thought of King Jessop. What father would willingly sacrifice his own son for military gain? "Father is the problem. He planned this. His orders killed Doren. He must be held accountable."

"You have no proof. I cannot believe our father would have instructed Oberus to kill our brother. It is treason to think such."

As Cassan went to lift his tankard again, Brumaine grabbed his wrist to stop him. "No, Cassan, I am not convinced. Both Varamanthu and Oberus revealed details to me that preach otherwise. Father needs to answer some hard questions, as well do those others who planned the mission. An inquisition is needed."

"Father would never agree to it."

He released his brother's arm, allowing Cassan the freedom to drink his mead. He waited until the mug was placed anew on the table. "Then you must force him."

Cassan spewed the beverage and broke into a coughing fit. Wiping the mead from his beard and nose, he glared at Brumaine. "What? Are you insane? How would I do that?"

Brumaine rose, and, grabbing his brother by the arm, pulled him up to stand then dragged him to the open door. Outside of the tavern, Morican troops were busy building temporary shelters to hide from the rain. The morning had seen a deluge of water and, as evening approached, it looked like the sky might break open again. He waved at those in the street. "You have an army."

Cassan drew his brows down and stared intently into Brumaine's eyes. "Be careful what you speak. You would have me openly revolt?"

He smiled. The trials over the past weeks had renewed his love for his siblings, something he had lost in the court machinations in Morence. "More than that. I would have you seize the throne. Morica needs a new king. One who is just and honest. One who loves his people, not power. You are that man, Cassan. You must do it."

Eyes now wide, Cassan stared into the street. "Such a thing. Is it even possible? Would these men follow me in such a quest? To usurp the throne?"

Chuckling, Brumaine clapped his brother across the back. "Why not? You are the god-slayer. They will follow you anywhere."

"Humph. The god still lives."

He nodded. "True, but only through the intervention of Gragnishozar. Had he not interfered, the god would now lie dead. Your men know that."

Cassan turned and walked back inside. Brumaine followed. This was the moment where his brother must decide. It had been a great risk to propose such a plan of action and, quite possibly, Cassan could reject it and try Brumaine for treason. It would result in a horrible death. There was no need for any further talk. He had to wait and see which way his brother went.

Lieutenant Var entered again to bring a new report. Cassan listened until it was finished. "Lieutenant, gather the officers. We will be leaving for Morica on the morrow. I am in need of every man in this army to support me. There is a great injustice to be corrected."

Var saluted and headed for the door, pausing at Brumaine's side. "Is it what I suspect?"

He nodded. "Yes, it is."

Var smiled. "May the gods be with us."

As the lieutenant left the tavern, Cassan sat at his desk, grabbed at some fresh papyrus, and waved him over. "Come, brother, we have much to plan."

Much to plan indeed.

***

It had been four days since the Moricans left. Although not displeased to see them go, Darlee was surprised when Prince Brumaine asked her to come with him. When asked why, he indicated his hope to wed her when she reached the age of ascension when such was allowable. Flummoxed at first, the thoughts of marrying the handsome young prince she had so pined for conflicted with her new sense of self. Politely, she had declined, much to the pleasure of Captain Brusk who had overheard the entire conversation. Brumaine had intentionally asked in Brusk's presence, he being Darlee's guardian and would wish the captain's consent.

The prince kissed her hand and wished her well then joined his brother on the trireme that led the Morican fleet out of the harbor.

Down at the wharf once more, she watched as the two lone fishing boats pulled into their docks. Morican transports really, but Prince Cassan had willingly left them as, with so many men lost and no war machines, he had more than enough to transport his troops home.

She wanted to say goodbye to her new friends because she would be leaving for home in the morning. When they alit on the pier, she went to the four women and gave each a hug, thanking them for all they had done. In the sea battle, the Piaxians had rescued as many of the Riazian fishermen as they could from the water, and they were once more now able to ply their trade. Thankfully, as fish was now the sole source of food on the island until goods could be brought in on trade ships.

Waiting on the wharf was Janina. The redhead smiled at her. "So, you leave tomorrow. If you ever decide to visit again, you can stay with me."

She hugged the woman. "I appreciate that. One never knows, but for now, I think home is where I want to be."

When they separated, Janina was crying. She looked into the woman's eyes. "What's wrong?"

Janina wiped at the tears. "I don't know. I guess I miss my friend Lasha. I don't think I can find another in this town to replace her. When you go, I'll be lonely."

Behind her, an old fisherman was hauling his catch onto the pier. "Janina, come help with this."

Janina kissed Darlee on the cheek. "I have to go. Take care of yourself."

She smiled. "Don't worry. I will."

Turning, she left the wharf and began to climb the hill into the city. Looking up the hill, she spotted Kero looking out over the bay. As she approached him, he smiled.

"It's nice to see you. I was hoping to get a chance alone before you left."

She wondered why. In truth, he must be happy to see her go. She had spurned him at times, even embarrassed him. She also had come to respect him. The maturity he had shown was beyond his years. He would become as good a man as any woman could hope for. "What did you want?"

"I'm not sure really, just that I wanted to see you."

There was something there, she knew it. He was still interested in her. She could tell. He was her age, albeit a couple of months older, which was practically nothing. He was a gentleman to the end. If she desired, she could stay, but despite everything, she did not think it would last. "Thank you for everything. You are a wonderful person and just the kind this country needs. I hope to visit again sometime when things are back to normal. If I do, will you greet me?"

He bowed. "With all my heart."

She leaned close and kissed him on the lips. "Though a pleasant thought, only good cheer will suffice. I will miss you, but home calls, and I must answer."

She left him where he was, and he turned to gaze out at the sea once more. She continued on until she reached the remains of Rock House. A fire glowed from inside, and she went to investigate, expecting to find Kero's guardian.

She found him in his private quarters, his brazier returned to where it had always stood, burning brightly. "There you are. Do you intend to rebuild? It was a wonderful inn."

Gragnishozar smiled. "Sadly, no. I have promised to leave the island, and in the morning, with the Piaxians, I will. I only wished to spend one final night in what was my home before going."

What would things be like in Riaz without the assassin lord? "Kero will miss you."

"And I...him, but it must be. In time, he will be stronger without me. His heart will heal."

For a moment, she felt sad. It was a shame the two must be parted. "Where will you go?"

"Where I cannot be found. That is all you need to know." He reached out and cupped her chin in his hand. "Before you go, there is a boon I could grant you if you would accept it. I could heal your eye. It is within my power. It would add to the beauty of your person."

She touched the eye patch. To see with both eyes again. No more would she think of herself as ugly, as scarred. It would, indeed, be a great gift. She pondered the decision. Would the restoration of her eye and the loss of the patch change her? Would she forget the horror with which it was wrought? Would, over time, she forget all that was lost? Her eye? Her home? Her parents?

No. Those memories were forever burned into her. "I accept your offer. It is most gracious."

He lifted the patch away. "Be still now. I must first open the wound, which will hurt immensely, but if you suffered this once before, I have no doubt of your fortitude to do so again."

She braced her arms against her, fists tight, and closed her other eye. "I'm ready."

A searing pain erupted where the eye had been. She swooned slightly, but the pain began to ebb away. When she could feel no discomfort, she opened the one eye that had always been good and saw Gragnishozar smiling.

"It is done. You can open them both now."

Ever so slowly, she pried open the other eye. For a moment, she was disoriented. Everything looked slightly different. She stumbled, and Gragnishozar caught her.

"Go slowly. It will take time to adjust to seeing with two eyes."

She grabbed his arm and hugged it. "Thank you. It's wonderful." From the restored eye, a tear fell. "I will miss you...brother."

He patted her head. "And I, you...sister. Now be off before I become sentimental like you."

She kissed his cheek goodbye and headed outside. It was dusk, and the sun was setting on the horizon. The sight was beautiful. In the morning, she would be on a boat heading home. Perhaps, when she got there, she might let a certain young soldier named Jango ask her out on a date. She was ready.

***

Two weeks had passed since the Piaxians had sailed taking Kero's guardian, Gragnishozar, and Darlee away. With each day, he had pined over their absence, but it no longer hurt as much as it had then.

Petrius had taken over the assassin guild. In a couple of days, Kero would turn sixteen, reach the age of ascension, and be able to join.

He had decided he would not.

Gragnishozar had left him with a sizable amount of gold coin, in the care of Bashar. With some of it, he was having Rock House rebuilt. He would be a respectable inn owner. It would help when the time came around for the elections to the soon-to-be-formed city council. He intended to run for one of the seats.

For now, along with his friend Derak, he was walking the basalt path that had once been the lava stream. The molten rock had stopped flowing when the god left and the mountain, though some smoke still rose, had remained quiet.

In a shout of glee, Derak raced off to his left and dropped to his knees on the ground, pawing at it. Stepping off the flow, he knelt beside his friend in the dark grey muck that covered the island. Forcing their way through were the green shoots of plant life. He recognized the vegetation. Wine vines. He smiled. Standing, he scanned the area. Everywhere, the plants were pushing through.

The rebirth of his country had started.

OTHER NOVELS by MICHAEL DRAKICH

GRAVE IS THE DAY

In October of 1957, more than Sputnik fell to Earth...

Set against the back drop of the Space Race and the Cold War, both the United States and the Soviet Union have a new issue to deal with, aliens from outer space. Both the Braannoo and the Muurgu are at war with each other and Earth becomes the newest battleground in their struggle. Spanning time from the launch of Sputnik to the near future, the interplay of historical events from a new light make you ask the question, could this all be true? The capture of aliens near small town USA unites three players from different quarters, Commander Kraanox of the Braannoo, First Lieutenant Wayne Bucknell as his captor and seven year old Justin Spencer, the first to make alien contact.

Grave Is The Day is a superb read! This story is a must read for all the science fiction, extraterrestrial lovers on Earth. Grave Is The Day has earned my rating of 5 stars! --Ramsey's Reviews

I have read books that meld fantasy with historical events before, but never one that takes such minute details and blends them so thoroughly. This is a great read and an exceptional rewrite of history for all ages. – Bitten By Books

He created each character with amazing attention to detail and development. I thoroughly enjoyed this book and found myself identifying with more than one of the delightful characters. --Paranormal Romance Guild - Beth Price

THE BROTHERHOOD OF PIAXIA

Years have passed since the overthrow of the monarchy by the Brotherhood of Warlocks and they rule Piaxia in peaceful accord. But now forces are at work to disrupt this rule from outside the Brotherhood as well as within! In the border town of Rok, a young warlock acolyte, Tarlok and his older brother, Savan, captain of the guard, become embroiled in the machinations of dominance. While in the capital city, Tessia, the daughter of Piaxia's most influential merchant, begins a journey of survival. Follow the three as their paths intertwine, with members of the Brotherhood in pursuit and the powerful merchant's guild manipulating the populace for their own ends.

Great, well-rounded characters? Magic running rampant? A lost princess? Yes, this book has it all. – tHe crooked WorD

If you love fantasy that mixes magic, lost royalty, sacrifices, heroes, and strong characters, I would suggest The Brotherhood of Piaxia. – Captivated Reading

The Brotherhood of Piaxia is what it wants to be - a real entertaining fantasy story. It comes along with more characters than you normally get but a lot less then you meet in a famous series you can watch at HBO. It has definitely more magic than a famous fantasy trilogy you could see in cinemas. There is less blood and gore than in a book with a title how to serve a drink. It is also a book which does not drown in romance. For me is a book which you like to read when you want to have a well dosed mix of well-known books. Or in simple words The Brotherhood of Piaxia is like the espresso you enjoy after a good meal. – Edi's Book Lighthouse

LEST THE DEW RUST THEM

Terrorism in America has a new game…decapitations!

Homeland Security Director Robert Grimmson faces the task of catching five men in New York City. They call themselves the Sword Masters with a single minded plan of terror through decapitations.

Barely has the task begun when a new arrival at JFK is a man importing thousands of swords! Alexander Suten-Mdjai is a trainer in the deadly art of swordsmanship and Robert cannot help but believe there is a connection between him and the Sword Masters.

As he goes about the task, each step in his search is made more difficult through the interference of politicians, the media and his own government.

Robert's examination constantly draws him back to Alexander who regales him with a tale of swordsmanship from his lineage featuring events of mankind's bloody past and often oddly having a connection to the case before him.

With the clock ticking as New York collapses into a deep panic, he must catch the Sword Masters before it is too late!

This one of the best suspense thrillers I have read in a long time. – Voracious Reader

This book was really, really good. It was action packed from beginning to end. I could hardly wait to finish and see what would happen. – The Book Worm

This entire book was nothing but entertaining. I have never read a crime-type book that I liked and this book was so good that it's going on my favorite's shelf. – Angels In The Underworld

THE INFINITE WITHIN

Going into outer space calls to Astronaut Brooke Jones like the sirens of old, and when the chance to be part of the first manned mission to Mars arises, she is ecstatic. But little does she know the fate that awaits her on the surface of the red planet or the results of her encounter when she gets back to Earth.

This book is very entertaining. It will grab hold of you, and keep poking at you to finish it. I would recommend this story to science fiction readers that enjoy something a little different. This will not give you the highs of the shoot-em-up in outer space. It takes place place on earth, for the most part. It could be a real story and has enough elements be good fiction. I look forward to reading more by this author. – Charles Kravetz – Keeping Dreams

I loved the uniqueness of the story and the high-caliber action scenes. The adventure and the sense of awe kept me reading late into wee hours. – Laurie Jenkins – Laurie's Thoughts and Reviews

Wow. First off I'll start by saying the book was amazing. In the beginning I was a little iffy about the whole deal then the book got better, and better, and obviously better. I was surprised at the level of detail in the storytelling – Ezekiel Carsella – Books N Tech

DEMON STONES

It's been almost a hundred years since warlock meddling freed the demons from their underground domain. Their eventual capture has encased them in large stones across all the lands. They became known as the demon stones. Over time, the truth of their imprisonment devolved into legend and tales to frighten children. Now, the seven kingdoms are in upheaval. The demon stones are being opened and the vile creatures once more roam the land. War has broken open between realms as the fingers of accusation are pointed. Caught in the middle is Gar Murdach, a farm boy who recently passed the age of ascension of sixteen marking him as a man, and his younger sister, Darlee, as they both struggle in their separate ways to escape the horrors wrought by the demons and the war that swarms round them.

Sometimes a trip into a fantasy world, filled with the magic of the mind is a good place to go, add the intense story line, the detailed world and a young hero who clearly started out WAY out of his league and it becomes clear that sometimes fantasy characters mirror reality
– Diane at Tome Tender (Amazon Top 500 Reviewer)

> Die-hard fantasy fans, particularly those who like a bit of high fantasy,
> will adore this book just as I did
> – Kyra – The Review List

I would recommend this book to those who enjoy a good fantasy which is well-written and easy to follow. Well done, Mr. Drakich
– S. A. Molteni – And So It Begins...

I AM

Genius, wealthy and life regenerated, Adam Spenceworth is living the dream aboard his custom spaceship run by Mum, his first designed AI, protected by Gort, his first robot, and occupied by Eve, his sexbot. With each regeneration he returns to start over as a twenty-five year old man ready to enjoy the pleasures of his success. What could go wrong? Except, maybe, planetary wars, territorial space battles, alien invasions, and the disturbing fact that each regeneration is taking exponentially longer than the one before bringing him into one galactic crisis after another. A frolicking space drama filled with references sure to strike home with any science fiction aficionado.

Michael Drakich's I Am is a brilliant space opera about one man's journey through eons of time in a futuristic world where worlds and galaxies collide in wat, join in peace, and may only survive through Artificial Intelligence that almost believes it is alive.
Diane @ Tome Tender Book Blog – Top 500 Amazon Reviewer

One of the top five independent author'd kooks of all time.
Lilyn @ sciFiandScary, Reviewing Both Independent and Traditionally Published Works

Everything I love about science fiction was in this book. The aliens, the robots, the advanced technology, and the humor make this book an enjoyable and engaging read from start to finish.
Tori@ Tori Lex, Judging Books Beyond The Cover

Overall, the story meets all my criteria for an excellent science fiction. It's epic scale, rich world, plausible futures, and focus on the people (both organic and not) make this one for the bookshelves, definitely worthy of reading over and over again. I'd highly recommend this to folks who love science fiction, hard, epic, space opera and otherwise.
Patricia @ Pure Textuality, Book Reviews, News & Everything In Between

ASSASSINS OF RIAZ

In Riaz, the profession of assassin is an honored one. Hired throughout the other eight realms, their use of powerful magic to complete assignments makes them a valuable commodity. When a regional trade negotiation is scheduled in their capital city of Lymos, the demand for the skills of the assassins is sure to change the dynamic of the meetings. Caught in the maelstrom of political intrigue is young Kero, the ward of the assassin lord. He's joined by Darlee, a girl from Sechland with her own magical powers, and Prince Brumaine of Morica, as each of them struggle to navigate the affair in their own way. Will old animosities prevail, or can new alliances alter the path toward all out war?

Michael Drakich writes for all ages and brings a tale to life that will entice any reader who looks for engaging storytelling, characters to admire or detest and a richly detailed plot that unfolds with mind-boggling energy! Easy to read, hard to put down, highly recommended reading that never lets up, page after page!

Diane @ Tome Tender Book Blog – Top 500 Amazon Reviewer

One of the things I liked about the story is that it feels bigger than it is. Feels like part of a greater story, even though it wraps up nicely in one volume. I got the impression of a greater world, an important aspect in any epic fantasy.

Trish @ Pure Textuality Book Reviews, News & Everything In Between

REQUIEM FOR A GENOCIDE

JAK037 is a warbot.

Built for the sole purpose of killing the enemies of Dalrea, he has survived longer than any other and is the last of his generation still in operation. Being the last JAK model, he is simply referred to as Jak, no unit number necessary. When word comes of a treaty with their nemesis, Carthia, Jak holds out hope his final days will be ones without war. It is with disappointment he learns the treaty is so a new front can be opened against a race of settlers from another world.

Humans.

In the coming conflict, can Jak and his comrades of aged warbots survive against an enemy with superior technology? In a mission to wipe out the settlers, will it succeed? Or will Jak's days finally be numbered. With the aid of a human child, a seven-year-old girl named Hannah, Jak hopes to end the war and save his people from what he believes is a looming disaster. It's a race where not only humans but Carthians, Dalreans, robotic laws, and his own failing body all conspire to stop him.

"Requiem for a Genocide", by Michael Drakich, is a completely compelling science fiction novel that fans of classic sci-fi and new sci-fi will love. I can't remember when I've enjoyed a robot-themed novel this much, and I highly recommend it for sci-fi fans everywhere. It has the kind of universal appeal that underpins a good sci-fi movie. - READER VIEWS GOLD MEDAL AWARD FOR SCIENCE FICTION

This heartwarming sci-fi action drama is like the love child of I, Robot and The Iron Giant. In a way, it comes across as a political parable with an appeal that comes from the touching relationship between a child and a thinking machine. It's a plain and simple story, but one that Michael Drakich has explored dramatically to deliver a strong plotline and compelling characters. Jak may be a machine, but he is oozing with humanity so it is not difficult to identify with him. It has a nice structure to it, with a fast-paced writing style that gives enough details without boring you. Requiem for a Genocide is fiction that feels realistic because it has something to say. It is a story that will win the hearts of both young readers and adults. - READERS FAVORITE

The first-"person" narrative gives us a chance to see into JAK's mind, and what I loved most about the book was his intelligent and down-to-earth philosophical musing about things like war, ethics, free will, and life in general. 5 STARS - Angie Boyter, Amazon Vine Voice ranked in the top 1000 of Amazon's ranked reviewers.

www.ingramcontent.com/pod-product-compliance
Lightning Source LLC
Chambersburg PA
CBHW072024020726
47501CB00006B/1937